By Dean Murray

Reflections	Dark Reflections	The Awakening
Broken	*Bound*	*Reborn*
Torn	*Hunted*	*Immortal*
Splintered	*Ambushed*	*Endless*
Intrusion	*Shattered*	
Numb	*Burned*	**A Broken World**
Trapped		*The Society*
Forsaken		*The Destroyer*
Riven		*The Founder*
Driven		*The Desolation*
Lost		
Marked		

Reflections	The Guadel Chronicles
(Dean Writing as Eldon)	*Frozen Prospects*
The Greater Darkness	*Thawed Fortunes*
A Darkness Mirrored	*I'rone*
	Brittle Bonds
	Shattered Ties

Marked

Dean Murray

Marked is a work of fiction. Names, characters, places and incidents are the products of the author's imagination or are used fictitiously. Any resemblance to actual events, locales, or persons, living or dead, is entirely coincidental.

Copyright © 2014 by Dean Murray

Published by Fir'shan Publishing

ISBN 978-1-9393634-3-5

www.FirshanPublishing.com

First Edition

For Katie

This isn't the first book I've dedicated to you and it probably won't be the last. Thanks for being there to help pick me up each time the world knocks me down.

Chapter 1

Adriana Paige
Interstate 15
Western Montana

I was running.

The sense that something terrible was chasing me was simply too strong for me to do anything else. I knew I was dreaming—my surroundings were too beautiful to be explained by anything else—but even that knowledge wasn't enough to make me stand my ground. It was like there was some kind of evolutionary cutout at work. The part of me that was advanced enough to talk and use tools was no match for instincts developed over thousands of years—not when faced by something that ran hunched over, with claws that dripped a combination of venom and blood.

It felt like I'd been running for hours, but given the way that time seemed to skip and stretch inside of dreams, there was no way of being sure how long I'd been fleeing. I jumped over a fallen tree, clearing the eight-foot-tall obstacle without breaking my stride. The trunk, a dark bar covered by faintly-glowing moss, sailed by with a speed I never could have managed in the real world. It was one more sign that this was nothing more than a nightmare, but I didn't slow my pace.

I was running on two feet, darting between softly glowing pillars that I knew had to be trees, and that felt wrong too. I was seeing the world the same way that Alec and the rest of my friends who were shape shifters saw it. It felt like I should be running on four legs, but there wasn't time to stop and make myself change shapes—even assuming that I was capable of something like that inside of a dream.

Heedless of the noise I was making, I crashed through a set of tall bushes that looked like some kind of glowing, new-age glass sculpture, and then I was free of the forest. The ground I was running across now couldn't possibly have supported the kind of dense forest that I'd just left. Rather than the soft black soil I'd been expecting, it had shifted to hard red rock.

It had been dark in the forest, but I exited into sunlight that was so bright it was almost blinding. I stumbled, squinting as I tried to continue forward, but before I'd even finished taking my second step the sun had vanished. It didn't set, it just disappeared, leaving me in a darkness that was so profound I felt like I'd stepped into some kind of void.

Only the feel of the rock underneath my feet gave lie to the idea that I'd stepped into a realm of nothingness. There wasn't anything living on the rock, nothing to provide even the barest hint of illumination to my borrowed, supernatural vision.

Before the light had disappeared the ground before me had been flat, but now it sloped upwards in a set of irregular steps that tripped me. I caught myself with my hands, but the impact sent shooting jabs of pain up my arms.

As I scrambled back to my feet, I heard something come crashing out of the forest. I knew I would be better off not looking back to see what was chasing me, but I couldn't help myself. It was big, much bigger than any hybrid, bigger even than the werewolf that had nearly killed Isaac and Jasmin in New York.

I'd only thought that the night around me was dark, but now I could see that I'd been wrong. The night still felt dark, but it was nothing compared to the darkness that streamed off of the creature. It was like nothing I'd ever seen.

I wanted to say that it was a dark light, but even with my heart trying to tear itself free of my chest I still knew that was a contradiction. Darkness was an absence of light, but this darkness acted like light, reached out with greedy tendrils in an effort to fill the space around the thing slowly advancing toward me.

The blackness was strong enough that it was hard to make out details. I'd already registered the fact that it was huge. The claws flexing at the ends of its fingers were longer than my arms and I got an impression there were more teeth crammed into its mouth than could have physically fit inside of the pit housing them.

The ground shook slightly as it approached. I needed to get away, needed to run—until my heart exploded inside of my chest if necessary—but I was having a hard time looking away from its eyes. They were green and seemed to flicker, moving inside of the deep sockets in its head as though they were made out of some kind of grotesque fire.

I'd always thought of green as a color that symbolized life, but in this instance green had been perverted into something unclean, something that devoured life and left behind only ruin.

"You can't escape me."

Its voice sounded like plates of chitin sliding across each other, like a billion insects chittering in unison.

"What do you want?"

It was stupid. In the back of my mind I knew that nothing I was experiencing was real, but part of me couldn't help but act as though this was all real, as though the creature was something that could be reasoned with.

"The death of everything you hold dear, the destruction of everything you stand for."

I opened my mouth to tell it that I didn't understand, but before I could get the words out, it sprang towards me. Nothing that big should have been able to move so quickly. I'd spent most of the last six months watching werewolves and shape shifters fight. I'd been exposed to unbelievable speed, to people who were so preternaturally fast that they could cover a dozen yards before I could even blink, but this was more than that. It didn't just cross the distance between us, it was as though it teleported, as though the space simply ceased to exist for one critical instant.

The impossibly long claws took me in the stomach, pierced my flesh at the same time that they sent me into a state of shock. I tried to push myself off of them in a vain attempt to get free so that I could flee from something faster than thought, but it picked me up.

"So easy. I thought maybe you would be a challenge, that you would be stronger than your friends. Will you beg for me to end your life too?"

Its words didn't make any sense. I'd never been the strong one. Alec, Jasmin, Dominic and even Rachel all had sources of strength that I'd never possessed. The very act of trying to understand what its words meant pulled my mind out of the shock that had been cushioning me from the pain up until then.

It was like having bars of liquid fire shoved into my gut. I'd spent months suffering from emotional wounds that had come within inches of destroying me. I'd thought that nothing could equal the agony I'd felt then, but this was a whole new kind of pain. It was like agony and despair all rolled up into one terrible package.

For a split second I balanced on the edge of disaster. I wanted to give up, to give into the pain and surrender, to let it carry me away into oblivion, but then I thought about Alec.

He needed me. Shawn's gift had settled that particular question as far as the future of the rebellion went. As hard as it was to believe, without Alec and me, the rest of my friends were doomed. With me by Alec's side they had a chance, slender though it was.

It was more than that though. I'd heard enough stories about how life in the pack had been while I'd been gone to know that Alec had been under incredible stress after I left Sanctuary. He'd dealt with things with admirable determination, but when you came right down to it he needed me in the same way that I needed him.

I wasn't going to give up and sentence him to a life of loneliness simply because fighting back against this thing hurt.

MARKED

Thinking about Alec sent a warm rush of energy humming through me. The pain was still there, but the tingling power that had filled me to the point where I nearly couldn't contain it had somehow muted the pain to a point where I could function again.

"I'm not scared of you."

Even as I said the words, I kicked off against the creature's arm with every ounce of strength I could muster. In the real world I never could have hoped to muster enough force to tear myself free of three-foot claws, but in this particular dream I did exactly that.

The pain spiked as I hurled myself back and up, but I'd known that would be the case and I gritted my teeth in a vain effort to stop myself from screaming again. The creature started to bring its other hand around, trying to rip me out of the air, and I knew that would be the end of everything.

In that instant I needed to be faster, and this time reality conformed itself to my needs in the way that dreams sometimes allow. I sailed up over the grasping, deadly points of the creature's claws seemingly moving in slow motion, but still somehow managing to be faster than the nightmare that had been chasing me.

I should have crashed to the ground on my back, but instead the dream once again molded itself to my needs. I tucked my legs and turned what should have been a disastrous, leg-breaking landing into a graceful backflip.

It wasn't something I could do in real life. I didn't even know how to tumble, let alone have the guts to do it in the middle of a fight for my life, but somehow it all came together for me and for one impossibly long second I felt a kind of weightless, perfection that would have probably haunted me forever if I'd been able to dwell on the feeling.

Rock shattered, crushed into powder under my feet from the force of my landing, and then I spun and took off at a run.

It was insane. I was still bleeding and I hadn't been able to outrun the creature even when I'd been at my best, but apparently I was firmly in flight mode.

I could hear the creature behind me, claws chipping away at the rock as it used them for extra traction while giving chase. My mind whirled desperately, looking for a weapon or a refuge, but this time my surroundings proved stubbornly uncooperative.

I took another step, hands forward to help propel me up the incline, and then I was at the top of the climb. I was trapped. There was twenty feet of flat ground and then beyond that a ravine that was more than fifty feet across.

Alec would have turned and attacked the creature, using his superior position to get at its head and neck, but I wasn't Alec. I was already gasping for breath, but I reached deep inside and tapped into some of the energy that had brought me this far. It was leaking out in time with the blood that had already soaked my pants, but there was enough left for one more good sprint.

I crossed the open expanse of rock in three impossibly long strides. I took my speed as a good sign, as proof that my dream was about to conform to my needs, and then threw myself across the ravine.

There was a glimmer of something on the other side that looked like it might be a safe landing spot, and that was what I was aiming for. I reached towards that spot with my mind and pulled with everything I had, willing the future I wanted into being.

I heard the creature scream in rage, a raspy roar that made my blood freeze, but it was too late—I was already two-thirds of the way across the ravine and showed no signs of slowing. A grin started to force its way past my concentration, and then suddenly the cliff seemed to get further away from me.

The shock as I started to fall was so complete that for a second my mind refused to function. I was dead...only a tiny voice kept trying to tell me that it was impossible to die in a dream.

Was I dreaming? Suddenly I wasn't so sure. Maybe I'd simply had some kind of psychotic break from the stress of dealing with the attack on the estate. It was possible for multiple psychological blows to send someone over the edge like that.

First there had been Dad and Cindi dying in that car wreck and then I'd nearly died more times than I could count. Really, it was a surprise that I hadn't completely melted down when Alec and I had broken up.

It hit me with a suddenness that took my breath away. What if everything that had happened since the accident had all been nothing more than some kind of massive hallucination? What if none of it had been real?

The universe felt like a crystal goblet vibrating a hairsbreadth away from high C. All it would take was the slightest change in pitch for everything to shatter. Life had gotten a lot harder since the accident, but that had always felt like a fair trade in exchange for having Alec in my life. The thought of going back to how I'd been, a broken little doll with nothing to look forward to, no purpose other than just getting through the day, was more than I could handle and something in the depths of my mind started to unravel.

I probably would have blacked out again, returning to the welcome oblivion of one of my panic attacks, if not for the warm, tingly energy flowing through me. That energy was Alec's. It had been one of his defining characteristics for as long as I'd known him.

MARKED

I could very nearly feel his arms wrapped around me and that pulled me back from the edge of insanity. Alec was too amazing to be nothing more than a figment of my imagination. Even in the middle of the worst kind of psychotic break, I still wouldn't have been capable of imagining a version of reality where I ended up with him.

People sometimes say that someone—or something—is too good to be true, but this was the exact opposite of that. Alec was too good *not* to be true, and that was all the reassurance that I needed. Besides, I wasn't sure that it was possible to feel this much pain in the middle of a hallucination.

Then again, it wasn't supposed to be possible to feel pain in the middle of a dream either. That was worrisome. Alec being real didn't necessarily prove that I wasn't falling. In fact, it actually made more sense that a mind facing death would come up with reasons why nothing it was experiencing was real. There were probably lots of people who fell to their deaths convinced that they were just about to wake up from a nightmare.

No, I could see myself doing that, but everything that had happened during the last few minutes was too far outside even the normal dream craziness for me to believe it was all real. This had to be a dream. Maybe the pain was just a side effect of the dream power that Mallory was convinced I had.

I was still falling; my brush with insanity had taken no more than a second, but I was moving impossibly fast and the ground wasn't very far away.

This wasn't my first falling dream and I relaxed as I fell the last hundred feet, expecting to wake up in the instant before I would have crashed into the ground. I started to drift free and then some kind of heavy pressure pushed me back into my body.

I screamed again, my mind clawing desperately for some escape, and then another wave of energy crashed through me and my eyes popped open.

I was safely in my bed at the back of Alec's massive RV. The chase and fall had been nothing more than a bad dream, a dream that was swiftly slipping away from me despite my best efforts to hold onto it for analysis.

There was something about what I'd just experienced that put it in a category all of its own. It was more than just seeing the world in shades of glowing white or the fact that I'd felt such intense pain. There was something fundamentally different about this dream, something that felt important.

It was right on the edge of my mind, like I'd started to say something and then had the word I'd wanted to use dissolve out of my memory. Maybe I would have managed to pin it down if I hadn't realized a second later that Alec's warm, muscular arms were wrapped around me.

"Are you okay, Adri?"

I couldn't think of a better surprise to wake up to. Alec and I were still sleeping separately despite the temptation to do otherwise. Waking up and finding Alec in bed with me sent thoughts of my nightmare tumbling out of my skull.

"I think so—what happened?"

"I was about to ask you the same question. You started screaming a little while ago. I came back to check on you and saw that you were thrashing around hard enough that you'd broken the bookshelf."

I didn't want to give Alec a reason to let go of me, so I didn't move very far, but I turned my head enough to see the pile of books on the far end of the bed.

"Wow, I'm lucky I didn't get brained by one of them."

"Yeah. In hindsight maybe it wasn't the best idea to mount a shelf above the bed like that. I was worried you were going to break the other one as well so I immobilized your arms. I've been trying to wake you up for nearly five minutes. Bad dream?"

"Yeah, I guess."

"You want to talk about it?"

"Actually I do, but I don't seem to remember much about it. I think something was chasing me, but that's about all that stuck with me."

"You're sure there's nothing else?"

"I don't know…maybe the sense that it wasn't a normal dream, but I couldn't tell you for sure what made it special. I'm sure exhausted though. I feel like I've been running for hours—I was less tired than this when I went to bed."

"There's a lot of that going around."

It was the kind of casual remark that I'd caught Alec making from time to time lately. I wasn't even sure he was aware of what he was doing, but it almost seemed like he was trying to give those around him a heads up without actually coming right out and saying point blank that there was a problem with something.

It was the kind of thing that could be problematic in a leader if he wasn't doing it on purpose, but I hadn't been able to bring myself to point it out to him. Most everyone else didn't know him well enough for it to be a problem and I was reluctant to make him any more of a closed book than he already was.

I opened my mouth and then decided once again against saying anything. Instead I turned in his arms so I was facing him. It was a calculated risk. There was always a chance that he'd take my moving as a reason to let go of me and sit up, but I kept his right arm trapped underneath my body and this time he didn't move.

Looking into his eyes was like entering an entirely new universe, one where I was completely happy. Alec could fake a lot of emotions on those occasions where it became necessary, but he couldn't fake the level of love and commitment that I saw reflected back at me in the quiet moments when it was just the two of us.

If his comment had been the slightest bit less concerning I would have just sat there gazing into his eyes for as long as he was willing to remain in one place, but I knew there was something important he wasn't telling me.

"What's going on, Alec?"

"This isn't general knowledge, so don't say anything to Donovan or the others, but it doesn't look like Dream Stealer has lost interest in Kristin. All the signs point to him having singled her out as the weak link in the pack."

"What does that mean? I know a little bit about Dream Stealer, but obviously not enough."

"It means he's torturing her every night in her sleep in an effort to break her. He doesn't do it often, but he's taken down entire packs this way. He picks out a target, either someone he thinks is weaker than the rest of the pack or someone who's got access to something particularly important, and then he makes every night hell until they finally snap. Once that happens they'll do anything to get him to stop hurting them.

"For someone who's been through that, there's no secret they won't disclose, no ally they won't betray, no murder they won't commit.

Sometimes he only has to break one person, sometimes he has to break half the pack, but in the end he's always managed to achieve his goal."

"That's...well, it's beyond terrible. Are you sure he's targeted Kristin?"

"Yeah. Ash says that she's thrashing around in her sleep every night and she's so tired that she drops off to sleep as soon as she stops moving. It was questionable before, but it's become pretty clear lately that she's his target."

I closed my eyes to stop them from tearing up. Kristin wasn't my favorite person. She was a little too pushy for the two of us to ever be close friends, but she didn't deserve to be put through what Alec was describing.

"She mentioned that she was having issues with him before the attack on the house, but she seemed pretty sure that he would leave her alone if she could just tough things out for a week or two."

Alec gave me a sad smile that told me he knew exactly what I was feeling. "Yeah. So far that's all that anyone has been able to do where Dream Stealer is concerned. He's not omnipotent so if you can manage to fight him off for several nights running then there is a chance that he'll reassess the situation and come at the pack through someone else."

"So if you win then it just means that he'll go after someone else close to you? That doesn't seem like much of a victory."

"It's not. For the last few decades he hasn't even had to break people to accomplish his ends. Once it becomes apparent that he's decided to target a pack, it usually just disintegrates as everyone tries to get far enough away from each other that there's no reason for him to continue to target any of them."

"He turns families against each other."

"Yeah, I'm afraid so. There's a reason that nobody has come out in open rebellion against the Coun'hij since they killed my father. Between Agony, Dream Stealer and Puppeteer there's never been any doubt as to where the balance of power rests. Agony was their scalpel, Puppeteer has always been a blunt instrument, and Dream Stealer is like a virus, just looking for a weakened host he can use to create a pandemic. Even someone like Jaclyn Annikov has had to be very circumspect about disagreeing with the Coun'hij in public."

"We can't let him do this to Kristin, Alec. There has to be a way to stop him. You've already killed Agony and you proved that Puppeteer isn't unbeatable. If we can find a way to neutralize Dream Stealer, then the Coun'hij will fall overnight."

"I wish that was true, Adri. I killed Agony, but we beat Puppeteer as much by luck as anything else. It's going to be a long road to defeating the Coun'hij, but I promise I'm doing everything I can right now. There isn't anything

I can do directly to protect Kristin, so Ash and Isaac are going to take her somewhere they can keep her isolated and make sure she can't hurt herself or the rebellion either one.

"To be honest, I'd hoped initially that I'd be able to stop Dream Stealer from getting at any of my people. I seem to be able to nullify most other powers. I stopped Agony's cuts from scarring like they should have, I can stop Grayson from being able to send people into convulsions, it didn't seem that much of a stretch to think that I'd be able to nullify Dream Stealer's ability to dream walk, but that doesn't seem to be the case."

"You didn't stop Dominic from being able to heal people and you didn't seem to do anything to nullify Shawn's gift either."

"Yeah, unfortunately there's still far too much that I *don't* know about my ability. I need time to explore its limits, but time is the one thing that we don't have. Many of the shape shifters who gathered in Sanctuary before the attack did so because they thought that my gift would protect them from Dream Stealer and Puppeteer. Now that they know that's not the case we're going to have a much more difficult time adding to our numbers."

"Are you second-guessing the decision to split everyone up?"

"A little, but I still don't see another way forward. Dream Stealer always does more damage in bigger groups. It's harder for him to get his hooks into someone unnoticed in small groups, and by compartmentalizing our operations we can limit the amount of information he has access to at any one time. When you throw in the fact that Puppeteer can only be in one place at any given time, it just makes sense to try to make sure we don't offer them a big, stationary target to come after."

"So we scatter and hide while Kristin suffers."

"For now. It all comes back to us needing to find the Coun'hij's base. If we can do that then we have a chance of forcing the fight on terms that favor us. I can't fight Dream Stealer on his home turf, but if we can pin him down in the real world then Jaclyn, Grayson or I can easily make sure he never tortures anyone else again."

Alec had been serious about compartmentalizing his plans, but so far I seemed to be one of the few exceptions. I appreciated that fact because it gave us one more reason to spend time together, one more thing to talk about, but it created a potential problem that we were going to have to talk about.

I told myself that I wasn't bringing that issue up because there was something else more important that I needed to ask Alec, but even as I asked my other question I knew I was mostly just waiting because I was scared of what his reaction might be.

"You don't seem as confident in our ability to defeat the Coun'hij as I expected you to be. I thought it has always just been an issue of us not knowing where they are located."

"That's the main thing, the only thing that I can point to as being a concrete problem, but there are a lot of unknowns. For decades there have been rumors that there are other members of the Coun'hij who keep their identities hidden, hybrids every bit as powerful as Agony or Dream Stealer or Puppeteer."

"Why would they do that? Wouldn't it make sense to present the scariest front possible in order to make sure that the packs are too intimidated to rise up against the Coun'hij?"

"Your guess is as good as mine. There is a lot to be said for making sure everyone knows exactly how big a stick you're wielding, but there is also something to the idea of keeping your enemies guessing. The less they know about your true capabilities the less they can do to neutralize your advantages through superior planning. You could argue that between Puppeteer, Agony and Dream Stealer the Coun'hij had a plenty big enough stick to threaten the packs with."

"You're not convinced that's the reason though."

"Not entirely. There are rumors that some of the Coun'hij hide their names and abilities because their gifts are so terrible that if the packs knew about them they'd rise up in a united group and try to overthrow the Coun'hij despite the blood bath that would almost certainly result."

"And if those rumors are true, then the mere fact that you're being so successful puts us in more danger, because that's the kind of thing that would cause the really scary members of the Coun'hij to finally get involved."

Alec nodded gravely. "Exactly. It's one of those things I can't plan around because I don't have enough information, but it's there in the back of my mind with every decision I make. It's like my own personal boogeyman."

I'd already wrapped my arms around Alec after turning to face him, but now I squeezed him harder. "It's going to be okay, Alec. You're going to find a way through this. We don't know what's coming or who else we might be up against, but we do know that it's possible for us to win."

"You're putting an awful lot of trust in Shawn's gift, and he never said we could win, just that it wasn't guaranteed that we were going to lose."

"No, I'm putting an awful lot of trust in you. Shawn's gift was just a nice confirmation of what I already knew. If you really put your mind to it there isn't anything you can't do. Your gift has fully manifested and we have an impressive list of allies that include Jaclyn and Grayson. You can do this, Alec, and I love that you've chosen to stand up to the Coun'hij. You're not doing it because you want the power; you're doing it because it's the right thing to do, the thing that will give your people a chance to be free for the first time since the monarchy fell."

He looked at me in amazement and this time the smile that was tugging at the corner of his mouth was a happy one. "You do realize that most people don't consider living under a monarchy to be a shining example of freedom, right?"

"Most people don't have to deal with the complexity of shape shifter existence. You were right all of those months ago when you told me that shape shifters can't live by the same rules that humans live by. Even the weakest of you are still incredibly dangerous and when you throw in the fact that you're in the middle of three wars while trying to keep your existence a secret from the humans, it becomes painfully evident that your people need a stronger central authority than would be ideal for a bunch of suburban soccer moms. Besides, living under the rule of a Graves is the one sure way to guarantee that you'll be treated justly."

That earned me an eye roll. "My ancestors weren't perfect and I'm even further away from perfection than they were."

"I don't know, you look pretty perfect from right here."

MARKED

That broke through the last of Alec's defenses. He was always less guarded around me than he was around most of the rest of the pack, but my favorite times were when all of the walls came down and I saw him without any pretenses.

There was an incredible gentleness to Alec Graves that he kept carefully hidden for fear that his enemies would use it against him. He wasn't wrong to do so. Someone like Puppeteer would do anything to exploit something he perceived as a weakness, but it wasn't a weakness, at least not in my book.

Alec fought so hard precisely because he cared. He would attack despite all the odds because he couldn't bear to let someone he cared about die if he had a chance to save them. The Coun'hij wasn't capable of understanding that any more than Brandon had been.

Every momentous change in our life could be traced back to that one thing and it had caught our enemies by surprise each time. Alec had fought Brandon to save me and triggered his power, and then he'd faced off against Agony in order to save Jasmin and Isaac and brought his power fully under control.

Even his decision to try and reestablish the monarchy had resulted from the fact that he couldn't bear to see packs being torn apart by the likes of Dream Stealer. The smart thing would have been for Alec to take a less confrontational approach, pretend to ally himself with the Coun'hij and bide his time while he gathered allies. It would have been the smart thing to do, but it wouldn't have been the right thing to do and so he'd never even considered it.

"Adriana Paige, I don't deserve you, but I'm very glad that you came into my life. I never would have made it this far without you."

I opened my mouth to tell him he wasn't giving himself enough credit, but he didn't let me get the words out. He kissed me and there wasn't anything hesitant about this kiss. I had a split second to be glad I'd switched to that new, longer-lasting mouthwash and then I was swept away in the moment.

Alec's arms around me tightened to the point where the pressure was just short of painful and I loved every second of it. It was like the ultimate expression of strength and manliness. He could have crushed me without even trying, but he wouldn't because even now Alec was in complete control of himself. That control was sexy in ways I couldn't even begin to explain.

I reached up and cupped his face as I returned the kiss, shaking from the thrill of having him close to me, giddy from the buzz of his shape shifter energy coursing back and forth between his bare skin and my hands, face and arms.

His lips were perfectly firm and insistent against mine, and I wanted to let myself go fully, but I knew I couldn't do that. I needed to tell him about my concern and if I didn't do it now then there was a chance that I wouldn't ever do it.

It was one of the harder things I'd ever done up to that point, but I pulled back from Alec and rather than keeping me there like some guys would have, he immediately relaxed his arms. He didn't let go of me completely, but he gave me the option of breaking free if that was what I wanted.

"As much as I would love to stay like that forever, there is something we need to talk about."

The old Alec would have become at least a little guarded after a lead-in like that, but all he did now was raise one eyebrow in a questioning manner. I took a deep breath and then forced the words out.

"What if I'm being attacked by Dream Stealer?"

"No, that's not possible…"

I cut him off before he could finish. "Alec, you have to be rational about this. I was thrashing around and screaming. I feel like I didn't get a wink of sleep, and I have no recollection of what I was dreaming about so I can't vouch for the fact that I wasn't being tortured."

He looked like he wanted to interject something, but I gave him a stern look and just kept on speaking.

"You said that Dream Stealer likes to target the weakest individuals in a given pack, especially if they have access to important stuff. In case you haven't been keeping score, that's basically a perfect description of me. You need to start cutting me out of some of the planning. I probably already know too much, but at least if you start keeping me in the dark now you'll be able to limit the amount of damage I do when he breaks me."

Alec shook his head at me. "Are you done?"

"Yeah, I guess so."

"Thank goodness. I was half expecting you to say something about locking you in the bathroom until we could make arrangements to ship you off to some kind of makeshift prison four states over."

I shrugged. "Now that you mention it, that's not a bad idea. I would have eventually suggested something like that—I just hadn't thought things out completely yet."

"I guess I should just be grateful that distancing yourself from me wasn't the *first* thing that you thought of."

His light, joking tone brought a smile to my face despite my best efforts, which just made me want to punch him in the arm.

"This is serious, Alec."

He sighed. "I agree, but I don't think there is a need to do anything drastic right now. Dream Stealer is something of an enigma, but while we don't know very much about him as an individual, the packs—even the sympathizer packs—have been keeping as close an eye on his activities as possible for the last couple hundred years. There's never been any kind of evidence of him working on two people at one time.

"There have been about a dozen times where he took a pack apart by breaking two of its members and even a few instances where he turned three people in order to accomplish his goals, but he always attacked them one at a time, even when he appeared to be working under some kind of a time limit."

"So as long as he's still trying to break Kristin that means I'm safe."

"Yes, which means that your nightmare was just that—a normal, subconscious-acting-up nightmare. Ash will keep a very close eye on Kristin and as soon as there are any signs that Dream Stealer has either succeeded or given up trying to break her, we'll get a call letting us know that we need to start keeping a closer eye on everyone else."

I closed my eyes for a second as I tried to think through all of the ramifications of what he'd just told me.

"I suddenly feel like an even bigger jerk than I did a few seconds ago. Kristin is suffering unspeakable things just so I can be safe. It doesn't make any sense. Out of all of the possible options, why choose her? It makes more sense to go after me."

"That's not true, Adri. It actually makes a lot of sense to get Kristin out of the picture. In a lot of ways her visions make her the ultimate wild card. As long as she's in play and on our side there's no way for the Coun'hij to guarantee that she won't ruin their plans by telling us something that we couldn't possibly know."

"But her visions are so unpredictable..."

"Yeah, but even so they could make all of the difference. If Dream Stealer hadn't locked her into some kind of feedback loop she would have been able to warn us of the attack against the estate. If we'd known that was coming even just ten minutes before the werewolves actually arrived, we could have changed the outcome there in a big way."

"You're right. If we'd been close together and waiting for them we wouldn't have lost most of the people who died that night."

My words came out rough, but that wasn't a surprise, not considering the way that my throat seemed to be trying to close itself off. Alec pulled me close again, but this time there wasn't any passion to his embrace, just the comfort that I so desperately needed.

"I'm so sorry, Adri. I know how much Carson meant to you. I wish I'd been there to help him."

I shook my head. "It's not your fault. If things had gone even a little bit differently your mom would be dead. Besides, Carson died the way that he lived—protecting someone who couldn't protect themselves. He wouldn't have wanted it any other way."

"I'm not sure it was a worthwhile trade. I'm not sure even now that Mother really understands that Rachel is gone."

Part of me wanted to pull back in shock, but I understood why Alec had said it. It wasn't that he didn't love his mother; he was just struggling with losing so many people.

"She's still there somewhere, Alec. You just need to give her more time to come back from that kind of a loss."

Alec sighed, but he finally met my eyes again. "How can you be so sure when I'm plagued with doubts? Tactically speaking, going after my mother was the worst decision I could have made."

"I'm sure because you couldn't have made any other decision and still have been the man I love. I'm sure because I knew Carson much better than you did and I know that he hated the fact that his life had been spent pursuing violence. The only thing that made his choices bearable was the fact that he was able to use his skills to protect people who were weaker than him. He never would have agreed to let your mother die in exchange for saving his own life.

"More than that, I have a pretty good idea just how devastated I would be in your mother's position. It was all I could do to keep on going when I left you and that was *my* decision. It would be a hundred times worse if you were *taken* from me. She's retreated inside of herself because she's trying to protect what's left of the woman who must have been head over heels for your father. That's good though because it means there's something there to protect, some fragment worth trying to preserve. I'm not sure I could have done as much in her place. I would have just gone catatonic."

Alec kissed my forehead, a chaste brief kiss, but one that still left my skin feeling like it was on fire, a pleasant, energizing fire. "You're a lot stronger than you give yourself credit for, you know."

I snuggled in closer to him, tucking my head into the spot where his shoulder and neck joined up. "Maybe you're right, but I didn't start out this way. Before I met you I was a shallow little girl who was little more than a collection of razor-edged shards. You are the one who put me back together and gave me a chance to become a real person again."

"I think in this instance we're going to have to agree to disagree."

Alec's words were little more than a whisper that teased stray strands of my hair into motion. He was making me feel tingly all over again, but this time it didn't have to do with the otherworldly energy that he gave off by virtue of being a shape shifter. This was wholly the result of him making me feel like someone who was special enough to be worthy of him.

"There aren't very many people who could have done what you just did, Adri."

"What do you mean?"

"Dream Stealer's power is dangerous, but it wouldn't be half as bad if everyone was strong enough to tell someone when they thought he was after them. You *are* strong. A weak person would have just stayed quiet and hoped that they were just having a string of normal bad dreams."

"I almost didn't say anything."

"But you did. You're going to make a fine queen someday, Adri."

Normally a comment like that would have been enough to give me the shakes, but I was too blissed out to let it worry me very much. I'd raised the possibility that I was being attacked. I'd done my part and now I could happily stay where I was, cuddling with Alec, for as long as he would hold still.

Unfortunately a few seconds later my phone started ringing. I tried to ignore it, but Alec wasn't the type to ignore calls.

"Adri, are you going to get that?"

"No, voicemail was invented for precisely these kinds of moments. Nothing that anyone could be calling me about this early in the morning could possibly be important enough to get in the way of spending more time with you."

"Isn't that your mom's ringtone?"

"Yeah."

"I really think you should answer it. Your mom doesn't call very often—she probably has something important to tell you."

I shook my head, still steadfastly refusing to open my eyes. As long as I couldn't see Alec's face he couldn't employ his most dangerous weapon against me. His words were already persuasive enough—I definitely didn't want to have to try and resist the earnest, concerned look I knew was currently being directed at me.

"My mom doesn't call about important stuff, Alec. *You* get important calls—you know the ones where someone's life hangs in the balance. My mom just calls once a week or so to make sure she's fulfilled her motherly duties."

"She's trying to change, Adri, but if you don't give her a chance you can't complain that the two of you still aren't as close as you'd like to be."

"Fine. You win, but don't think that there won't be consequences later on. The last thing you want is for my mom to decide to relocate to wherever we end up living once all this is over. It's going to be very difficult for me to look very queenly if I've always got my mom hounding me about the fact that I'm not going to college like a good, sensible girl."

"No consequence is too dear if it means a happy future mother-in-law. Be sure to tell her it was me who convinced you to answer her call."

Alec rolled off the bed and ducked out of my room with a twinkle in his eye while I was still struggling to come up with a response. I threw my pillow at the swiftly closing door and then reached over and answered the phone.

"Hi, Mom."

"Hi, Adri. Did I wake you?"

"Normally you would have. We just left Oregon yesterday so I'm still on Pacific Time, but I had a bad dream that woke me up earlier than normal."

"Sorry, sweetie. I didn't know. I just figured that you were still in Utah."

"It's okay, you didn't know that we've been travelling lately. If I get really off of Utah time I'll put my phone on silent before I go to bed. How did your latest shoot go?"

Talking about her work was always safe territory and it was a good bet that she'd just finished an assignment sometime in the three days since we'd last talked. Russ was having a good effect on my mom when it came to convincing her to be less of a workaholic, but it was going to probably take years before she toned things down to the level most people would have called normal.

"It was really good. That's the first time that I've been down to Belize. You wouldn't believe how beautiful it was down there and the shoot went acceptably. The models were all great to work with, my equipment all arrived on schedule, and the weather cooperated completely."

"Wow, Mom. I think your standards are getting even more stringent. If the weather and models were all taking orders and you had your gear it seems like that's the definition of perfection to me."

"Adriana Paige, you may be a millionaire and living on your own, but that doesn't mean I can't show up and spank you if you get too big for your britches."

Part of me wanted to take exception with her tone, but mostly I was too busy envisioning Mom storming into the RV and being served tea by Donovan while he calmly explained to her that it simply wasn't done to administer any kind of physical discipline to the future queen of the North American shape shifters.

Alec, on the other hand, would probably hold her coat for her while she tried to administer said punishment.

"Sorry, Mom. You do have to admit that there isn't much more you could ask for on a photography shoot, though..."

"I suppose you're right. The work side of things was fine. I guess I was just sad that Russ wasn't able to fly down with me. We were scheduled to go down together, but then Patrick called at the last minute with something urgent and everything changed. It put me really out of sorts. Then you throw in the fact that my bodyguard was hassling some of the support staff, and it felt like the whole world was collapsing in on itself."

Bodyguard? That was new—I'd thought I was the only Paige forced to deal with having a minder less than twenty feet away at all times. I went to ask Mom what she meant, but she'd already moved on, talking as fast as always.

"Adri, Russ hasn't been acting like himself lately. Do you think that he's losing interest?"

I almost dropped the bottle of water that I'd just finished uncapping. "Seriously, Mom? This is Russ we're talking about. He's the last person you need to worry about stringing you along."

"I don't know, Adri. He's acting really different lately. He's been travelling a lot more than normal, and he's stuck me with a bodyguard. It was bound to happen really. Once the initial excitement wore off, there was no way I was going to be able to keep someone so eligible interested for the long haul."

I recapped my water bottle as I reflected on just how alike we were. We had so many differences that it was sometimes hard to remember that my mom and I shared a lot of the same insecurities.

"Mom, I don't think you're being fair to Russ. He's not the kind of guy to leap without looking. If he proposed to you then you're exactly what he's looking for. I know he could have almost any girl he set his eyes on, but I know a little bit about dating those kinds of guys. If something is bothering you then you need to sit down and talk to him about it."

There was a long pause as my mom digested my words. "You're right. You're not telling me anything that I haven't already told myself, but I just haven't been able to bring myself to broach the subject with him. What if I don't like the answer he provides? I'm not sure I'm ready for all of this to end."

"Who says it has to end?"

"There's something going on, Adri. Maybe you're right and he's not losing interest in me, but that doesn't mean that things are okay. For all I know, he's started trafficking drugs. Actually, that would explain a lot."

A chill worked its way up my spine. "What do you mean, Mom?"

"I don't know. There's the bodyguard, despite the fact that Belize isn't any more dangerous than any of the other places I've been to recently, but there's also the fact that when I stopped by for lunch last week Russ was seeing some guy out that isn't one of his usual associates."

"Some guy?"

"Yeah, you know the type. Tattoos, piercings, looked like he could bench-press a small car. It didn't look like they were on the best of terms either."

I closed my eyes for several seconds and then took a deep breath. "You said that your bodyguard was causing problems at the shoot—tell me more about that, Mom."

"I don't know, I wasn't watching. I was changing lenses and looked up as Jonas put some poor guy in an arm bar and then threw him off of the location. I'm right, aren't I? Russ is working with the Mafia or something, isn't he?"

"Is Jonas there with you now, Mom?"

"No, he picks me up whenever I need to leave and then checks the house when he drops me off, but he doesn't stay here in the apartment with me. Adri, how bad is this? Is Russ some kind of criminal?"

"I think it's too soon to be jumping to those kinds of conclusions, Mom, but I don't think it's too soon to begin taking some precautions."

"What do you mean when you say precautions?"

"I mean you need a bodyguard of your own, one who's on your payroll rather than on Russ'. Ideally you ought to get two bodyguards until you get to the bottom of whatever is going on right now."

"I don't...wait, you seriously think that I need three bodyguards? I wasn't even thrilled about the prospect of having one bodyguard and now you're telling me that I need *three*?"

"No, I'm telling you that you need a bodyguard you can trust who can worry about external threats without having to worry about what Jonas is going to do."

"Adri, you're completely overreacting! What has gotten into you?"

She was aiming for indignant, but she wasn't succeeding. She sounded exactly like what she was, scared but trying very, very hard to hide it.

"Mom, this is my world now. If I had questions about photography I'd come to you and I'd listen to your advice. Worrying about bodyguards and assassins is my photography. You need to pay attention to what I'm telling you."

I had her on the back foot for the first time in a very long while and I wasn't going to let up now, not when her life might very well depend on it.

"Listen, Mom. As soon as we're done you need to call the two most successful models you've worked with and ask them for bodyguard suggestions. Models, the really successful ones at least, probably deal with stalkers on a regular basis. I'll go talk to Alec and see if he has anyone he can put you in contact with, but his guys are going to stand out like a sore thumb in the kind of circles you run in."

It sounded like she was on the verge of hyperventilating.

"Mom, get a pencil and some paper and write this down. You need to get two bodyguards hired before the day is out and then you need to schedule a conversation with Russ. Make sure that you pick the location. Make it somewhere public, but run it past whoever you hire before you finalize things with Russ."

"Adri, you sound like a spy."

"Mom, I don't hear you writing. This is important."

"Russ is going to feel like I don't trust him. I don't think I can do this. I'm not sure I can afford to hire one bodyguard, let alone two."

"Right now you *already* don't trust him, Mom. Best-case scenario right now is that he's keeping something back from you, something dangerous enough that he thinks you need a bodyguard. The worst-case scenario is that he's put Jonas there to make sure he can control you. If Russ is just worried about you then he's not going to resent you taking your own precautions. As for the money, you aren't paying that ridiculous tuition now that I'm here, but if you need more money I can send you anything within reason."

I could hear the sound of a pencil on paper and some of the tension inside of me started to loosen now that she was taking the situation seriously.

"Okay, Adri. I'll start making calls as soon as I hang up. What should I be looking for as far as qualifications for a bodyguard?"

"I don't know for sure, Mom. I've never been the one actually hiring our people. Once you've got some names ask the candidates to evaluate the other names on your list, that should help weed out the guys that are totally unqualified, but it's still not perfect. I guess if you can find someone who helped protect a head of state that would be a bonus. Let me go ask Alec."

I stood and started towards the door, but my mom brought me up short with a single question.

"Adri, how much danger are you in? When I was in Utah last time you made it sound like Alec was just being paranoid with all of the security arrangements. That wasn't the case, was it?"

"I didn't say anything that was untrue, Mom, I just let you think what you wanted to think."

"Adri, I'm serious, how much danger are you in?"

"A lot. Probably more than you, but the difference is it was my decision to get involved with Alec and put myself in harm's way. I knew what I was getting into. Russ is keeping you in the dark, which means you can't even make an objective evaluation regarding how much danger you're in."

"What has he gotten you into, Adri? Is *Alec* some kind of drug dealer? I always thought it was suspicious that he had access to so much money. Have you even met his mother? The rumor back in Sanctuary is that she's been dead for years."

"Yes, I've met Samantha Graves and Alec didn't 'get me into anything,' Mom. Like I said, I chose this. Alec isn't doing anything wrong. The danger I'm in—that we are in—is because Alec is trying to stop some very bad people from doing terrible things."

"Then he should call the police, that's what they are there for, Adri. Don't let him drag you into some kind of vigilante-inspired quest for glory."

I wanted to yell at her, but I forced myself to keep my voice under control. My mother was older and more experienced than I was, but she wasn't ready for the world I'd been living in since we'd arrived in Sanctuary. She was obsessing about my situation as a way of denying the seriousness of her own circumstances.

"The police can't help us, Mom. They can't do anything until after a law has been broken, and even then, sometimes there are criminals they aren't qualified to deal with. You're in the same situation now. The police aren't going to be able to save you—you need to take steps of your own to make sure that you're not a soft target."

I opened the door to my room and looked out at the rest of the RV, but rather than the calm, ordered environment I'd grown to expect from our time on the road, I found the desperate motion of a group of people who were one step away from disaster. Alec was talking on the phone and the hand holding his cell had gone white from the effort of not crushing the device.

"What do you mean you don't have eyes on them? I specifically told you to keep their compound under observation. Buildings don't just disappear. If the satellite is still working then you should be able to see the compound and be able to confirm whether or not they've started evacuating."

Alec turned towards Donovan and pointed at the laptop the butler was working on. "Fine, send the feed to Donovan's machine. I want to see what you're talking about for myself."

Donovan's inbox chimed as an email arrived, and then his screen flickered as he clicked on a link and a video feed started playing. It took me several seconds to realize what I was seeing. There was so much smoke filling the center of the screen that it was only the large fountain on the bottom left-hand corner that made it possible to tell that we were looking at an overhead view of the Bishop Compound in Chicago.

A heartbeat after I finally registered what was going on all of the phones in the RV started ringing at the same time.

"Mom, I'm sorry, but I have to go. I'll call you back as soon as I can, but in the meantime make sure that you get those bodyguards."

Chapter 2

Adriana Paige
Interstate 15
Western Montana

It would have been impossible to adequately describe the chaos of the next few hours as call after call came in from our people letting us know that they had somehow picked up Coun'hij tails and that they needed help.

It wasn't surprising to find out that our RV had been set up with advanced communications equipment—that was exactly the kind of foresight I'd come to expect out of Alec and Donovan. What was surprising was the fact that we came frighteningly close to exceeding its capabilities and it was the only thing keeping our people from being cornered and defeated in detail.

None of us knew how it had happened, but somehow the Coun'hij had managed to track most of our people from the time that we'd split up. To be honest, most of us didn't have the time to think about the bigger picture. We left that to Alec and just focused on our little piece of the puzzle. Everyone was pressed into service in some capacity or another—even Vik, the hulking Tonopah hybrid who was currently serving as my bodyguard, ended up manning a headset.

Somewhere along the way both RV's started moving again, but I was too busy to notice. My world narrowed down to the laptop in front of me and the procession of voices coming through my headset. I never had time to change out of my pajamas—I barely even had time to understand what I was supposed to be doing.

All of the calls into Alec's personal cellphone were routed into the main switchboard and from there sent out to Vik or me for verification. Once the caller's identity was established I ran through a checklist of questions and entered their responses into my laptop.

"Are there any indications that you're being followed?" "Are you currently in motion?" "Where are you right now and where are you headed?" "How long do you have before you'll run out of gas?"

The questions were the kind of straightforward thing that I should have been able to memorize after my first time through them, but the sheer terror in their voices made it hard to type in their responses—I was pretty sure that I wasn't physically capable of anything more complicated than that.

As bad as the terror was, in some ways the ones who weren't alarmed were even worse. They were confident that Alec would find a way to save them, which made it easier to get the information I needed out of them, but it was hard not to disabuse them of their faith considering that I could turn my head and see the flurry of activity taking place around Donovan's desk.

Alec had a big map of the Western United States up on the giant touchscreen mounted on the wall and he was desperately trying to create a plan that would allow our people to survive what was coming next.

Yellow dots popped into existence every time a new call came into the switchboard. As I finished inputting the information from my current caller, a middle-aged woman from the Las Cruces pack named Daphne, a dotted line appeared around her location in Southern Utah.

The dotted line formed a circle that represented how much further she thought she could drive before she would run out of fuel. The single black dot orbiting her position on the map meant that she was being followed by only one Coun'hij vehicle.

"You'll send help, right?"

I tore my eyes away from the screen and forced a smile on my face, hoping the old adage about people being able to hear the smile in your voice was true. "Yes, we've had a few calls like yours come in today, so Alec is just tracking down which of our people are best placed to intercept the group that is currently following you. For now, turn back north the first chance you get. It looks like Cedar City is probably your best bet, but give me a call once you're headed north so I can confirm your location and the amount of fuel you have left."

"Thank you, Mistress Paige. I swear I've been careful ever since I left the main group in Nevada. I don't know how they managed to find me like this."

"Given the circumstances, I think it would be just fine for you to address me as Adriana, Daphne. I'm sure that you were careful, but we'll worry about how they found you after you're safe. For now you just concentrate on driving and Alec or I will get back to you as soon as he's arranged for someone to meet up with you."

"Thank you, Mistr...Adriana. Thank you very much. I knew that your fiancé wasn't the kind to leave his people hanging in the wind. That's why I was so willing to swear fealty to him when I arrived at the estate. Oh dear, listen to me go on. I'll let you go take care of your other duties."

It nearly broke my heart to hear such trust in her voice. She was old enough to be my great-grandmother and she was in an incredible amount of danger while I sat in a comfortable, climate-controlled RV and made promises I wasn't sure I was going to be able to keep.

I looked at the monitor at the top of my screen and confirmed that there wasn't anyone else in the queue. I flashed Vik a 'stay there' gesture and stood so I could walk over to Alec and Donovan.

"How many of our people are still unaccounted for, Donovan?"

Alec's voice was starting to sound a little strained, but Donovan didn't seem to notice. "We've had roughly seventy percent report in on their own. I've managed to get through to another ten percent and per your instructions I've instructed them to fill up their vehicles and prepare for some kind of rescue operation, but our connection to the outside world is becoming less and less reliable."

I shook my head. "What do you mean? It's been nonstop calls in for Vik and me. We haven't had anyone disconnect on us."

Alec nodded, but he didn't look away from the screen. "Donovan diverted most of our hacking resources toward keeping the incoming lines open, but it looks like the Coun'hij has finally entered the computer age. They are keeping constant pressure on our communications. It doesn't really matter at this point whether they are hoping to track us down or if it's simply an attempt to stop us from mustering any kind of coordinated response to the attack on our physical assets. At some point we're going to have to address their growing capabilities."

"Those are people out there, Alec. They aren't just assets."

Alec's knuckles went white and I realized that I'd pushed too hard. He was too much of a gentleman to say so, but he didn't need me jostling his elbow at a time like this.

"I'm sorry, Alec. I guess the pressure is getting to me. The calls keep coming in and I can't offer them anything solid. I feel like I'm just lulling them into a state of complacency rather than letting them know just how bad things are. *I* don't even know how bad things are."

"Bad. Really bad, but you don't need to apologize. You're right, I need to make sure I don't get so caught up in playing a giant game of chess that I forget that those are real people out there."

Alec turned toward Donovan, rewarding me with a smile in the process, and for the first time I realized how tired Alec looked. His eyes were bloodshot and he had dark circles under them. It seemed impossible that he was the same person I'd been cuddling with such a short time ago. He was under even more stress than I'd realized if he'd gone downhill so quickly and I suddenly felt even more guilty for my recrimination.

Alec hadn't ever forgotten that he was dealing with real people, not if he looked like that.

"Donovan, please add back in the location information for the ten percent of our people who aren't currently being followed. Color us, Grayson and Jaclyn red so I can decide where exactly I want to position the interceptions."

A dozen blue dots materialized on the map. The blue dots were just as scattered as the yellow dots, but they were still surprisingly comforting despite the fact that they were so few in number. I started to feel better about our situation right up until I realized that there was only one red dot on the map.

"I'm sorry, Master Alec; it looks like we've still been unable to contact Jaclyn or Grayson."

Alec closed his eyes as though momentarily unable to face the reality we found ourselves in. "That's going to make this a lot harder. Even if we manage to get ahold of the other twenty percent of our people we're still going to be looking at something like six-to-one odds."

"Indeed, sir. I'll divert some of the IT assets to establishing a secure line out now that the calls in have started to taper off and I'll personally try to get ahold of both of them."

Alec nodded absently as he started selecting blue and yellow dots. "Sync these seven up and then calculate a least-time intercept here on I-70. Try to bring the ones without tails together with whoever is the furthest east with enough time that they can fight the first round and still have time to get set before the next batch shows up."

It was like watching a special kind of symphony, one that used space, time and numbers in place of woods, brass and strings. We were too outnumbered to get away with just throwing all of our people into one big fight. Instead Alec wove a complex ballet of movement that resulted in our people coming together in ways that gave them sufficient numbers to have a chance of beating the opposition.

It felt like I stood there watching Alec for hours, but the truth was that the whole process took less than five minutes. At the end, Alec stepped back from the board and surveyed the results with a worried look.

"That takes care of the first round. I'm not sure it's wise to try to lock anything else in at this point. Too much will depend on how the first set of fights go."

"What about those two groups in the center? You've diverted almost everyone else who could help out away from those groups."

Alec nodded. "It was never going to work to try and cherry-pick them off anywhere but on the fringes. Donovan, are we still headed back the way we came?"

"Yes, Master Alec. I'm sorry to say though that I've still been unable to reach Grayson or Jaclyn."

"Fine. If we speed up just a little bit we'll be in a position to bail out this group here about the time the first of them runs out of gas."

Alec picked up a headset and keyed in a number from memory. It was obvious after the first second or two that he was going to go through to voicemail.

"Tasha, it's me. Look, I know you're not particularly happy about everything that has happened over the last couple of months, but this is bigger than you or me. We've had some kind of massive security breach. More than two-thirds of our people are being tailed right now by what we have to assume are Coun'hij forces. I've redeployed my remaining people, but there's simply not enough of us to deal with this problem by throwing bodies at it. I need you and Grayson in Nephi, Utah within the next hour and fifty minutes. Faster if you can manage it, but you absolutely have to be there by then or a lot of people are going to die, including a few from your pack."

Alec hung up on her and then turned back to Donovan. "Get me someone important in the Del Rio pack and then get started directing traffic out there. We've almost waited too long if we're going to make some of those intercepts work. I kept hoping that we would be able to get in contact with more of our people, but it can't be helped now. Once we have all of the intercepts in motion we can go back to trying to contact whoever we still haven't heard from. I doubt we'll be able to use them to set up any more intercepts, but maybe they will be able to tip the odds further in our direction at some of the fights we're already committed to."

Donovan nodded and began pulling up the number Alec had asked for. Alec gave me a tired smile. "They are going to need your help on the phones, Adri, if we're going to make this work. Just hang in there for a few more hours and things should calm down enough that we can start rotating people out for breaks."

"I know, don't worry about me. I'll call as many people as I have to."

Donovan looked up and pointed at Alec's headset. "I'm putting you through to a hybrid named Tiffany Marks. The last information I got out of Del Rio is that she's the one calling the shots right now."

I walked back over to my laptop and slipped on my headset as Alec adjusted his boom mike.

"This is Alec Graves. Am I talking to Tiffany Marks? Good, I have a business proposition for you. No, I don't care about your supposed neutrality. You're going to listen to me. Why? Because I'm the reason you're in power right now. Without me your whole pack would still be under Lori's thumb."

Alec's voice was completely emotionless. It was like nothing I'd ever heard out of him before and it was driven home to me once again that Alec had grown up in a very different world than I had. I was completely lost when it came to high-stakes negotiations, but Alec was perfectly at home in a world where showing the wrong emotion at the wrong time could result in people getting killed.

"I'm sorry, but a simple 'thank you' isn't going to balance the ledger between us. Yes, you could hang up on me, but if you do that I'll burn your entire pack to the ground and salt the earth as I leave town. Don't tell me that you don't think I could do it. We both know I wouldn't even have to see to it myself."

My hand was hurting, but I didn't understand why until I realized that it was clenched around the red coffee mug that I'd filled with water hours before.

Alec continued on, oblivious to how much distress he was causing me.

"No, you're right, on the face of things, that's not very much in keeping with my public persona of justice and mercy, but I know something you don't. You see, I'm fully aware that you've kept Everett locked up in a cage since shortly after you realized that he and his daughter have spent the last ten years playing you all for fools. I know that you've kept Lori in a drug-induced coma for weeks now, and that you killed Everett's right-hand man when he protested against what your little cabal was doing.

"How is that relevant? It's relevant because your entire pack has done enough wrong over the course of your coup that I'm sure I can find a pretext for executing you and the rest of the ring-leaders once I come to power. You have a choice—you can hang up on me now and hope that the Coun'hij succeeds, or you can do me a favor in exchange for leniency after I come to power.

"I want Lori, Everett, and anyone else you can spare on a plane to Utah in the next ten minutes. You have exactly one hour and forty-eight minutes to have Lori on the ground in Nephi, Utah and she needs to be awake and able to use her power against the Coun'hij enforcers who will be rolling into town five minutes after your arrival.

"I'm fully aware what that will mean. I suggest you leave half the pack behind to start packing. You'll want to be out of town before the Coun'hij can reposition one of their strike teams to come after your people.

"You don't have the option of sitting on the fence and we both know it. Right now you're down three hybrids, and without Lori you don't have anyone who's capable of playing the kinds of diplomatic games that have allowed you to stay neutral up until now. It was only going to be a matter of time before you were going to have to pick a side. All I've done is move up the schedule a little bit."

I didn't get a chance to listen in on the end of the conversation because my headset started ringing as Donovan finally got the outbound call details fed into the queue.

Chapter 3

Adriana Paige
Interstate 15
Western Montana

The next two hours were every bit as much of a nightmare as I'd expected them to be. On the one hand it was good, because Donovan kept me busy making dozens of phone calls to reroute our people to the ambush sites that Alec had picked out, but it was exhausting to project an air of calm assurance while knowing just how fragile Alec's solution really was.

I caught bits and pieces of what was going on around me. When we stopped for gas, Mallory tried to change over to our RV from the other one where Alec had assigned her when the calls had first started coming in. She wasn't happy when Alec told her there wasn't room for her inside of our vehicle, but she didn't have Donovan's computer expertise, she couldn't take over as the driver, and both Vik and I were in the middle of calls so she couldn't kick either of us out.

I heard Alec try to call Shawn and Ulrich at least two or three times to no avail. I got the impression when he finally got ahold of Jaclyn that she was too far away to be of any help. Alec asked her to go to Chicago instead and see what she could dig up on Ulrich's people.

That would have been depressing enough all by itself, but I also got the feeling that neither Tasha or Grayson had gotten back to us, which meant that everyone I was sending toward Nephi at varying speeds so that they would all arrive in town at the same time was probably headed into a gigantic trap.

The worst was when Daphne came up on my queue. I took a deep breath and then pushed the dial button.

"Hello?"

"Daphne, it's me, Adriana Paige again."

"Oh, thank goodness. I have to admit I was starting to get worried after so long without hearing from you. I called back in to let you know that I'd turned around as you instructed, but your bodyguard refused to let me through to talk to you."

"I'm sorry about that, Daphne. We got you headed north, which was the most important thing, so there were some other...issues that needed handling before I could get back to you. We're going to have you meet up with several of our people in a little town called Nephi. Do you still have enough gas to make it there?"

Apparently something in my voice gave me away—even over the phone. Daphne was quiet for several seconds and then sighed. "You're going to have to work on that, Adriana. Even good queens have to keep secrets from people. I hope you don't mind some unsolicited advice from an old woman who's way out of line right now, but you need to spend some time with someone you trust practicing the art of misdirection. How bad are things, really?"

"Pretty bad. You aren't the only one who is being followed by enforcers. Alec is redeploying people to try to ambush the Coun'hij teams, but we're awfully spread out and some people had a lot less fuel in their tanks than you did when they realized that they'd picked up a tail."

"Is there actually anyone waiting for me in Nephi?"

"Yeah, there will be, but most of them have tails of their own. Alec is trying to get one or more of our powerful hybrids down there to give you all the edge that you'll need to come out on top, but I'm not sure if they are going to make it there on time. Stay in your car for as long as possible and if push comes to shove change shapes and make a run for the location I'm texting you right now."

It wasn't much, but it was all that I could offer her, and we both knew it. After my call with

Daphne, things slowed down enough that I was able to catch more of what was going on, albeit in a second-hand manner, but for some reason it refused to integrate into any kind of cohesive picture. All I registered was fragments of information, pieces of scenes.

At one point Donovan looked up from his computer, hand pressed against his headset to make sure he could hear what was being said.

"The first ambush was a success. Louis reports that they drove off the enforcers with only three casualties."

Alec didn't even blink. "What was our loss ratio and how many of them did we kill? I need to know if we're losing ground to them."

"We lost two wolves and a hybrid in return for three of their hybrids."

"Fine, that means the odds shifted slightly in our favor. Tell Louis to get everyone there consolidated into the largest three or four vehicles and get on their way. They can bandage each other up while they are driving—we need them at the next site as soon as possible or the Coun'hij will beat them there."

I was on the phone for the next fight. I'd been guiding one of our wolves who was having a hard time finding the industrial park where we were staging the next fight. I'd just asked him if he could see the rendezvous site coming up on his right when he swore and floored the car. Two seconds later a terrible crash was the last thing I heard before the line went dead.

I didn't find out until later that the Coun'hij had correctly guessed his destination and tried to set up a counter-ambush. They'd underestimated how many of our people Alec had waiting there and the numbers were almost even right up until our guy slammed his car into one of the Coun'hij's hybrids. The driver ended up with a concussion and all of our people got injured in one way or another, but that time we managed to kill two hybrids before being chased off by the arrival of the car that had been tailing the wolf I'd been on the phone with.

They were going to be in for a long, tense drive, but they had a full tank of gas, which meant that they had time before they could be forced into another fight. Alec moved them to the bottom of the priority list and started scrambling for another way to fill in the hole that had been created by our not managing to leave the ambush site without a tail.

I watched the clock slowly count down to the time for the ambush in Nephi and my insides clenched tighter and tighter with each passing minute. I was so focused on the impending massacre in Southern Utah that I completely forgot about the fact that we'd been headed to Idaho with the intention of setting up an ambush designed to save the other half of our people.

It took me completely by surprise when the massive RV gently shuddered to a stop. Alec was at my side before I even managed to get out of my chair.

"I want you to stay inside the RV, Adri. This should be a quick, easy fight, but there's still no reason to risk you."

I wanted to argue with him, wanted to tell him that I belonged by his side, but I knew exactly how tight our timing was on this particular operation. I couldn't bring myself to argue with him, not this time, not when I knew doing so could end up costing lives.

"Fine, I'll stay inside, but I want you to take Vik with you. If things go badly I want you to have all the help possible out there."

"Okay. I'll take Vik and Donovan can stay here to drive the RV in case we need to bug out quickly."

"No, take Donovan out there too. I can drive the RV."

Alec wanted to argue with me, but I could see the same understanding in his eyes that was in the forefront of my mind. We simply didn't have time to waste, not if we were going to save our people. I got a short nod and then the rest of the shape shifters started filing out of the vehicle.

I worked my way up past all of the laptops and settled into the driver's seat, unrolling the passenger's window so I would be able to hear what was going on.

MARKED

Whoever had picked this location for the ambush site had been nothing less than brilliant—it was that perfect. We were situated in some kind of low, natural amphitheater in the middle of a lava field. We were parked on a large stretch of blacktop that seemed to indicate someone had been planning on building something out here at some point in the past, but if so they'd never followed up.

Paul, Alec's bodyguard, had parked our vehicle so that we were facing back the direction we'd come from, but I noted that only because it meant that I wouldn't have to turn the beast of an RV around if we did have to leave in a hurry. The other RV was parked just to the left of me, and I looked over expecting to find Mallory sitting behind the wheel, but the driver's seat was empty.

A few seconds of searching let me find Mallory, who was obviously in no condition to be in the middle of any kind of fight. That didn't seem to be stopping her though and even Donovan's beseeching looks in her direction didn't seem to be having any kind of effect on her. She had some kind of pistol hanging from the end of her arm and seemed to know how to use it.

"I want everyone to spread out in an arc. Stay far enough back that you don't get caught up in the area of effect of my ability, but if something goes wrong be ready to jump in and help out the new arrivals."

Alec's orders got a round of nods and then everyone turned towards the entrance of the amphitheater. A few seconds later I was able to hear it too, an engine under hard acceleration. The white subcompact that raced into view caused Alec and Donovan to look at each other in astonishment.

"I thought we were expecting someone in a black SUV first, Donovan."

"Indeed, sir."

The white car was followed by a red mini-van which was in turn followed by a pair of black SUV's, which would have been good except for the fact that these SUV's were sporting flecks of red and white paint from where they'd tried to run our people off of the road.

"They've learned from the other ambushes so far—they're being more aggressive. They want to get their people here all at once rather than letting them come in piecemeal. Why didn't we know this was developing? This is going to have major strategy implications, Donovan."

"I'm not sure, Master Alec. The logical answer is that they must have used their IT resources to shut down our communications."

"Once we're clear of this we're going to need to invest in some dedicated communications equipment. It's not going to be possible to get by just using the commercial providers like we've been doing up until now."

MARKED

The car and the minivan both screeched to a stop less than a dozen feet away from the RV's, but rather than following them, the two SUVs stopped back by the entrance to the amphitheater. I realized what was going on at the same time that Alec did.

"They're trying to trap the rest of our people and kill them before we can get there!"

The words came from a throat that was no longer human. Alec had thrown himself forward, shifting to hybrid form mid leap. The rest of our people—everyone but Donovan—followed less than a second behind, charging the two SUVs and the six heavily-tattooed men who were already exiting the vehicles.

Donovan was the last person I would have expected to lose his nerve, but then again maybe I wasn't being fair to him. It had been decades since he'd last fought in anything other than the financial arena, and there was something to be said for the idea that he was too valuable to be risked in a grand melee where luck would play just as much a part in his fate as his rusty combat skills.

I opened my mouth to call Donovan back, to order him into the other RV as a way of saving face, when it happened. The sound was a kind of crack, with an odd kind of vibrating echo that seemed to hang in the air afterwards. At first I didn't understand what had happened. Even after I finally registered that what I was hearing was gunfire, I initially thought the shot had come from Mallory who was limping along behind everyone else. Only her gun was still pointed down toward the ground.

By the time the second shot rang out, Alec was less than a dozen feet from the Coun'hij enforcers and based on the way that they'd crumpled to the ground, his power was active. The first shot had taken him in the left shoulder, but he didn't even slow down.

Afterwards I would ask myself again and again whether he initially just didn't realize that he'd been shot or if he knew but threw himself forward regardless, desperate to neutralize the enforcers who were guarding the only usable cover in the kill zone that the parking lot had just become.

Ash would have told me that the first shot out of a cold barrel is always the least accurate one. The sniper had missed Alec's heart by inches with his first shot. The second shot should have taken Alec's head off, but somehow he managed to twist aside at precisely the right instant to make the second shot miss him and tear through one of the SUV's instead.

I didn't remember starting up the RV, but I started it forward with a vague idea that I needed to be there with Alec rather than sitting here uselessly dozens of yards away. I started to veer to the left to avoid running Donovan over, but the only sign of his presence was fragments of black and white cloth that hadn't even had a chance to finish fluttering toward the ground yet.

Some of our people had figured out what was going on, but they still weren't fast enough. The third shot took Alec through the chest and he went down in a spray of blood that I knew was much worse than any other injury he'd ever sustained.

The two wolves and the hybrid who had arrived in the white car and the minivan scattered in an effort to avoid the incoming gunfire. Even Vik started towards the SUV's as though intent on saving his own neck. Only Paul acted the way that a bodyguard was supposed to.

Alec had started falling as a hybrid, but by the time he slammed into the ground he'd shifted back to his human form. It was a bad sign, he wouldn't have abandoned the safety of his hybrid body unless he was forced to. That meant severely injured...or dead.

Paul scooped Alec up with one hand, barely breaking stride as he charged towards the SUV's. His massive hybrid claws tore into Alec's flesh, but there wasn't anything to be done about it. Paul was right—the first priority had to be getting Alec out of the line of fire.

The Coun'hij enforcers that Alec had laid out so casually with his power were starting to stir now that he wasn't actively draining them. We still had at least a second or two before they would recover enough to pull themselves up to their feet and be a threat, but our people were too scattered. We needed them concentrated around the SUV's so that they could take advantage of the small window of time during which the enforcers were vulnerable, but if they'd stayed together they would have been too easy for the sniper to pick off.

All of that went through my mind in a flash as the RV finally got up to twenty miles per hour. I was contemplating trying to run the hybrids over, as unlikely as that was to work considering just how fast they were, and then I saw Mallory. She hadn't gone over to try and get Alec out of the line of fire, but then again given how crippled Agony had left her it was unlikely she could have done anything to save him.

Instead she continued limping toward the SUV's with the same determined gait that she'd used so far. She was less than twenty feet away from the enforcers when she raised her handgun and sighted in on the first hybrid.

They really weren't that far away in the grand scheme of things, but I couldn't imagine a world where *I* could have hit someone from so far away. Luckily Mallory wasn't me; her first shot was perfectly placed in the chest of her target and the next one followed up a split second later.

MARKED

The sound of the handgun was nothing more than muted pops in comparison to the crack of the hypervelocity rounds from the rifle. As another shot rang out from the sniper I absently wondered how I'd ever thought that first shot had come from Mallory. This time the sniper hit Paul. I didn't see where the shot landed, but Paul went down with a suddenness that initially made me think that he'd just tripped.

Mallory was still working her way through the enforcers. The third one had pulled himself to his knees by the time that she started in on him and it took three shots to put him down. Vik was past the initial shock of being shot at for the first time and he blurred into motion. I shouldn't have been able to follow him—maybe I simply visualized what I thought was happening, since my mind wasn't capable of following his actual motions—but it looked like he raked his claws across the throat of one enemy and then put his fist into the chest of a second enforcer.

I felt a tiny thrill of hope that we might be able to salvage the situation and then the sniper fired again and Vik rocked backwards as his shoulder turned into a mess of red. Mallory swapped magazines and resumed firing, scoring a shot on the last enforcer as he lunged toward her.

Mallory was as good as dead. In her human form she was faster than I was, but even if she hadn't been crippled she still wouldn't have been a match for a hybrid.

I had a fraction of a second to begin mourning her and then Vik was there. His left arm wasn't working, but that didn't stop him from tackling the other hybrid like an NFL lineman. The two of them hadn't even come down from their first bounce before Mallory put another bullet into the enforcer's head.

It was the kind of risky shot that meant she and Vik were going to have words later, but I didn't have time for worrying about that. After what felt like forever, I was finally pulling up next to Alec and Paul.

I angled the RV so that the right side was facing the sniper's position, and then bailed out of the driver's seat into the tiny sliver of ground that was hidden from the sniper's view. I wasn't under any illusion that the RV was actually going to stop a bullet; the best I could hope for was that he wouldn't hit anybody if he couldn't see us.

A second later another shot rang out, punching a hole in the aluminum skin of the RV that was bigger than both of my fists put together. I ducked despite knowing that it wasn't going to make any kind of difference. If the next shot had my name on it then nothing I did was going to change the outcome.

Somehow Mallory had made it over to my side. I looked at Paul and my mind blanked out. I'd registered that Paul had gone back to human form, but that was all my mind was willing to let me see. It wasn't the first time I'd seen a dead person, but it was the first time I'd seen someone killed by a high-powered rifle round.

"Get him off of Alec!"

Mallory's voice was loud in my ear. I started to comply, but she grabbed onto my arm. "Not you, him."

Vik was standing in front of me as if by magic. He'd shifted back to human form and his arm still hung limply at his side, but he was moving, which put him in better shape than Alec or Paul.

Another bullet tore through the side of the RV and then a scream cut through the echo of the most recent shot. After all of the shooting I shouldn't have been able to hear anything, but somehow my ears were still working well enough that I was able to register the fact that the scream had ended with an abruptness that wasn't natural.

A second later Donovan's voice drifted down to us. "The shooter has been neutralized. Get Master Alec inside before the next group of enforcers arrives."

Chapter 4

Adriana Paige
Interstate 15
Southern Idaho

We didn't make it away before the next two carloads of our people arrived, Coun'hij enforcers in hot pursuit. Actually, we didn't even come close. Our people were still running back to the RV after having scattered six ways from Sunday.

I thought we were all dead. Realistically we should have been. We had a slight edge in numbers, but not enough of an edge to make up for the fact that we would be pitting wolves up against hybrids. We were obviously in a state of disarray when the enforcers arrived, so they didn't seem to be in much of a hurry, at least not until the first of Donovan's shots slammed into the big hybrid at the center of their formation.

Up until that moment I hadn't even realized that Donovan even knew how to use a firearm, let alone that he was a crack shot capable of bringing down moving targets from a couple hundred yards away with an unfamiliar weapon.

I watched in awe as Donovan dropped three of the new enforcers in the couple of seconds between when the new arrivals stepped out of their vehicles and when both sides crashed into each other in a whirling frenzy of fangs and claws.

I'd been standing next to the driver's seat of the RV, paralyzed by a combination of shock and fear as our remaining wolves and hybrids tore into the last three enforcers, but Mallory's yell got me moving again.

"Where is Donovan? He's the best doctor the pack's ever had, but if he doesn't get here soon even he isn't going to be able to save Alec!"

I threw open the door and hung out of the RV, heedless of the fact that I was probably making our vehicle a priority target.

"Donovan, we need you down here right now!"

A second later something big knocked me completely away from the RV. My world rotated a couple of times as I went sailing through the air, and only the fact that I landed looking back towards the fight allowed me to piece together what had happened.

One of the Coun'hij hybrids had managed to break away from the fight and charge the RV. Vik had knocked me out of the way and then shifted forms as he leapt out of the RV and intercepted the enforcer.

It wasn't a fair fight, not with Vik unable to use one of his arms, but a pair of wolves had been nipping at the heels of the enforcer and once he and Vik finished skipping across the concrete they made short work of the outnumbered hybrid.

Donovan appeared at my side, as if by magic, and helped me to my feet. I turned to thank him and almost tripped over my own feet as I registered his appearance. He was wearing a standard, pack-issue ha'bit which meant that for the first time I was able to see the wiry musculature that his butler's uniform had always concealed before now.

Donovan wasn't going to be featured on any swimsuit calendars in the near future—he was still obviously an old man—but there was a solidness to him that I'd never noticed before. He looked like a sixty-year-old, but he looked like a sixty-year-old who worked out.

All by itself that would have been enough to give me pause, but it was the blood smeared across his face that really threw me for a loop. The sight of Donovan with his hair in disarray and a massive rifle in his left hand was nothing in comparison to visible proof that he'd just killed the sniper using nothing more than his fangs.

I tried not to be obvious about my shock, but Donovan noticed my lingering gaze and bowed his head slightly in apology.

"I profoundly regret my appearance, Miss Paige, but I'm afraid there simply isn't time for me to do anything about it. Please, we must hurry back into the RV if I'm going to be able to save Master Alec."

I shook myself out of my stupor and hurried back towards the RV. I would have insisted that Donovan go before me since he was the one we needed to get to Alec's side, but I wasn't sure that he would bend protocol that much, even with Alec's life on the line. It was easier and quicker to just move as fast as I was able.

A few seconds later we reached my room at the back of the RV and Donovan was pouring rubbing alcohol over his hands as Mallory used her free hand to finish laying out the supplies from the medical kit stored in the front of the RV.

Donovan fished out a pair of tiny clamps and then moved Mallory's hand out of the way. He talked as he inserted both clamps into the hole in Alec's chest and then went back for more.

"We're expecting one more car, but the fact that it hasn't arrived yet means that they are probably already dead. Every minute we stay here increases the odds that we're not going to be leaving. Mallory, someone has to get the convoy moving. Please see to it. Out of all of the people we have left, you have the most derived authority given your close association to Alec."

For a second I thought Mallory was going to argue that I needed to be the one to organize our remaining forces. She'd known Alec for longer than I had and obviously wanted to be there at his side if these were his last minutes on earth.

Donovan looked away from the needle he was threading through the ruin of Alec's chest for just long enough to shoot Mallory a stern look. "It has to be you. I need Miss Paige here to communicate with our IT assets. Some of them refuse to use a phone and you don't even know how to type."

Mallory would have been less incensed if Donovan had physically slapped her. The expression on her face said that he would pay for that comment later on when there weren't any witnesses around, but she spun on her heels and headed out of the room without saying another word.

"Miss Paige, I need an assistant, but don't waste time trying to find the perfect candidate. Please grab the nearest submissive you can find, and bring them back here. I should have thought that particular need through minutes ago. You're going to need both of your hands to fulfill your task. It will do us no good for me to save Alec's life only so that all of us can die in prison cells, assassinated by Coun'hij agents a month from now."

I nodded and ran to the front of the RV. Mallory was already giving orders and apparently Donovan had been right about the amount of authority Alec had invested her with because nobody was arguing with her.

I spent less than a second looking over the crowd of people starting to disperse to the various tasks that Mallory had assigned them. My time with the pack had taught me a lot about body language and the short brunette on my side of the group had submissive written all over her.

It would have been a very bad idea to grab the arm of most shape shifters, but I grabbed her arm and didn't even think about the possible consequences until later. Apparently she was even more submissive than most, that or my status as Alec's fiancé gave me even more weight to throw around than I'd thought.

"I need you to come with me. What's your name?"

"But Mallory just told me to..."

I looked over at Mallory. "I need this one—find someone to fill in for her."

Mallory didn't look happy to be taking yet another set of orders, but I didn't give her a chance to argue with me. I stepped into the RV, still pulling Donovan's newest assistant forward by one arm.

"What is your name?"

"Ruby, your highness. My name is Ruby."

"Good. Do you have any first-aid training, Ruby?"

"A little. Louis made all of us take some classes, but I really don't know very much."

"That's okay, you don't need to know much. Mostly you just need to be able to follow directions. Donovan, this is Ruby—Ruby, meet Donovan. Help him with whatever he needs. Alec's life depends on it."

Ruby turned so white that I thought for a moment that she was going to pass out, but either she was made out of sterner stuff than I would have originally guessed or the habit of obedience was just too ingrained to allow her to do anything other than follow orders. She nodded and then stepped towards the bottle of rubbing alcohol.

I brushed a lock of hair out of the way as I forced myself to look away from Alec's bleeding form. "Okay, Donovan, what do you need me to do?"

"Please get my laptop, it has all of the necessary protocol installed on it."

The next two hours passed in erratic stops and starts. When I was deep in the middle of communicating with one of Donovan's hackers I was temporarily able to forget that Alec was bleeding to death less than four feet away from me. When that was the case time flowed by at a normal speed. The rest of the time it felt like I was balanced on the edge of a cliff, like I'd already slipped and had started to fall and only the fact that time was holding still had stopped me from plummeting to my death.

Donovan steadfastly refused to answer any of my questions about how the surgery was going. Initially he simply didn't acknowledge that I'd even asked them. It took several attempts before he finally looked up from Alec's chest and frowned at me.

"With all due respect, Mistress Adriana, I'm at the limits of my capability. I can operate on Master Alec and I can probably direct you with sufficient skill to get us away safely, but my attempting anything more than that will simply guarantee that I'll fail at one or both of those other tasks."

After that I shut up and other than asking questions directly related to what he needed me to communicate to his hackers, I let him focus on sewing up Alec.

The first two hours were more intense than I would have guessed they would be. I had multiple chat windows open and was trying to answer four or five hackers at the same time at any given moment. I couldn't even keep straight who was asking what, but Donovan kept track of all the personalities and what they were asking without even seeming to break a sweat. There were even several times where he anticipated a question before it was asked.

Up to that point in my life there hadn't been very many chances to watch a true master practice their chosen vocation. My mom had probably been the first. She'd started out as a terrible photographer, but the last shoot I'd gone to with her in New York had been nothing less than amazing. That was probably the first time that I'd really understood why she'd turned our lives upside down twice in an effort to follow her dreams.

Mom had owned the entire location. She'd kept the shooting schedule in her head at the same time that she'd worked with one model and monitored the progress of three others who'd been in various stages of getting into wardrobe or having their makeup done. The level of respect that everyone there had accorded her had bordered on awe—and I'd completely understood why they'd felt that way.

As good as Mom had been, Donovan was even more impressive. I don't know if anyone else in the world could have accomplished that kind of surgery in a moving vehicle, bags of blood swaying in the air next to them, while working with an untrained assistant, and directing counterintelligence operations against the best cyber-talent the Coun'hij had managed to bring to the event.

At one point I couldn't help but stop what I was doing and just sit there and watch Donovan's sure, deft movements. He was in his element in a way that I'd never experienced before because I didn't have an element. All I could do was continue relaying his instructions and hope that his skills were sufficient to save Alec.

Mallory got the RV moving and back on the interstate within minutes of me arriving back in the bedroom with Ruby. She even sent someone back to the bedroom to ask for the number to the last car, the one that had been supposed to meet us back at the amphitheater but which never showed.

I didn't find out until later that the driver of that last vehicle never answered his phone. All we could assume was that Donovan's fears had come to pass and the Coun'hij's people had managed to run him off of the road sometime before he could make it to the rendezvous point.

Somewhere along the way Donovan instructed me to go out into the main section of the RV and get Vik back on the phones so we could resume relaying instructions to the rest of our people.

The data that started flowing in once the switchboard was manned wasn't pretty. The initial ambushes had gone well, but once the Coun'hij had figured out that Alec and Donovan were luring them into traps things had gotten ugly. Our people went from having slight numerical advantages to fighting outnumbered.

We'd had a few surprise upsets—hybrids who outfought some of the Coun'hij's best or wolves who bailed out of their cars and then proceeded to outrun their pursuers on four legs—but we'd lost a lot more people, people we couldn't afford to lose.

The only truly bright spot was the fact that throwing those kinds of numbers at us required time for the enforcers to reposition. Occasionally they guessed wrong with regards to where we were trying to set up our ambush, so whoever was running their side of the operation wasn't infallible.

Even when they guessed right sometimes they weren't able to get people shifted to the location in time, and even when they did, that meant whoever they had been following before being ordered to redeploy to the supposed ambush site was then free and clear.

When it became clear that we couldn't continue to count on winning our ambushes, Donovan and I started instructing our people to start trying to lose whoever was tailing them. I would have given almost anything right then to have access to Ash, but he steadfastly refused to pick up his phone.

Donovan indicated that Alec had talked to Isaac earlier in the day, but Isaac and Kristin had gone completely dark too, which meant that we had to use the next best resource we had. I hated calling Dominic more than almost anything. Calling her meant that I was putting her, James, Andrew, Addison and Alec's mom all in danger, but I couldn't come up with any other way of giving the rest of our people who were still being chased a chance of surviving the next few hours.

Dominic was the one who seemed to have picked up the most tradecraft from Ash in the weeks and months leading up to the attack on the estate. That was probably part of why Alec had chosen Dom and James to guard the pack's noncombatants. So far Alec's trust in Dom's skills was being vindicated, but after the way that the Coun'hij had managed to track down such a large percentage of our people, I wasn't sure how long even her luck could last.

Donovan seemed to be focusing on the idea that we'd been outmaneuvered by the Coun'hij's cyber-assets, but I wasn't so sure of that. We'd go ahead and take all of the precautions Donovan wanted to implement now that we couldn't be positive that we had the edge when it came to hacker talent, but I didn't really think that we were being tracked by way of our phones. I was pretty sure that the Coun'hij had just unveiled one of their secret members, one of the ones Alec had been worrying about earlier that morning.

Dominic graciously agreed to do whatever she could to talk the rest of our people through trying to lose their tails, but I could hear the doubt in her voice even as she agreed to my request and I handed her off to Vik to route her to whoever was the closest to running out of gas.

I didn't say anything to try and reassure her because I knew she was right. It isn't easy to lose someone who is determined to follow you. It's possible, but only if you knew what to look for. Dominic could explain the principles over the phone, but the chances of someone correctly implementing them on their first try in a real-world situation were not very good.

Once everything else had been dealt with, I finally turned my attention to piecing together what had happened in Nephi. I'd already caught bits and pieces of information as Vik and whoever was helping him updated our database. It didn't sound good, but I'd told him to put the highest-ranked individual we had on the ground there in charge and then I'd buried myself in everything else that needed to be done.

I knew it was a questionable decision. All of those other people I'd chosen to put at the front of the queue were important too, but Nephi was our biggest single concentration of assets and it was hard to legitimately value anything ahead of that.

I could tell that Donovan had picked up on my hesitation to pursue the situation in Nephi, but he didn't press, either because he was too focused on trying to keep Alec alive, or because he didn't want me to lose face in front of Ruby. I didn't analyze it too much because that would have pulled my own feelings out into the open where I couldn't continue to ignore them.

The situation came to a head when my screen flashed with an incoming call that I hadn't asked Vik to put through to me.

"What in the hell were you thinking, Alec?"

I'd exchanged maybe ten words with Natasha Annikov since I got back from New York and found out that she and Alec had been days away from sealing an alliance between the Tucson and

Sanctuary packs by getting married like a couple of feudal nobles. Despite not having heard her voice more than two or three times, I recognized it instantly. Call me jealous, but everything about Tasha was burned into my memory. She'd come very, very close to taking Alec away from me forever and the worst part was the nagging little voice in the back of my mind that kept telling me I couldn't hate her because it had all been *my* fault for having walked out on Alec in the first place.

"I'm sorry, but Alec isn't available to talk to you right now, Tasha. Perhaps I can help you in some way or another."

"Adri Paige. It will be a cold day in hell when that's the case. Put Alec on the phone."

"This may surprise you, but I'm not in the habit of repeating myself. Alec isn't available right now. If you legitimately need something then tell me and I'll make sure it gets taken care of. Otherwise get off of the phone line so I can get back to helping people who aren't so poisoned by jealousy that they can't even see straight."

I thought for a second that Tasha was going to choke on her own spit, but after a couple of seconds of strained near-silence she got to the point. "I don't know what Alec was thinking leaving everything up to a voicemail like that, but Grayson and I managed to get to Nephi just before our people started rolling into town."

"Good, I'm glad you were able to make it in time. What happened after that?"

"The enforcers timed their arrival so that they all showed up at once. There were a lot more of them than anyone told me to expect."

"I see. And did you call back into headquarters once you got Alec's message or were you too busy fuming to realize that the prudent thing would have been to find out if we had any kind of revised force estimate for you?"

She didn't like that. I didn't have to be there in person—or even know her very well—to know that she was probably bleeding off metaphysical energy like a sun on the point of going supernova.

"Grayson and I were focused on trying to make Alec's little deadline. We didn't have time to waste calling in to plead for updates that *you* should have been sending *us*."

"And ironically, Alec and the rest of our people were too focused on trying to save dozens of people scattered across nine different states to waste time repeatedly calling an operative who hadn't even bothered to let us know that she'd received her orders and was on the way to try and fulfill her mission. You didn't call in, so we wrote you off and Alec made other arrangements."

"You mean that whore from Del Rio."

"If you're referring to Lori, then yes, I believe that Alec made arrangements for her to be in

Nephi in case you and Grayson couldn't be bothered to follow orders. If you have a problem with that then you'll have to wait to take that up with Alec when he's got a few minutes to waste. I fully agree with his decision."

That wasn't even a little white lie. If there hadn't been so much else going on when I'd overheard Alec make the call to Del Rio—and if there had been a way to talk to him without undercutting his authority with everyone within earshot—I would have had a thing or two to say to Alec about the idea of recruiting the slut who'd tried to use her lust-creating power to steal him away from me.

Saying that I fully supported Lori being on the ground with our people was about as big a lie as it was possible for me to tell, but I figured I was angry enough right then that Tasha wouldn't be able to tell for sure that I was lying.

Actually, it was too bad. Hating Lori was probably the only thing that both Tasha and I could really get behind. Still, I wasn't going to give away the upper hand now that I had it, not against Tasha Annikov.

"Do you have any idea what she did?"

"Why don't you just go ahead and tell me your version of events. I'll be calling her shortly to get her version."

"Grayson had the situation under control. The enforcers were on the ground convulsing and our side was executing them. Everything was fine until she arrived and short-circuited his ability. One minute we had everything under control and then a wave of lust washes over everyone on both sides and Grayson's eyes roll back in his head. I thought for a second that all of the guys and half of the females here were going to rip her apart in their effort to be the first to get to her."

"I take it that she survived?"

"Yeah. It was the eeriest thing I've ever seen. She asked for silence and no sooner had the words left her mouth than you could have heard a pin drop. Then everyone lined up in two lines just like she asked them to, and she told the enforcers that she wanted them dead, that it was the sacrifice she needed out of them if they were going to please her."

I wanted to say that was terrible, but I wasn't sure how well that would fit with my current persona, the act that so far had done the impossible and made Tasha toe the line. Tasha continued before I could decide what the appropriate response was.

"I've never seen anything like it. Some of the enforcers slit their own throats. Most of them just stood there and let our guys kill them without even trying to defend themselves. Only a couple in the whole group managed anything even remotely like effective resistance, and even they were swarmed down in seconds. I saw wolves well into their second century, wolves with enough experience to know better, throw themselves directly into the claws of some of the baddest hybrids on the planet like they were hotheaded kids with more brawns than brains."

"How many did we lose?"

"Only one, but it was one we didn't need to lose. If she'd just stayed out of things then Grayson could have held them all in place for the minute or so more we would have needed to dispatch all of them. That death is on her head; more than that, it's on Alec's head and if you supported his decision then it's on your head too."

Chapter 5

Adriana Paige
Interstate 15
Southern Idaho

I wanted to throw up, but I hadn't eaten anything since the evening before so there wasn't anything in my stomach to come back up. I couldn't have said how I got off of the phone with Tasha, but I had vague memories of telling her to make sure that everyone was taken care of and that they cleared far enough out of Nephi that the authorities wouldn't be able to track them down.

There were two calls waiting for me in the administrator phone queue, but I couldn't bring myself to answer them. I looked over at Donovan, who now had blood smeared all the way up to his elbows in addition to the blood on his face from when he'd killed the sniper.

"I have to know, Donovan. Is Alec going to survive or has all of this been for nothing? I'll get back on the phone and lie to all of those people if that's what needs to happen to make sure that the wheels stay on long enough for Alec to take back over, but I can't do it if he's not going to be around to pick up the pieces when I fall apart in a few days because of all the stress and the lies."

Donovan looked up at me and for the first time I could remember he looked old in the I-have-one-foot-in-the-grave-and-it's-only-a-matter-of-time-before-the-rest-of-me-follows way. I'd seen Donovan face with equanimity the destruction of the house that had been his to maintain for more years than I'd been alive. I'd watched as he dealt with Rachel's disappearance with the kind of serenity few parents could have hoped to match, but now he looked exhausted in ways that went much deeper than just a lack of sleep.

"Ruby, you've been an outstanding assistant, I'm sorry to have to do this, but I need your word that you won't breathe a word of what has transpired in this room to anyone."

"Of course, Mr. Harringsford."

"I'll need you to bind your beast to it."

"Very well. I promise not to breathe a word of what has transpired in this room to anyone."

"This ye so swear, unto this you bind yourselves?"

"Yes, this we so swear. Unto this we bind ourselves."

"Thank you, my dear. You can leave now. Please activate the white noise generator on your way out and then shut the door behind you."

Donovan watched until Ruby was gone and then resumed working on Alec for several seconds before he finally sighed.

"I can't say for sure, Mistress Paige. To be honest I should have lost Alec four or five times in just the last hour. The bullet passed within a centimeter or two of his heart."

"So it missed it then, that's good, right?"

"With a different bullet, yes, but a bullet of that caliber moving at supersonic speeds doesn't just tear through flesh it creates a shockwave that destroys everything in a cone around the entry wound. By everything I've seen since I began practicing medicine Alec should have been dead before he hit the ground."

"But he's not, right?"

"No, he's not, but we've used our entire store of whole blood and there is still severe damage to the area around his heart. I think that I've got the bleeding stopped, but if I don't then he could very easily end up dead before we can find more blood."

"What's his blood type? He can have a pint of mine."

"I don't think that's a good idea, Mistress Paige."

"You're not even going to ask what my blood type is first?"

Donovan didn't even look up from his sewing. "No, I'm not. Your idea has merit and if in an hour his blood pressure has continued to drop, I'll search among the rest of our people for someone who has the correct match, but we will not be using your blood."

"Why not, Donovan?"

"Because you are Alec's heir and we are still in the middle of a war. I'm not going to do anything that might put you at risk."

"That's ridiculous. People give blood all of the time. It's perfectly safe."

"Indeed that is the case for civilians, but what do you think it would do to your chances of survival if you were injured just after giving blood? You're too important to the monarchy to risk in such a way. You need to be preserved at all costs so that you can rule over our people."

I was almost too shocked for words. I had to shake my head incredulously several times before I finally managed a verbal response.

"Donovan, we both know that isn't true. The only thing that makes me even remotely important is the fact that Alec cares about me. I'm not fit to rule over anything. If I'd been the one in charge today everyone would have died. You were the one who killed the sniper, you were the one who operated on Alec, and you were the one who sent the police chasing their tails so that we could flee the scene of the battle."

I took a deep breath and said the words that we both knew needed said. "Donovan, you need to be the one in charge of things until Alec is back on his feet. I can't do it, I'll just get everyone killed."

Donovan looked up just long enough to give me a sad smile. "Quite to the contrary, Mistress Paige. You are the only one who can hope to keep Master Alec's coalition together in his absence, temporary or otherwise. My close association with Master Alec has imbued me with a certain amount of his authority, but I'm a shape shifter and that means that I'm part of the normal dominance hierarchy. No matter how good my opinions actually are, I will eventually be challenged for my position and the fact that I am or am not viewed as Master Alec's logical successor will never even enter into the equation.

"You on the other hand are a human being. That means you stand outside of the normal dominance hierarchy and the fact that you're gifted with an ability means that you're still somewhat of our world. More importantly you'll be viewed as a fairly neutral party.

"The authority Master Alec has invested you with will guarantee your position for at least the next several days, possibly as long as a few weeks. With any luck, Master Alec will be back on his feet by then, but if the worst should come to pass, you'll have had a period of time in which you were able to show yourself as a reasonable, competent, fair ruler. If you can come to a favorable arrangement with Jaclyn Annikov or Grayson there is a chance that you'll be able to cement your position and continue ruling long past the time when the Coun'hij is defeated."

"I don't have anything to offer Grayson or Jaclyn."

"You have Alec's half of the Graves fortune, but more importantly you have the qualities that Master Alec saw in you so long ago. You have the potential to be an excellent queen, you merely need time to grow into the role."

"And if I say no?"

"Then it won't matter whether Master Alec lives or dies. In the absence of a strong central authority, especially after a setback such as we suffered today, our coalition will evaporate in a matter of days or possibly even hours. With no other significant distractions to worry about, the Coun'hij will hunt all of Alec's closest confidants down and none of us will survive the month."

Chapter 6

Adriana Paige
Interstate 15
Northern Utah

After Donovan put things like that I couldn't refuse to do whatever it took to try and hold things together. I took a deep, bracing breath and then I put my headset back on and answered the first of the calls that were waiting for me.

"This is Adriana Paige, what do you need, Ms. Marks?"

The communications software on Donovan's laptop told me who had been waiting to talk to me, but I knew far too little about Tiffany Marks. I was about to continue the high-stakes negotiation that Alec had started with her a few hours previously with nothing more to go on than an overheard conversation between her and Alec.

"I was told I was being put through to Alec Graves. Nobody said anything about making me dance for his skirt."

"Really? I rather suspect that you were told you were being directed to the person in charge. Right now that is me, and I'm feeling generous right now, so I'm going to let you apologize and start over rather than telling Alec to go ahead and carry out the threat he leveled against you earlier today."

I could tell based on the lungful of air that she sucked in that she was about to reply with something hasty, so I beat her to the punch.

"I'm the one who has been sitting in on Alec's conferences for the last two months, Ms. Marks. Unlike you, I know what's really going on and if you cause me even a single moment more unpleasantness you're going to find yourself very, very alone in the middle of a world that is much, much more dangerous than you've been led to believe."

A tiny part of me wondered what Daphne would have thought of my performance. I wasn't any better at misdirecting people than I had been earlier in the day, but this time I was the one calling the shots and that was surprisingly liberating. I didn't have to dance around the truth because as long as Vik and the rest of our people were willing to obey me, in a very real sense I could create my own reality and the reality I could see for Tiffany Marks could become very bleak indeed.

"You're much more than I was told to expect."

"That's the funny thing about rumors, Ms. Marks. They rarely turn out to be accurate. I'd suggest you spend some time pondering that little gem of wisdom over the next few days. I suspect there will be some very wild rumors spawned because of today's events. Now what do you need? And be quick about it. I have a number of other pressing things that still need to be done."

"Graves steamrolled me into helping, which means that everyone else in my pack who didn't fly here on the plane with me is currently in cars headed north with no destination in mind and very little cash. It took everything we could scrape together on short notice to charter a jet that had any hope of making the deadline we were given."

"It will be some time, a few hours at the very least, before I can give you a solid idea of where your people should be headed, but I'll see to it that you are all taken care of. I'm going to transfer you back to Vik and he will see to it that a reasonable amount of money is made available to you. Tell him I told you to ask for two hundred thousand dollars."

I heard a soft inhalation and wondered how Tiffany had ended up running the Del Rio pack. Even I could tell that she was much too transparent to last long in the position. It was a useful piece of information, as was the knowledge of just how impoverished her fellow pack mates were. Money couldn't buy loyalty, but it could buy obedience and I was more than happy to settle for that for now.

"The money is for *all* of your people, Tiffany. If you try to run off with it, things will not go well for you."

"You're not afraid of throwing your weight around, are you?"

"I'm simply doing what needs to be done, Tiffany. It's not always pleasant, but right now there is more to be done than Alec could possibly get to."

"I guess there are a whole lot of people who've underestimated you."

I started to say goodbye, but Donovan's words about needing allies were still ringing in my ears. I was pretty sure that I'd taken things as far as I could with Tiffany for now, but that was okay. She wasn't any more or less powerful than any other hybrid. In fact, the only reason that I was talking to her was because Alec had made promises to her and the only reason that Alec had called her in the first place was because she was the one currently holding Lori's leash.

The real question was whether she understood that, and if she did whether she actually wanted to be responsible for keeping Lori from doing something even worse than what she'd already done.

"Tiffany, what have you done with Lori?"

"She's sitting in a rental car with two of my people who are ready to cut her throat if she so much as twitches. I would have drugged her up already, but we left home in such a hurry that we forgot to grab the tranquilizers. Now that you're sending me some cash I'll go make a quick trip to a veterinary supply store and buy something strong enough to put an elephant under."

"I want to talk to her."

"Why on earth would you want to do that?"

"Because I'm a relatively neutral third party and you're currently sitting on the back of a tiger and praying it doesn't realize that your arms are getting tired. There's a small possibility that I can work this situation around to one that benefits both of us."

She wasn't happy about giving Lori the phone, that much was obvious from the way that she stomped over to the car where Lori was being held, but she went and for now that was all I could ask.

"Someone wants to talk to you."

"H-hello?"

"Lori, you and I haven't ever met, but my name is Adriana Paige. Do you know who I am?"

"Alec Graves' girlfriend?"

"More precisely, I'm Alec's fiancé and future wife. I'm the one you tried to screw over by using your powers to manipulate him into being your sockpuppet."

"I didn't want anyone to get hurt. You don't know what it's like to be part of a small pack that's besieged on all sides by enemies. All I've ever done is try to protect my father and keep our pack from getting caught up in your little war."

"Actually, I know exactly what that feels like. We've had a knife to our throat for the entire time I've been part of Alec's pack. The difference is that we've never taken away people's ability to choose their own path."

"Whatever helps you sleep. I've heard enough stories to know that isn't true. Alec isn't any different than any of the rest of the pack alphas. He's used force and intimidation to get nearly everything he's ever wanted."

"It's logic like that, Lori, that made me think I was probably wasting my time talking to you. Threats and intimidation are part of the world we live in. I don't like them, but sometimes that's the only way to get someone to see the situation they are actually facing. At the end of the day though, they still have a choice. That's why your ability is such a deviant thing. Someone under your influence doesn't have the ability to choose anymore."

She took a breath, probably to respond with righteous indignation, but I beat her to the punch.

"How did it feel to take control of all those people and then order the enforcers to kill themselves?"

Based on how long it took her to answer me, I'd caught her completely off guard. "It...it was scary. It was the first time I've ever taken out all the stops on my gift like that. Before Alec outed me, I always took a lot of effort to make sure that I used my gift in subtle ways. My father always told me never to push anyone so hard that afterwards they would question a decision they'd made in our presence."

"Maybe I was wrong about you, Lori. A lot depends on where you choose to go from here."

"What do you mean? I don't have any choices. Tiffany is going to drug me again so I'm safely unconscious until the next time somebody needs me to wipe out an enemy army for them. Even if that wasn't the case, nobody is ever going to trust me now that everyone knows about my ability."

"That's the funny thing about trust, Lori. We all trust people who could hurt us, but we trust them because of their past actions. Spend some time thinking about that, and while you're at it try to figure out which side of this war you want to be on."

"What if I don't want to pick a side?"

"That's not going to be an option and you know it—at least your dad knows it. That's the only reason for the two of you to have come to

Sanctuary in the first place. Now hand the phone back to Tiffany, I have other people I need to talk to."

There was a pause, almost like Lori was having a hard time wrapping her mind around what I'd just said, and then I heard her pass the phone over.

"You get enough do-gooder points to salve your conscience after running roughshod over me?"

"Think what you will, Tiffany, but that was a very necessary conversation. I want you to leave Lori awake. Make sure that she's well-fed, that she's got clothes and is otherwise treated like a human being—her dad too, wherever he is."

"Are you out of your mind? Lori is one of the most dangerous hybrids in the entire world. I'm not going to just let her run around and build up some kind of army."

"I didn't say anything about letting her go. I want you to keep her under guard, I just want you to show some humanity in the process."

"I can't keep her under guard. The only way this has worked up to this point is because we've been able to keep her under sedation. I don't have enough people to keep her under a twenty-four-hour guard and fight off every male if she decides to make them attack us like she did a little while ago with the Coun'hij."

"I'm aware of the unique challenges involved in what I'm requesting. I'm authorizing you to recruit from the rest of Alec's people to fill out your rotation of female guards and I'll furthermore provide a salary of two thousand dollars per day to each of your guards to recompense them for the long hours they are going to be putting in."

"I don't think that you're listening to me. It isn't possible to hire enough guards to stop every male in the state—shape shifter, human or vampire—if she sends them all at us at once."

"I heard you just fine the first time, but you're failing to register the most important fact of all. Lori could have done that already and she hasn't."

"Only because we've had our claws at her throat the entire time."

"Maybe, or maybe she's just not as far gone as all of us assumed. Make this happen for me, Tiffany. Hire however many guards within reason that you think you need, prohibit any of our men from approaching closer than fifty feet, take whatever precautions a prudent person would take in your situation, but make sure that Lori is conscious and well taken care of. An awful lot may depend on it."

"Fine, but if this all goes wrong and she goes off the rails then I'm coming for you personally. And not even your boyfriend can protect you while he's sleeping."

"*If* Lori 'goes off the rails' then I rather doubt either of us will be around to worry about anything, but your threat has been noted."

I hung up on Tiffany and pulled up the call queue, but Donovan cleared his throat before I could patch the next call through.

"What are your plans with regards to the Del Rio girl, Mistress Paige?"

"I'm not honestly sure, Donovan, but it's like you said, if things go badly I'm going to need someone higher up the food chain to back my play. Lori may or may not be that person, but it feels right to start positioning myself as her white knight."

"And if she 'goes off the rails' as it were?"

"Then we'd better hope that Alec survives this, because he may be the only person in the world capable of stopping her again."

"Part of me wishes I could attribute that statement to the kind of hyperbole your generation seems so fond of, Mistress Paige, but I'm afraid you may be all too correct there."

"Yeah, I know. Here's to hoping that I read her correctly."

"What are your other plans?"

"I'm not sure; so far I've just been fighting fires."

Donovan paused, needle held only inches from Alec's chest. I looked down at Alec's bloody skin for only the briefest of moments and then looked away again. You would think that spending so long in the same room while Donovan operated on Alec would have inured me to all of the blood, but it hadn't. Maybe it would have been different if it had been someone else lying there on the bed, but it wasn't someone else. It was Alec and not only did I love him, the survival of a lot of other people who were important to me depended on Donovan saving him.

"Given everything that has happened in the last day, it is entirely understandable for you to be in crisis mode still, Mistress Paige, but that is a dangerous mindset for a leader to be in. You need to be thinking further ahead than that or you'll find yourself boxed in and unhappy with the options that remain open to you."

"I'm open to ideas, Donovan."

"Call James and ask him to come back here. You need a bodyguard you can trust. I saw Vik's response when Master Alec was shot. Vik is a passable fighter, but you need someone who will interpose themselves between you and danger rather than ducking for cover themselves."

"You don't think that will cause more problems? Vik isn't going to like being demoted and James isn't always a prime example of dependability and restraint. If he knows that Alec is injured then isn't there a chance that he'll try to take over? Besides, if I bring James and Dominic back here that means I'll be putting Addison, Andrew and Alec's mom in danger with us."

"It's a possibility that having James here will cause more problems than he will solve, but I think he's started maturing enough that he understands the real stakes for everyone involved. As far as your other concern goes, the truth is that our entire pack is already in an incredible amount of danger regardless of where they happen to be right now. Telling ourselves anything else is nothing more than wishful thinking."

"Even Rachel?"

"Especially Rachel. I don't understand what has happened to her, but I certainly hope that you're right and she can see the future. She's out there all alone in a world full of people who would prey on her simply because of her link to Master Alec. Her odds are not very good."

The thought of Rachel brought back memories of the last night that any of us had heard anything from her. That was the night that the Coun'hij had razed the mansion to the ground...the night that Dominic had healed Donovan's leg.

I suddenly felt like such a fool.

"Donovan, bringing James back means that we'll have Dominic back here too. There's a chance that she could heal Alec and have him back on his feet in hours rather than days."

I'd expected Donovan to greet my idea with relief. I didn't expect him to all but collapse against the wall behind him.

"I've failed Master Alec, the entire pack and the rebellion as a whole. How could I have been so blind? Even as I walk around on a limb that was made whole by Mistress Sanchez, I still somehow forgot that there was a much better way to save Master Alec than my feeble skills."

I found myself at Donovan's side without remembering standing and crossing the distance between us. I grabbed his arm and stopped him from sliding down the wall.

"This is not your fault, Donovan. You've worked a miracle in keeping Alec alive and you can't be blamed for not thinking of Dominic's gift after so many decades where your skills were the best solution—the only solution—for any hurt suffered by the pack. Alec isn't dead, this isn't about saving his life anymore, it's about getting him back up on his feet as quickly as possible."

"But it could have been the difference between Master Alec living or dying and it never even crossed my mind. What else have I failed to consider, what other mistakes am I making even now?"

"You're going to make mistakes, just like I'm going to make mistakes, Donovan, but we have to just do the best we can. Everything you said about me is just as true about you. There isn't anyone else who can fill your shoes; if you try to step down people are going to die. I can't do this on my own, Donovan—I need you."

I shouldn't have been able to hold him up. I was the least athletic person in the world and lately I'd started losing weight again much like I had done right after Cindi and my dad had died. I was the last person who should be able to hold up a grown man by his arms, but I was doing it and that worried me almost as much as Alec's injury.

Only a few hours ago I'd been thinking just how fit and wiry Donovan looked. Somehow Alec's condition had hit the old butler so hard that he'd shrunk in on himself to the point where he looked like a stiff wind would carry him away.

It took several seconds for my words to cut through the despair-filled haze that had overcome Donovan, but he finally shook himself and regained his feet. "You're right, of course, Mistress Adriana. We must all soldier on regardless of our failings. Knowing that Master Alec isn't there to catch my mistakes is harder to deal with than I realized it was going to be. I had much of the privilege of teaching him, but even at a young age he displayed incredible insights."

"I know I'm no Alec, but with any luck Dominic will have him back on his feet in no time flat. They can't be more than a few hours' drive away from us, not if we change direction and meet them halfway."

"I wish I could share your optimism, Mistress Paige. Mistress Dominic has accomplished some truly incredible things, but so far her gift does not seem to be under conscious control."

"You're right, but there's still a hope. How long before you can finish closing Alec up? I want you to get some food in yourself sooner rather than later."

"If I may be so bold, Mistress Paige, you are in dire need of some sustenance as well."

"Yeah, I kind of missed breakfast, but I'm going to call Dom before I go, so if you finish up first I hereby order you to go eat and I'll stay here with Alec until after you're done."

"Very well, Mistress Paige. I won't contest your orders so soon after having convinced you to assume command."

"That's right, otherwise I might disappear with Alec never to be heard from again."

"A quote about the unwise nature of making threats which one is unwilling to fulfill comes to mind."

That drew a chuckle out of me which was interrupted by a yawn as I realized just how exhausted I was. Considering that I'd woken up feeling like I hadn't gotten much sleep, it was nothing short of a miracle that I was still functioning at all considering everything we'd been through since dawn.

I punched up Dominic's number and waited as the phone rang.

"Hello?"

"Dom, it's me, Adri."

"Hello, Adri. I thought you were going to try and avoid calling us."

"Yeah, but then I realized just how much we need you and James here. We are in Northern Utah right now. Where would be the best place to meet you?"

"I'm not sure. Something unusual just happened and it might not be the best idea for us to be driving right now."

"What do you mean?"

"Andrew got a call from Isaac earlier. Shortly after he got off of the phone he lost consciousness. We've been unable to wake him since then."

I wanted to start pulling my hair out by the roots. Every time I thought I had a handle on things and knew what we were up against another issue jumped out of the bushes and ambushed me.

"Does Andrew seem to be in any kind of immediate danger?"

"No, but..."

"In that case, I need you to pack up and get on the road within the next hour. I've got people here who might not make it if we can't meet up very soon. I'm sorry to hear about Andrew's condition, but this has to take precedence. I'd say that we would call and tell Isaac what was going on, but I've been trying to get through to Isaac, or Ash or even Kristin all day. I can't believe he called Andrew but blew me off. What did they talk about?"

"I'm not sure. Jess, I think, but beyond that I couldn't say."

"Okay, where should we meet you?"

"Adri, there are other considerations that you aren't giving me a chance to tell you about. Andrew isn't the only one who's unconscious. I went in to check on Alec's mom a little while ago and she's completely unresponsive."

"You don't have any idea what happened to either of them?"

"No…well, there's one thing. Addison says that she was walking past Samantha's room earlier and she saw flickering lights. Addison thought at the time that Samantha was just watching television, but James said that when we checked in the manager gave us a discount because the television in Samantha's room wasn't working."

"Dom, why didn't you call and tell me this was going on?"

"Because you told me we were supposed to be keeping a low profile. James and I thought it would be best to wait a day or two and see if they woke up on their own."

Dominic sounded hurt, but I couldn't entirely blame her. Some of my frustration had bled through into my voice despite my best efforts. She had no way of knowing what I was dealing with or how things that were happening to her and the people she was watching over might impact all of the rest of our people.

"I'm sorry, Dom. Please just get everyone in the car. I think the Coun'hij might have just unveiled another weapon and we need to know as soon as possible if it's something that Alec's power can counteract. If not, and the Coun'hij can just pick us off one at a time by sending us into comas, then we're in even hotter water than any of us realized."

Chapter 7

Adriana Paige
Interstate 15
Northern Utah

Donovan finished sewing up Alec about the time I finished up with Dominic. In the end he convinced me to go get something to eat while he washed up. I exited the bedroom to find that the only people sharing the RV with us were Ruby, Vik, and a driver who was so focused on the road that he didn't even seem to notice me.

The fact that Mallory was in the other RV bought me some time given that Ruby and the guys weren't going to push me about Alec's exact status. They asked, but I told them something reassuring and vague and then focused on microwaving some food for Donovan and me.

Once we'd both eaten, Donovan and I slept in shifts in one of the bunks outside of the bedroom.

I tried to convince Donovan to go first based on the fact that he was obviously exhausted, but he pointed out that the next couple of hours were especially important when it came to monitoring Alec's blood pressure.

In the end, I gave in and went to sleep and enjoyed a few blissful hours where I didn't dream even once.

I woke up to my phone ringing, which really threw me for a loop. Not only was I waking up somewhere other than where I'd expected to, my phone wasn't next to my head like it normally was. I finally managed to fish it out of the waistband of my shorts about the time it rang for the fourth time.

"Yeah?"

"Adri, what is going on there?"

I recognized the voice—it was Jaclyn Annikov. I closed my eyes and focused on controlling my breathing. This might be the most important conversation I would ever have. I needed Jaclyn—we needed Jaclyn.

"What do you mean?"

"I've been trying to call Alec for the last fifteen minutes and getting nothing, it's not even going through to voicemail. It's a good thing Alec entered your number into my phone before I left or I would still be sitting here wondering whether to stick around the Bishop Compound or get back to my main mission. Can you please hand your phone to Alec?"

I rolled out of my bunk and slipped into Alec's room. Donovan started to get to his feet, but I waved him back down as I closed the door and turned the privacy box back on.

"I can't hand you to Alec. This stays between you and me, but he was hurt in our last fight with Coun'hij forces."

"How?"

"They must have figured out beforehand where we were going to ambush them. They had a sniper waiting up on the lip of the amphitheater. He got two bullets into Alec and killed Alec's bodyguard before Donovan put him down."

"Alec's still alive though?"

"Yes…"

"You're obviously worried he won't make it though or you wouldn't be asking me to keep his injury quiet. Why are you telling me of all people?"

"I need you back here. If Alec doesn't survive then I'm going to need help keeping the wheels on."

Jaclyn swore. "It would go down like this. I finally come out in full rebellion against the Coun'hij and Alec has to go get himself shot. You realize none of us have any kind of chance without him, don't you?"

"I wouldn't go that far. There are other resources out there that I'm currently in negotiations with. We lost a lot of people today, but the Coun'hij lost nearly as many and they have more demands on their personnel than we do. It's entirely possible they'll blink first and if that happens we'll have the neutral packs joining us left and right."

"Well, you certainly don't lack for ambition."

"It's not ambition, it's loyalty. I'm not going to just stand by and let everything Alec has been building come crashing back down. Are you with me? Will you come meet up with us and help me?"

"Those two things aren't mutually exclusive. I can be 'with' you and not meet back up to hold your hand. Please give my regards to Alec when he wakes up and let him know that I've continued on with the mission he originally gave me. As things stand, *that's* the most important thing I can be doing."

For a split second I considered trying to force the issue with her, but I had very little in the way of leverage to work with.

"Fine, I wish you the best of luck in your search, but before you go I'll need you to report your findings."

It was a small first step along the road towards her reporting to me for real, but it was a step and we both knew it.

"I don't think so."

"You swore an oath to serve my fiancé, Jaclyn. I'd hate to have to tell him when he wakes up that you've been remiss in your duties."

She was silent for several seconds before she finally responded. "Very well, I'll play along for now, but when he wakes up I'll expect you to tell him that I cooperated with you."

"I'll be telling Alec everything that happens while he's out of commission. I'm sure he will reward everyone commensurate with their level of…cooperation."

If she chose to read the slightest of veiled threats into that comment then that was just fine with me.

"You're on a phone with data capabilities, right?"

"Yeah, how come?"

"Hold on just a second and I'll send you a video feed request."

A second later my phone chimed and once I accepted her request I was greeted with a scene of desolation the likes of which I'd never seen before. The aerial view had been bad enough, but it was nothing compared to what Jaclyn was showing me.

The grand old house that I'd last seen when Shawn had taken me back to face off against Agony was completely leveled…only leveled wasn't the right word for it. The compound had been built on top of a large underground structure that had contained, among other things, the challenge arena for the Chicago pack.

That subbasement was visible now, more than visible in fact. It was as though someone had set off a massive bomb underneath the house. Pieces of concrete had been hurled into the air and returned to the ground dozens upon dozens of yards away from where they'd started.

The Bishops had a significant amount of ground—especially for a place like Chicago—but even so the wreckage from the house had still shattered several of the closest houses. A fire had started at some point as well and spread to the east, taking out at least three of the neighboring mansions before the local fire department had been able to get it under control.

Up until that moment I hadn't realized just how much security I'd derived from the knowledge that we had the Chicago pack waiting backstage to help out if it became necessary. We'd never depended on them other than to use Shawn's ability to know when someone truly meant their promises, but even so I'd always known that we had an incredible tide of hybrids and wolves who could be sent our way if Alec could convince Ulrich it was time to come out openly in support of Alec's claim to the throne.

"How many dead?"

Jaclyn shrugged, jostling the video feed. "I don't know. I suspect that the authorities are still trying to arrive at a final number. By the time I arrived they'd already started moving the bodies. I waited until they finished loading up the body bags and then I snuck in through the back way. I had to shock a couple of cops unconscious to get this far, and I can hear them moving rubble around just on the other side of that hill, so I'm not going to be able to case out any more of the wreckage than this, but it's bad. It wouldn't surprise me if they lost as much as half of the pack depending on what was going on here when the bomb went off."

"Is there any sign of where they might have gone?"

"No, none."

"What about any evidence as to who did it?"

"It was obviously the Coun'hij...wait, you think it wasn't a bomb, that this was the result of someone's power? Do you have proof that the rumors are true? Are we really up against a bunch of unknown hybrids with top-tier abilities who have managed to keep their powers hidden for the last few decades?"

"Nothing conclusive yet, but the circumstantial evidence is starting to pile up. Alec thinks we got hacked, that the ambushes our people walked into were just a case of phones being tracked, but I'm not so sure."

"No offense, Adri, but I sure hope you're wrong."

"None taken—I feel exactly the same way, but I can't afford to base all our plans on the theory that we've seen everything the Coun'hij has available to them. That would be a good way to get the rest of us killed."

Jaclyn stopped walking and panned the camera around in a slow panorama. "There was a guy that

I saw loitering nearby when I first got here. A tall redhead wearing a black leather jacket. He looked out of place enough that I noticed him."

"That's not much to go on."

"I know. You're not going to be able to track him down using Donovan's hackers or anything, but put the word out to the rest of your people to be on the lookout for him. They'll know if they run into him."

"How can you be so sure of that?"

"Because he tripped every mental alarm I've developed over the course of almost two hundred years of fighting for my life against creatures most Americans don't even suspect exist. Something about him was giving off a really dangerous vibe."

"How dangerous?"

"Dangerous enough that I kept my distance."

"I guess that tells me enough. Be safe, Jaclyn. Alec is going to need your help, we all are."

I spent several seconds after she hung up looking at my phone and the final frame of video that she'd sent over. I'd thought the destruction of Graves Manor was bad, but that had been nothing more than fire—this was something else entirely, something that left me feeling somehow unclean and cold.

"How is he doing so far, Donovan?"

"So far so good. His blood pressure seems to be holding steady, his oxygen levels are good and I haven't picked up anything odd about his heartbeat, so there aren't any overt signs that it is about to give out."

"How long until we can say he's out of the woods and that we don't need to worry anymore?"

"I wish I knew for sure. A couple of days at least, but even after that it would be best if we could get him to an MRI machine and have a specialist look his heart over."

"Except then they'd figure out that he's not a normal human."

"I suppose that's a possibility. I'm not sure how drastic the differences in our cardiac system are when we are in human form. I was more concerned that checking Alec into a hospital might bring the Coun'hij down on our heads, but it seems as though there is no end of concerns."

"Alec was a hybrid when he was shot; there isn't any chance that he'll have some kind of residual damage that only manifests in hybrid form, is there?"

Donovan opened his mouth and then closed it and shook his head. "I'm afraid I must once again say that I just don't know. The normal rule is that we shape shifters recover from anything that doesn't kill us, but I've never seen anyone survive this much damage before. I'm simply unable to make even an educated guess regarding much of anything where Master Alec is concerned at this point."

"I'm sorry to press, Donovan."

"No, it's quite all right, Mistress Paige. I understand entirely."

"Well then, I guess it's time for you to go get some sleep. What should I be watching for while you're gone?"

Donovan handed me his stethoscope. "You'll want to spend some time listening to his heartbeat now to familiarize yourself with it and then check him every twenty minutes to make sure it hasn't changed. Beyond that, make sure he's not having any difficulty breathing and that his color doesn't change."

As I draped the stethoscope around my neck similarly to how Donovan had had it just a few seconds before, the RV began to slow and then stopped.

"Do you know where we are?"

Donovan shook his head. "I haven't left this room since you went to sleep, Mistress Paige."

I looked at Alec and sighed before turning back to the door. "I'd better go be leader-y. You can go ahead and go to sleep, Donovan. I'll be back here momentarily to take care of Alec."

"If it's all the same to you, Mistress Paige, I'd just as soon stay here until you return."

He gave me a tired smile as I stepped out of the room.

"Why are we stopping?"

Ruby looked back at me from the driver's seat. "Mallory flagged us down from inside the other RV. I think we're stopping to get gas."

A couple of seconds later Mallory was pulling herself up into the RV. "Where's Alec? It's been *hours* without any kind of an update."

"I told you that we had the situation under control."

"Under control? That's medical doublespeak. What in the hell is going on?"

Mallory made as if to push past me, but she was the one shape shifter I figured I had a decent chance against in a purely physical confrontation. She was still stronger than me, but she hurt so badly when she moved that she couldn't apply that strength very well. I didn't give way before her.

"Mallory, you need to stop. Ruby, you can stay; I want the rest of you out of the vehicle. Turn on the noise generators on your way out."

Vik shot me a look that said he was suffering from a bout of professional concern at leaving my side. He wasn't entirely out of line considering the way that Mallory had started shaking, but the fact of the matter was that shifting forms would be so agonizing for Mallory that she would incapacitate herself if she did so. If things were headed for some kind of physical confrontation between the two of us then it wasn't going to involve claws or fangs.

"Now, Vik."

I got another frown, but a second later Vik followed our nameless driver down the steps and closed the door behind him.

"Get out of my way, Adri."

"You need to calm down, Mallory. You're going to hurt…"

I was suddenly looking down the barrel of the pistol Mallory had used less than twenty-four hours previously to execute some of the Coun'hij enforcers that had come so close to killing Alec.

"You don't get to tell me what to do, *Adriana Paige*. I've known Alec since before he was born. You are going to stand aside and let me in to see him or I will put a bullet through that pretty little forehead of yours."

It was one of those defining moments, one of those exchanges that determined who was dominant to whom. Mallory might be too grief-stricken to realize it, but I wasn't. I could feel three futures stretching out before me. In one I backed down, let Mallory in to see Alec and then over time she proceeded to gain the upper hand in the rest of our interactions to the point where eventually she ran the show—right up until the rebellion shattered into a million pieces.

It wasn't pretty, but Donovan was right. Mallory couldn't hope to keep control over a bunch of shape shifters, not in the crippled old body Agony had left her with.

In the second path I refused to back down and she killed me. Once I was dead then it was still only a matter of time before the Coun'hij came out on top. The third path was the only one that promised a chance of survival for all of the people that I'd grown to care about so much.

I had to convince her to back down because that was the only way forward that offered a chance of me remaining in control of Alec's people. Even then there was no guarantee that I'd be able to successfully navigate the perils awaiting me, but right or wrong, somehow I'd come to believe that I really was the best person for this particular job.

It was a moment of clarity that I hadn't expected. I'd always thought that being a dominant was a matter of aggressiveness and posturing, but it turned out sometimes dominance was nothing more than a certainty that you were right, that if you didn't stand up to someone bigger and stronger than you, everything you cared about would be destroyed.

I smiled, and even without a mirror I knew that the smile was somehow calm and unconcerned. It wasn't that I didn't care if I died, but for the first time in ages I wasn't second-guessing myself.

"Mallory, you need to think about what you're doing. Pulling that trigger isn't going to get you what you want. You pulling that trigger and killing me will just mean that Ruby will rip your throat out."

"I'll kill her too. I may be old and slow, but I'm not that old and slow. I can turn and get off at least two or three shots before she'll be able to close."

"Maybe, but then what? How do you think Donovan is going to feel about you shooting me? How do you think Alec is going to feel? You'll be lucky if he just exiles you. More than likely he'll feel he has no choice but to have you executed. Imagine what that will do to Alec—imagine what that will do to Donovan."

"Stop talking! You're just trying to confuse me. None of that matters if Alec is dead."

"He's not dead, Mallory, and I'm willing to let you see him, but you're going to do so on my terms."

"You don't order me around!"

I saw her finger start to take up the slack on the trigger and then the door behind me opened and I felt Donovan at my back.

"Indeed she can't, Mallory, not until you decide to let her, but you should know that Mistress Paige has my loyalty in full. Only Master Alec stands higher in my esteem than she does. If you try to harm her, it will be the end for us. I will fight—and even kill—to protect her."

"I just want to see Alec. What is so wrong with that, Donovan? I've sworn an oath of loyalty to him."

I could hear the pain in Mallory's voice and a tiny part of me wanted to give in and let her have what she wanted, but the armor of my certainty was just enough to resist the urge. The pain in Donovan's voice was even harder to ignore.

"You've spent nearly your whole life as a dominant, my dearest. There are some lessons you've never had to learn. Sometimes it is not for us to question our leaders, not in a time of war. You must trust that Alec and Adri have your best interests at heart.

"The question isn't whether or not your request is reasonable, it's whether you trust Adri's judgment. I do. The last twenty-four hours have removed any doubts I might have had, but you can't rely on my judgment, you must come to your own decision—otherwise you'll never be willing to live with the consequences of following her. Above all else, loyalty is a choice."

Mallory was still shaking with the tiny, uncontrollable tremors of a shape shifter only heartbeats away from a transformation, but somehow that entire time the barrel of her gun hadn't moved at all. It seemed to take hours, but finally she let it fall back to her side. She still hadn't stopped shaking, but I stepped forward and wrapped one arm around her in a hug as my left hand reached down and carefully took the gun out of her unresisting grip.

"I'm sorry, Adri. I don't know what's gotten into me. I just feel so lost. I don't know who I'm supposed to be anymore. I can't be the person I was before I was injured—I'm not in any shape these days for ruthless dominance games—and I can't be the person I was in my cabin for the last two decades. She doesn't belong in this world.

"I left my own personal refuge to come back here and help Alec, but he keeps me on the outside of things more often than not. I just want to go back to how things were."

I handed the pistol back to Donovan and then wrapped my left arm around Mallory so that I could give her a proper hug.

"I'm sorry, Mallory. I wish I could promise that things were going to get easier, but I can't. If you'll swear fealty to me and promise to keep my secrets then I can start including you in on things that you've been excluded from up to this point."

"I can't swear fealty to you and Alec both."

"I know, but I've been thinking about that. Swear a secondary fealty to me where you only have to obey when it doesn't contradict Alec's stated wishes and that will be enough."

Mallory stepped back from me and wiped a tear from her eye. "Okay, if you promise to take me to Alec after this then I'll give you the oath you're after."

Donovan and Ruby witnessed the oath and then I asked Ruby to step outside and have someone fuel up our RV. Donovan led Mallory back into the bedroom as I watched Ruby leave to go fulfill my orders.

Once she was gone I stepped into the bedroom and put a hand on Mallory's shoulder. "As you can see, Alec is alive, but Donovan isn't entirely certain he's going to survive. If the worst comes to pass I'm going to need your help keeping everything from falling apart around us. Donovan thinks there is a chance that I'll be able to bind enough shape shifters to me personally in the next few days to keep the rebellion from splintering."

I pulled the door to the room shut behind me and then paused in confusion. I'd expected Mallory at least to run to Alec's bedside, and there was every reason to think that Donovan would want to take the chance for one last check on Alec's condition before he went to catch up on the sleep he needed so badly.

That was what I'd been expecting, but instead the pair of them had stopped only one step into the room. It was like they were too stunned to move and I could only think of one reason for them to be shocked like that.

I pushed between the two of them, my heart in my throat, and then fell to my knees as soon as I was able to see Alec.

He wasn't dead, not yet at least, but that didn't mean he was okay. Every single muscle in his body was clenched tight as though he was fighting for his life, but it was his eyelids that gave things away.

I couldn't smell his terror, but I didn't need to when I could see his eyes moving around underneath his eyelids. It was obvious he was dreaming and based on Donovan's and Mallory's responses it wasn't a normal dream.

At that very moment Alec was fighting against Dream Stealer. His power wasn't going to be able to save him this time any more than it had been able to save Kristin.

Chapter 8

Adriana Paige
Interstate 70
Western Colorado

It had seemed like I was just starting to get my feet underneath me. Finding out that Dream Stealer was targeting Alec was like getting blindsided by a semi-truck. I didn't know if that meant Kristin was dead or if Dream Stealer really was able to break two people at once, but I was certain that we were in even more trouble than I'd realized.

Alec was strong and determined, but nobody could last forever against the kind of torture Dream Stealer was said to employ. Donovan, Mallory and I spent several minutes staring at Alec in shock before something brought me out of the haze of despair that I'd been wallowing in. I stood and turned so I could face Donovan and Mallory.

"This isn't the end of the world. It's a complication, but it's one that we'll deal with. Mallory, you need to pull yourself together and get back out there and keep our people from falling apart. We need to make the meet with James, Dom and the rest. I need a bodyguard I can trust fully and we need to see if Dominic has gotten her ability in hand well enough to be able to heal Alec and then hopefully you too."

"What good will it do to heal his body if his mind is shattered beyond repair?"

Donovan sounded so crushed that I reached out and placed a hand on his shoulder. "This isn't over. Dream Stealer never breaks someone overnight. We have a window of opportunity in which to find him and kill him. If we can do that quickly enough then we can save Alec."

Mallory looked at me in astonishment. "You're talking about finding the Coun'hij's base as though it's not something that people have been trying to do for hundreds of years. Even once we find them that doesn't guarantee anything. Nobody was quite sure that we'd be able to take down the Coun'hij even *with* Alec. Without him we don't stand a chance."

I resisted the urge to shake her. She'd promised fealty, but that was much the same as promising obedience. I needed more than that, I needed loyalty and that was a living, breathing thing that I was going to have to nurture over a long period of time.

"You don't know everything that's happened, Mallory. I'm going to try to bring you further into the loop, but that's going to take some time, time that we don't have right now. Even once we have a few quiet minutes you're never going to know quite as much simply because your role is going to be different than Donovan's role."

"What is my role going to be exactly?"

"You're going to be my strong right hand where the rest of the shape shifters are concerned. Everyone knows that you have been Alec's secret counselor ever since he first manifested an alternate shape. You will keep our low-level people in line and working towards our goals."

"It won't work. A broken-down wreck of an old woman will never be able to accomplish that."

"Dominic is going to heal you. Weeks ago Alec told me that need was what finally triggered his power. We *desperately* need Dominic to heal Alec and we need her to heal you. It's going to work this time."

"You can't make plans like that. It's like trying to build a house of cards on top of a beach ball. Besides, even if I could whip the rank and file into shape, that still wouldn't solve our problems. We need someone with a game-changing ability if we're going to have any chance of taking down Dream Stealer. He's going to be protected by dozens of hybrids at the very least."

"We already have top-tier ability available to us."

"Grayson isn't going to be enough, not when Puppeteer can throw an endless stream of werewolves at us."

"I'm not talking about Grayson; I'm talking about Lori from the Del Rio pack. She can force the Coun'hij enforcers to turn on each other, can force them to fight Puppeteer's werewolves for us. She just neutralized the entire group of enforcers down in Nephi."

"Careful, or you're going to actually convince me that you're out of your mind, Adri. Lori can't be controlled by anyone, let alone me. Her, Grayson, Jaclyn, none of them can be controlled by anyone other than Alec. I can't make them toe the line for you."

"I don't need you to *make* them do anything, Mallory. You just worry about the people we've got here for now. They are already taking your orders and the passage of time is just going to make it more and more natural for them to keep doing so. Once Dominic gets here we'll see about getting you back to one hundred percent physically and then you can worry about the rest of our people. Leave Lori, Jaclyn, Grayson—and whoever else we manage to turn up—to me."

"This is never going to work, you know that, right?"

I started to respond to Mallory's question, but Donovan beat me to it. "No, Mistress Paige is right. This is the only way. It's by no means guaranteed, but it does have a possibility of being successful. We need to do exactly as she says and pursue the war against the Coun'hij with every resource at our disposal."

I rewarded Donovan with a smile. "I know you're exhausted, Donovan, but while Mallory gets everyone back on the road, I need you to take a look at the communications equipment. Once that is done, you can go take a nap."

"Is there a problem, Mistress Paige?"

"I'm not sure, but Jaclyn said that she had to call my phone because she couldn't get ahold of Alec's phone and Mallory had to flag Ruby down just now."

"Very good, I'll check up on Master Alec and then I'll look into the communications suite right after that."

"I'll go ahead and check him, if you don't mind, Donovan. That way if I have any questions I can ask them before you go to sleep."

Donovan turned to go, Mallory half a step behind him, but I stopped her with a word. "Mallory, as soon as things calm down I need you to spend some time examining all of our surviving hybrids. I want to know if anyone is hiding an ability like Lori has been doing for the last few years."

"It's very unlikely. I've interacted with nearly everyone at this point. If they had an ability of any real power I would have seen it already. I only need to really examine someone if I'm looking for potential or if their ability is very weak."

"I know, Alec indicated as much, but I want you to look all the same. Just because someone's ability doesn't have a lot of raw power doesn't mean it can't be useful to us. Given the way that things are stacking up, I want to know about every potential weapon in our inventory."

"Understood, I'll get started on it as quickly as I can. What do you want me to tell everyone about Alec? They are going to ask now that they know I've been in to see him."

"Tell them the truth. Tell them that you've been in to see him and that while his injuries are severe, he is in stable condition and based on the inherent advantages of being a shape shifter, only a fool would expect anything other than that he would recover from any wound which hadn't killed him already."

"The truth?"

"Yes, the truth. A certain version of it at least. You're going to have to sell it, Mallory, or they are going to start asking questions and if that happens it's only a matter of time before they trip you up."

For the first time since the ambush had gone south, Mallory smiled. "I've been dancing rings around the truth since before you were born, Adri. I'll make it work—I just needed to know what the official party line was going to be."

Once both of them were gone I turned down the privacy box so I could hear Donovan working in the computer closet just through the wall, and then I began examining Alec. It was eerie to be next to him while he was so stiff that I could occasionally hear his muscles creaking from the strain he was putting on them. Alec would never knowingly hurt me, but all bets were off if he started thrashing around in the throes of some nightmare.

As much as it pained me to consider tying Alec down, we needed restraints. It was the only way to make sure that he didn't accidentally hurt Donovan or me. Not only that, it might actually help him. If he started thrashing around he might re-open his wounds. I added it to the list of things that needed to be done as I put the stethoscope in my ears and warmed the metal against my arm.

His heartbeat sounded fast to me, and he felt feverish, but his color looked good and he seemed to be breathing as normally as you could expect for someone locked inside of a supernatural nightmare.

I left my hand resting lightly against the bare skin of his uninjured shoulder and wished that I had time for tears. Maybe if I'd had a few more minutes I would have convinced myself there was time to break down and cry, but a second later Donovan stepped back inside of the room and turned the privacy generator back up.

"I have bad news, Mistress Paige. The communications array has been rendered inoperable."

"How is that possible? It's been working for the last several hours. Things don't just stop working."

"Indeed, that was my thought as well. I've examined it in detail and it appears that one of the shots that punched through the skin of the RV caused ancillary damage to the communications equipment, damage that didn't manifest itself until recently when a jolt in the road caused some of the wiring to finish pulling loose."

"Appears?"

"Yes…appears. The odds of something like this happening seem very slim. I worry that we might have a saboteur amongst our number."

I could feel a headache starting to build. It was bad enough that we had the entire might of the Coun'hij trying to hunt us down. The possibility that we had been infiltrated, that someone had made it past all of our precautions, that they had managed to swear fealty during one of the windows when Shawn hadn't been around to measure their intent, that they were such a good liar that nobody had picked up any unusual vibes from them, was enough to make me want to scream.

"I'm out of my depth, Donovan. I don't know the first thing about running some kind of counter-intelligence operation. What do we do now?"

"We need to confirm who has been inside of our vehicle since the ambush and then we need to keep those individuals away from each other. Given just how good a liar we must be dealing with if this really was sabotage, there is little chance that we'll be able to catch them by way of casual questioning and it would be wrong to use harsher methods on people who haven't done anything wrong. Our best bet is to make sure that their access to our operations is limited enough that if they strike again it will be obvious which of them is our culprit."

"Okay, that makes sense. Anything else? Can we get the equipment working again?"

Donovan hesitated before finally shaking his head. "I'm afraid not. Even if it was a possibility, the chance that it's been tampered with would preclude our using it. I'm simply not expert enough to guarantee that it hasn't been modified somehow to serve as some kind of tracking beacon."

"Is it even going to be possible for us to remain untraceable without that equipment?"

"No. Our IT assets can do quite a bit in that area, but much of our current security protocols are designed around the capabilities of this particular equipment. I simply don't think there is a reliable way to mask and scramble our signal while using stock cell phones."

"You realize that means all our saboteur would need to do if they wanted to lead the Coun'hij to us is leave their cell phone on?"

"Assuming we really do have a saboteur…then you are completely correct. We need to collect the cell phones of all of our people and turn them off. Also, we need to take measures in case we've already been found on a satellite feed. We're not going to be safe until we've changed vehicles somewhere that would preclude any kind of remote surveillance."

"*If* we have a spy in our midst. We're going to have to assume that we have one because to do otherwise would be like committing suicide. Even though taking people's phones away is going to cause a lot of ill will. I really hate this kind of double- and triple-think, Donovan. Well, a deal is a deal. Go get some sleep. I'll get Mallory started collecting everyone's phones."

"If we simply drop off of the radar we're going to end up causing an incredible amount of concern among the rest of our people, many of whom have just escaped from enforcer kill teams."

"Yeah, I know. That goes double for anyone who already knows that Alec was injured in our ambush or who manages to get in contact with someone who knows. Don't worry, I've got an idea there too."

Ruby was back sitting in the driver's seat, but by some miracle we hadn't started moving yet. Under other circumstances that would have frustrated me to no end, but it had worked out in my favor this time so I didn't say anything chastising to Mallory when I found her standing outside of the other RV.

I pulled her inside of her vehicle and shut the door to the bedroom so we could speak without being overheard. "Donovan thinks that there is a chance that the communications suite in the other RV was sabotaged. I'm going to need you to collect everyone's phones before we get back on the road."

"You don't ask for much, do you?"

"Believe me when I say that I would pursue another course if I felt like it was even remotely possible it would keep us all safe."

"This is going to require more than just my say-so."

"Is my say-so going to be enough?"

"We'll never know until we try."

I took a deep breath and nodded before turning to lead the way back outside. I found Vik and our unnamed driver waiting not too far away from the RV, and waved them over.

"I need each of you to go gather up as many of our people as you can—please hurry."

It took less than three minutes for a respectable crowd to gather, but I was fidgeting the entire time. It was more than just the fact that we needed to be back on the road and headed towards our meeting with James and Dominic. I was exhausted again and not entirely sure that I would stay awake if I sat down in the camp chair that Mallory offered me.

I'd been feeling pretty good initially when I'd woken up from my nap, but sometime between the time when I'd hung up from the call with Jaclyn and when I'd exited the RV all of my energy had drained away. It was one more thing to worry about and I made a mental note to make sure that Donovan, Mallory and I all checked each other at night while we were sleeping. If Dream Stealer really was capable of going after more than one person at a time then none of us were safe.

I looked around the group gathered in front of me, and then began speaking. "You may have noticed that our phone service has been spotty. It turns out that our communications equipment—which is integral to the security measures we've put in place to keep the Coun'hij from being able to track us by way of our cell signals—was damaged during the ambush. Donovan kept it running for as long as he could, but it's officially beyond repair.

"Given our current circumstances, it's going to take some time before we're going to be able to get replacement equipment installed. I hope that you've all been complying with the communications protocols that force your phone to only connect to the cell network through the RV's communication suite, but given Alec's current injuries, it's just too dangerous to the group as a whole to leave unregulated cell phones out there. Mallory will be organizing groups of three individuals to go around and collect everyone's cell phones."

A murmur of unhappiness swept through the assembled group of shape shifters, but I almost thought I was going to get away with it until a big guy towards the front of the group spoke up.

"And what if we decide we're not going to give you our phones? I didn't sign up to be some kind of slave."

I recognized him from back in Utah. I couldn't remember his name, but he was one of the hybrids who had come through and sworn fealty to Alec. I thought he was from Louis' pack, but I wasn't positive about even that.

I'd known something like this was coming, but honestly I'd been hoping to make it a little bit longer first. Oh well, no time like the present.

"Nobody said anything about anyone being turned into slaves. I could bring up the fact that you swore fealty to Alec, but I won't. Alec doesn't want anyone here who doesn't want to be here and I feel exactly the same way. You're here because this is where Alec is. You're here because he offers you his protection in return for your loyalty and service to him."

The rabble-rouser in the front was grinning like I was headed exactly where he'd wanted me to go, but I refused to let that rattle me. I couldn't just keep my feelings off my face, not when I was dealing with a bunch of shape shifters. I had to not feel doubt or all was lost.

It should have been impossible, but I simply refused to give those negative feelings any room inside of my head. Alec was going to be okay. I was going to see to it.

"Alec is many things, but he's not foolish, and trying to protect people who are actively working to make protecting them more difficult isn't just foolish, it's pointless. Anyone who wishes to retain their phones may do so, but you will not be accompanying the convoy if that is the case. You have exactly two minutes in which to make your decision."

"You can't force us into making some kind of snap decision."

"Forcing you into making decisions is an unfortunate consequence of the fact that we've been traveling for several hours while being unaware that our security precautions had potentially been compromised. Allowing some kind of protracted debate would be irresponsible on my part and would put everyone here in even greater danger than we're already in. That is the last thing that Alec wants to have happen.

"You now have one minute and thirty seconds before the rest of us will be leaving."

A dark-haired woman at the back of the crowd was next.

"Is Alec okay?"

It was the question I'd been preparing for ever since I'd agreed to take over, but I didn't bear her any ill will for asking it. She wasn't trying to cause problems; she was just understandably concerned about our situation.

"He's been shot—not once but twice. If he'd been a human he would have died on the spot. Luckily, you all have much better regenerative abilities than that. He's still alive and you all know that anything that doesn't kill a shape shifter within an hour or two of the injury is something that you'll eventually come back from."

The big bruiser at the front cocked his head to one side. "That sounds suspiciously like what Mallory just finished telling those who asked."

"What are you implying?"

"I think you've hatched a story between the three of you and you're trying to make us think Alec Graves is going to survive when in fact he's going to die at any moment."

I'd been struggling so hard to make sure I didn't feel any despair that I hadn't steeled myself against anger. A wave of rage crashed through me with a suddenness that took my breath away.

"To most of you, Alec Graves is nothing more than a meal ticket. At best you're actually willing to do as he commands in return for the protection he offers, but even so, most of the risk is his. Unlike all of you, I was there before Alec manifested his ability. I stood by his side in the midst of terrible danger even though nothing I could do would make even the slightest bit of difference. I did that because I love him.

"If you think that I would be out here wasting my time verbally sparring with you if I thought Alec was going to die at any moment then you are sadly, sadly mistaken."

It was right on the edge of believability. I could see it on the faces of the people arrayed before me. There was only one thing left to do. I knew it was the only route open to me, but I was still surprised when my mouth opened and the words poured out.

"I'm no more able to see the future than any of you, but I will say this as clearly as I'm able so that there is no room for doubt. Alec Graves *is* going to recover from this injury. You now have thirty seconds in which to make your decision. Personally, part of me hopes you all stay here, but I know that isn't what Alec wants to have happen."

I turned and walked away without looking back. Two seconds later I heard a rush of people moving forward towards Mallory in an attempt to make sure that they got their phones handed in before the time limit ran out.

Chapter 9

Adriana Paige
Interstate 70
Western Colorado

Donovan was asleep when I got back, but Ruby was still sitting in the driver's seat. "What's going on?"

"The communications equipment is down, so I just told everyone that they need to hand over their phones if they want to continue traveling with us. Now that we don't have a way of scrambling our cell signal it's just not safe for people to be using their phones."

Ruby digested my words for a second and then pulled a slender flip phone from her pocket. "Here, it sounds like you need this."

"Thanks, Ruby. We should be on our way again shortly. We've got some lost time we need to make up."

I started back towards Alec's bedroom, but stopped after just a couple of steps. "You haven't asked me if Alec is okay."

"I figure there are some things I'm better off not knowing, Miss Paige. What I don't know I can't accidentally let slip. Don't get me wrong, I'm hoping that he makes it through, but either way I'm a lot safer here with everyone else than I would be off by myself."

"Would you be willing to swear fealty to me, Ruby?"

"I...I don't know. I'd have to think about it."

"That's fine. I'd rather it be something you didn't just jump into. It would be subordinate to the oath you've already sworn to Alec or your alpha, but there isn't any rush. Just continue to keep your mouth shut about everything that happened back there earlier and I'll be a happy camper."

"I can do that."

I gave her a smile and then walked the rest of the way back to the bedroom. I checked on Donovan on my way. He was sleeping peacefully, which was good because it meant we hadn't woken him with our chatter and he wasn't being targeted by Dream Stealer.

We were just about to start moving again, which meant that this was probably as good a time to make one last call as any. It was still dangerous, but it couldn't be helped. I dialed the number that had burned itself into my mind the last time that I'd seen it.

"What now?"

Tasha didn't sound particularly happy to be answering my call, but then again I wasn't happy that I was having to call her. I briefly wondered what she would have sounded like if I'd called using Alec's phone. That of course reminded me that we needed to get Alec's sim card out of the communications equipment. People were going to be calling his phone still if they needed something.

"We've run into a problem. Our communications equipment has given out on us, which means that we don't have the ability to scramble and mask our calls. We're going to have to go dark for a while until we can get it replaced."

"So you're calling everyone you know to tell them, thereby sending up a massive signal fire as to your current location?"

The scorn in her voice was palpable and for a second I almost changed my mind, but she really was the only option that made sense.

"No, I'm calling you and only you. I want you to take over as a kind of temporary communication node. Get ahold of as many people as you can and let them know to keep their heads down for a few days until I can get us back online."

"Why me?"

"Because you've got Grayson and Lori both there with you. Until Alec is back on his feet and able to fight again, your group is our strongest, most secure force. Your group has the best chance of surviving if the Coun'hij track your calls and come after you."

"Best chance of survival is a long ways off of guaranteed survival. Neither of those two is going to be worth spit against a group of werewolves."

"I know. You'll want to keep moving, use burner phones, and batch your calls so you have a chance to drop out of sight afterwards. Hopefully it's only for a couple of days."

"You're basically giving me the keys to the castle here. You realize that, right? If I've got ambitions for taking over everything this is my golden opportunity. Why me? There are a lot of people here in this group who could do the job."

"I'm not an idiot, Tasha. I know very well that this is a risky move, but the fact of the matter is that I have to put someone in charge. Whoever I put in charge would have the option of trying to wrest control away from Alec, but that's quite simply a waste of time. Once Alec is healthy again it would be futile for anyone to try to keep control of people who are already sworn to his service."

"And if he doesn't recover?"

"He's going to recover, but this is the part where you are expecting me to threaten you so I'll oblige. I'm tapping you for this job because you'll have the threat of your mom backing you up, but if Alec doesn't survive and you try to wrest control of our people away from me then

I'm going to make you wish Alec had survived to deal with you. He's got a soft spot where you're concerned because of your history together. I'm not laboring under that disadvantage. Do a good job on this and *when* Alec recovers he'll reward you. Try to screw Alec and me over and I'll make sure you suffer as a result, even if I have to pull the trigger myself."

Mallory opened up the door to the bedroom within seconds of me hanging up on Tasha. "You have a second?"

"Are we having problems? I was serious about being on the road. Anyone who gives you problems needs to just be left behind."

"No, nothing like that. After you left that same guy tried to convince everyone that you were bluffing, that there wasn't anything you could do to stop them from just tagging along behind us, but I reminded him that Donovan is a crack shot with the sniper rifle he took off of the shooter back at the ambush site. That shut him up instantly."

"That one's going to be a problem."

"Yeah, but that's not why I stopped by. I've got teams of three people each collecting cell phones. We'll be moving again within the next two or three minutes."

"I'm glad my performance did the trick."

"Actually, that's what I wanted to ask you about. Do you realize how much of a chance you took back there?"

"Yes—that's actually why I took it. It was a risk, but the alternative was having people press harder and harder as time went on. I needed to nip the rumors in the bud or everything was going to fall apart in the next few days."

"How did you know you could pull a lie of that magnitude off? I've been around some pretty high-level players and I'm not sure that any of them would have done that, even if they could have. When Alec dies you're going to have zero credibility with these people."

"I'm aware of the risks, Mallory, but it was the only choice I could live with."

"You're playing a risky game, Adri. One that is going to eventually come back to bite you, but I'll stick with you. You're the only game in town and Donovan believes in you, but be careful. Now that you can get away with lies like that it's going to be very difficult to stop yourself from lying any time you run up against a truth that you don't like. The problem is the more lies you throw out there the harder they are going to land when they come home to roost."

"Thank you for your concern, Mallory. I'm managing the risks. Please get us on the road as quickly as possible. I had to make one last call to Tasha just now so it's important that we get moving. Hopefully Alec's hackers are still managing to keep our images off of the satellite feeds. I need to check up on Alec again."

Despite what I'd said, several long minutes passed after Mallory's departure before I moved from the room's only chair. I really did understand Mallory's worries, but at the same time they felt like something with no relevancy to my world.

I could see the appeal to being able to lie about anything and having people believe you because their very senses told them you were telling the truth, but I could only lie about one thing. Alec was going to survive this and he was going to come out the other side sane and very much still his own person.

It was going to happen because I was going to use up myself—and everyone else around me if it came to that—to *make* it happen.

Chapter 10

Adriana Paige
Downtown
Denver, Colorado

Seeing Dominic again was like seeing the sun again for the first time after a long, cloudy winter.

We were reunited amongst a flurry of activity that went much better than I expected it to. I was still worried that the Coun'hij was tracking us via preternatural means, but even if that was the case, it was only a matter of time before the bullet holes in our RV occasioned some kind of attention from law enforcement. The logical answer was to change vehicles, but I'd been reluctant to insist on it because of the difficulty involved.

I raised the question with Donovan though once he woke from his nap and came in to check on Alec. It took us less than five minutes' discussion to decide to change up every vehicle in the convoy.

The actual logistics ended up being both easier and more difficult than I'd been expecting. The only thing Donovan was worried about salvaging from our existing RV was the trio of aerodynamic antennae affixed to the top of the roof and the large touchscreen attached to the wall. Beyond that, everything else was easily moveable.

It took another ten minutes to draw up a list of things we were going to need and tasks that were going to need to be done, and then I began splitting the tasks into separate lists for Mallory to distribute out to the teams she was going to have to put together.

We rolled into town forty-five minutes before the arranged meeting time with Dominic, and stopped at a large truck stop half an hour away from the meeting place. A short conference was all that it took to bring Mallory up to speed and then we all sprang into action.

A couple of burly guys who looked like they knew their way around power tools started grinding off the serial number stamped into the engine as soon as Mallory got the other RV in place to screen their activities from anyone driving past on the road.

Most of the rest of the group was sent off, either shopping or dumping their cars in a variety of different manners, all of which should help make sure that they wouldn't surface and lead the Coun'hij back to us anytime soon. That was actually one of the more dangerous parts of the plan. I didn't like having everyone spread out like that, but neither Donovan nor I had been able to come up with a way around it any more than we'd been able to find a way around replacing our vehicles without putting large sums of money in the hands of the people tapped to go do the actual purchasing.

The last three cars to leave all waited to go until after we'd extended the large canopy that was one of the features of the RV. We backed each of the three cars up next to the RV in turn before they left. I was in the second vehicle, a minivan that we'd dropped the two back seats down in so that they formed a large flat surface that was an adequate bed for Alec.

Donovan cleaned Alec up and draped a clean sheet over him before we moved him with a second clean sheet used as an improvised stretcher. Alec still looked bad, but he looked good enough for people to think that he was on the mend, and the top sheet hid the fact that we'd tied him up so that he wouldn't flail while being moved and thereby let everyone know he was being attacked by Dream Stealer.

Mallory had carefully picked the group that had been left behind to see Alec and our hope was that she'd correctly picked people who weren't inclined to ask a lot of questions, people who would be relieved to see Alec was still breathing, and most importantly people who would be believed when they said that Alec looked like he was in a peaceful, healing sleep.

I'd been most nervous about having our people dispersed, but Donovan had been most concerned with the idea that Alec and I were going to be driven around by Ruby. I could understand his worries—frankly I wasn't as sanguine about the whole thing as I tried to let on.

Ruby had a one-in-three chance of being the Coun'hij agent who had ruined our communications equipment, if indeed that was what had happened. Mallory had obliquely questioned all three of our possible saboteurs without any of them mentioning that they'd noticed anything odd, but that still wasn't proof that the malfunction had been solely the result of shrapnel from the bullet that had punched through the communications closet.

Being only a wolf, Ruby wasn't particularly dangerous compared to most of our people, but she didn't *need* to be very dangerous to be a threat to Alec and me. Donovan had wanted me to use someone else as a driver or barring that to drive us himself, but in the end simple logic made him agree that she was the only option. Donovan was the only one who could do some of the shopping that needed to be done and Ruby already knew—and seemed to be keeping secret—the true extent of Alec's injuries. I didn't trust Ruby, not totally, but I didn't want to risk anyone else finding out that Alec was in such bad shape.

All of which explained the great degree of comfort I took from the pistol that Mallory slipped me just before Ruby, Alec and I left. Ruby couldn't attack me while she was driving the van, and now that I was armed I had the ability to make sure she didn't take us somewhere I didn't want to go.

It wasn't a perfect plan, but it wasn't that big of a departure from what we were already doing. We'd let her drive the RV because there hadn't been any other way to both isolate her and keep her too busy to get into any mischief, and she hadn't wrecked the RV, so there was a reasonable chance that she wouldn't crash the minivan.

Ruby didn't say anything until we'd been driving for nearly a minute. "You don't trust me, do you?"

"You can smell the gunpowder?"

"Yeah, a little bit. Mostly it's the gun oil."

"No, Ruby, I'm afraid that I don't trust you, not completely. I'm sorry if I'm doing you a disservice, but I just can't afford to take that chance right now."

"That's fine, it's better than fine actually. Believe it or not, I want Alec to come through this every bit as badly as you do."

"Okay, for now just keep to the route we talked about and get me to Dominic and James."

The rest of the trip was thankfully uneventful. Twenty minutes later we pulled under the overpass and something unknotted when I saw the large, black van waiting for us.

A tiny part of me had been convinced that Dominic and James were never going to arrive, that I was going to have to try to keep Alec alive with no more help than what Donovan and Mallory could provide. Knowing that I was going to have two more friends with me, friends I could trust without question, took away some of the burden that I'd been carrying since Alec had been shot.

Ruby parked a couple of feet behind the black van and then turned off the engine and handed the keys back to me without having to be asked. I still half expected her to try to make a run for it as soon as she was out of our minivan, but she simply stood between the two vehicles while I locked all but one of the doors and then exited myself.

As soon as they could see me, James and Dominic both climbed out of their vehicle. Dominic crossed the distance between us in a flash and pulled me into a hug before I could even blink.

"I'm so glad to see you, Adri. I've spent this whole time worrying that something was going to happen to you and Alec before we could meet up."

"Yeah, I was worried about you too. Have you had any more luck with your ability?"

She looked so crestfallen that I wished I'd waited to ask until later. "No, nothing yet. I've tried a dozen times to heal James' mother of her scars, but it's all been to no avail."

She'd pulled back a little while acknowledging her failure, but I reached forward and gave her hand a squeeze before turning to James, who was keeping a wary eye on Ruby at the same time that he tried to keep a watch out for other threats.

"Thanks for coming, James."

"Yeah, how's Alec doing?"

"Not as well as I'd like, but a lot better than he could be doing. This is Ruby. So far she's been very cooperative and helpful, but I'm still not completely positive I can trust her, so watch yourself around her."

"I was already planning on doing exactly that."

"Good. Can you two please move Alec to your van? There's room, right?"

"Yeah, just barely, but it's not like Andrew or Mrs. Graves is going to notice if we crowd the two of them a little."

Apparently James could smell the gun I was packing too. It was the only logical reason for him to be treating me like I was actually capable of backing him up if Ruby suddenly went crazy. It was flattering, but I was actually a lot less confident in my ability than he seemed to be. Shooting someone from less than five feet away who was seat belted into one spot was probably something I could manage, but anything beyond that was pushing things.

James kept an eye on Ruby while I unlocked the back of the minivan and then once I had a clear line of sight to Ruby again he went over to help Dom move Alec.

"Oh, no. He's hurt so badly!"

"Yeah, that's why I've been so anxious to get you and him in the same place."

"I'll do my best, Adri, but I'm just not sure I'll be able to help. I'm starting to think the past healings are some kind of cruel prank, that or just a fluke."

"No, one time could be a fluke, but you've healed more than a dozen people on two different days. You've got a power, it's just a question of how long it will be before it manifests fully."

"I hope you're right."

Once they had Alec safely tucked away in the back of their van, I stepped forward and handed James a slip of paper.

"We need to ditch the minivan. James, can you take Ruby with you and lose it somewhere reasonably close to the Park Hill area, please? That will put you close enough to make the rendezvous point in plenty of time."

"Yeah, I can do that. Take care of Dom and the rest of them for me until I get back."

I nodded and tossed Ruby the keys. Dom was already climbing into the van. I followed her, taking a seat in the passenger's seat next to Addison, who favored me with a dirty look.

"You just couldn't let well enough alone, could you? You had to drag all of us back into the crosshairs with you."

The old Adri probably would have let her get away with it, but I knew I couldn't allow that kind of blatant disrespect. Alec could, simply because he was so much more powerful than the rest of us that it almost didn't matter if he had two or three people openly sniping at him. My position wasn't anywhere near as secure as that.

"Listen, Addison, I'd like to get one thing straight. I'm not going to put up with that kind of garbage from you. Not now, not in the future, not in private and definitely not in public. You know as well as I do that we are alive for one reason and one reason only. Alec has put his life on the line for all of us repeatedly and while that doesn't make him some kind of infallible saint, it should earn him some pretty profound respect."

She opened her mouth, but I cut her off with a glance.

"If that doesn't cut it for you then know this. It's the Graves money that has been putting food on your table since you were injured. Alec may feel some kind of vicarious guilt over what happened when Agony came through here and killed his father, but I don't share that feeling. If you have constructive ideas or legitimate concerns then I'm all ears, but if you keep digging at me or Alec, either one, I will see you thrown out on your ear so fast you won't even know what hit you. Maybe then you'll realize that you've had a target on your back since before Kaleb died."

"You wouldn't dare. I'm the one who takes care of Samantha. Alec would be furious."

"Maybe, maybe not. I can hire any nurse off the street to take care of someone in a coma, it's not like Samantha would notice a difference. Actually, come to think of it that would probably be the case even if she was conscious."

That last bit hadn't been something I'd been planning on saying, it had just kind of happened, but it obviously struck home in a major way. Addison's eyes narrowed and she went bright red.

"If you send me away then James will come with me."

"Don't you ever get tired of using your own son as a bargaining chip? I'm not so sure that James would follow you off into an exile that you earned for yourself, but if he did then that would be fine by me. I need James, but I need a James I can count on. If his loyalties are that divided then I'm better off without him. For however long Alec is out of commission I'm going to need people I can trust."

MARKED

She shook her head at me as she turned the van on and put it into gear. "My, my. Somebody put on her big-girl pants today."

I reached over and turned the key in the ignition, killing the motor as I grabbed the burner phone I'd brought with me out of my pocket.

"Take the phone and get out. I'll give James your number when I see him at the rendezvous. He can call and let you know whether or not he's going to accompany you into exile."

Her knuckles went white on the steering wheel, and in that moment I was very aware of the fact that despite her no longer being able to participate in combat operations she was still a shape shifter and I was very much within arm's reach of her.

I could almost see her juggling through responses, picking between options that would either escalate or defuse the situation.

"I'm sorry, no disrespect was intended."

"That's a lie, Addison. I don't have to be a shape shifter to know that. You absolutely meant disrespect; you just didn't think that I would back up my earlier threat. You were testing me. The only question now is whether you've learned your lesson. Next time I won't be so generous as to offer you a phone when I kick you to the curb."

"I'm sorry, it won't happen again."

"It better not. I don't make idle threats and you just used up your one get-out-of-jail-free card."

The rest of the drive went about like would be expected after that heated confrontation. Dom made a couple of half-hearted attempts at breaking the strained silence and then just gave up. Addison and I exchanged the least number of words possible given that I was navigating and she didn't know where we were headed. The twenty-minute drive felt like it took an hour and a half before we finally arrived.

In all fairness, part of that was all of the precautions we were taking to avoid being followed and to hopefully make anyone trying to watch us using satellites lose track of us. I was glad we had Dom with us. I never would have spotted most of the opportunities she so effortlessly found.

After what felt like forever we finally pulled into the massive underground parking garage that Donovan and I had picked out before arriving in town. It was actually one of three separate locations where we were assembling before leaving town again.

Like everything else about the plan today, our decision to go with three different locations was the result of a long series of tradeoffs. It should mean that the Coun'hij would have a harder time finding us. The tradeoff in this instance was that if they did find one or more of the assembly points then we were going to be too spread out to offer any kind of effective resistance. Then again, with Alec still unconscious, we weren't in much of a position to fight off anything much tougher than a troop of Boy Scouts.

The biggest remaining concern that I'd had was whether or not the parking garage was going to have enough clearance for the RV's Donovan was supposed to have purchased. I breathed a sigh of relief when I saw the pair of long RV's idling in an empty corner of the lowest level of the structure.

Donovan met us within seconds of Addison pulling up next to the outside motorhome.

"I'm so glad you're all okay. You didn't run into any problems?"

"No, let's get Alec into whichever RV you've picked out for him. I want him out of sight before everyone else shows up."

"Very good, Mistress Paige." Donovan helped Dom open up the back of the van and then paused for a moment. "I didn't anticipate how hard it would be to see them all there unconscious like that. They are three of the people who've contributed these last twenty years to making the estate feel like home. So much changed the night that Master Kaleb died and yet not these three, not Rachel. I will truly miss the time that Andrew and I spent tending the grounds at the estate."

I put a hand on Donovan's shoulder. "We'll go back and rebuild when this is all over."

"Yes, Mistress Paige, I expect that we will go back and I expect that we will rebuild, but it won't be the same. The old house is gone and the grounds were devastated by the fire and the emergency crews."

"You're right, Donovan, it won't be the same. It's going to be better. Andrew is going to be able to walk around the grounds with you rather than being confined to a wheelchair, and you won't spend every minute of every day wondering if Brandon or the Coun'hij are only hours away from destroying everything you've worked towards."

Donovan squared his shoulders and nodded. "Indeed you are right. I'm sorry to wax sentimental. Let's put Master Alec in the outside vehicle. They are identical from the outside, but the interior of that one is several steps better than the other one. It will make for a much better mobile command center."

Donovan and Dominic picked up the sheet and carefully carried him towards the designated RV. I hurried on ahead of them to make sure that the doors were all open, and then once I was satisfied that they were, I went back out to the van.

Addison was still standing at the back of the van as though not sure what to do. I stopped next to her and then pointed at Mrs. Graves. "I don't think I can manage Jess' dad, but I'm game to help carry in Alec's mom if you are."

She hesitated for just a second and then nodded. "I could probably carry her in by myself, but it would be very undignified. If you'll get her legs then I'll get her shoulders."

Once we were inside, Donovan motioned us into a tiny bunk room that butted up against the master bedroom. It was a shrewd choice for him to have picked this RV given that Andrew and Samantha weren't going to be complaining about cramped sleeping arrangements anytime soon. I was however surprised to find that they had put Alec in the bottom bunk.

"That's not going to work, Donovan. Alec needs to sleep in the master bedroom."

"I understand your hesitancy to usurp the master bedroom, Mistress Paige, but Alec won't know the difference. Not only that it will go a long ways towards cementing you as the leader of the core leadership group."

"I understand, Donovan. It also means that you've got everyone who needs constant care all in one place, but I'm not going to kick Alec out of his bedroom. Please move him in there so that we can go get Andrew."

For the briefest of moments it almost seemed like Donovan was going to argue with me, but in the end he nodded and Dom stepped forward to help him lift Alec. A couple of seconds later Alec was in the bed and Donovan headed back out to help Addison with Andrew.

Dominic slowed down as she walked past the sniper rifle that Donovan had carried away from the failed ambush in Idaho. I didn't even begin to have an idea what kind of expression Donovan had received when he had carried that into the RV dealership on foot.

"Where did that come from? I don't remember that being standard issue for Alec's bug-out vehicles."

"It's not, but after the last little while I think it probably will be. That's the rifle that the Coun'hij operator used to shoot Alec. Donovan circled around behind the sniper, killed him, and then put down most of the next batch of arrivals without even blinking. I never would have guessed that Donovan was such a crack shot."

Dominic smiled. "I learned long ago never to underestimate Donovan, but even so he still manages to surprise me on a fairly regular basis. I'm starting to wonder if there's anything that he *doesn't* know how to do."

Donovan and Addison were back with Andrew and Donovan shook his head as though embarrassed. "There are an infinite number of things that I'm unable to do at all and even more things that I'm unable to do well, Mistress Sanchez, as you well know. Mistress Paige, it appears that the first of our people have just arrived."

I nodded and headed back outside, passing another set of three wooden bunks on my way out and a small area that contained a kitchenette, a table and a small desk that was done in the same dark knotty alder as the rest of the trim.

The next half hour went better than I'd worried it might. Mallory had split everyone into groups of two or three and assigned them to meet up with one of the teams responsible for procuring new vehicles so that gear could be transferred at suitably low-key locations similar to the overpass where Ruby and I had met up with Dominic and the others.

Nobody had been given the option of picking their own groups, which we hoped would reduce the likelihood of a Coun'hij spy taking the opportunity to pick up another phone. All that was left was to see whether our plan had worked.

I'd half expected our people to come back tired and cranky from their various assignments, but they were almost uniformly in good spirits and it only took me a couple of minutes to realize why. It was the new vehicles. Mallory had sent people to three different lots and each team had negotiated a discount for purchasing several brand-new vehicles at the same time. I'd made it clear to everyone before we split up that the new vehicles were going to be theirs to keep, since I was making them abandon their original cars.

If I'd stopped to think about what that meant I might have anticipated that the announcement might have a positive effect on the guys, but even then I would have been surprised by how much of an impact it ended up having on the females. Maybe it was just because I'd never owned a vehicle of my own. I'd barely been able to drive before Dad and Cindi had been killed in the car accident and after that I hadn't had much of an inclination.

Apparently the new vehicles were all upgrades over what everyone had owned before and that had bought me an incredible amount of goodwill. It was a good lesson for me to have driven home.

The Graves fortune was the next best thing to limitless, which meant that I could fund nearly any conceivable spend for as long as I cared to, but I was under no illusions as to how long the goodwill would last. You couldn't keep throwing money at people and expect it to keep them happy forever. At some point they would have everything they wanted and the money would stop motivating them.

Alec had said at one point that Ulrich Bishop used his fortune to keep an equilibrium inside of his pack, but he obviously knew something that I didn't. For now I just circulated among the returning shape shifters and checked up on them. I didn't say anything to remind them that I was the source of their good fortune, but I figured it couldn't hurt for them to associate my presence with the near euphoria they were feeling at that moment.

Fifteen minutes after the first car rolled in we were all ready to get back on the road. James and Ruby were the last two to arrive and I saw James give the black van he'd come to town in a sad look just before he boarded the command RV.

"Don't worry, James. Your Accord will be waiting for you when you go back to wherever you left her."

"Maybe, but I'm not going to count on it. I put a ton of time into that machine and I'm really going to miss it."

"When this all blows over, if your car really is gone, I'll buy you something with even more potential to modify. If it's still there then I'll buy you a new turbo or something else that's nice and shiny."

That earned me a smile. "If we make it through this I'm going to hold you to that promise and it's going to be something very shiny."

"Don't think he's joking about that, Adri. Some of the parts that James has been talking about putting on his car are ridiculously expensive."

I turned back to Dom and smiled. "I'll actually be kind of disappointed if he doesn't come up with a part that is roughly as expensive as most new cars."

James rolled his eyes at Dom and me, but the gentle chiding seemed to have cemented his good humor. Donovan came out of the bedroom with his burner phone in his hand.

"I'm sorry to intrude, but I've now heard back from the other assembly points. They are both ready to go and it's past time for us to be on the road. If I can slide past you all, I'll go start up the engine to our vehicle and we can be on our way."

Ruby had followed James into the RV a little hesitantly—almost as though not entirely sure she was still welcome. She opened her mouth as though planning on offering to drive, but Addison beat her to it.

"I'll drive, Donovan. You have other things you need to be doing and it's not as though Samantha is going to need me for the next little while."

She said it with a kind of nonchalance that I knew had to be on purpose. Only time would tell whether or not Addison had really turned over a new leaf, but the offer to drive had the feel of an apology to it. I nodded my agreement and then turned to Dom.

"I'm sorry to push, Dom, but would it be possible for you to try to heal Alec now?"

Dom looked like she wanted to refuse, but I knew that wasn't because she was unwilling to help. Dom always wanted to help, but she was terrified of failing yet again. After a second she nodded, but her eyes were bright, almost like she was fighting back tears.

I waited until we'd made it back to the bedroom and shut the door before saying anything.

"It's going to be okay, Dom. Even if you can't heal him we aren't going to kick you to the curb. We all loved you even before you started being able to heal people. It's a useful skill for you to have—one that's saved a lot of lives already—but that isn't why we are your friends."

"But what if I fail and then Alec dies because of me?"

"I don't know what's going to happen, Dom. I keep thinking that it's impossible for Alec to die now that he's made it this long, but Donovan is still really skittish about the state of Alec's heart. What I do know is Alec dying—if that's what really happens—isn't going to be your fault. I would love for you to get to the point where your power came when you called it, but if you're not there yet then you're not there. Just give it your best shot."

Dom reached over and gave my hand a squeeze. "You always seem to see exactly the thing that is bothering me. Thank you for the vote of confidence, I'm ready now."

I nodded as she released my hand and then knelt down next to Alec's bed. Dom gently rested her hands on the bare skin of Alec's chest and then she closed her eyes and slowed down her breathing.

Time seemed to grind to a standstill. I'd been present the last time Dom had healed someone, and that time the people she touched had gotten incredibly hot while she'd healed them. I wanted to get up and move closer so that I would be able to tell if Alec's skin started to heat up, but at the same time I was terrified of breaking her concentration.

Dom could be shockingly self-confident regarding certain things, but her healing ability wasn't one of them and despite my words earlier, a very tiny part of me was worried that each failed attempt at healing reduced the chance that she would ever be able to heal again. At some level, if you believed that you really *couldn't* do something, it was bound to eventually become a fact.

If Dom could get her gift under control then the possibilities were almost endless, but I wasn't thinking about all of the people she could save. I was thinking about Alec, about the fact that I needed him to live, that while I might be able to guide our people into hunting Dream Stealer down and killing him, there wasn't anything I could do to fix Alec's heart if it really was only seconds away from tearing itself apart.

The RV rumbled into motion, but I barely noticed. All of my attention was focused on Dom and I barely even breathed because I was so worried about disturbing her. Minutes stretched into what felt like hours with no discernible change in Alec's condition.

MARKED

I was nearly ready to tell Dom that she could stop trying, that we would wait and try again tomorrow, when I felt *something* happen. It was hard to describe and it was so subtle that I almost didn't notice it. The air picked up a faint hum at the same time that the tiny hairs on the back of my neck all stood on end.

Dom hadn't moved at all, but for the briefest of instants it almost seemed as though she expanded to the point where she took up the entire room. Despite my earlier determination not to jostle Dom's elbow, I opened my mouth to ask her what was going on, but before I could get the words out she collapsed to the side, hands sliding off of Alec as her body hit the carpeted floor underneath her.

Her lips were blue and she wasn't breathing. I screamed for Donovan as I tried to start mouth to mouth on her.

Chapter 11

Adriana Paige
Interstate 70
Eastern Colorado

I thought we were going to lose Dom. I'd had a CPR class back in Minnesota as a way of getting extra credit in one of my classes, but I barely remembered any of it. For all I knew, I was doing more harm than good, and it seemed to take forever for Donovan to arrive.

I could tell that I was in shock. I was barely functioning, but I still managed to tip Dom's head back and breathe into her mouth several times before the bedroom door opened behind me. Moving with the speed of a shape shifter and the economy of a practiced professional, Donovan knelt down at my side and straightened out Dom's body so he could start doing chest compressions as soon as I paused the rescue breathing.

"James, Ruby, I need one of you in here now! Adri, stop."

I pulled back from Dom and Donovan started doing chest compressions as I heard James' heavy footfalls as he ran towards us.

"Get the crash paddles charging! Adri, go."

I'd been staring at Dom rather than counting compressions like I should have been, so Donovan's order to resume rescue breathing caught me by surprise. I bent down and put my mouth over Dom's as James reached us.

"Where are they?"

"In the plastic case on the other side of the bed—no, curses, that was the other RV. They should be here somewhere, Mallory assigned someone to make sure that they were moved out of the old vehicle. My turn, Adri."

The sound of ripping cloth next to my ear nearly drowned out the order, but once again I moved out of the way as Donovan resumed compressions on Dom. Another set of footsteps approaching from the front of the motorhome momentarily threw me for a loop. I hadn't felt Addison stop the vehicle, which meant that it couldn't be her.

"Here. It was in that load of gear that was dropped off just before we left the garage."

Ruby's voice was the most welcome sound I could imagine hearing at that moment.

"Thank heaven. Get them charging, it's the—"

"I know, the switch on the top...charging."

The whine of the charging paddles nearly drowned out Addison's yell from the front of the RV.

"Tell me what's going on. Is she going to be okay?"

"Your turn, Adri. We're doing everything we can, Addison. Ruby, I need the gel."

Something cold and wet splashed onto my cheek as I finished my second breath and then Donovan was pulling me backwards as Ruby leaned in.

"Clear!"

The thumping sound of the defibrillator discharging was jarring, but it was nothing compared to the way that Dom's body bounced on the carpet as the electrical jolt caused preternaturally strong muscles to instantly contract. Ruby had positioned herself so as to get nearly her entire bodyweight resting on Dom's chest, but even with that she was still thrown back into Donovan and me with enough force that I hit the wall behind me.

James stepped forward and steadied the two of us as Donovan placed his fingers on Dom's wrist to check whether or not the shock had worked. A second later that question was answered as Dom started breathing on her own again.

I collapsed to my knees as James let go of me and wrapped his arms around Dom. It seemed impossible that we'd come so close to losing Dom such a short time after Alec being shot. Part of me wanted to rage against our string of terrible bad luck, but I was careful to keep my mouth shut.

James seemed convinced that Dom was fine now, but I wasn't so sure. People didn't just stop breathing for no reason. I was pretty sure that we hadn't seen the last of the fallout from me having pushed Dom to try and heal Alec.

I lost some time after Dom's brush with death. For several days everything felt like it was completely up in the air. Dom was still alive, but she could barely get out of bed. Andrew on the other hand woke up a few hours after we put Dom in the bunk below him. He was still weak and more than a little disoriented, but he was awake, which was definite progress compared to when he'd first been carried onto the RV.

Donovan was having a hard time tracking down a suitable replacement for the communication equipment that had stopped working after the sniper had shot Alec. Apparently it wasn't as off-the-shelf as I'd thought. Even the fact that it was more or less restricted hardware wasn't the full extent of the problem. The real holdup was trying to get the equipment to interface with the custom software or firmware—or some kind of ware—that was a key part of the magic that made everything work.

It meant that we were still dreadfully out of contact with Tasha and the rest of our people, which was bad, but it was also the only thing that saved me as I spiraled into a kind of dark haze like nothing I'd experienced since my panic attacks had stopped.

It was all that I could do to function well enough to stop rumors from starting on the few times that we stopped the convoy to refuel or grab something to eat. Everyone in our RV knew I was struggling, and I was pretty sure that Mallory knew that something was up, but the rest of our people seemed to still be on a high over the fact that we'd managed to get out of Denver without having to fight the Coun'hij.

I tried to smile in the right places and ask after their welfare. I didn't do an especially good job of it, but everyone seemed to think that I was just preoccupied over all of the things that still needed to be done to keep the rebellion from falling apart.

It really was a critical time. I needed to be cementing my control over our people—preferably over all of our people, but at the very least the shape shifters in our group. It was only a matter of time before people started asking after Alec again, and when they did it wasn't going to reassure them in the least that he was still bedridden. Even without knowing that Alec was being attacked by Dream Stealer, people were going to start panicking if Alec didn't make an appearance soon.

I knew all of that, but just couldn't seem to make myself function beyond the bare minimum required to keep the wheels from coming completely off. Donovan didn't say anything recriminating, but then again he didn't have to. I could feel his eyes on me no matter where I went inside of the RV.

I tried early on to apologize to Dominic for nearly getting her killed, but I couldn't really get the words out, not like I wanted to, not with James standing protectively nearby. It wouldn't have made much difference if I'd managed to say what I'd wanted to say, not given how out of things Dom was, but maybe it would have made me feel a little better.

As it was, it was just one more failure to be thrown across my shoulders and carried forward into a future that was going to be nothing more than more failures until the weight of them finally crushed me. More than ever I wished Alec were around to talk to. I needed to be able to talk to someone else who really understood what it meant to have the ultimate responsibility over so many lives.

At some point after we got Dom's heart started again I moved completely into the master bedroom. I could still feel Donovan's worried eyes looking my direction, but it made things a little bit easier. I cut my interactions with the rest of the pack to the bare minimum. Food, when I remembered that I needed to eat, a shower each morning, and a status report from Donovan each day to find out how close he was to getting a new set of communications equipment in. I simply couldn't manage anything more than that.

I started sleeping a lot too. Not just more than was normal, more than was probably healthy, but in that too I didn't seem to be able to stop myself. Mostly I fell asleep while sitting in the chair next to Alec's bed. Usually it wasn't even something that I meant to happen. I'd be sitting there trying to convince myself to get up and go out where I could interact with the rest of the pack and then the next thing I'd know, I was waking up from a six-hour-long nap that left me feeling not at all rested.

After the second time that happened I started to worry that maybe I was being attacked by Dream Stealer. I tried to blame it on the fact that I was only catching snatches of sleep here and there. I even tried to explain it away as the result of sleeping fully dressed while sitting up in a chair, but after it happened a third time, I realized that I was doing the same kind of thing that Alec said happened every single time Dream Stealer went after someone.

I had to know. I changed into some shorts and a tank top and after making sure that Alec was okay I lowered myself down on the bed next to him and closed my eyes. If I woke exhausted yet again, then I was going to go straight to

Donovan and tell him that he couldn't trust me anymore, that he needed to lock me up until they managed to kill Dream Stealer...if they managed to kill Dream Stealer.

Right before I finally drifted off to sleep I reached out and took hold of Alec's hand. I was asleep within seconds of touching him.

I knew I was dreaming again. It wasn't just the fuzziness of my surroundings, it was the way that just as I'd dropped into slumber I'd felt like I was dropping down a long, dark chute. For the briefest of moments, as I felt myself start to be sucked down into the dream, it almost felt like I was dying. I landed in the dream with my adrenaline flowing and my heart pounding.

Only calling it a dream didn't do it justice. I'd landed in a nightmare that was beyond anything I'd ever experienced before. I seemed to be in a jungle, but the plants were all spines and leaves that were stiff and sharp enough to cut. I could hear something—or maybe multiple *some-things*—moving around just out of sight.

For the first time in recent memory I was glad that I didn't have as keen of a sense of smell as Alec and the rest of the shape shifters. The stench that was assaulting me was strong enough to bring tears to my eyes and make me gag. The melody of scents I was picking up overwhelmingly smelled of death.

All of that would have been unsettling enough if that was the only thing that was off about my surroundings. Unfortunately it wasn't. The plants all gave off a kind of dark light that was hauntingly familiar.

When I finally realized what was so odd about what I was seeing, I almost wished that I hadn't ever put the pieces together. What I was seeing was almost the complete inverse of what I normally saw when I shared a dream with Alec.

Rather than giving off the pure, soft silvery light of living things, these plants seemed to be eating the light. It turned the plants into malevolent entities, but that wasn't the complete story. I'd seen this kind of living darkness once before—in the nightmare from the morning before Alec had been shot.

I'd forgotten most of the terror-filled dream that Alec had woken me from, but now that I was once again dreaming I was suddenly certain that this wasn't some kind of terrible coincidence. The dreams were similar not because they had both originated from the same dark slice of my subconscious but because they had both been created by an external force.

I was being stalked by Dream Stealer just like Alec was, just like Kristin had been. That meant that there was no longer any question as to whether Dream Stealer was capable of breaking multiple people at once. He was. I just needed to remember that piece of information once I woke up, that or go through with my resolution to talk to Donovan about my recent lack of quality sleep. I wasn't very optimistic about either outcome.

I looked down at myself and realized for the first time that all of the light I could see was coming from me. It made the light-absorbing, darkness-emitting plants around me feel even more sinister. It wasn't just that they were absorbing the light, they were absorbing *my* light—they were devouring me one photon at a time.

It was beyond disturbing, but it also meant that I would stand out like a bonfire for anything else that happened to be out there and able to see my glow. There wasn't any guarantee that the creatures I heard moving around in the darkness could see the light from living things like a shape shifter could, but I wasn't going to just blindly assume I was invisible to the things that I sensed were already stalking me.

I'd been in countless dreams where I'd changed some aspect of the dream—often without meaning to—so it seemed worthwhile to try to change my surroundings to something less dangerous. I visualized the dark jungle morphing into a bright, cheerful meadow, but nothing happened.

I tried concentrating harder, but it still didn't seem like anything was happening. I could hear something circling around behind me, setting up for an attack, but all my efforts so far had gained me was the beginnings of a splitting headache.

It was time to change my strategy. I needed some kind of equalizer. The image of the massive sword that I'd seen so many times in Alec's bedroom came unbidden to my mind and this time when I visualized it as being part of my dream I felt an odd kind of...catch...as my mind grabbed onto something and forced the sword I wanted into existence.

Only it wasn't exactly what I'd wanted. My focus must have wavered at the last second because rather than the dark, gleaming steel I'd imagined I got a weapon that was the same size, but which gave off the cool white light of a living thing. Luckily my faulty concentration had also resulted in a weapon that was much, much lighter than the real weapon I'd been using as my model.

I wasn't stupid enough to think that having a sword meant I knew how to use it, but the softly glowing weapon still gave me a sense of power that I hadn't expected. I took a couple of tentative practice cuts with the sword and smiled as it effortlessly sliced through a spiky tree that was as big around as my wrist.

I spun in place, using my weapon to clear an area more than ten feet in diameter. It wasn't much, but I wanted room to move around in and I now had at least a modicum of space. I turned my head from side to side in an effort to locate the creature that had been circling me, but the movement had stopped.

MARKED

A shiver worked its way up my spine as I realized that meant whatever I'd been hearing was ready to pounce. Silently cursing the stupidity that had made me spin around and lose track of whatever was out there, I put the point of my sword in the direction I thought I'd last heard movement coming from and steeled myself for what I knew was coming.

I thought I was ready, but when it jumped out at me I still almost wasn't fast enough. I'd been wrong about where it was located and my sword was out of position, but I somehow managed to bring it around enough to score a long slash on the creature's side as it closed with me.

There was an odd tugging feeling on my left arm as my blade cut it, but for a second, as it recoiled back out of range of my sword, I thought that I'd made it through the first exchange of the fight without getting hurt. It wasn't until I looked down at my arm that I realized the tugging motion had been the creature slicing into my arm with its claws.

It was funny, but the cut didn't hurt until I saw the blood leaking out of it, but once it started hurting it was pure agony. I tried to force the pain to the back of my mind, but that didn't do anything about the fact that my left hand wasn't working quite right now.

I could feel tears gathering at the corners of my eyes, but in that moment I couldn't have said for sure whether they were tears of pain, fear, or rage. I was scared out of my mind, and telling myself that I couldn't actually die from anything that happened inside of a dream wasn't doing anything to lessen my terror.

On the other hand, I was so incredibly tired of living in a world where I was constantly outclassed. The *thing* I was up against right now wasn't Dream Stealer, but that just meant that it could be killed and I wanted it dead.

Once again grateful that my weapon was so light, I shifted it fully to my right hand and studied the creature that was slowly circling me. It was vaguely humanoid, with a head, two arms and two legs, but even so it made my skin crawl in a way that was usually reserved for spiders.

It was nearly six feet tall with the muscled body of a gymnast, but its skin was a rough, black material that made it hard to follow in the near darkness and each of its fingers was tipped with foot-long claws that looked purpose built for rending and tearing.

That alone would have been enough to convince me that what I was fighting had no real-world counterpart, but it was its mouth that was the most unnatural. It opened its mouth to hiss at me and I saw rows of teeth emerge from the darkness. It was like getting a close-up view of a shark only much, much worse because its jaw was hinged in such a way as to let it open impossibly big. It also looked like its teeth must retract somewhat when it closed its mouth because there was no way that teeth that long would fit otherwise.

I turned in place to keep my sword between the two of us, and the creature hissed at me again, multifaceted eyes tracking my movements. Just as I realized that it didn't have a tongue it sprang at me again.

I tried to stab it, but it slapped my sword aside with its claws and slashed at my head. I should have died right then, but as I was backing away from it I tripped and my fall caused its claws to pass just over the top of my head.

I slashed in the creature's direction with my sword as I fell and was rewarded with a strike to its arm. It was a weak blow, so much so that it barely qualified as such, but it was better than nothing. Luckily it was enough to make the creature back off again, which was a good thing because I'd reflexively used my left hand to catch myself and the pain nearly caused me to black out.

I was shaking as I rolled back to my feet. I just wasn't fast enough. I needed to be faster if I was going to survive, which was impossible...except making a sword appear out of thin air was unarguable proof that this really was a dream.

I went on the offensive, trying to buy myself time to think. I stepped forward and slashed at the creature, but it easily dodged my sword, darting backwards and then lunging towards me with the same preternatural speed it had demonstrated so far in the fight.

There was no way I could possibly get out of the way in time. I was too slow but I *willed* myself to move faster, to match the fiend that was about to rip out my throat. It shouldn't have worked, I'd misjudged just how little time my attack would buy me and my mind seemed to be moving so slowly.

I caught a dark flash out of the corner of my eye, something too fast for me to completely register and then I felt the same odd catch in the back of my mind at the same time that my headache exploded into something far more severe even than the pain in my wrist.

It felt like someone reached inside my head, grabbed ahold of one of the hemispheres of my brain, and proceeded to rip a big hole in it. I screamed in spite of my best efforts to keep it all bottled up inside. It was the kind of pain you got when you'd damaged something in a way that you could never fully heal from. It was silly to worry about something like that when you were about to have your throat ripped out by some nightmarish creature, but somehow the idea that I'd somehow inadvertently ruined myself was scary in a way that dying wasn't. You could only die once, but you had to live with a crippled mind or body forever.

MARKED

I'd been screaming for what felt like forever, but the creature still somehow hadn't hurt me. I opened my eyes and found that the creature's claws were still headed towards me, but they were moving as though through molasses.

It was impossible, but it was happening and I did my best to take advantage of it, but I was moving just as slowly as the creature. The air felt like it had the consistency of water and I simply wasn't strong enough to power my way through it faster than it wanted to let me move.

I wasn't going to have enough time to dodge backwards, so instead I stepped into the creature, angling my sword so that it would be correctly placed to block the follow-up strike that I knew would be coming as soon as my enemy realized that I was too close for its leading arm to get me.

From there it was natural to let the momentum my sword already had send its hilt up into the bottom of the creature's mouth. In the precise instant when the hilt of my weapon collided with the thing I was fighting, the pain in my head hit a new crescendo.

The impact of metal on flesh was still satisfying. I'd hit the creature hard enough to launch it into the air, but I hardly noticed all of that because I was too busy trying to clutch my head with my free hand.

I staggered back to my feet at the same time as the creature. I reached past the pain and tried to speed myself up even more, but something inside my mind had been pushed as far as it was capable of being pushed. The creature opened its mouth to hiss at me again and I had the pleasure of seeing dark, black blood pouring out of the wounds its own teeth had inflicted on its mouth when I'd hit it with my sword.

We circled, and this time I raised the point of my sword slightly so that it was pointed at the creature's head. That seemed to make the creature more nervous than anything else I'd done so far. It kept moving its head from side to side, changing the angle between it and my sword—much like I'd done earlier when I'd been trying to locate it based on what I could hear of its movements through the underbrush.

I took an experimental stab at my enemy, the kind of half-hearted attempt that I thought would help me avoid getting too far out of position, but rather than missing by a mile like I'd expected to, I scored a shallow gash on the creature's cheek. It still seemed to be having a hard time following the movement of my sword.

I stepped back and slashed at the creature, and nearly lost my grip on my sword from the sheer force of the creature's block. There was something there I could work with, but I didn't have much longer, not at the rate I was currently losing blood.

I took a deep breath and then launched two more short slashes at the creature that triggered the same kind of brutal blocks that I'd come to expect so far, but this time I was ready for the force behind the counters and I got my sword back into position each time before the creature could get into striking range of me.

Based on the way that it was batting at the air in front of it in an effort to knock the point of my sword away, it was getting frustrated. I pulled my sword in closer, still keeping it angled so the creature couldn't see it, and then as it stepped closer to me, I also stepped forward and rammed the point of my sword towards the creature's head.

Once again it saw my sword coming towards it at the last second, but this time I was moving too fast for it to dodge to one side. Under other circumstances the feeling as the sword went home in the creature's flesh would have made me sick, but this time all I felt was relief that I'd managed to survive.

I was shaking as I tried to pull my sword out of the creature's head, but I wasn't sure if that was because of the blood loss or if it was just the result of coming down from all of the adrenaline. Either way, I'd already lost too much blood.

Somewhere along the way I'd ripped holes in the bottom of my tank top. Based on the scratches on my stomach and back, I must have rubbed up against some of the nearby thorns during the fighting. In a way it was a good thing. The damage to my clothing was the only reason that I was able to rip a section of material off of the bottom of my tank top so that I could tie something around the gashes in my left arm. I never could have done it using only one hand otherwise—the material was just too strong.

The whole process took less than two minutes, but I could hear other things moving around in the jungle the entire time and my nerves were stretched to the breaking point by the time I finally finished up and pulled myself to my feet.

I worked my sword loose of the creature's corpse and was debating what to do next when a massive monster came crashing through the jungle. I reflexively raised my sword before I realized that this monster was glowing in much the same way that I was, and he was a spitting image for Alec's hybrid form.

"Alec, is that you?"

I started to drop the point of my sword, but was forced to dodge to one side as the hybrid before me took a swipe at my head. In its own way that was as jarring as anything else I'd seen so far in this place. Even in a dream it shouldn't have been possible for me to dodge a hybrid's attack.

"You won't be able to trick me that easily, Dream Stealer."

It was Alec's voice. It was rusty-sounding as though he hadn't used it in a dreadfully long time—or maybe as though he'd spent dozens of hours screaming—but it was definitely Alec's voice.

He slashed at me again with his claws and I was forced to turn them aside with the flat of my blade, but once again he was too slow. The real Alec, if he really believed I was his enemy, would have killed me with the first exchange.

As he started to circle me I realized that while he was glowing with the light I'd come to expect from all living things, he wasn't glowing like me. His glow was dimmer except for two brightly-glowing spots—one in his chest and one on his shoulder. He looked like a guttering candle, like he was just one stray whisper of breeze from being extinguished forever.

It was his voice that decided me. Either he was the real Alec and he suspected I actually *wasn't* one of Dream Stealer's twisted constructs, or he was the real Alec and he was truly that close to the end of his reserves. Either way I wasn't going to fight him.

I dropped my sword and watched as he stopped in mid attack.

"Is that really you, Adri?"

"Yes. I guess my ability must have kicked in again. You have no idea how good it is to see you."

He'd shifted back to human form and wrapped his arms around me before I'd even gotten two words out, but as I finished he went tense.

"You can't be here, it's not safe. Dream Stealer will be back soon."

I tried to prolong our embrace, but he gently tore himself free of me and picked up my sword.

"This way. We need to hide you. I know a place. I used it once before. I've been saving it for a later time, for a time when I couldn't take any more of this, but it's more important that you be safe. He can't have you, I won't let him."

"Alec, you're not making sense. Isn't Dream Stealer here now? Doesn't he have to be here in order to trap you like this? Hasn't he been here the whole time?"

Alec grabbed my uninjured arm and began pulling me deeper into the jungle. "I'll try to explain, but we have to move. If we stay motionless for too long the shadows will attack."

We crashed through the underbrush as though Alec was completely unconcerned about leaving a trail or attracting the attention of whatever I could hear moving around still just out of sight.

"I initially thought the same as you. I thought that Dream Stealer had to be here in order to keep me locked inside of the dream. He'd been torturing me for days even before I got shot, but I could never remember it when I woke up. Something changed though when I was injured. Before then I could usually control my surroundings at least to a limited extent."

Alec turned back to make sure I wasn't having any problems keeping up with him and I wanted to cry over the mess the leaves and thorns were making of his poor body. His shoulders, stomach and chest were all deeply lacerated, but he hardly seemed to notice.

"After I was shot, he pulled me into this place. It's different. I can't control any of it, and the shadows—the creatures like the one you just killed—are always here, even when he's gone. He leaves them to make sure that I don't get any rest here, that I'm always worn down when he arrives."

I pulled on Alec's arm, trying to force him to stop and talk to me. "I don't understand, Alec. How is any of this possible? How can you hide from Dream Stealer?"

He stopped for just a second, and the look on his face was the scariest thing I'd ever seen. He was starting to wonder if he'd been wrong, if I actually wasn't me, if I was just another of Dream Stealer's tricks. Even worse, I could see a touch of madness skittering around in the backs of his eyes.

I held up my free hand beseechingly. "I'm sorry, Alec. I don't mean to ask anything that would make you doubt me, but maybe there's something that you're missing, something I'll notice that we can use to get you out of here."

"Everything has rules, Adri. Sometimes the rules seem inconsistent, but they are always there. This place isn't any different. It's been hard to learn them though because they are built on a combination of things from my mind and some things from Dream Stealer's mind."

"So once you understand the rules then you can use them to your advantage..."

"Yes, exactly. My hiding place only works because I understand at least part of how his mind works. It's..."

I stopped him with a shake of my head. "Don't say it out loud. I don't want to know where it is—it's not worth the risk that he'll somehow find out about it. Instead tell me about these rules. How do you know when Dream Stealer has returned?"

"Everything around me changes subtly. It's hard to explain, but when he's gone this world feels like something I could have almost imagined on my own if I'd accessed the deepest part of my subconscious. When he comes back it's different. It's crueler somehow and it feels more alien because it molds itself more to his will than mine.

"The shadows, the creatures you fought, they are faster and stronger than anything that size should be, but their compound eyes struggle when it comes to seeing detail. They can see us because we are so bright, so there isn't any way to hide from them, and they are great with registering movement, but I've killed several of them with improvised spears and if an attack starts out with my hands close to my body they lose track of my hand until it's too late for them to dodge it."

I shook my head in astonishment. "I did something similar with my sword. I didn't know the reason why, but it seemed to have more difficulty with straight thrusts, so I used that."

Alec nodded. "I don't even remember where I heard that bit of trivia about compound eyes, but it's been the only thing that has allowed me to make it this long. I've been hunting them each time Dream Stealer leaves and dispatching them as quickly as possible. New shadows don't arrive until Dream Stealer returns and creates them again, so I've been getting more of a break than he realizes."

"Aren't you worried he'll figure out what you're doing?"

"Yes. I'm certain he would if he returned to find a host of dead, cold shadow corpses, but I don't kill them immediately. I cripple them, wound them and then leave them there to die over the next few hours. I figure that will throw him off as to what's going on."

It was all I could do not to pull away from Alec's hand. I told myself that the shadows weren't real, that Alec was merely doing what he needed to do in order to survive, but it was still surprisingly hard to push the image of him maiming something that *felt* alive and then leaving it to suffer.

"What else can you tell me about this place, Alec? How far does it stretch? Is it all just jungle? Is it ever day?"

"It's always dark, there's a stone pyramid in the center of the jungle where Dream Stealer takes me once he's defeated me each night. He straps me down to a stone table and…"

Alec swayed a little on his feet and closed his eyes. "Sorry, you don't need to know the details there and it's better if I don't think about those times."

I wrapped my arms around Alec, hugging him from the side. It wasn't much in the face of everything he'd gone through, but it was all that I could offer him in that moment.

"I'm sorry to keep asking, Alec, but what else can you tell me? We have to get you out of here and so far nobody knows how to find Dream Stealer in the real world."

"What about Jaclyn? Has she found the Ghost Pack yet?"

"I…well, the truth is that I don't know. That's partially because our communications equipment was damaged at the same time that you were shot, but mostly it's because I've been spectacularly useless since Dominic tried to heal you and nearly killed herself in the process."

That got Alec's attention. "When did that happen and what do you mean she almost killed herself?"

"I'm not sure. I've lost track of time since then. Maybe three or four days ago she tried to heal you. She sat there for a long time and then I felt this sense of pressure and heard a hum in the air right before she stopped breathing and collapsed."

"It shouldn't be possible, but it's too much to think it's just a coincidence..."

He was staring off into space and mumbling to himself in a very un-Alec manner. I shook him, trying to get him to snap out of it.

"What shouldn't be possible?"

"Time is hard to track here too, but about the same time you're talking about I felt this place change. It was the oddest thing. I felt stronger, like maybe there was still a chance for me to outlast Dream Stealer, but at the same time the jungle moved closer to Dream Stealer's vision of it than my version. The next time I went to the edge of the cage the bars were thicker. I think that might have been because of Dom."

"What bars?"

"You're sure that you don't want me to hide you?"

"Is there room for both of us? Will we be able to talk so you can tell me more about what's going on?"

Alec paused for a second and then shook his head. "No. It would just be you there and you'd have to be completely still or he would hear you."

"Then show me these bars. I'm not going to hide away here while you suffer."

"Okay, step back—we don't have time to walk there. I'll shift and then carry you."

I stepped back and watched Alec shift into the same tired, battered hybrid that I'd almost not recognized from before, and then l climbed up and put one arm around his neck. He cradled me with his left arm while carrying my sword in his right hand.

He set out in a course nearly one hundred and eighty degrees opposite from the direction we'd been traveling in before then. We made good time. In fact, Alec pushed so hard that he couldn't carry on a conversation and still maintain the punishing pace he seemed to feel was merited.

I wanted to beg him to slow down so that we could talk. There were things that I still needed to know about this place, but that wasn't the only reason. I wanted to talk to him just because talking to Alec was helping to re-center me. I could now see just how stupid I'd been. I'd spent the last few days pretending that I was getting by, that I was doing what had to be done to keep the wheels from falling off, but the truth was that I'd completely lost sight of the larger picture.

Survival wasn't enough, not if I wanted to save Alec. I had to do more than just keep the rebellion from falling apart. I needed to kill Dream Stealer, which meant that I needed Jaclyn Annikov to find the Ghost Pack. Failing that I needed some other plan. I needed a double agent inside of the Coun'hij or some hacker to find a way to track the Coun'hij down. It was all stuff that I'd known before, but I'd let grief over what had almost happened to Dom blind me to what *had* to be done.

As much as I needed to talk to Alec and tell him about the rest of my mistakes, I wasn't going to question his judgment about the speed required to get us to the 'bars' before Dream Stealer returned. He might be starting to come apart around the edges, but he was still Alec and I would continue to trust him until I had positive proof that he couldn't be trusted anymore.

It felt like we ran forever. Alec went beyond anything I thought even a shape shifter was capable of. By the time we finally came to a faltering, stumbling stop, he was gasping and his fur was soaked in sweat. He set me down on the ground and then collapsed into a panting heap, but when I made as if to stay by his side he waved me forward.

I almost refused, but after a couple of seconds I picked up my sword and walked towards the rock face he'd pointed to. After so long being surrounded by the brutal thorns and cutting leaves of the jungle, it felt odd to leave all of the black vegetation behind me, but the plants all melted away as I got closer and closer to the cliff that had originally been all but hidden in the darkness.

The stone that made up the rock face was different than anything else I'd ever seen. It wasn't black, not compared to the living black of the plants, but it was close enough. It was cold to the touch and had a glassy texture similar to obsidian.

I knew without having to ask Alec that this cliff couldn't be scaled, not even by a hybrid. The smooth surface was unmarked by seams or cracks that could be used as finger holds and when I experimentally tried to chip the stone with the point of my sword I nearly cut off my left arm. The black rock didn't just resist chipping, it deflected my sword away with as much or more force than I'd used to drive the sword forward at the wall.

"It circles the jungle for as far as I've been able to explore so far and all the rest of it is just as featureless and unclimbable as this."

Alec still looked exhausted, but he was back on his feet and his breathing was nearly back to normal. I would have rushed over and given him another hug, but he was still in hybrid form and with the way he was shaking his claws were even more dangerous than they were normally.

"There aren't any openings?"

"Only one that I've found so far. Here, it's this way."

We traveled less than twenty feet before coming to a cave entrance. If I'd been by myself I probably would have been too scared to go inside, but I followed Alec into the darkness without hesitating.

MARKED

A few steps later we came around a corner and I found myself looking at a set of pewter-gray metal bars. Just on the other side of the bars was a barren, mist-filled landscape that made me want to cry for joy. Barren and gloomy was an infinite step up from the nightmarish existence we'd been subject to up until now.

I took an involuntary step towards the bars and shifted my sword so it was leaning against me. My fingers were only inches away from the dull metal when I realized that Alec hadn't moved forward with me.

I looked back and was confronted with a vision of the future. I was still looking at Alec, but now he looked like he'd aged two hundred years over the last few steps. His fur was a patchy white and he was hunched over as though bearing the weight of the world across his shaking shoulders.

"What is this place, Alec?"

"It's the exit. Every place has to have a way out, and this is the way out of Dream Stealer's domain."

"How do you know this isn't just another trap, something designed to make you waste your time and effort here instead of spending it fighting back?"

"There isn't any other possible exit. The cliffs can't be climbed. I tried digging on my third day here, but I only made it down five feet before I hit the same kind of impenetrable rock the cliffs are made out of. This has to be the way out because there has to be a way out. That is a belief at the core of me, something that Dream Stealer couldn't have entirely subverted."

There was an element of madness to Alec's voice and I realized in that instant that this was part of what was keeping him going. Alec needed to believe there was a possibility of escape or he would simply give up and die. I couldn't take that away from him.

"I'm sorry, Alec, I didn't mean to second-guess you. You're the expert when it comes to this place. Honestly I'm surprised that it's this big. I would have thought that would make it harder for Dream Stealer to find you."

"Yeah, I would have thought so too, but he never seems to have any problem in that area. I tried to get lost in the jungle on the first two days I was here—that's actually how I found this cave—but simple distance never seems to matter. He finds me...and then we fight, and once he's beaten me nearly senseless he drags me back to the pyramid, but the trip back only takes a couple of minutes for him."

"Why are you staying so far back away from the bars, Alec?"

"They make me weak. It's like they suck the life out of me. From here it's bad enough, but if I get closer it gets worse and worse until eventually I pass out."

I moved my hand a little closer to the bars and left it there just a couple of inches away from the metal that was apparently Alec's own personal brand of kryptonite.

"I don't feel anything. Do you think I need to be closer?"

"No, I think it doesn't work on you. I think that Dream Stealer designed the exit to be as impenetrable as possible to me within the rules of this place, but he never even considered that I might have help from the outside."

"Okay, well, I guess there's only one way to be sure."

I reached out and grabbed hold of one of the bars with my right hand, unsure whether I was going to have my soul pulled out through my fingernails, or whether the experience was going to be completely anticlimactic.

I was completely unprepared for a third option.

When I was in ninth grade I got hit in the face with a basketball during gym class. I can still remember how it felt at the exact moment the ball hit me. When you're completely unprepared for something like that the shock is more than just physical. It was like the ball hit my face and the force of the blow continued past my skin and bone and tore something inside of my brain.

This was like that. When I touched the bar it delivered a shock that wasn't electrical, but which still rocked me back on my heels. I tried to let go, to distance myself from the bar, but my arm felt almost disconnected from the rest of me.

I dropped to my knees, but I retained just enough awareness to yell at Alec. "Stop, don't get any closer."

"What just happened, Adri?"

I opened my mouth to tell him that I didn't know, but before I could get the words out I realized that my eyes were closed...they were closed but I could still see everything around me.

All of my senses seemed to have been thrown into overdrive. I could hear Alec's heart beating from three feet away, could smell one of the creatures—one of the shadows—approaching from more than a mile away. I was aware of my body in ways that I'd never been aware before.

The dull pain in my arm beat a slow counterpoint to the sharp pain of my headache and it seemed almost as though I could feel each separate pain neuron firing off to tell my brain which parts of me had been pushed too far.

I felt a god-like sense of awareness regarding what was going on around me, but all of that paled in comparison to the scene that had painted itself on the backs of my eyelids. Alec was still a figure of pure, silvery light, but he was less distinct now—like someone had poured white fire into a container that was only vaguely man-shaped.

Alec was brighter now too, but that was only the beginning of what I could see. Every single bit of our environment seemed to be made up of shining golden threads that were so fine even my new vision almost couldn't see them.

It would have been impossible to trace it all back to its source by following one of the threads, but it turned out that I didn't need to find the source that way. Instead I merely followed the brightness of the light coming off of the threads. They got dimmer the further away from us they were, but they never truly went completely dark.

I turned my head, surveying the furthest extent of the dreamscape we were trapped in. The miles of distance that it covered didn't serve as any kind of impediment to my sight, I could see it all. The pyramid was exactly as Alec had described, a hulking stone edifice in the exact center of the jungle.

I saw the remaining shadows that were slowly closing in on our cave and felt a tremor of fear at facing six of them at once, but even terror wasn't capable of tearing my mind away from the vista before me.

The black, glassy walls stretched around the jungle, unbroken just as Alec had guessed, except for the spot where we were standing. From the ground previously I hadn't been able to follow them up very far, but now the darkness concealed nothing from me and I traced their route up as they arched back over top of us and met miles above in a black dome.

In every direction I looked but one, golden threads wove an impenetrable barrier. Alec had been right, there was no other way out. These bars were the key, but in more ways than just one. The threads all got brighter the closer they got to us, but it was the bars that were where the brightest threads were located.

They were so bright that I couldn't see the misty landscape on the other side of them, but they weren't so bright that I couldn't see the glowing rope that ran from Alec to the bars. Even as I watched, Alec— nearly overcome by worry for me—shifted closer to the bars and the threads that made them up got even brighter as the rope between them and Alec swelled with yet more light.

I brought my injured left arm up and watched as my free hand got closer to the bars. Tiny golden threads shimmered into existence, joining me to the bars with ribbons of light that flowed only in one direction.

"You were the key all along. It really is devouring us, but you most of all. You should be dead already..."

"Adri, what are you saying? Come away from there, I don't like what it's doing to you."

I looked more closely at Alec and felt my vision sharpen yet again. There were other threads attached to him, threads that I could somehow feel weren't stopped by the walls that Dream Stealer had built around Alec.

Light flowed along these as well, some in one direction, some in the other, but I got the feeling that the net effect was positive. It was the only explanation for why Alec was still alive after days of having his light pour out to sustain the very prison entrapping him.

"You said that you found this cave on one of your first days here?"

"Yes. Why?"

"You didn't think that was odd? Dozens, maybe hundreds of miles' worth of wall and you came directly to the exit. It boggles the mind."

"I...I could feel it pulling at me. No matter where I go inside of this place I can still feel it."

I opened my mouth to explain what it was I could see, but instead a harsh, almost mocking laughter came out. There was an edge of hysteria to it that scared me, but I couldn't seem to stop. I'd seen stuff that the human mind wasn't equipped to deal with, and now I was paying the price.

"Adri..."

Whatever Alec was going to say was interrupted as the world around us shivered. There was no telling what Alec saw, but for me the rate at which the bars sucked light out of Alec increased noticeably and I could see the light being sucked from the threads by another creature of light that had materialized at the pyramid. *That* was enough to cut off my laughter.

"Dream Stealer just arrived, Adri. We need to get you somewhere safe."

"I know, I can see him. There isn't anywhere safe for me to go though. It's too late to get to your hiding spot."

I tugged on the bars with my right hand, but it was pointless. I wasn't strong enough to bend metal—for that you'd need the muscles of a hybrid at the very least. I started to tell Alec to run and then I noticed the feather-light weight of my sword which was still leaning against my chest.

"Alec, take my sword."

"I don't know how to use it, Adri. It won't be enough for me to stop Dream Stealer."

"No, not to use against Dream Stealer, to use against the bars. It's the obvious solution."

Alec shook his head as he started back the direction we'd come, obviously intent on making sure that he wasn't going to have to worry about being pushed back into the bars during his fight with Dream Stealer.

"I already tried that. I tore a small tree out of the ground when I first found the bars and tried to use it to knock a hole in the gate while staying back far enough that I wasn't being drained, but it didn't work."

I grabbed my sword and ran after Alec, desperate to convince him before Dream Stealer arrived.

"No, you don't understand. Anything from this place isn't going to work because it's all you and the bars are designed to stop you. Use my sword; it comes from somewhere else. Look, no threads."

Alec didn't seem to have heard me. He'd already started walling the external world out, leaving himself just enough awareness to be able to fight while burying as much of his core identity as possible down where Dream Stealer would have a hard time getting at it once the torture commenced.

I could see Dream Stealer headed our way. He was moving faster than any living thing should have been able to move and I knew that we had only seconds left. I dropped my sword and wrapped both arms around Alec's arm in an effort to stop him.

"Trust me, Alec, please trust me. This is the solution!"

Something got through to him. I couldn't tell whether it was the sound of my voice, the feel of my bodyweight hanging from his arm, or the clear bell-like note that rang out as my sword hit the rock under our feet, but *something* made him stop and look at me.

"You're sure?"

"Yes, but *hurry*. Dream Stealer is almost here."

Alec turned and scooped up my sword with one smooth motion. I wanted to yell at him to run faster, but I knew he was hurrying as fast as he could already—it was only my altered time sense that made it seem otherwise.

I followed after him, but whatever I'd done to myself to make me able to see and think as fast as Alec wasn't enough to actually let me match his speed. I looked towards the bars as he got nearly to within striking range, and neither his body nor the stone blocking my line of sight was sufficient to stop me from seeing the golden pillars that he needed to destroy.

The rope running from Alec to the bars tied into their middle and then from there the light fed out of the tops and bottoms of the bars to the rest of the nightmare world around us.

"Cut free the middle third of each bar. Hurry!"

My sword was like a living flame in Alec's hand, and now that it was further away from me I could see the silvery thread that ran from me to the weapon. Alec lifted my sword in both hands and then lashed out with it.

The impact of my weapon against the metal bars was an event that happened on multiple levels, some of which I was only vaguely aware of. It sounded like someone had struck a huge bronze bell, but I barely noticed because of the way the world around us seemed to quiver.

I looked back at Dream Stealer and saw him stumble and fall to one knee, in the split second before the white line of my sword flickered. It was like someone reached into my gut and started pulling my insides out. My headache reached new levels at the same time that strength started pouring out of me.

There was a split second there where I could have severed my link to the sword. The temptation was almost overwhelming, but I forced myself to feed more strength into it instead. Without the sword we weren't going to be able to get out and I was willing to pay any price to free Alec.

The light flowing down the thread towards my sword grew to the point where I could see it even when I looked away, but this time when Alec slashed through the bar it cut much more cleanly and didn't flicker in time with the blow.

The second blow had cut one of the bars entirely free and I rejoiced as all of the threads around us got a little darker. Alec gasped as the bar hit the stone floor and disappeared. His glow was brighter now and he stood taller as he cut through the top of the second bar. More importantly the destruction of the first bar seemed to have slowed Dream Stealer's progress. He was running more furiously now than he had been before, but whatever advantage he'd enjoyed when he'd arrived seemed to be gone—he wasn't any faster than a normal hybrid.

Another blow with the sword and the second bar dropped away. I thought my head might split in two, but I managed to keep from crying out until Alec made the first cut on the third bar. Each of the blows had taken something out of me, and now that Alec was regaining some of his strength he wasn't resting as long between blows.

My scream brought Alec around. "Adri!"

"Keep going, cut a big enough hole for you to get through."

He took me at my word and sheared through the bottom of the third bar. I tasted blood and realized that I'd bitten down on my tongue in an effort to keep from screaming. I hadn't succeeded and Alec ran over to me.

"Adri, you're bleeding!"

Alec had somehow shifted forms without me noticing. I tried to tell him that I was fine, that the blood was nothing, that my tongue would be okay, but there was too much blood hitting the stone floor for it to be just coming from my mouth. Alec's fingers on my cheek came away wet.

My eyes were bleeding, but that was just a symptom. I could feel my soul starting to tear free of my body as the stress of keeping my sword from shattering pushed me beyond the limits of anything my ability had ever been meant to do.

"He's almost here. One more bar, Alec. Cut through one more and then you can shift to human form and get us both out."

"Not if it's going to kill you."

Alec dropped my sword to the rock next to me and then shifted back to his hybrid form. A few seconds previously he couldn't have gotten close enough to attack the bars with his claws—he had barely been able to get close enough to hit them with my sword—but with each destroyed bar the amount of light being drained away from him had decreased to the point now where he had no problems walking right up to the grate blocking our escape.

Alec's claws stretched out to full extension and then he hit the next bar in sequence with a titanic amount of force. Whatever his claws were made of was sufficiently hard and strong for the task and the top of the bar was sliced away, but Alec staggered as though he'd been punched in the stomach.

Contact with the bar, even just once, had sucked a tremendous amount of light from Alec. He staggered away from the grate, desperately trying to catch his breath, but Dream Stealer was close enough now that Alec could hear him crashing through the underbrush. We were out of time.

Alec turned back towards the grate and slashed at the bottom of the last bar we needed removed in order to escape. I grabbed my sword up off of the stone floor and used it as a crutch to get myself back to a standing position as I yelled for him to stop, but he was already in motion by the time the words left my mouth.

Alec's claws cut through the bar, which shattered as it hit the ground, and then his body shimmered and he was back in his human form and falling towards the metal spikes left at the bottom of the grate after he'd cut the bars away. I felt something tear inside of me as Alec was impaled through the stomach by two of the bars.

The sight of the shards of metal sticking out of his back was almost enough to make me vomit, but I steeled myself as I reached his side and picked him up by his waist. I wasn't even close to being strong enough to lift all of Alec's bodyweight—especially with my left arm not working correctly—but Alec hadn't lost consciousness and did what he could to help lift up his midsection.

"You need to go, Adri. There isn't any time."

"I'm not leaving you, Alec. You're dying, I have to get you back to the real world—maybe Dom can heal you this time."

"I can't die here, I'll just lie there until my body heals enough for me to move again. It's happened a dozen times already."

I pulled upwards as hard as I could and his body finally came free of the metal spikes. I pushed him the rest of the way through the grate and then picked up my sword as I heard footsteps behind me. The thing that came around the corner was only slightly bigger than a hybrid, but other than that and the fact that he was full of light instead of darkness, it was the same creature I'd been running from in my nightmare the morning of the ambush.

I was meeting Dream Stealer for the second time and I was already wounded and tired.

"You should have done what he said, Adri. You're lower down my list, but I will be coming for you eventually. You needn't be so eager to remain in my care."

"I'm going to kill you."

"You hardly seem in any condition to be making threats, child. You can't even open your eyes. How are you going to beat me without the use of your sight?"

My crazy laugh was back. It was the same borderline hysterical cackle as from before, but this time I welcomed it.

"I don't need these eyes to be able to see you. I can see you better this way—I can see everything better this way. I can see the way that you've been stealing Alec's light. You're weaker now that you don't have as many bars funneling his strength toward you."

I'd clearly caught him off guard, but it only took him a second to regain his equilibrium. "Fancy tricks won't save you here, Adri. This is my domain. I've been hunting here for longer than your *parents* have been alive."

"I'm not scared of you, Dream Stealer. I'm coming for you in the real world. You can beat me here, but it's only a matter of time before I find you and when that happens even people who don't like me are going to fall in line to make sure that they get a chance to put you down. How many people have you ruined over the centuries? How many packs have you forced to bend their knees to you? All of those people, all of their friends and families are going to be gunning for you."

"I've touched more lives than you can imagine, but that's irrelevant because you're never leaving here. You're not like Alec, you're like me. You're here more strongly than a casual dreamer—it gives you the power to change things you shouldn't be able to change, but it means you can be hurt, means you can be killed."

I hefted my sword and smiled. "Thanks, it's nice to know ending you here will save me having to hunt down your body to make sure that you're really gone."

He looked at the six-foot-long jet of living flame that was my sword with a trace of uneasiness and then shook himself and smiled. "You're just a human."

His attack was fast—much faster than Alec had been moving, but enough of my altered time sense still remained for me to see him coming. Even so, having something that big lunging toward me was too intimidating for me to charge forward and meet him.

I hopped backwards, easily clearing the spikes that were still wet with Alec's blood, and stabbed him in the stomach with the point of my blade a split second before he hit the grate with so much force that the entire mountain above us shook.

I was feeling quite pleased with myself until I stopped falling backwards. For a second I couldn't figure out what had happened. I'd made it safely through the grate and the opening I'd used was much too small for him to fit through in his current form.

MARKED

I was safe and the fact that I'd managed to wound him in the process was just an added bonus. If he tried to come through the grate I would have no problem taking his head off before he could get through and have space to move around again.

I should be stumbling backwards, desperately trying to reverse my momentum before I got too far away from the grate to stop him from shifting forms and coming through.

Only I wasn't.

Something tugged me forward and I finally realized that Dream Stealer had hold of my shoulder with his claws. It shouldn't have been possible, but he'd somehow made his arm stretch at the last second. The claws on the end of his fingers were gripping my shoulder blade like it was some kind of dinner plate, while the claw on his thumb had punched right through my upper chest. I could feel the razor-sharp edge of his thumb claw slicing through my flesh, but I couldn't feel anything at all from my left shoulder down. No pain, no pressure, no sensation at all.

He'd severed the nerve. He'd said I could be killed here in the dream...did that mean that the paralysis was going to be permanent as well? I pushed the worry out of my mind. It didn't matter; I was probably going to bleed to death before I ever got a chance to find out. Really, even that was a stretch given how fast he was pulling me towards the opening in the grate.

I wanted to give into the despair, to beg for mercy, but that wasn't an option. Someone like Dream Stealer had to have been born without mercy to have fallen so far, and I'd already given into despair once since Alec had been shot. I wasn't going to do that again—I wasn't going to go down without a fight.

I tried to slice my sword upward through his body—tried to take him with me—but I only had the one hand and the leverage was all wrong. Contrary to what you see in the movies, it takes a lot of force to cut through flesh—and to get at anything vital I was going to have to go through more than just muscle.

Dream Stealer was still pulling me forward and I used that to shove my sword deeper into his stomach. My blade was angled upwards, but I was still pretty sure there wasn't anything important in its path. My suspicions were confirmed when I felt the tip of my weapon grind to a halt between two of the ribs in his back.

I pushed harder against my sword, trying now that it was stuck against his ribs, to use it to keep my distance, but it was wasted effort. He just kept up the pressure on my shoulder and I was faced with a choice between moving toward him or having him slowly rip my arm off of my body.

I needed a miracle. I needed the rules to change in my favor...except that was actually possible in this place. I'd been envisioning Alec's sword when I'd conjured my sword out of thin air, but his sword wasn't the perfect weapon I'd initially thought it was. I needed something even sharper…something so sharp that even a puny human girl could use it to slice through a hybrid—even if she could only use one hand to wield it.

What I needed formed in my mind. It was identical in all respects to the sword I already had except the edge narrowed down to something sharper than anything could possibly be. I'd heard some of the geeks back in Minnesota talking about a monofilament knife, a weapon that had an edge that was only a single atom across. I envisioned my sword slimming down like that and then forced my desires to become reality.

I felt the welcome, painful catch in the back of my mind and then a pulse of light shot down the thread that connected me to my weapon and I felt it shudder slightly in my hand. This time as I pulled up on it—using the point, which was still stuck on Dream Stealer's ribs, as a fulcrum—it started slicing effortlessly upward.

The slight shudder as my blade had changed must have alerted Dream Stealer; that was the only explanation for how quickly he sprang away from me. I felt ribs part as my blade applied the slightest of pressure on them, but then Dream Stealer was off of my blade and I was falling backwards now that he wasn't pulling me toward him.

I had just enough presence of mind to make sure that my sword was well out to the side, far enough away from my body that there wasn't any chance that I would cut myself, and then I crashed to the ground, only it was a much softer ground than I'd been expecting. I turned my head and found that I'd landed on Alec.

His eyes were starting to go a little glassy from blood loss, but he managed a smile for me just before my whole world went dark.

Chapter 12

Adriana Paige
Interstate 70
Just west of St. Louis, Missouri

It took longer than normal for my awareness to return. At first I thought maybe that was because I was dead, but as I slowly started to register the amount of pain I was in I decided that couldn't be the case. My skin felt like it had been rubbed off with a cheese grater and I was sporting a truly world-class headache, but I was pretty sure I was still alive—and that made all of the pain nothing more than a secondary concern.

The faint, steady rumble of the RV's engine underneath me was a welcome reassurance that I'd made it back to the real world, but it was still several minutes before my brain was working well enough for everything that had happened to come back to me.

My first thought was of Alec, but my eyelids refused to respond when I tried to open them. For one terrifying moment I thought I was blind, but then I realized that the problem really was my eyelids. They were sealed shut. I could feel the eyelashes pulling against each other. It was still a concern, but I forced myself to remain calm.

Even groping blindly it only took a second to find Alec with my right hand. He was warm and still breathing. A wave of relief crashed through me, but it wasn't enough. I needed to know whether or not he'd managed to escape with me.

It took me a couple of tries to get my voice to work. "Alec, are you awake? Please tell me that you're okay."

For one agonizing second he didn't respond, but then his hand closed around mine. "I thought I was still dreaming. I didn't want to open my eyes and have to go back to that hell."

I started to shake as I realized that we'd done it. We'd beaten Dream Stealer at his own game. Alec was free—he was going to be okay.

Alec groaned as he slowly rolled up onto his side. I heard his breath catch as he got his first good look at me.

"Adri, what happened to you? Your eyes are bloody and you look like you haven't eaten anything in days..."

"I'm not sure. I think I remember my eyes bleeding at one point there at the end of the dream. I guess some things transfer between that reality and this one."

"You told me that you were having a hard time, but you didn't say that you'd stopped eating."

"I didn't stop. I've been eating—I mean I think I've been eating. Everything is a little blurry."

I let go of Alec's hand and ran my hand over my stomach. He was right, I could feel my ribs. Actually that had been the case for a while, but they were much more prominent now than they'd been when I'd fallen asleep—my hips too.

"How are you feeling, Alec? Are you up to helping me to the bathroom? I want to clean up my eyes."

"Weak. I feel really weak, and my chest and shoulder hurt, but I think I can manage to roll out of bed if I'm careful."

I shook my head. "No, don't risk it. I'll call for Donovan, I'm sure he's close enough to hear me if I yell."

I took a deep breath, but before I could get anything out a tremendous commotion broke out on the other side of the wall.

"Where am I? Kaleb! What's happening?"

It took me a second to place the voice—it wasn't one that I'd heard very often before—and even once I recognized it, I still had a hard time believing that I was really hearing Alec's mom. She didn't sound anything at all like the foggy, only marginally attentive woman I'd interacted with the few times that our paths had crossed since I'd first visited Graves Manor.

"Mother?"

I felt Alec move like he was going to get out of bed, but I grabbed at his arm, desperate to keep him from moving.

"Please, Alec. You had a hypervelocity bullet pass within centimeters of your heart. The shock wave should have killed you and Donovan is still worried that your heart may have suffered permanent damage. You have to hold still or you could trigger a heart attack."

Whatever Alec might have said was preempted by the bedroom door being thrown open. I could only assume it was Samantha I heard gasp.

"Who are you and why did you call out for me? Why do I feel like I should know you?"

"Samantha? Have you really returned to us?"

Donovan's voice had a reverent quality that I'd never heard before from him, but that was nothing compared to what I heard in Addison's voice.

"Please let it be so! What do you remember?"

"Donovan? Addison? What has happened to the two of you? You look different—Addison, you look like it hurts to walk. Where is Kaleb and where are my children?"

"She doesn't know."

Donovan's voice was filled with such regret that I knew he wasn't going to be able to tell her. I would have waited and let Alec or Addison tell her, but I wasn't sure that Addison would be able to bring herself to break the bad news either and I didn't want Samantha's first memory of Alec as a man to be him telling her that she'd lost her husband and the last two decades of her life.

I didn't want to be the one to tell her either, but if she was going to hate someone, better me than one of the last few links she had to her deceased husband and the life she'd lost.

I still couldn't see anything, but I forced myself to roll onto my side and then worked myself into a sitting position. It was harder than I'd expected it to be—my left arm seemed to have fallen asleep—but I managed and then once I was sitting, I turned so I was facing the door to the bedroom.

"Mistress Paige, your eyes..."

Donovan's voice was so full of concern that I wanted to reach out and give him a hug, but instead I held up my good hand to cut him off.

"I'm very sorry to have to be the one to tell you this, Mrs. Graves, but your husband, Kaleb Graves, is dead. He died almost twenty years ago in a fight against Agony. You've spent the intervening years in a state of disassociation due to the effects of having the Ja'tell bond severed.

"The young man behind me is your son Alec. He was recently shot during a fight against Coun'hij forces in Idaho. Your daughter Rachel disappeared a week or two ago about the same time that Graves Manor was destroyed by a

Coun'hij strike force consisting of hybrids and werewolves.

"Alec's power has finally manifested and it is a doozy, which has caused him to directly oppose the Coun'hij. So far Alec has managed to kill Agony and a number of the Coun'hij's enforcers, but we've been unable to find their home base and we don't currently have a good counter to Puppeteer's ability to throw werewolves at us.

"You're currently in an RV located somewhere in the Midwest and you've spent most of the last week unconscious for unknown reasons which I suspect relate to the fact that Alec has been under psychic attacks from Dream Stealer."

My voice had gone hoarse by the time I finished, but I forced myself not to wilt under the pressure of all the eyes I could feel resting on me. Once I was done, there was silence for several seconds before Samantha Graves finally broke it.

"And who are you whom I just found in my son's bed, who orders my staff around as though they are hers, and who presumes to tell me what I need to know?"

My chin came up in response to the derision in her voice. "My name is Adriana Paige."

"She's my fiancée, Mother, and we would have been married before now if not for the attack that destroyed the manor. What's more, she's the glue that has held everything together while I've been injured and unconscious."

"It hasn't been just me; Donovan and Mallory have done most of the real work."

Donovan cleared his throat. "I'm sorry to contradict you, Mistress Paige, but neither Mallory nor I could have accomplished anything of significance without you. I feel it important to add that the two of you have been introduced prior to this and you were welcomed into the house by Mistress Samantha, albeit in the same distracted fashion that has been her way during these many long years since Master Kaleb was taken from us."

I got the feeling Samantha still wasn't happy, that in some way Donovan sticking up for me just fanned the flames of her anger, but Alec resumed talking before she could say anything.

"Adri is the reason that I'm able to talk to you right now, Mother. She's not a shape shifter, but she's got a dream walking ability that is very similar to what Dream Stealer is able to do. She came in after me and nearly killed Dream Stealer on his own turf. She is due every respect as my future wife, but more than that, she's due every respect many times over as a result of what she's accomplished all by herself. Donovan, please help Adri to the bathroom so that she can wash the blood away from her eyes. I'd do it myself, but she said that my heart may still have some residual damage from that second bullet."

"Indeed, Master Alec, it would be best for you to avoid any kind of activity. Right this way, Mistress Paige."

A moment later Donovan was at my side, helping me to my feet. He was a solid, reassuring presence that went a long way towards balancing out the unfriendly stare I could feel coming from Alec's mother.

With Donovan's help I managed to make it to the RV's tiny bathroom without stumbling, but it was more of a challenge than I'd expected it to be. My left arm was nothing more than dead weight and that threw off my balance by a significant factor.

Washing the blood out of my eyes with only one hand seemed to take forever. The process felt even more awkward because nobody said a word the entire time I was in the bathroom.

Despite the brave front I'd tried to put on for Alec, I'd actually been more than a little worried about my vision. I was shaking by the time the last of the clotted blood came free of my eyelashes, but I opened them to a wonderful world full of all of the colors and details that I'd been worried might be lost to me forever.

I grabbed the sink with my right hand to steady myself as a tsunami of relief crashed through me. The feeling passed after only a second and then I looked up and caught my reflection in the mirror for the first time since I'd come back from Alec's dream. I looked…disturbing.

The whites of my eyes had turned a dark crimson that I'd never seen on anyone else before in my life. I looked like I'd been possessed—that or beaten nearly to the point of death. My left arm, still hanging limply at my side, didn't do anything to combat the illusion that I'd been through hell and back recently.

I stepped out of the bathroom to find that Donovan had gone to Alec's side and had his stethoscope pressed up against Alec's bare chest. Ruby was driving again, James and Dominic were sitting on the couch, Andrew was sitting at the desk, and Addison was standing in the doorway, looking at Samantha with an air of reverence.

It was Samantha who looked over at me first, and while her gasp wasn't entirely surprising, it still stung.

"What happened to you?"

"I was injured while fighting Dream Stealer."

"What about your arm? Was that the result of your fight with Dream Stealer as well?"

That made me pause, but I still answered before my mind had finished picking at the fragment of memory that was trying to surface.

"No, I must have just slept on it funny. I think it just fell asleep."

Alec looked up at me with a concerned expression on his face. "That doesn't sound right, Adri. I seem to remember something happening during the fight...didn't Dream Stealer stab you?"

"Maybe. Now that you mention it I think you're right."

Donovan crossed the distance between him and me in a flash and prodded my arm. "Can you feel this, Mistress Paige?"

I shook my head. "No, like I said, it's asleep."

"Do you feel pins and needles yet?"

"No, but I haven't been up for very long."

Donovan met my eyes with a concerned look. "Enough time has passed that you should be able to feel something. I'm sorry to be the bearer of bad news, but I think the nerve damage is permanent. I'm afraid your arm has been paralyzed."

Chapter 13

Adriana Paige
Interstate 70
Just west of St. Louis, Missouri

Alec lurched out of his bed, desperate to get to my side, heedless of the possible consequences of stressing his heart. He only made it half a step before his legs gave out on him. It was a good thing that his mother was already in the room.

Samantha wasn't anywhere close to being strong enough to support Alec's full weight, but she managed to slow his fall and pull him just far enough to the side to stop him from slamming his head into the small bedside table just to his left.

I made it to Alec's side a split second before his head would have hit the floor and managed to help cushion his fall.

"Alec, you can't take those kinds of risks!"

He'd gone a concerning shade of white, but he managed a smile as he shook his head at me. "I didn't even think about the fact that I might not make it to your side. That doesn't matter—what are we going to do about your arm, Adri? It's my fault you got hurt."

I shook my head as his words brought the end of my dream back to my memory. It was all I could do to tear myself away from reliving the moment when I'd been paralyzed. "We don't know that the paralysis is permanent, but even if it is, this wasn't your fault. Dream Stealer is the one who did this, but it's a small price to pay in order to get you back."

Alec grimaced as Donovan lifted him back onto his bed and began checking his vitals. "You're right, maybe it's just temporary, but either way it was far too dear of a price to be required of you."

"Master Alec, please be still. I'm attempting to diagnose things that normally require very large pieces of equipment that we don't have access to. Unless you are prepared to take the risk of visiting a real hospital I'm going to need your cooperation."

Alec's mom took me by the arm, the one that still worked, and pulled me out of the room. "What are you?"

"I don't know what you're talking about."

"Don't you? I saw you move just now. You made it to Alec before *Donovan* even got turned around. No normal human could move that fast. I don't know how you've managed to trick Alec and the rest into believing your lies, but I'm not going to let you get away with it."

I suddenly felt incredibly tired. It wasn't just the days of poor sleep or the night I'd just spent doing battle with Dream Stealer—although both of those were part of what I was feeling. My exhaustion also had to do with the fact that even with everything else that was going on, I was still having to deal with all of the usual problems of normal life.

You expected there to be problems with your fiancé's mother, but I'd thought I'd sidestepped that particular concern due to the fact that Samantha Graves had spent most of the last two decades barely aware of the outside world. Speaking solely for myself, I could have been perfectly happy if she'd remained the way she was, but I knew this was what Alec and Rachel had been wanting for years.

I was willing to sacrifice anything for Alec, I'd just been hoping this wasn't a sacrifice that I would end up having to make.

"I'm sorry, Mrs. Graves, but I really am exactly as I've presented myself to Alec and the others. I'm a normal human girl who happens to have the ability to touch people's dreams, an ability which I just used to save Alec."

I never even should have seen the blow coming. I'm no martial artist, but Samantha didn't do anything to signal the fact that she was about to hit me. One second she was standing there in front of me with her hands on her hips and a scowl on her face, and then in the next she'd thrown a punch directly at my throat.

It was all the more surprising given the fact that Alec's mom looked like a stiff wind would blow her halfway across the state, but then again she apparently knew enough to pick a target that didn't require a lot of force to put someone down.

I wanted to panic and scream, but her fist seemed to be moving in slow motion and I found that I had plenty of time to dodge to the left as I raised my one good hand up to knock her arm to the side. It was surreal because I seemed to be moving just as slowly as she was, but even with the air dragging at me I was still able to move quickly enough to save myself.

I bounced off of the wall next to me and threw myself hard to the right in an effort to avoid Samantha's next attack. Seeing everything happening in slow motion was a huge advantage over the normal state of affairs for me, but it wasn't a magic bullet. I was faster than I normally was, but that wasn't enough to compensate completely for the fact that Samantha was some kind of hand-to-hand ninja and I could only use my right arm.

In my effort to get out of the way, I went too far and would have fallen if James hadn't grabbed me from behind. Samantha's second punch whipped past my ear, but James easily blocked her follow-up kick with his shin as he moved me around behind him, safely out of her reach.

"I don't know what's going on, but Alec isn't going to be happy if you hurt Adri."

"My son is being tricked by this *thing*. You saw how quickly she moved—there's no way she's what she claims to be."

"James, don't you dare lay a hand on Samantha! Come away from there."

James shook his head in response to his mom's order, that or maybe in response to Samantha's accusation. We never got a chance to find out which, because at that instant Samantha threw herself forward in an attempt to get past James so that she could take me down.

Alec and Ash were the only members of the pack who seemed to have spent any real amount of time learning to fight in their human form, which wasn't necessarily a black mark against James. In a fight against almost any normal human, James' superior speed and strength would see him through without too much problem and any fight against another shape shifter would always end up escalating to claws and fangs.

James would have been fine in a normal fight, but he was handicapped by the fact that he didn't want to seriously injure Alec's mom.

Samantha apparently wasn't operating under the same kind of concern.

She raked him across the cheek with her fingernails a split second before she threw a knee at his groin. Whatever had sped up my time sense was apparently still in effect because I was able to follow not only Samantha's attacks but also James' responses to them.

It was obvious that James hadn't actually been expecting Samantha to attack him. He pulled back enough that she missed his eyes, but then had to check his reflexive slap that probably would have snapped Samantha's neck.

That slowed him down so much that Samantha was easily able to duck underneath his blow. The knee she threw at his crotch was as perfectly executed as anything I'd ever seen before. Even now, *I* couldn't have hoped to get out of the way in time, but James simply punched her in the leg, stopping her strike with enough force that I knew Samantha was going to have bruises all of the way down to the bone.

Against another shape shifter James would have followed up with something designed to put Samantha down for the count, but rather than doing that he backed up half a step as though trying to give her a chance to reconsider what she was doing.

That was a much bigger mistake than I would have expected it to be. I heard the door to the bedroom thrown open at the precise instant that

Samantha reached back and pulled out the hair sticks that had been holding her bun in place. A split second later she shoved the one in her left hand into James' leg.

I was close enough to James that I could feel him start to sway forward as his leg began buckling. As Addison screamed, I stepped forward, trying to get around James so that I could intercept the chopstick in Samantha's right hand. I didn't actually expect to be able to successfully stop Samantha—I was probably going to end up being stabbed instead of James—but I wasn't going to just sit there and do nothing.

My world had narrowed down to the shiny silver stake in Samantha's hand, so much so that it took me a second to realize what had happened. As Samantha dropped bonelessly to the ground I looked up to find Donovan stepping through the bedroom doorway and Alec looking at his mother with his hand outstretched. Alec couldn't rush to my side, but that didn't mean that he couldn't use his power.

"Enough, Mother! That is the last time that you will attack Adri, James, or anyone else currently in this vehicle. I want your word on it."

"You don't know what you're facing, Alec. I can't make that kind of promise!"

Alec was obviously still weak, but he pushed himself into a sitting position with a grimace.

Donovan looked back and forth between James and Alec.

"Master Alec, it's not wise…"

"Be still, Donovan. I'm realizing that we don't have time for you all to baby me along. Please see to James."

Alec looked back down at his mother and sighed. "I will have a promise out of you, Mother, or I will have you locked up in a cell somewhere safe. I'm grateful that you gave me life and took care of me during those first few years before Father was killed, but your knowledge is woefully out of date at this point. I need Adri and James for what I suspect is coming, but more importantly, they are my friends—more than friends really. They've stood by me for long enough for me to know their hearts and they aren't guilty of what you seem to think they are."

Alec's gift was still going strong, still potent enough that his mother couldn't pull herself to her feet, but he apparently toned it down at least slightly because she pulled herself up into a sitting position.

"You don't know what's out there. You're too young to know what you're up against."

"Then tell me, Mother. What is it that I'm up against? I killed Agony. My people and I drove off Puppeteer's werewolves, and I've spent the last several days fighting Dream Stealer. During that time I've always known where James and Adri stood. Even when they couldn't support me they still at least gave me the courtesy of telling me they were leaving before they left. What's more, I've stood next to Adri as she promised to do everything she could to support me in my war against the Coun'hij. I heard the truth in her voice when she promised to help me, but even beyond that, I had her intent confirmed by someone whose ability is such that they know the intent behind such promises."

To everyone else Alec probably looked stern and resolute despite being confined to a bed, but I knew him better than that. He was only a hair's breadth from breaking down and telling his mother just how much betrayal he felt from all of her years of neglect. He was nearly to the point of telling her that Donovan, Mallory, Jasmin, Isaac and even James had all been a much better family to him than she had.

It was an understandable urge, one I could relate to because of how absent my own mother had been for various parts of my life, but it was the wrong thing to do. I wasn't even sure that the woman who'd offered me a distracted welcome into her home was the same person as the one who'd just stabbed James. Either way, if Alec said what he wanted to say right now, in front of all of these witnesses, he would destroy any chance of having a meaningful relationship with his mother.

I shook my head slightly, praying that Alec would understand, but he was so focused on his mother that I wasn't even sure that he saw me.

"I'm not a child, Mother. You've been gone a very long time and I grew up. If you're going to continue traveling with us then you're going to do it under the same terms as everyone else here. You'll do it having sworn fealty to me."

I would have said that nothing could shock this new, ultra-confident Samantha Graves. She'd listened to everything up until then without even blinking, but the mention of swearing fealty drew a gasp out of her.

"That hasn't happened since the monarchy."

Alec nodded. "I've declared myself to be the third king. I will restore the monarchy or die trying."

As I'd scooted forward and to the side to make room for Donovan to see to James, I'd accidentally brushed up against the very edge of what Alec was doing to his mother. It wasn't the first time that I'd been exposed to his power in action, but it had been a long time since I'd had it focused, even indirectly, on me.

Even back when Alec had used his ability to defeat Brandon his absorption ability had been incredible, but he'd apparently gotten more powerful since then. Just brushing up against the edges of the field that was draining the strength from Alec's mom left my feet feeling like a couple of blocks of wood. It was nothing more than pride and determination that kept me on my feet after that. I was impressed that Samantha was sitting up and carrying on a conversation. If there had been any question about just how determined this new version of her was, then it had just been settled.

I was even more impressed by what happened after Alec said that he was going to restore the monarchy or die trying. Samantha looked like she'd just had an electrical current sent through her. She went from slouched against the wall to sitting straight up and even looked for a second like she was going to make it up onto her knees.

"...Restore the...oh, Kaleb. What have you done? All those memories hidden away for all of this time... We've been operating blind...such a tremendous risk that you took and I never even..."

Samantha collapsed mid-sentence and I somehow knew that the ripples from what had just happened were going to be far-reaching indeed.

Chapter 14

Adriana Paige
Interstate 70
Just west of St. Louis, Missouri

Apparently I still hadn't completely assumed the tough-as-nails persona that I'd been projecting since Alec had been shot. Despite everything Samantha had done to me since she...woke up, I still reached for her as she collapsed. In the heat of the moment I'd completely forgotten about Alec's ability, but he must have already shut it off by then because I got only the faintest shadow of a tingle as I reached for Alec's mom.

Her breathing was fine and I was checking her pulse when I looked up to find Alec kneeling just across from me.

"Is she okay?"

"Her vitals seem normal as far as I can tell, but I'm not the expert..."

Donovan called out from the sofa where he was tending James. "Master Alec, do you want me there or can I finish up on James first?"

Alec wasn't any less conflicted about his mother than he'd been a second ago, but he took a deep breath and then shook his head. "Make sure that James is out of any danger first. Mother was the aggressor, it wouldn't be right to take care of her first."

In all the confusion I'd forgotten about Dom, but in that second she stepped out of one of the tiny rooms that contained the sets of bunk beds and shook her head. "She's your mother, Alec. I'll go finish up with James. Donovan can see to her."

Just saying that Dom looked bad wasn't enough. She looked like she'd aged at least two or three decades since she'd tried to heal Alec. Her hair was still the same color, but it had lost its luster and her skin had age spots that should have been an impossibility on someone her age.

"I'm sorry; I should have gotten up and helped before now...I've just been so tired lately."

Alec shook his head as he stood and grabbed hold of Dom's arm to steady her. "You shouldn't even be up right now, Dom. Go back to bed. My mother can wait."

Dom's smile was a thing of beauty. It transformed a face that had felt ancient and alien just a second ago into something that belonged to the girl we all knew and loved. "You're one to talk, Alec. Neither of us is supposed to be out of bed yet, but here we both are. Really, I'll be okay—it will probably be good for me. I don't feel as bad now that I'm up and moving around."

Alec hesitated for a second, hand still on Dom's arm, before finally nodding. "Thank you, Dom. Not just for this either. I appreciate what you did for me earlier too. I'm not sure I would have lasted this long without your help. If it gets to be too much for you let us know and Donovan will jump back over and help finish up with James."

"*Sí*, Alec. Things will be fine."

"No healing him, Dom. We can't risk it right now. Take care of him the old-fashioned way."

There was a heartbeat there where I thought that Dom was going to argue with Alec, but in the end she nodded her agreement and hobbled past us. Actually, hobbled wasn't the right word—she started out moving with obvious difficulty, but Alec steadied her for the first few steps, after which she seemed fine.

Alec looked at me with misery written large across his face. "This is my fault."

"Don't say that. You can't control your mother any more than you can force any of the rest of us to behave. Besides, James is going to be fine and your mother didn't manage to actually lay a hand on me."

"No, you're right about the rest, but that wasn't actually what I was talking about. My mom being unconscious is my fault. I was trying to keep her from getting back up and attacking anyone; I had my gift open just a crack, just enough to keep her down, but then there at the end there was such a surge of power out of her that I had to increase the amount of energy I was pulling in or she would have been able to get up."

"I don't understand, Alec."

"I drained away the surge of energy to wherever it is that I send stuff with my ability, but then her power level dropped so quickly that I wasn't ready and didn't rein in my absorption fast enough. I took too much from her, Adri. I tried to stop, but it's hard when it's wide open like that. There at the end I could feel her life force guttering. I almost killed my own mother."

"But you didn't, Alec, she's going to be just fine."

"Is she? I may not have killed her, but I did send her back into a coma. Who knows when—or even if—she'll wake up again."

"Don't talk like that, Alec. This isn't your fault—you don't even know that she's in a coma yet."

"She is…I can feel it, Adri. Maybe I'm the one who put her into a coma the first time around. I'm not safe to be around, not even for my own mother."

I put my hand on the side of Alec's face and pulled his head around so that he had to look at me. "You're right, you are very dangerous to be around—that's exactly the reason that we're all here. If you'd been even a smidgen less dangerous we'd all be dead. You're dangerous, but you're infinitely better than the rest of what's out there. We *need* you to be dangerous, but right now you need to be back in bed."

Alec looked at me uncomprehendingly for several seconds before shaking himself as though waking from a dream as Donovan knelt down next to us. "There isn't time for that, Adri. Donovan, please see to my mother—I'm afraid that I'm going to be unable to wait at her bedside as protocol might demand."

Alec stood up and started walking back towards his bedroom, but he was still moving as though in a daze, so I was easily able to jump over his mother's legs and catch up to him.

"Alec, you *have* to lie back down. If we lose you then we lose everything."

"There isn't time, Adri. If I don't take this opportunity to circulate among our people then we're still going to lose everything. You said that we lost the communications equipment—how are we keeping in contact with Mallory and the rest of our people?"

"We're using burner phones, but you should really..."

While I'd been talking Alec had stripped off his shirt and I got my first good look at his chest since before we'd fought Dream Stealer together.

He wasn't fully healed, but the angry red scars that had persisted for so much longer than they should have were almost completely gone. His shoulder looked like it had never been injured, and all that was left of the gunshot that had nearly destroyed his heart was a mass of white scar tissue that looked like it was years old.

"How did that happen? I thought you were still weak when you woke up—you couldn't even make it out of the bed."

"I was weak—I could feel a flutter in my heart and it was all I could do to move my arm, but sometime between now and then all of that went away. There's still no guarantee that I don't have some kind of critical damage to my heart, but if so the simple passage of time probably isn't going to make any kind of difference."

"You're telling me that your chest healed during the course of less than five minutes? That's impossible, even for a hybrid."

"I know it's hard to believe, Adri. I don't have an explanation, but the thing I keep thinking about is that this was how my father used to be before he died. It doesn't make any sense, but we don't have time to stop and question it—I need to talk to Mallory and the others and then I need to make about a dozen calls. There are things that need to be set into motion if you...if we are going to have any chance of winning this war."

I wanted to run over to him and wrap my good arm around his bare chest. I'd only just barely gotten Alec back and it didn't seem fair to lose him to the demands of his duty already, but he was right. I'd already neglected our people to a dangerous degree and there was no telling how much work he had ahead of him repairing the damage I'd done.

"I'll go get a couple of burner phones and wait for you out with everyone else."

I turned to go, but Alec was suddenly blocking my way and his arms had wrapped themselves around me so fast that I didn't even see them coming.

"I'm sorry we aren't going to have more time to just be together without all of the rest of this craziness right now, Adri."

I wiped a tear away from the corner of one of my eyes, hoping that I'd managed to catch it before he noticed. "No, it's okay. I understand—I really do. Maybe if I hadn't made such a mess of things it would be different, but I did, so it's not."

"You can't say that, Adri. You've done an amazing job. You provided the direction needed to keep our people from splintering into a dozen different pieces. Not only that, you did battle with Dream Stealer himself and brought me back. You've been incredible in every way."

"It doesn't feel like I've been incredible. It feels like I started out decently and then cracked under the pressure after I nearly got one of my best friends killed. You would have done a lot better if you'd been in my shoes."

"I was in your shoes not too long ago, Adri. You were gone and I made an absolute mess of things. You've managed to keep a group of complete strangers headed in the same direction—I nearly alienated my closest friends, people who were ready to give me the benefit of the doubt over and over again. You've exceeded anything I could have hoped for and I wouldn't be here if not for you. You're the most amazing person I could have hoped to end up with. I'm so sorry about your arm."

He kissed me, one, long glorious kiss that seemed to transport me to somewhere else, to a location where we didn't have to worry about Dream Stealer or the rest of the Coun'hij. I wanted to stay there in his arms, pressed up against the bare skin of his chest, forever, but in the end, I was the one who broke the contact.

"You're right, we need to get moving. I'll be waiting for you as soon as you finish changing."

Donovan had just finished lifting Alec's mom into one of the bunks as I pulled the bedroom door shut behind me.

"How is she?"

"Resting. I fear that Master Alec is right and she's slipped back into a coma, but I'm most worried about Master Alec."

"You're going to have to see it for yourself, but it looks like his hybrid healing has finally kicked in. His chest is almost completely healed."

Donovan had to reach for the wall to steady himself. "How is that possible?"

"I don't know, but it couldn't have come at a better time. I need to grab some burner phones so Alec can call Mallory. I suspect that he's going to want to make some calls to the rest of our people, which means that we need a city, something big enough that we have a chance of losing ourselves in the crowds while Alec makes calls to numbers that are almost certainly being tracked."

Donovan nodded. "Of course. I think that we're within an hour or so of St Louis. I'll get on with our IT assets now and ask them to start encrypting random calls going out of the city. It won't do anything to hide the fact that there is something going on in the city, and it won't stop someone from triangulating the calls if they know what numbers we are calling from, but it will keep the Coun'hij from listening in on our conversations at least."

Alec came out of the bedroom wearing designer jeans and a long-sleeved shirt that he hadn't bothered to button up. I handed him one of the three burner phones I'd grabbed out of the supply we'd picked up in Denver and he smiled his thanks as he turned towards Donovan, already sitting at the desk typing.

"Donovan, I grabbed my phone off of the table next to my bed, but it's missing my sim card. Did you guys get that out of the communications equipment before you changed vehicles?"

Donovan went white. "No, Master Alec, I should have remembered—I knew that your sim card was at the heart of the equipment that we left behind, but I failed to instruct our people to remove it from the device before setting the RV on fire…"

"It's okay, Donovan, you come pretty close, but nobody is perfect. You and Adri have picked up quite the load since I was injured. I'm no Isaac, but I can probably manage to clone my sim card before we get to the closest city. I know I can't use this phone until we're almost ready to leave, not without bringing Coun'hij kill teams down on our heads, but by now I've probably got a hundred messages that need to be gone through. The people with Tasha will have known not to call this phone, but we'll have other people who are more out of the loop than that and I need to get back to them as soon as possible."

The next twenty minutes went by in a blur. Alec called Mallory and let her know that he wanted to stop in St Louis so that she could handle all of the logistics of finding a safe spot to stop inside of the city and making sure that we didn't lose anyone along the way. From there Alec hooked his phone and a new sim card up to his laptop and began trying to get his phone cloned.

I ate and then kept myself busy with whatever small tasks I could find to help with that didn't require two hands. I handed Dom medical supplies as she finished taping up James, I helped Ruby carry Andrew to and from the couch, and I fetched extra burner phones for Alec and Donovan as needed, but mostly I watched the pack watch Alec.

There was a sense of reverence to the way that they all looked at him. It was obvious that on some level each of them had been convinced that he wouldn't be coming back, that they would never see him again and that our cause was doomed. That belief seemed to require that they touch him and exchange a few words with him before they could really accept that they'd been wrong, that they still had a chance of surviving.

Even James, who I was pretty sure didn't always like Alec very much, and Donovan, who I'd thought had more faith than me, stopped Alec on some pretext or another and spent a couple of seconds making sure that it was really him, that he'd really come back to us healed and ready for another round of fights.

Alec handled each interruption with the regal bearing that he'd started demonstrating more and more lately. He'd always been polite and understanding, but it seemed like he'd come to understand his people on a whole new level recently. He didn't resent the interruptions because he knew it was the price that had to be paid if he was going to keep everyone motivated and pulling towards the goals we needed to achieve.

Mallory outdid herself when it came to selecting our stopping place. Rather than the dark parking garage that I'd been expecting, she directed everyone to the largest music festival I'd ever seen. It was brilliant because all of the musicians and a surprising number of the fans had arrived in motorhomes and tour buses similar to what we were driving.

Even better, the festival was due to run for nearly a week—with different musical styles each day—so I was guessing that there would be a steady stream of RV's coming and going each day. Against that kind of backdrop we would blend into the noise so well that it would take a miracle for the Coun'hij to find us.

We pulled into the massive parking lot a few minutes behind Mallory and then, after turning around, parked close enough that our canopies nearly touched once they were extended. We were safe from aerial observation as well as being watched from two directions, which was about as much as we could ask for without drawing an inordinate amount of attention to ourselves, but Donovan still handed out sun glasses and hats as we exited the RV.

Alec took the accessories with a smile as he put his phone in his pocket, but he didn't put them on. "I know it's a risk, Donovan, but they need to see me. I'll put them on before we go into the city to make the rest of the phone calls."

"Very good, Master Alec."

Mallory was waiting just outside of our vehicle as if worried that going inside would break some kind of spell and return Alec to his injured and helpless state. Alec carefully hugged her as soon as his feet hit the blacktop.

"Thank you for supporting Adri. I knew I could count on you."

"Apparently she hasn't told you the full story."

He looked back at me with a raised eyebrow, but I wasn't about to go into that particular tale with so many other ears around.

"Things got a little tense at one point, but I was able to bring Mallory around to my point of view. The negotiations were understand-ably…energetic."

Mallory snorted. "I underestimated this one, Alec. I was feeling my oats and started thinking that maybe I should be calling the shots like I used to do when I was your dad's enforcer. I'm glad she was here to remind me that I'm nothing more than a tired old lady these days."

"Well, however it happened I'm glad that the two of you were able to work together with Donovan. How much longer before all of our people will have arrived?"

Mallory shrugged. "It's hard to say for sure. The last car is supposed to be a good five or ten minutes behind you, but given the reason we're stopping it wouldn't surprise me to find out that they've been crowding up closer than that. I can read them the riot act if you want, but honestly I can't blame them too much for wanting to see you with their own eyes."

"No, you're right. We'll have to hope they don't draw any extra attention our way, but I can't really blame them. Besides, given how short we are on time it's probably for the best anyway."

"Is something going on that I should know about?"

"Nothing so urgent that we need to get into it out here. Don't worry, I'll make sure you're fully briefed on everything before too much longer."

Mallory looked like she wanted to press Alec, but she knew as well as I did that anything we said right now would end up making the rounds among our people. After everything that had happened so far today, the gossipers among our people were going to be putting in overtime.

"Did you serve as the heavy for my dad a lot back in the day?"

"Yeah. That's something you should keep in mind, actually. It's something that you see a lot on navy ships. The first mate is the one who deals with most of the punishments and the like, which means that the captain can remain above that and retain the crew's loyalty even through very trying circumstances. I'm not saying that

I'm the ideal person to take that role any more, but you ought to have someone who can throw their weight around from time to time when the circumstances call for it."

I gave Mallory a surprised look. "Isn't it a bad idea to talk about something like that out here where everyone can hear you?"

"Maybe, but the best strategies often work on people at a subconscious level. You can know that I'm playing a role to a certain extent, but that's probably not going to change the fact that you won't like me if I come down on you. By the same extent, you'll always be inclined to think that some of my enthusiasm is beyond what Alec would strictly want to take place, which means that you'll be predisposed to like him even though you know he's the one who put me in charge of disciplining you."

Alec stifled a yawn. "Sorry, it's not the subject matter. Resting while injured this time around was surprisingly unrestful. The old-time captains learned a lot of lessons over the years and their situation wasn't all that different than what we're up against.

"Out on your own, cut off from any kind of communication, and in charge of a bunch of trained killers, some of whom were there only because they didn't have any better options open to them, some of whom you could count on to stand with you no matter what. I'm open to any suggestions you might have where that kind of thing is concerned, Mallory, but it looks like most of our people are here now."

Mallory surveyed the group of people standing a respectful distance away from us and then looked over at a silver SUV that had just parked forty feet away from us. "Yeah, that Escalade is the last of them. You can start with whatever you want to say as soon as they get here."

Shape shifters were normally capable of carrying on a conversation in what was the sub-audible range for humans, but maybe the background noise from the nearby performance made that impossible—that or maybe Alec just wanted me to be able to hear what was said. Either way, he spoke loud enough for his voice to easily carry to the farthest member of our group.

"I'm sure some of you probably doubted Adri when she took over command and told all of you that I was going to recover. I'm here to tell you that while I understand your doubts, they were misplaced."

Alec hadn't ever buttoned up his shirt and now he slipped out of it, making it so that everyone could see his unblemished shoulder and the mass of white scar tissue next to his heart.

"I appear to have made a full recovery, and I vindicate Adri's decision to take over while I was unable to perform my usual duties, but that's not the most important thing I called you all here to hear. I made a full-scale rebellion possible because I'm more powerful than any of you."

Alec lifted his hands to shoulder level and then closed his fists. This was a demonstration of power like I'd never seen from Alec before. I was standing less than a foot from him, safely out of the zone he was impacting with his ability, and this time I was able to feel *something* happening as the people in front of us all dropped down to their knees. It felt more than a little like the metaphysical wind I often felt from Alec and the others during dominance displays, but rather than flowing out away from Alec it was flowing to him.

I didn't even begin to have an idea how much power Alec was pulling away from the thirty-plus shape shifters in front of us, but I once again got the impression that Alec's power had increased. Unlike in Chicago when dropping Agony's enforcers had strained Alec's ability nearly to its limit, this time he didn't evidence any kind of strain from the amount of energy that was passing through him.

Alec dropped his arms and the gale I'd been on the fringes of disappeared between one second and the next.

"I was the reason that the rebellion was able to make it this far, and in some ways I'm more powerful than all of you together, but in other ways you're more powerful than me. I can only be in one place at a time, you can be in many. It only took one man with a single rifle to nearly kill me, but Donovan easily dispatched the sniper. The way ahead of us will be difficult, you must not forget your power, you must not forget that it is only when we are together that the Coun'hij fear us, but they fear you as much or more than they fear me."

Alec looked around the gathered shape shifters, all of whom had pulled themselves back up onto their feet. "We have a lot of work that needs to be done in the next hour or two. Donovan is working on obtaining the communications equipment we need, but it will do us no good until the three antennae have been installed.

"Mallory will be organizing a team to handle the installation of that hardware, other teams will be in charge of purchasing supplies, and I'll need a group to come with me into the city so I can make calls to Natasha and the rest of our people currently carrying out other necessary tasks. Remember, if an order comes from Adri, Donovan, or Mallory then it comes from me."

Alec shrugged his shirt back on and then motioned for Mallory to take center stage. The next hour was incredibly hectic. Just organizing everyone took a full half hour and even then it wouldn't have been possible without Mallory and Donovan's help. Once those plans were laid I found myself in one of the SUV's with James, Dominic and Alec.

By any logical measure neither James nor Dom should have been on bodyguard duty. James was walking with a slight limp and while Dom no longer looked prematurely old, she was still obviously exhausted and functioning on little more than sheer willpower. Alec would have probably left them back with the RV to watch over everything there, but they'd both insisted and there was no denying the fact that we needed people we could trust with us.

The thought of James or Dominic taking a bullet for Alec was enough to make me feel sick to my stomach. Alec apparently believed every word he'd just told our people about them being as important as he was. Maybe he was even right, but for now—at least until everyone else believed it—James, Dom and I all knew he was more important than any of the rest of us.

I didn't want to see James or Dom die, but I couldn't deny them the privilege of possibly dying, not when I was also perfectly willing to take a bullet for Alec.

We spent the drive into downtown St Louis with me trying to get Alec up to speed on everything else that had happened while he'd been unconscious. I wracked my brain trying to make sure that I got it all out there for Alec to judge and either approve or disapprove.

My consolidation of power into Tasha's hand was met with a nod, as was my decision to use Lori as backup security along with Grayson.

Really Alec seemed happy with nearly all of the measures that Donovan, Mallory and I had come up with. The sole exception to that was our not having been able to get the communications equipment back up and running.

I finished up with my summary just before we pulled into the parking garage underneath the mall, and the first thing that Alec did once he got out of the car was call Donovan.

"You've got to get some kind of solution up as far as communications go, Donovan. We simply can't fight a war like this. I know you've got limits, but call back our hackers and push them on this. *Something* is better than nothing. We need to understand exactly what the issue is."

A few seconds later we met up with the two hybrids Mallory had detached to back up James and Dom as bodyguards. I hadn't caught either of their names before we left and was too embarrassed to ask once they were within earshot. I kept thinking that James, Dom or Alec would let their names drop at some point during the outing, but the new bodyguards were so competent that nobody ever had to address them directly.

We made a slow, meandering trip through the airy, sunlit mall, Alec and I holding hands as though we were just like any other couple, Dom and James a few feet to either side of us, and the two new guys following a dozen feet behind.

Alec spent the whole time on the phone. I lost count of the number of calls he made. Most of them were short, designed primarily to make sure whoever he was talking to knew that he was still alive, that he had a plan, and that he might be using me to interface with them from time to time.

I heard calls to Rebekka, Louis and Tasha, but I didn't actually pick up on most of what was said because I was so worried about how tired Alec looked. He'd been so vibrant and alive when he'd been talking to our people before we'd left the music festival that it was hard to believe this was the same person.

I counted six yawns in his two-minute conversation with Tasha and his steps were slowing at a noticeable rate. I looked up and caught Dominic looking at Alec with concern, which only made me more worried because that meant we had one less set of eyes focused outward looking for trouble.

I couldn't blame Dom for being concerned, but after that I spent as much time watching our surroundings as I did Alec. I wasn't going to lose him to another surprise attack that we could have stopped if we'd been paying a little more attention.

"That's the last of the calls that I know I need to make."

Alec's announcement caught me by surprise. I turned back to him and saw big, dark circles under his eyes.

"Does that mean we can go back and let you get some sleep?"

"Not quite yet—I need to turn on my phone and check my voicemails."

"So things are about to get dangerous."

"I'm afraid so. We should be fine unless the Coun'hij has a team already inside of the city, but things are going to get very hot in St Louis sometime in the next hour or two—we're going to want to be gone by then."

"I guess this is as good of a place to do it as any. From here we could be down to the car in less than thirty seconds if we ran."

"Let's hope it doesn't come to that—I'm not sure I've got a thirty-second sprint left inside of me."

"Are you okay, Alec? I know that Dr...I know that you haven't been getting the kind of sleep that you should have been getting, but I've never seen you this exhausted before."

"Don't worry, Adri, it's nothing that a little quality rest wouldn't fix."

Alec checked the time on the burner phone and then sighed. "I didn't think it would catch up to me this fast. I thought I would have another hour or two, but by now Mallory and Donovan should have our people resupplied and the antennae mounted to the top of the RV."

We'd stopped moving, but it still seemed like it was all Alec could do to keep from tipping over. I looked around the department store we were in, but it wasn't like most stores wasted valuable floor space with chairs anywhere but in the shoe section. After a second I took his arm and led him over to a floor-to-ceiling window that looked out over the city.

We were only on the second story, but that was still enough to discourage me from taking in the view. My nervousness around heights wasn't bad enough to qualify as a fear, but I wasn't on a first-name basis with heights or anything.

"Sit here and make your calls and then we'll go back to the RV."

Alec gave me a smile. "I really don't know what I would have done without you, Adri. Thank you for holding everything together and thank you for coming in after me when...you know."

We most definitely didn't want word of Dream Stealer's attacks on Alec to get out. Dom and James already knew, but there wasn't any question but that we could count on them to keep our secrets. The new bodyguards were another matter entirely though and the fact that Alec had come so close to slipping up and saying something he shouldn't around them told me that he was even worse off than I'd realized.

I needed to get him home, preferably as soon as possible. If I could have, I would have stopped him from turning on his phone—he wasn't mentally in a state fit for entering into any more high-stakes negotiations—but I knew he wouldn't stand for that. I was extremely worried about what he might let slip on the next call he made, but by the same measure he was right that we needed to make sure that one of our people wasn't in trouble somewhere waiting on us for help.

"Turn on your phone and check your messages, Alec. We need to get out of here."

"Yes, ma'am."

I rolled my eyes at his subservient expression, but honestly it was reassuring to know that the same old Alec was still there underneath all of the exhaustion. Despite everything that he'd been through, Dream Stealer hadn't managed to break him.

Alec took a deep breath and then powered on his phone. I knew there was no way the Coun'hij was going to have people in place to come after us for at least a little while, but I still tensed up. Based on how jumpy our bodyguards were acting, I wasn't the only one who was nervous about what might happen next.

As a general rule Alec didn't skimp on his tools and his phone was a tool—maybe not in the same way that Isaac's phone was a tool, but it was still a necessary tool. I knew that Alec had paid a pretty penny for this particular device, but even top-of-the-line, not-yet-available-to-the-public phones take time to boot up and the seconds that passed by as Alec waited for it to become usable seemed to drag on forever.

It finally finished powering on and then Alec dialed his voicemail. A few seconds later he frowned and pulled the phone away from his ear so that he could key in some numbers. I pulled myself away from my obsessive scanning of our surroundings long enough to ask him what was wrong.

"I'm not sure. My voicemail isn't working."

"What does that mean? Why wouldn't it work?"

"It could mean that I screwed things up when I tried to clone the sim card, or it could just be some kind of automated security feature that was tripped because it's been so long since I've logged in."

"But if that was the case you would just be able to re-enter your PIN, right?"

"Yeah, except I just tried to enter it twice and it's not working."

"You mean someone changed it?"

"Maybe, or maybe I don't remember it."

"Well, we know that isn't the case. You've got the best memory out of anyone I know. You basically never forget anything."

Alec looked at our new bodyguards for a second before responding. "I...I don't feel like myself. It's like I'm trying to reach through a brown haze to get at my memories. I'm not sure I'm as unscathed after everything that's happened as I would have hoped."

I felt like I'd been punched in the gut, but I knew I had to be strong for Alec's sake. He'd spent years trying to mold himself into the kind of leader who would have a chance of standing off his pack's enemies. He depended on his memory and intellect as much as he depended on his strength and speed when it came to keeping the people around him alive.

Even after his power had manifested, Alec had spent agonizing hours worried that he might not be capable of beating the Coun'hij and saving all of us. The idea that he might be somehow less than he was before had to be absolutely terrifying for him—even more terrifying than it was for me.

I shook my head. "You didn't forget it. Somebody changed it. Maybe the Coun'hij hacked into your voicemail because they figured that was a perfect way to spy on us."

Alec didn't just look tired now, he looked like someone who had just been thrown into a world they didn't understand. "That doesn't make sense, Adri. I can see them trying to hack into my mailbox—that's part of the reason that I change my PIN so often—but if they managed a successful hack like that they wouldn't change my PIN. It's too easy for me to get it reset—all that would do is tip me off to the fact that they were listening in."

"Fine, I don't know the answer, but I know you aren't forgetting things."

Alec still looked tired and lost, but he seemed to draw a measure of strength from the fact that I needed him to be strong.

"Wishing something was a certain way doesn't make it so, Adri. We have to face the reality that is, even if it's not the reality we wish it was."

Alec squared his shoulders as he spoke and I wondered how many times in his life Alec had wanted to give up but forced himself to go on because he knew someone else was depending on him. In a way that was reassuring because it meant that Alec was still Alec, regardless of what he might have lost, but in other ways it was still terrifying.

It made me wonder. How would Alec Graves deal with a world where people desperately needed him but he wasn't capable of making a difference?

"Maybe we have to deal in the world as it is, Alec, but that doesn't mean that you're right about this. There's another explanation—you'll feel better once you've had a chance to catch up on your sleep."

"I wish I had your faith in the world, Adri."

"It's yours to borrow any time you need it, but it's not faith in the world, it's faith in you."

Alec turned and looked out the window—almost as though unable to continue to meet my gaze. When he looked back at me something had changed.

"Can you please have everyone spread out? We're too conspicuous standing this close together."

He needed a moment, needed some privacy so he could have a chance to try to pull himself back together.

"Okay, Alec, I can do that. We'd better get moving back to the rest of our group pretty soon though if we want to avoid problems."

"Thanks, Adri. I'll be along pretty soon."

I was pretty sure that the other four had already heard everything Alec and I had said, but they all played along and pretended like they didn't know it was coming when I asked them to move further back. A few seconds later we were all back far enough that even the shape shifters couldn't possibly overhear anything Alec might be saying.

Dominic followed me over to a collection of swimsuits that I pretended to be looking at while keeping an eye on Alec through the intervening racks of clothing.

"May I examine your arm, Adri?"

I started to move my right arm in her direction, but stopped as I realized that wasn't what she was asking for.

"Yeah, go ahead."

"You really can't feel anything?"

"Nope, just a big old dead weight out on the end of my shoulder."

I tried to keep my voice casual, tried to hide the pain of my most recent loss in the fight against the Coun'hij, but I knew I wasn't completely successful based on the sympathetic look Dominic gave me.

"Do you remember what happened?"

I looked around to make sure that the two new guys were far enough away that they wouldn't be able to hear us. When I looked back at Alec he had his phone up to his ear.

"Mostly. Sometimes when my power throws me into someone else's dreams I don't remember everything clearly, but I think I've got all of the high points from last night. Dream Stealer's thumb claw went in about right here and sliced me up pretty good. I guess he must have severed the nerves that used to run down into my arm."

Dominic shook her head in amazement. "I wouldn't have believed such a thing if I hadn't been able to see it with my own eyes. To think that you could be hurt so cruelly inside of a dream makes me not want to ever close my eyes again."

"I think you're safe. Dream Stealer did a lot worse to Alec before I ever arrived, but it didn't result in any kind of lasting damage for him. If Dream Stealer was capable of killing people in their dreams, he would have done so a hundred times over already. I must just be uniquely vulnerable because of my ability. It's probably no less than I deserve."

I fidgeted with a blue and green two-piece while Alec pulled his phone away from his ear and input a number.

"I don't blame you for what happened to me, Adri. Even if I did, I still wouldn't want something like this to happen to you, but I really don't blame you."

"I know you don't, Dom, but that's because you're too nice for your own good. That just means that I have to make sure that *I* blame myself. You nearly died because I was pushing you so hard to heal Alec. That isn't the kind of thing you should casually dismiss."

Dominic stepped in front of me, momentarily blocking my view of Alec to make sure that she had my full attention. "I'm not being casual about anything right now, Adri. What happened wasn't your fault any more than it was Alec's fault. You were the one who brought me back, but I could have said no at any point along the way. The truth is that I would have eventually tried to heal Alec even if you hadn't asked me to."

"That's nice of you to say, Dom, but we both know that I pushed you into doing something you weren't ready for and it was only luck and Donovan's skill that kept you here with us."

I stepped to one side so I could see Alec and this time Dom didn't get in my way. Instead she just sighed as she looked back down at my paralyzed hand and arm.

"I think I learned something from the experience, Adri. I've been trying to heal things in the same manner as Mrs. Valencia got me to heal the scar on my face. I've been trying to relax, but with Alec that wasn't what I did. I tried to find the same peaceful, calm feeling that I felt in New York, but this time there was so much riding on my ability that when it wasn't working I got mad. I got so very mad that something changed."

"What do you mean, Dom?"

"I mean I felt *something* inside of me. Maybe Mrs. Valencia wasn't all the way wrong. It was like there was a still, cool pool of energy inside of me, but I couldn't access it until I was feeling a strong emotion, something powerful enough to make me move the boulder that normally keeps it hidden out of the way."

I tore my eyes away from Alec, who was running one of his hands through his hair while talking into his phone, and finally saw the glimmer of excitement that had been lurking in the back of Dom's eyes.

"I know it sounds crazy, like I'm supposed to do two opposite things at the same time, but in some ways it actually makes a lot of sense—it's a better fit for when I healed everyone back at the estate at least. I wasn't calm that time—maybe I seemed calm on the outside, but I was so incredibly angry with the Coun'hij for sending people to attack us, to burn down our home and kill our friends. I wanted to do something to stop them."

"And you did."

"But that was the thing, Adri. I didn't think I could. I knew that I wasn't fast or strong enough to fight them. I wanted to do something, but I was at peace with the fact that I couldn't actually make a difference."

"You're right, that sounds pretty crazy."

"*Sí*, but it worked and what I felt when I tried to heal Alec was very similar to that, only…"

"Only what, Dom?"

"Only this time I can still feel the pool of energy inside of me. It was gone when I first woke up and was so muddled, but it's been slowly filling back up, drop by drop, and now I want to try and heal your arm."

I pulled away from her in shock. "No."

"Think of it, Adri. You could have the use of your arm back. I know it hasn't been very long yet, but surely you're already noticing how much harder things are."

"Of course I've noticed. If I let myself stop and think about anything other than trying to stop the Coun'hij I would break down and cry. Trust me, I've thought about how much my life is going to suck because of this, but I'm not going to let you risk your life just so I can tie my shoes without help."

"Adri…"

"No, I'm not going to do it, Dom."

"Then I will risk my life to remove Mallory, Addison and Andrew's scars. My gift is too valuable to leave untapped and you can't forbid me from trying to master it."

She was right. There wasn't any way for me to compel her to never put her life in jeopardy like that again, but I would have said it anyway and risked ruining our friendship if Alec hadn't collapsed to the ground right then.

I hadn't been born with shape shifter strength and speed, but I'd been watching Alec rather than looking outward, so I still made it to Alec's side before anyone else.

"I need to call Isaac."

Alec was slumped against the wall, phone on the floor, apparently having dropped out of fingers that no longer had the strength to hold it. All I could think was that he was having complications with his heart, that he hadn't healed as completely as he'd thought he had.

"We need to get you back to Donovan. Isaac can wait. You can call him tomorrow or the next day."

Alec shook his head weakly. "He's left me messages—he thinks that I'm holding a grudge for how everything went down when Jess lost her memory. I need to call him and tell him that it's okay, that there aren't any hard feelings on my end."

Alec wasn't strong enough to resist me, but I likewise wasn't strong enough to pick him up and manhandle him back to the car. I started to turn towards the two new guys to ask them to pick him up, but I saw Alec's eyes start to flutter so instead I asked him the first question I could think of in an effort to keep him with us.

"I thought you couldn't get into your voice-mail, Alec."

"I couldn't but Rachel left me a message telling me how to get in."

"How would Rachel know? For that matter how could you get her message telling you how to get into your voicemail without first being able to get into your voicemail?"

Alec smiled, but it was a weak movement. "She didn't leave me a message on my phone. Look out the window, Adri."

He was sounding weaker by the moment and he was obviously delusional—just talking to him wasn't going to get him through whatever was going on.

"You and you, pick him up and get him back to the car. I think it's his heart; we don't have any time to waste."

Dom grabbed my arm. "If it's really his heart then he needs a hospital—now, not after Donovan has had a chance to look him over."

"No, a hospital will just be signing his death warrant in a different way. The Coun'hij almost certainly has people headed to St Louis right this instant. They probably already have people running background checks on every patient in any hospital within sixty miles."

"Then let me try to heal him."

It was an infernal choice. My fiancé—the love of my life—balanced against the life of one of my best friends. Even worse, if I said yes and let Dom try to heal him again then there was a really good chance that I would lose them both.

Alec weakly shook his head. "No, I'm not dying, I'm just tired. Don't try and heal me, Dom."

His words were slurred—in fact he looked worse than he had even a few seconds before. I could see Dom poised to try; her hands were already resting on his chest. I opened my mouth, but James cut me off.

"He's not delusional—look out the window."

The billboard was so big that I wondered how we'd missed it on our way in, but that wasn't what was unique about it. It was nothing more than simple green text across a blue background.

Big Brother,

2425. Lose everyone else and lie to Jas. If you go help her then everything is lost and we'll never see each other again.

Rach

My heart skipped a beat, but Dom spoke before I could manage to say anything. "How did Rachel know we were going to be here at this exact time?"

"My little sister is full of surprises these days."

Alec still looked exhausted, but his speech was a little better and he looked like he could have almost stood on his own—he didn't look enough better though for me to wave off either of the guys currently supporting him by his arms.

"I thought you didn't believe my hypothesis that Rachel could see into the future."

"I think you're right about the fact that she's seeing time in a different way than the rest of us do. I just wish we could sit her down with Mallory so we could get a definite idea of what's going on. I'm not sure her gift—if she really has one—is the kind of thing I would trust to take care of her out in the world all by herself."

"But you trusted her and her gift enough to wave us all off."

"Yeah, enough to lie to Jasmin when she called just now too."

"How is Jasmin?"

Alec looked up at me with tortured eyes. "It's not good, Adri. She's got the answer to everything we need. She says that she knows where the Coun'hij is based and she's going in there tonight, with or without me."

It was an impossible choice, and I was simultaneously glad that Alec was back so that I didn't have to make it, and sorry that he had to carry such a burden. Help the friend who was depending on you to save her or believe your possibly crazy younger sister who had so far shown a remarkable penchant for predicting the future.

A buzz from Alec's pocket saved me from having to say anything. Alec made a weak attempt to get at his burner phone, but I knew he was going to struggle, so I reached into his pocket and grabbed it. The caller ID was flashing the number of Donovan's current burner phone.

"Hello?"

"Mistress, you all need to get back here as soon as possible. Our IT resources have gotten a number of hits on the facial recognition algorithms. The Coun'hij already has at least two kill teams in the city."

"We're on our way."

I hung up and shoved the burner phone in my back pocket and then I reached down and grabbed Alec's phone off of the floor.

"Get moving everyone. We could have company at any moment!"

I powered Alec's phone down as the other four collapsed in around Alec and half carried him towards the escalators. We made better time than I expected us to; we were even almost fast enough. We made it to the elevators down to the parking garage without any problems other than the fact that Alec seemed weaker and weaker with each step.

Whatever second wind he'd found about the time our bodyguards had first arrived back at the window to prop him up vanished after just a few steps and it seemed to be all he could do to keep his eyes open.

I was the first one off of the elevator when the doors opened, which meant that I was the first one to run into the Coun'hij kill team. The lead enforcer did a partial shift on his right arm without even breaking stride and then slashed towards my neck with a kind of lazy power that told me he knew exactly who I was and that there was no possible way a human could avoid even a half-hearted blow from him.

I should have died in that instant, but I was even less of a normal human than I'd been just a few days ago. I threw myself backwards with everything I had and was once again forced to watch five deadly claws arc towards my unprotected neck in slow motion.

The blow came so close to ripping my throat out that I felt the air pushed on ahead of the enforcer's claws tickle my bare skin, but I managed to get out of the way of the first attack. I could hear movement behind me as the others carried Alec out of the elevator, but I knew they weren't going to be able to save me—they were too far back there and the enforcer was serious about killing me now.

The second attack was a backfist that was moving fast enough that I knew the impact from the oversized arm would snap my neck, but there wasn't anything I could do about it. I was already moving backwards as fast as I could, off balance and falling.

"Adri!"

Alec's yell sounded only a split second before his ability kicked in. Between one instant and the next the enforcer's arm shrank back down to its normal size and went whistling past my head. The enemy operative dropped to the ground a second later and I realized for the first time that there were three more big, tattooed men behind him.

Apparently this batch had been fully briefed about what they were going to be up against. Rather than charging forward or staying clustered together like I'd seen their kind do in the past, all three of them pulled out handguns and they were moving with a speed that I wouldn't even have been able to follow without the augmented time sense I'd acquired during the fight with Dream Stealer.

The barrel of the closest enforcer came up, still moving at something that felt very close to normal speed, and then suddenly I felt the reassuring presence of someone big and muscular just behind me. The barrel of the gun suddenly started dropping as quickly as it had been rising a second before.

Alec stepped around me as I heard the sound of someone hitting the enforcer who had tried to take my head off. The last two guns hit the ground and I suddenly felt like I was standing in the eye of a hurricane.

All three of the enforcers in front of us tried to shift forms at the same time. I felt the characteristic flare of power from all three of them, but this time it was over before it even had a chance to get started. Their bodies flickered and then returned to human form now bereft of their tattoos and piercings. Through it all I could feel a metaphysical vortex of power circling Alec and me.

"I thought it took everything you had to force Jaclyn back into her human form."

"It did."

"How have you gotten so much stronger in such a short time?"

Alec looked back at me, confident that his ability would keep the enforcers down and immobile. "I don't know—I'm not even really sure that I have. The black hole on the other side of the conduit seems to be stronger than it was before."

"Weren't you worried at one point that it was going to fill up and your power would become useless?"

It was the kind of thing I probably shouldn't be talking about around Dom and James, let alone our new bodyguards, but I was in such a state of shock that I couldn't help myself. Alec didn't seem to mind though.

"Yes, I was. That doesn't seem like it's going to be a problem though."

"That's good then, right?"

"I'm not sure. I want to say yes, but I honestly don't know. I suppose it all depends on where all of the energy I drain away actually goes."

Alec stepped forward and ended the life of the closest enforcer with a single, surgical strike from his newly-transformed hand. It was like watching a completely different person. A few seconds before this, Alec had looked like he was on death's doorstep. It didn't seem possible for him to now be all but running across the parking garage to kill the last two enforcers.

"Alec, how are you doing this? You should be exhausted."

"I am exhausted. I can feel it pulling at my every movement, but right now there is something stronger that is keeping me awake and alert through sheer force. I've pushed myself too far—I can see that now. It was for a good cause, but it was still a risk I shouldn't have taken. My beast should have taken control by now and created nine different kinds of havoc. Only he's been so weak lately that at times I've started to worry that he had somehow disappeared."

"I didn't think that was even possible. I thought your beasts were a part of you, I thought that once they awoke during your first transformation that they *couldn't* leave."

"I don't think they can, not really."

"But you just said…"

The next enforcer was dead now and Alec started towards the last one. "I know; I said I was worried that he had disappeared, but I'm not worried about that now. He's back, he's what's keeping me awake right now, but everything feels wrong. My beast shouldn't be so subservient. I'm worried that something is changing him, which means that there is some external force that is changing me."

Chapter 15

Adriana Paige
Downtown
St. Louis, Missouri

Our trip back to meet up with the rest of the convoy took longer than the trip out to the mall because Dominic was in full paranoia mode, but I couldn't bring myself to complain. As worried as I was about Alec, it was vital that we make sure a Coun'hij kill squad didn't follow us back to the convoy.

After fifteen minutes of driving Dominic finally gave us the go-ahead to send Donovan a text letting him know what had happened.

Alec pulled out a fresh burner phone and typed in a message while I watched.

Incident at the mall—needs virtual cleanup. Go ahead and get everyone on the road, we'll meet you at the first location.

We made the rest of the trip without saying anything else despite the fact that there were about a million questions I wanted to ask Alec. All of the things we needed to talk about were the kinds of things that we couldn't risk getting out to the rest of our people.

It was hard, but I kept my questions to myself and just held onto Alec's hand like it was the only thing stopping me from drowning. Actually, in a way it was.

Alec didn't seem to be fading as fast this time around, but I could still see signs of exhaustion in the way he stared off into the distance for such long periods of time. It reminded me of the time I'd stayed up for thirty-six hours straight. I'd been prone to losing track of what I'd been doing and had ended up just sitting there with my mind wandering aimlessly for minutes at a time.

I breathed a sigh of relief when I finally saw our RV, sporting three new aerodynamic antennae on its top, parked in a rest stop an hour outside of St Louis. Donovan met us at the door to the RV.

"Our IT assets are confident that they've managed to delete all of the video feeds for the mall during the time that the six of you were there. The local police were alerted to the bodies—probably by the other kill team—within a couple of minutes of your departure from the parking garage, but so far don't seem to have any significant leads."

Alec nodded tiredly. "Thank you, Donovan, that at least is a relief. What's the status of the hunt for new communications equipment?"

"Frankly, the technical aspects of what I'm being told are still somewhat beyond me, but when I escalated the issue of the communications suite being damaged to the wider group, one of the hackers indicated that he would be able to write a program that would let a more conventional set of hardware accomplish most of the functionality we enjoyed with the specialized hardware."

"What is entailed in 'most' of the functionality?"

"We'll be able to scramble our location for incoming calls, but not for outgoing ones."

Alec sighed. "That's not ideal, but it's better than nothing. It will take some doing to set up a call schedule so that we get regular incoming calls, but it's doable."

"Indeed, Master Alec. It will also make us less nimble when responding to unexpected events, but I should have pushed for something like this days ago."

Alec gently patted Donovan on the shoulder. "Don't beat yourself up about it, Donovan. This solution isn't going to be as bulletproof as you're being told it is. Software solutions are never as reliable as hardware solutions. Besides, there was an element of risk in pushing the issue like this. I rather expect that we're going to see a decrease in the responsiveness of our hacker who specializes in communications hardware. Hackers tend to be difficult to work with at the best of times and he'll be feeling like we crashed his party. Hopefully we can salvage the relationship enough to get him to write the revised drivers when we've managed to get our hands on a proper set of hardware."

Addison was driving again and she got the RV moving forward at the precise time that Alec turned towards his bedroom. Under normal circumstances I would have expected Alec to seamlessly compensate for the change, but this time he actually tripped and fell, and he didn't just get right back up, it took the combined efforts of Donovan and I to get him back up to his knees.

"We don't have very much longer. I've been awake for too long. Can the two of you please help me back to the bedroom so we can review the last few things I have to tell you?"

Once we made it back to the bedroom Alec motioned towards the white noise generator. "Adri, can you please turn that on."

"There's no need. Get some sleep. None of this is so critical that it can't wait until you've had a chance to catch up on your rest."

"Donovan, please turn it on, there are things I need to say that shouldn't be overheard."

Donovan looked back and forth between Alec and me for nearly a full second before stepping around me and turning on the privacy generator. Once it was on, Alec turned back to me.

"I'm afraid this stuff can't wait, Adri. Today has been a godsend. It gave me a chance to still some of the rumors that were probably starting to circulate even beyond our group and it let me reinforce your position as my heir, but today was nothing more than a temporary reprieve. Once I fall back asleep Dream Stealer is going to pull me back into his realm and this time I won't be coming back unless you manage to find him and kill him out here in the real world."

I could feel tears starting to pool in the corners of my eyes, but I blinked them away. It had been there the whole time but I'd refused to see it. Even now I was still mostly in denial.

"That's not true, Alec. We beat him."

"Beat him, yes, killed him, no. He'll be back for me, I can feel it. I'm sorry I didn't say something earlier, but it seemed cruel. I wanted us to be able to spend today together as much as possible without him hanging over us."

"I beat him once, I can do it again. I'll go with you and we'll fight him together. This time we'll kill him and you'll never have to worry about him ever again."

Alec grabbed my hand and pulled me down so I was sitting on the bed next to him. "You don't have good enough control over your ability yet, Adri. You can't guarantee that you'll be able to make it back into my dream, and even if you did, you can't guarantee that you'll be able to time it so that you arrive when I'm fresh and able to help you. We got lucky last time and it still cost you the use of your arm. I don't want you to come back in after me."

"You won't be able to stop me."

"It's true, which is why I want you to promise me that you won't try. Go after Dream Stealer in the real world. We can't win these fights by going up against the Coun'hij where they are strong, we need to go after them where they are weak. Jasmin's idea is brilliant. If Jaclyn doesn't get anywhere when it comes to looking for the ghost pack then I want you to put our people to work capturing a vampire mentalist. You'll have to find one who's strong enough to get the job done, but not so strong that we can't keep him imprisoned."

Donovan hadn't heard the summary of Alec's call with Jasmin yet; he looked positively poleaxed. "Master Alec, that's brilliant. Why didn't she say something before now? Once we have a mentalist under our control then all we'll need to do is capture one of the enforcers and use the mentalist to pull the location of the Coun'hij's headquarters out of them."

"Jasmin has already done it. She tracked them to a state park in Tennessee, but she plain and simply doesn't have enough backup to get the job done."

I blinked in shock. Alec hadn't revealed that particular detail earlier. Donovan was so astonished that it took him several seconds to find the right words.

"Master Alec, why are we not headed to Tennessee right now to aid her? This is our chance to end the war once and for all."

"Because Rachel told me not to."

"You talked to Mistress Rachel?"

"Not exactly, more like she sent me a message telling me that I couldn't get involved in Jasmin's offensive."

Donovan appeared to be choosing his next words carefully. "It must have been difficult to let Jasmin head into that kind of situation on nothing more than faith in Rachel's apparent ability to see the future."

"Yes. Especially because it is almost certain that Jasmin's attack will result in the Coun'hij relocating. When we are ready to attack we're going to be faced with tracking the Coun'hij down again before we can actually strike. It was a hard decision, Donovan, but I'm confident that I made the right one."

"As you say, Master Alec."

"No." My voice came out oddly detached considering the raging torrent of emotions trying to break free of my tenuous mental control. "No, that's not okay. We need to go right now and help Jasmin. I'm willing to take a lot on faith where Rachel is concerned, but you are *not* going to throw away what may be our only chance at killing Dream Stealer. I'm going to tell Addison to make for Tennessee."

Alec grabbed hold of my hand with a gentle, but still unyielding strength. "We can't do that, Adri. I'm already on my last legs. By the time we arrive in Tennessee I'll be long gone. That means you would be going up against the might of the Coun'hij with nothing more than a few dozen wolves and hybrids. You can't win, not against those odds. I started out lying to Jasmin and refusing to help her because of Rach's message, but by the end I'd realized that it really was the only way forward."

I cast about for a counter-argument—I wasn't going to give up without a fight, not this time. "Use your ability. It propped you up earlier in the parking garage. Use it on some of our people and you can keep yourself awake until we arrive in Tennessee. That way when we go up against the Coun'hij we'll have you at our backs. It's the perfect answer."

"We don't know that the use of my gift was what gave me a second wind. It's entirely possible that it was nothing more than the result of my being positive for a second that you were going to die. I've never felt that much adrenaline hit my system at once."

"That's crap and you know it, Alec. I saw the same thing happen before then when you used your power on our people back at the music festival. Really it shouldn't have taken me this long to put the pieces together, but now that I've had a chance to think about things it couldn't be more obvious."

"You don't know that for a fact, Adri, any more than I do. Regardless, I won't do it. I nearly killed my mother. Who would you sacrifice in her stead just for the slim chance of buying me a few more hours of exhaustion-addled wakefulness?"

"You used it on your people after you put your mother back into a coma. It's too late to pick and choose now."

"I used it on all of our people at once and I used the smallest field I was capable of. That's entirely different than using it on two or three people. The risk is simply too great, Adri, and before you ask, no, I won't use it on you, not even if you volunteer. As you pointed out so recently, neither of us is capable of making the other do something we don't want to do."

"We shouldn't have killed those last three enforcers then. You could have drained them until the cows came home and if you happened to go a little too far and kill one of them it wouldn't have been any great loss. Man, why couldn't I have thought of that back then?"

"It wouldn't have made any difference, Adri. I thought of it before I killed them, but I wouldn't have agreed to that plan either. I'll use my ability on an enemy to defeat them or even to kill them, but will not agree to enslaving even a full member of the Coun'hij in that fashion. To do so would be to turn myself into something very little different than the vampires we've all spent so much time fighting."

"So I'm just supposed to sit here and watch while Dream Stealer destroys your sanity?"

"No, do as I asked. Re-establish communications with the rest of our people, especially Isaac—I don't want him to continue thinking that I'm holding some kind of grudge. I know you may not be able to call him for a little while, but if he calls again you have to promise me that you'll answer no matter what."

"Okay, Alec. It sounds like we probably need to do some testing over the next few days to make sure that the communications solution is working as intended, but after that I'll bump Isaac to the top of the list."

"No, this is important. If he calls you have to find a way to talk to him and tell him that I'm not angry."

"Are you saying that you want us to risk the lives of everyone else here in order to take Isaac's call?"

Alec closed his eyes for several seconds before shaking his head. "No, don't put everyone in danger—that wouldn't be right, but please do everything you can to find a way to talk to him. I get the feeling that Isaac's in a bad way and I'd rather not have him go to his death thinking that

I abandoned him because of something petty like that."

I looked over at Donovan, who seemed to be making a concerted effort not to get sucked into this particular part of the conversation, and could tell that he was thinking the same thing I was. This wasn't just because Alec was worried that Isaac's time was short. Alec was subconsciously worried that *Alec's* time was short. It made me want to cry, but I managed to hold myself together, receiving a nod of agreement from Donovan before turning back to Alec.

"Okay, Alec, I get it. We'll do whatever we can to fix things between the two of you. What else do you need to tell us?"

"Start analyzing everything we can get from Fort Loudon State Park in Tennessee in the hopes that we'll be able to track the Coun'hij if they move after Jasmin's attack, and be able to take them at a later date after you've had a chance to consolidate our people back into one group."

My sadness hadn't disappeared, but part of it was starting to morph into something else, the kind of white-hot anger that I only seemed to feel when I felt completely helpless.

"That won't make a difference though, Alec. Don't you see? Without you we still don't have a chance. Jaclyn and Grayson are both useless against Puppeteer's werewolves."

"I know, but they aren't your only weapon. Tasha is asking Lori to meet up with us in Kansas

City. She's the one who can shift the tide for us. Drop her in the middle of the Coun'hij's base and she'll have their own people climbing over top of each other to kill Puppeteer and his werewolves."

"She's dangerous, Alec. I don't know if we can control her."

"I know she's dangerous, but you've got to think in terms of winning her friendship. You've made a good start there, continue on in the same manner, but keep Dominic and a few of the other women you trust around. I wish I'd been able to get Jasmin to come back here for that reason if for no other. She and Lori would strike sparks off of each other, but she would go a long way towards keeping Lori in check."

I shook my head as the first of my tears escaped and made shiny tracks down my cheeks. "Please don't do this, Alec. Don't give up like this."

"I'm not giving up, Adri. I'm going to be fighting Dream Stealer with everything I have, but this is the only way for us to win, the only way that doesn't result in me turning into the kind of monster we're trying to defeat."

"I'm scared."

"You've still got Donovan and Mallory and now you've got James and Dom here to watch your back as well. You don't need to be scared. All of the pieces are in place; you just need to hold things together for a little bit longer and it will all be over. For the first time in centuries someone actually has a chance at toppling the Coun'hij. Be strong for just a little bit longer and everything will be okay."

I wiped my tears away and nodded. Alec gave my hand another squeeze and then looked back over at Donovan.

"When you finally get a shot at Dream Stealer and the others you're going to want to mobilize every resource we have, Donovan. That means Alexi and everyone else he thinks is remotely trustworthy."

"Are you sure, Master Alec? Even Alexi doesn't know the truth about us. He's been working for us long enough and cleaned up enough of our slipups that I suspect he's put together most of the pieces. He can probably be trusted to continue to keep what he sees a secret, but if we start bringing in other mercenaries we're liable to have the existence of our people get out to the public."

"I'm sure. The Coun'hij needs to be stopped regardless of the price. We take the best shot we can and we'll worry about picking up the pieces afterwards."

"Very good, Master Alec, is there anything else?"

"Probably, but I'm so tired I'm having a hard time keeping track of the pieces. Try and track down anyone we haven't heard from lately. Jess, Wyatt, Isaac, Ash and Kristin, along with whoever survived from the Chicago pack. We're probably going to need all of them before this is over."

"If it is within my power it will be done, Master Alec."

"I know it will be, Donovan. I...I'm grateful for everything. You've been one of the few constants in my life and none of this would have been possible without your support. You were the best father anyone could have hoped for, blood relation or not."

Now it was Donovan's eyes that had gone shiny with unshed tears. I didn't want to leave Alec's side, not now that I knew just how short our time together might be, but I also knew that this was a moment that I wasn't meant to share. I tried to stand again so I could give the two of them their privacy, but Alec still refused to let go of my hand.

"Please stay, Adri."

"No, the two of you should have a few minutes alone. It's only right."

Donovan blotted at his eyes with a handkerchief and then cleared his throat. "No, Mistress Paige, Master Alec is quite right. Over the last two decades we have said everything that needs to be said. He knows that I couldn't be prouder of him, and that I profoundly respect the man he's become. More than that though, there is no need because this isn't a time for goodbyes. I will see him again."

"Careful, Donovan, you're starting to sound like me. The next thing you know you'll be delusional and lying to people because you're convinced that you can will the future you want into existence."

Donovan gave me a very serious smile. "Mistress Paige, if your 'delusions' are capable of continuing to bring Master Alec back to us again and again, then one has to wonder if they're really delusions. I'll leave the two of you to discuss whatever else needs to be discussed."

"Donovan, please tell Mallory that I'm sorry we didn't get more time together. I meant to carve out a few minutes with her, but it just didn't end up happening."

Donovan bowed his head. "I think you'll find that Mallory is nothing if not a pragmatist, Master Alec, but I will convey your apologies."

Once Donovan had pulled the door shut behind him, Alec gave me a sad smile. "You still haven't promised me that you won't come in after me."

"I was kind of hoping that you wouldn't notice."

"Fat chance of that. I've thought about very little else since I first realized how terrible of a price you had to pay to come get me this last time. Please promise me?"

I debated for several seconds before shaking my head. "I won't give you the promise you want, Alec, but I'll agree not to just jump right in without looking. I'll give the effort of tracking him down in the real world my best shot and only come in after you if it seems like there isn't any other option."

"I guess that's probably about as good of a compromise as I'm going to get."

"I'm afraid so."

"Very well, I accept your terms on one condition. When you come after me you do so with the knowledge that the man you're trying to save might not be there to be saved anymore. You need to have Donovan here to put me down if it turns out that I'm too far gone to come back to myself after you kill Dream Stealer."

"Alec, no! You can't talk like that."

"I'm serious, Adri. I don't want to become a monster. My ability is too dangerous for that. The amount of destruction I could wreak if Dream Stealer makes me over in his own image would be unimaginable."

"Maybe you're right, but don't make Donovan and me do it…"

"It has to be the two of you, Adri. Nobody else knows me better. Maybe Jasmin or Rach could make the call as to whether I'm still me, but there's no guarantee that either of them will be around. You'll have to decide fast. If I've really gone off the rails then I'll be incredibly dangerous."

I tried to look away from him. I couldn't even begin to classify everything I was feeling in that moment, but my emotions were so overpowering they were causing me to shake. I wanted to scream, cry, and laugh hysterically all at the same time. Only Alec would put this kind of burden on two of the people who loved him the most, but he wasn't wrong to be worried about what he might become if Dream Stealer was allowed to torture him for weeks or even months.

"I'll do what needs to be done, Alec. If there's one thing I've learned from you it's a sense of responsibility."

Alec nodded hesitantly. I was pretty sure he knew I was telling the truth, but he could apparently also tell that I wasn't telling him the full story. That was fine. I wasn't about to start volunteering extra information—not after what he'd just made me promise to do.

I would live up to my end of the deal if it came to it, but I was going to do everything I could—up to and including going in after him sometime within the next week or so if it came to that—in order to make sure that there was still something there to save. 'No other choice' was one of those subjective kinds of phrases and that was what I'd agreed to.

Alec's head had started to bob, so I gently pushed him back onto his pillow. "Is there anything else you need me to promise? Any innocent children who need to be gunned down or schools that need to be burned to the ground?"

"Please don't be like that, Adri. I wouldn't ask if there was any other choice..."

"I know, but that doesn't change the fact that everything about this situation sucks."

Alec pulled me down next to him and helped me turn so I could rest my head on his chest. His heartbeat didn't sound like the heartbeat of a condemned man. It sounded slow and strong—too confident for someone who was about to be tortured.

"I know. I'm sorry—I really wish that things could be different. Maybe I shouldn't have declared war against the Coun'hij. Maybe I should have pretended to join them and then tried to destroy them from the inside."

"No, you couldn't have done that and still been you. You had to do what you did—this is all just part of the price for being you, Alec. It just sucks that we live in the kind of world that punishes the best and brightest. You deserve a lot better than this."

"I'm not sure I qualify as the best or the brightest, but I appreciate the sentiment."

We sat there in silence for several seconds. I was afraid that he'd fallen asleep, but I was too scared to check. It was an incredible relief when he finally spoke again.

"If Rachel shows back up—if she survives all of this—can you please tell her that I love her and that I'm sorry I didn't take better care of her?"

"You *are* going to survive—I think you took great care of her—but I'll tell her that's what you said."

"Thanks. Tell my mother that I'm sorry our last interaction had to go down like it did. I must have envisioned her coming back to herself a million times over the last ten years, but it was never like that in my imagination."

"Alec...I'm sorry about..."

"No, it wasn't your fault. I should have known that she would be like that. The distant, distracted woman I knew growing up never could have been such a polarizing figure inside of the pack. I should have expected something like this."

"Are you sure I'm the best one to tell your mom anything?"

"It needs to come from you. Sooner or later she's going to have to accept that you were the one I wanted to spend my last moments with."

"Okay, Alec. I'll tell her."

"Thanks, Adri. I never meant to drop all of this on you. Almost from the first moment we met I wished that I was someone else, that we could just have a normal life together without any worries about the Coun'hij or restoring the monarchy. I've wished so many times that I could just bring myself to walk away from it all so that you wouldn't have to see this side of the world."

"Never wish that, Alec. I wouldn't have fallen in love with you if you'd been the kind of person who could abandon people who desperately need you. Never apologize for who you are. I keep wanting to tell you to stop saying goodbye, but I guess I'm no better than you when it comes to that either. I would hate to miss the chance to tell you that you saved me. Not just from Simon and Nathanial or from Brandon. You saved me from despair.

"When I met you I didn't want to go on anymore. I wanted to curl up in a little ball and just wait to die. I felt like there wasn't anything left to live for, but you changed all of that. You showed me a world of terror and pain, but it's also a world of incredible beauty, one where it actually matters what we choose, one where I can help make a difference, even if just a small one. You've been everything I could have ever hoped for and I'm sorry for how much pain I caused you."

Alec shook his head. "You don't need to apologize for that, Adri. We both needed that to happen to get to where we are today. I'm so grateful that you came into my life when you did. In a very real way, everything I've accomplished in the last few months is because of you."

He sounded so tired. I was pretty sure that anyone else would have given up fighting a long time ago, but Alec just refused to go to sleep. His breathing slowed even more, but just when I thought he'd finally succumbed to his exhaustion he squeezed me tighter.

"Will you stay here until I fall asleep?"

"Of course I'll stay here, Alec. I'll make sure there is always someone here watching you, even when I can't be here, and I'll be here every spare minute I can manage."

"Thank you. That actually helps more than I would have expected."

I stayed there by Alec's side for twenty more minutes as he continued to fight off the sleep that would mean a return to being in Dream Stealer's power, but even Alec's incredible will eventually met its match and he drifted off to sleep. I finally knew for sure that he was asleep when every muscle in his body simultaneously turned to iron, but even then he didn't scream out.

Chapter 16

Adriana Paige
Interstate 70
Western Missouri

I was coming up on the end of my shift with Alec, which meant that it was nearly my bedtime and I was beyond exhausted. Frankly all I wanted to do was curl up in my bed and close my eyes, but Louis had other ideas.

"Adri, I'm afraid that I must insist you hand me over to Alec. I have something important to discuss with him."

I probably shouldn't have even answered Louis' call. Donovan and his team of hackers had our new communications equipment up and more or less running, but they'd encountered more of the 'unexpected problems' that Alec had warned us against. The hacker who originally had been in charge of our communications seemed to be passively resisting helping in the hopes that our jury-rigged solution would fail and vindicate him for not coming up with it himself.

On some level I could understand his frustration. He'd wanted to employ a bulletproof solution that wouldn't be vulnerable to all of the problems we were currently experiencing, but I didn't have six months to wait while he got all of the nitpicky little details squared away. I needed a solution now, one that would let me keep everything Alec had struggled to build from falling apart. I just needed something that would last long enough for us to find and kill Dream Stealer.

The real kick in the teeth was that our unhappy little hacker was right. The solution we'd chosen to go with was temperamental and seemed like it was ready to fall over at any moment. I was even less conversant with the technical details than Donovan was, but as nearly as I could tell we were involved in a kind of high-tech, programming arms race.

The Coun'hij's hackers were getting better and better at writing programs that had a chance to break through the security measures that masked our cell signal, while our people took more and more desperate actions to try and keep us from being tracked back to our actual location. It was like we were building a gigantic house of cards while the Coun'hij was pulling cards out one at a time from the bottom of the house. If we did everything right and worked at a frantic pace then we had a chance to stay ahead of them, but all it would take was for us to slow down a little or make a mistake and the Coun'hij would bring the whole house crashing down.

Donovan had two separate teams of mercenaries currently driving around the country in RV's with similar communications suites in them. Those teams turned on their equipment at semi-random times in an effort to distort the data being picked up by the Coun'hij, but each time I got on the phone to accept an incoming call the Coun'hij got a little closer to tracking us down.

Every IT resource we had access to had been pulled into the battle to keep control of the cellular networks and the satellite surveillance systems, but we were slowly being locked out of one critical system after another.

The trip to Missouri had taken twice as long as it should have due to the fact that we'd had to vary our course to avoid making it too easy for the Coun'hij's people to predict where exactly we were headed. Even with that and the two million dollars we were spending per day, we still didn't know for sure that the Coun'hij wouldn't have a big welcoming committee waiting for us in Kansas City.

I looked at the tablet next to Alec's bed, which was showing a risk level of fifty percent, and then rubbed my eyes before responding to Louis.

"Alec isn't available to speak with you right now, Louis. Like he said when he called you a couple of days ago, I'm fully up to speed on everything that is going on, so you can tell me whatever it is and I'll make sure Alec hears about it as soon as possible—assuming I can't just take care of it myself."

"With all due respect, Adri, you aren't Alec. I didn't swear fealty to you and I don't have to take orders from you. You can hand me over to Alec, or I'll hang up and maybe when he gets around to calling me back I'll be in a position to pick up *his* phone call."

"If you hang up on me you're going to be very, very sorry, Louis."

"Is that a threat?"

"No, it's a statement of fact. Alec told you to listen to me when the two of you last talked. If you hang up on me after a direct order to tell me what it is you called about, then you're effectively disobeying Alec. He's not going to forget that kind of thing."

"That sounds an awful lot like a threat to me, young lady, and it depends solely on Alec being alive, which I don't think is the case, not after some of the things I've been hearing lately."

I forced myself to smile despite wanting to throw something through a window. The tablet on the table was now showing a sixty percent risk factor, which meant that Donovan's hackers were probably scrambling one or both of the mercenary teams and turning on the other communication suites.

"Thank you, Louis, for pointing out that I've been too lax with you and the others. From here on out you may address me as Mistress Paige or ma'am. Alec Graves is very much alive and he's going to be very unhappy at the course this conversation has taken. He and I both thought that you were a man of your word, Louis."

"I am!"

"Then prove it. Either you're with us or you're against us. This is a critical time and we need to know exactly who we can depend on for the upcoming assault against the Coun'hij headquarters."

"You've really found them?"

"Yes, we have. Jasmin Bianchi traced them to a location in Tennessee before she dropped out of sight. There is a good chance that they've moved since then, but the simple fact that we've got them on the run will tend to create opportunities for us."

"You haven't really found them then."

"Louis, if I say that we've found them, then we've found them. They may drop out of sight for a little while, but we know how Jasmin did what she did and it's entirely repeatable. That's why I asked you to be on the lookout for Coun'hij enforcers who are operating in small enough groups that you might have a chance of capturing one or more hybrids."

"You can't just be planning on torturing their location out of them. It's been tried before—the enforcers have all bound their beasts to not reveal the location of the Coun'hij's base. They'll die before revealing anything useful to you."

"Louis, I simply don't have the time it would take to tell every single one of our people every aspect of Alec's plan. Our communications equipment is holding together with the IT equivalent of spit and duct tape. You're going to just have to trust us that we know what we're doing. Get to your real reason for calling so I can get off the phone and see to everything else that needs doing."

"There are rumors going around that you're relocating that Del Rio girl—Lori—to wherever you're headed…"

"I suppose I shouldn't be surprised that the back channel information flow is still healthy despite the fact that every call any of you make puts you at risk."

"I'm not going to let you dodge this question—that girl is dangerous."

I simply let the silence stretch out despite the fact that I could still see the monitor slowly tracking up as the risk that the Coun'hij would be able to localize us increased. As hard as it was to waste some of my precious phone time, I wasn't the only one running risks because of this call. Louis' signal was much more traceable than mine and there was a limit to how long he could stay in one place on the phone before he'd have to start worrying about a Coun'hij kill team coming for him.

When I finally broke the silence, I did so in a way that I hoped still gave me the upper hand. "I don't think you phrased that question the way you meant to phrase it, Louis. My patience is not infinite."

For a second I thought he was going to refuse to cooperate, but apparently I'd managed to be convincing enough with regards to the threat of what would happen if indeed Alec was still alive.

"My...apologies, ma'am. What I meant to ask was if the rumors were true, and if you felt that you'd properly considered the danger the Del Rio girl represents."

"Yes, the rumors are true. Alec started the wheels moving to have Lori meet us on the same day that he last called you. As to the second half of your question, yes, Alec and I are both very aware of the fact that Lori is dangerous. To be perfectly frank, she wouldn't be as useful to us if she wasn't so dangerous."

"With all due respect, ma'am, that's the kind of thing that is fueling the rumors that Alec is dead and you've engineered some kind of behind-the-scenes takeover."

"Is it?"

"Yes, people are saying that there wouldn't be any need for Alec to keep Lori alive if he were really still in control. Alec is already a near-perfect weapon, and with Jaclyn and Grayson to back him up, it doesn't seem justifiable to bring in such a loose cannon."

"Louis, I understand your concerns, but the next time someone calls you to chew the fat, please remind them that when we go in after the Coun'hij, we'll be up against Puppeteer and more than likely a whole host of werewolves. Alec beat Puppeteer's forces at the estate through a very fortuitous set of circumstances. As much as all of us might hope that we'll be able to replicate that when we go in after the rest of our enemies, it would be exceedingly foolish to count on something so out of our control.

"Lori's defense of our people in Nephi proved that she's got the potential to be a powerful weapon. Neither Alec nor I are inclined to set aside such a valuable tool—not considering the forces arrayed against us. All weapons are dangerous, Louis, it's just a matter of knowing what it is you're up against."

"Very, well, ma'am. I'll be sure to pass that message along should the opportunity arise."

"Thank you, Louis. Be careful though. I don't want you to end up with a kill squad in your lap. If you engage the Coun'hij's people I'd much rather it be on your terms rather than theirs."

I made my farewells to Louis as the monitor edged up to the seventy percent risk range and then looked out the window to confirm that the field we'd been traveling through for the last several hours had given way to the suburbs.

Andrew was waiting for me just outside of Alec's room. "Are you ready to call it a night, Miss Adri?"

"I wish, Andrew. Unfortunately I still have one more task to see to now that we've arrived in Kansas City."

"Well, I won't presume to tell you what to do, but do try not to let yourself get too run down—it seems to me that the best leaders are always the ones who make things look easy. You wouldn't want to be exhausted if we ran into a real crisis."

"Thank you for the words of advice, Andrew. I'll keep it in mind and try to make sure that I get caught up on my sleep. You're okay to watch Alec for me now?"

Andrew nodded and motioned towards Dominic and Ruby, who had both headed our direction as soon as I'd opened the bedroom door. "I've got a new novel that I've been meaning to read for several months now, and I think my trusty helpers are ready to move me inside. I'll be in good shape to keep an eye on Alec for at least the next few hours."

I smiled my thanks to Andrew and then made my way past him and the girls, carefully working my way towards the front of the RV. Donovan hadn't skimped on our transportation—it was a truly enormous vehicle, but even so it was feeling cramped with so many people living out of it.

Samantha was unconscious, and Alec wasn't moving around at all, but that still left six other people—plus whoever was driving—to try not to step on each other's toes. I'd considered asking Donovan to pony up the cash for a fourth RV, but I wasn't quite sure who I would move into the new vehicle if I did so.

I didn't particularly trust Ruby or Addison on their own, and I wanted to keep Dom, James and Donovan close at hand in case I needed them for something, which really only left Andrew and Samantha. I wasn't going to move Alec's mom into another vehicle where something might happen to her, and it didn't seem right to only kick Andrew out, not after how helpful he'd been with Alec. Besides, there wasn't any way to be sure that any of the rest of our people would properly take care of him.

No, we were all stuck together for at least the next little while. There was nothing to do but make the best of it and hope that we would be able to abandon our transient lifestyle before too much longer.

"Donovan, are we really in Kansas City?"

"Yes, Mistress Paige. Addison indicated that we're only a couple of minutes away from the location where we're supposed to be meeting Lori."

"Thank you, Donovan."

I hadn't bothered hiding the handgun that I'd taken from Alec's bedroom. There wouldn't have been any point, not given that everyone else in the RV could smell it as soon as I'd opened the bedroom door. Still, I slipped it into the front of my pants as I walked past Donovan and stopped just behind Addison's seat. I was a lot more careful to keep my hand free these days, especially when walking around inside of a moving vehicle.

"I think that's their vehicle right there, Miss Adri."

"Thank you, Addison, I think you're right. Bring us alongside of them, please. There's no need to find a parking spot—we're only stopping for long enough to swap out passengers."

That brought Donovan's head around. "Is that wise, Mistress Paige?"

"Probably not, but I'm sure Tiffany has some tired ladies in that vehicle with her, which means that they're all going to be even more on edge than normal. Given that I need to talk to Lori, either she needs to come here or I need to go there."

"Ah, yes, I can see your quandary. It would not be wise to bring her inside of our vehicle."

"Yeah, my thoughts exactly. So I'll be riding with Lori and her guards for the next little while. I'll want you all to keep a close eye on whomever she sends back to take my spot here. Don't let them back to see Alec, but we will hopefully win some points with them by offering them a place to sleep and a few hours where they don't have to be in a constant state of alert. I'll get a promise from them that they'll obey you for as long as they are your guest—that should go a long ways toward defusing any dominance posturing."

"Very good, Mistress Paige. We'll do our best."

"I've come to expect nothing less from all of you."

I fidgeted with the front of my shirt, trying to make sure that it did a decent job hiding my gun, and then Addison brought the RV to a ponderous stop and it was time for me to disembark. Tiffany climbed out of the passenger side of her vehicle and met me a couple of steps from the RV.

"I was starting to wonder if you were going to bother showing up after all of the times you changed up the schedule."

"I'm sorry about that, it couldn't be helped. I suspect that you've got some very tired people in there with you. I'd like to ride into the city with you, but if you'd like to detach one or two of your ladies they are welcome to sleep inside my RV."

"With all due respect, I'm not sure I want to be driving through a city this size down two guards, not if you're their only replacement. One human with a broken arm and a gun isn't going to be enough to stop Lori if she decides to turn the city against us."

I very carefully didn't look down at my left arm, which I'd taken to carrying around in a sling because it seemed less unnerving to those around me. "It's paralyzed, not broken, but maybe when this is all over I'll sit down and tell you the story about how it got paralyzed—I think it would change your mind about just how capable I am."

I watched as her nostrils flared. She could taste the truth of what I'd said, but she was still having a hard time believing there wasn't some kind of double-talk in my statement.

"Are you really trying to tell me that you're a match for two experienced hybrids?"

"That all depends on the circumstances, Tiffany. Out in an open field with nothing but my bare hands, I'm nothing more than a sitting duck, but there are circumstances where it's entirely possible that I could give your girls a run for their money. It's not like your people can really utilize the full range of their abilities while sitting in a vehicle like that—there's nowhere near enough space for you to shift in there. The best you could hope to do is partially shift and kill Lori with your claws."

"You're not wrong, but you're leaving out the fact that we can move as fast as Lori—you can't."

Tiffany's hand shot forward as she tried to make her point, but I'd come down the steps of the RV knowing there was a chance that I would be dragged into exactly this kind of dominance posturing. She'd seriously underestimated me. If she'd been in her hybrid form—or even if she'd put everything she had into the blow in an attempt to really hurt me—I would have barely seen the blow coming, but as it was I was not only ready, I had the advantage.

I stepped to the side as I grabbed for my pistol, and then as her fist went screaming past the side of my head, I stepped forward and put the barrel of my gun directly against her forehead.

"It's a good thing I know this was just more juvenile chest-beating, Tiffany, or you'd be dead right now."

"I've never seen any human move that fast before."

Her expression was so shocked that I figured I was safe putting my gun away, especially considering that I didn't want anyone to call the cops.

"I'm not surprised—you probably won't ever see another human move that fast. Are you going to let me ride with you or am I going to have to bring Lori inside of my RV with all of those hot-blooded males she's so good at manipulating?"

"Fine, you convinced me. Alec Graves knew what he was doing when he picked you to be our next queen."

"Does that mean you're ready to swear fealty?"

Tiffany snorted. "Not hardly."

"It's only a matter of time, Tiffany. Pick two of your people to go get some sleep, but I want a promise out of them that they'll obey Donovan while they are in there."

"You're not bashful about asking for the moon and the stars, are you?"

"Alec has high expectations and he's not going to want to be disturbed for *anything*."

Tiffany knocked on the window and motioned the driver and another of the women out of the car. They'd apparently all seen me draw down on Tiffany, because both of the women that exited the SUV looked at me with the wary postures of shape shifters who weren't sure how the dominance hierarchy was going to play out.

"Miss Paige has kindly offered us a chance to get some shuteye in there with her people. We'll sleep in shifts just like we've been doing, but with the added benefit of bunks and not having to worry about someone slitting our throats while we sleep."

The taller of Tiffany's companions, a solid-looking woman with a mohawk hairdo that was uncomfortably close to the kind of thing a Coun'hij enforcer would wear, gave me a sour look.

"How do we know we're not going to wake up and find one of her people's claws around our throats?"

I gave her what I hoped was a cold, imperious stare. "Because you have my word that my people will treat you with the utmost hospitality—as long as you follow the orders of my man Donovan."

"Graves' cripple?"

It was all I could do to keep from going for my gun. The derision in her tone touched off all kinds of protective instincts inside of me.

"Not a cripple anymore, but then again he never was—not in the way you're implying."

I turned back to Tiffany and motioned towards the taller woman. "I withdraw my offer of hospitality for that one. If you have another of your people you'd like to put forth for consideration you can."

"Now listen here! I've earned a break. I've been watching that little whore for the last thirty hours straight."

Mohawk took a step towards me, but I already had my hand on my gun and she was still four long strides away from me. It was a gamble after what she'd seen me do already, especially if she wasn't willing to shift. She froze in place, but it was hard to tell whether that was because of the possibility that I might be fast enough to shoot her, or if it was because Tiffany looked like she wanted to tear someone's head off.

"Get back in the car!"

"No, I want what's coming to me."

"What's coming to you is a coffin if you don't do what I say."

"Are you going to put me down now? After all we've been through together?" Mohawk stepped into Tiffany's space. It was time to intervene.

"Tiffany isn't going to have to put you down."

"Why? Are you feeling lucky, little woman?"

"Actually I am, but I don't fight peasants. I've got more than forty people sitting in the cars you see parked around us. If you really think that they aren't listening right now you're sadly mistaken." I called out a single name without breaking eye contact. "James!"

More than half a dozen doors opened in unison as my people exited their vehicles. James was at my back before anyone else could move. "You called, Adri?"

"Yeah, Mohawk over there is deciding whether or not she wants to be difficult. She insulted Donovan and then had the gall to be offended when I withdrew my offer of hospitality."

James stepped around me as though fully ready to go head to head with another hybrid on nothing more than my say-so. Mohawk tried to step forward to meet him, but Tiffany was there.

"Don't do this. He doesn't have to take you on by himself. For all intents and purposes we are in their territory right now. You can't win a fight against three or four of her people and the last thing we want is to bring half a dozen burly guys down here where Lori will have an easier time of influencing them. Don't throw away everything we've spent the last few weeks trying to accomplish."

Mohawk shook her head. "The slut won't do anything—Tasha still has Everett locked up."

I put my hand on James' elbow to stop him from continuing to close, but my eyes never left Mohawk's face. "I agree with Tiffany. There is no need to further inflame things. Get back into your vehicle and we'll pretend this never happened."

She wanted a piece of me, of anyone really, but me most of all. For a heartbeat I thought she was going to resist the order, but then she finally realized that I was planning on getting into that same SUV with her and driving away from James and the rest of my supporters.

Her smile as she got back into the SUV was a cruel thing, but I was still several steps ahead of her as I turned back to Tiffany. "You have anyone else you'd like to give a break? Preferably someone with more sense and less of a chip on her shoulder."

Tiffany waved one of the women from the backseat out. "Go get some sleep in the RV. While you're in there toe the line and do whatever the butler says."

They both nodded, but I held up my hand, stopping them before they could go to the RV. "I want a promise from each of you that you will obey Donovan for as long as you're enjoying my hospitality."

Once I had their promises I waved them in and nodded for James to follow them. Mallory appeared at my elbow. "I don't think this is a good idea, Adri."

Tiffany shook her head. "She'll be safe. Really, we've just exchanged hostages—nothing's going to happen to her as long as she's got two of my people in that RV."

I gave Mallory an inquiring look, but I wasn't surprised when she finally gave me a reluctant nod to indicate that Tiffany was telling the truth. The Del Rio hybrid wasn't the type to bow and scrape, but she also seemed to play things pretty straight.

"Tiffany, if you can drive I'd like to get started—we're running even further behind schedule now."

I opened up the door closest to me and sat down in the middle bench seat next to Lori. I would have rather sat down in the back seat next to Tiffany's fourth hybrid, but that wasn't the right way to start out what was probably going to end up being the most important negotiation of my life.

Lori was in obvious need of a shower and a hairbrush, but that somehow just managed to highlight how incredibly beautiful she was. It seemed like every second girl I ran into made me feel like an ugly duckling, but most of them had to do their hair and makeup to look that mind-blowing. Lori, on the other hand, just looked like she was slumming.

Her wrists were handcuffed together and her ankles were manacled to the chair frame beneath us. If Tiffany's group had been pulled over on their way east they would have ended up having to decide between killing a cop or spending the rest of their lives in jail, but Lori's condition wasn't entirely surprising.

They'd apparently stopped drugging her and she looked like she was at least getting something to eat, but that was as far as they'd been willing to go. It actually should make my job easier, but that didn't mean that I liked anyone being treated in such a manner—even the girl who had tried to seduce Alec.

I couldn't really blame Lori for ignoring me when I scooted onto the seat next to her as best I could with only one working arm. She was probably expecting me to take the opportunity to beat her with a baseball bat.

"Where are the keys to her restraints?"

"You're not freeing her!"

The protest burst out of the woman behind me with a force that said she was having a hard time believing that *anyone* would consider freeing Lori to be a good idea.

"Adri, meet Polly; Polly, this is Adriana Paige, our…patron. Go ahead and give her the keys."

"I don't care if she's the patron saint of leprechauns; I'm not giving her the keys."

"You'll do it or you'll be walking home. As much as I don't like it, it appears that she's the one in charge here. Graves backed us into a corner and we don't have much of a choice but to go along with whatever he's got planned."

Polly turned her head like she was going to spit, but then looked at the upholstery and changed her mind. "I'm a free woman, I've got all of the choices in the world."

"Yeah, you have the choice to let your daughter starve—or worse. You know as well as I do that we're screwed if Graves doesn't continue to give us cash. We left home with little more than the clothes on our backs and as long as this war is going on it's not like we're going to be able to settle down and work steady jobs."

"So we torture the whore and get at the money she and her daddy have stashed away."

"Yeah, good luck with that. Everett is no Alec Graves. He doesn't come from old money and the tithe from the pack was never enough to really get excited about. Besides, I'm not going to torture Lori, so you'll be on your own."

Mohawk shrugged without looking back at Polly, Lori or I. "Not on her own—I'd help."

"Yeah, which just means that you'd kill her after three hours instead of six. Neither of you know enough to do it properly without killing her before she breaks. Hell, you don't even know how to properly restrain her."

"Oh, I don't know, the cuffs seem to have worked just fine."

I cut into the conversation before it could go any further. "Yeah, cuffs and leg irons are just fine if you want to cut her hands off. You're lucky it wasn't a full moon or she might have lost control and bled out."

Mohawk gave me a dark smile. "You're coming at this from the wrong angle, Polly. If we want money we should be torturing the gimp princess rather than the whore. I'll bet that Graves would pay tens of millions to get her back in one piece."

Tiffany looked back at me by way of the rear-view mirror, but she didn't speak up. Apparently she wanted to see how I was going to handle myself. I shook my head at Mohawk. "Alec won't pay a single penny to get me back because he doesn't negotiate from a position of weakness. What he will do is take time away from the war with the Coun'hij to hunt down anyone who hurts me."

"That's no big deal, Polly and I have both been on the run before."

"Not from Alec Graves you haven't."

This time I'd slid my gun into the sling holding up my left arm rather than into my pants. My hand was already gripping the handle. Mohawk was on the far side of the car from me, I figured I had a decent chance of taking her out before she could reach back and hurt me, even assuming she was one of the relatively rare hybrids who could manifest a partial shift. The real problem was Polly, but she was sitting directly behind Lori, so I would probably have time for at least one shot. Polly was going to kill me, but not before I got Mohawk. It wasn't how I would have chosen to die, but not many humans could say that they took out a hybrid in the process of dying.

"Stop. You're not going to kill her or I'll make sure this car is ripped apart."

It took me longer than it should have to realize that it had been Lori who had finally spoken, but that was at least partially because Tiffany slammed on the brakes with so much force that my butt actually left the seat for a second.

Sometime over the last minute or two we'd entered the city limits and moved off onto a smaller road with stoplights and crosswalks, but that wasn't why we had to stop so abruptly. We'd stopped because more than half of the cars around us had come to a stop and even now people were getting out of their vehicles and approaching ours.

Polly had a knife at Lori's throat. "Release them!"

The slender length of steel had already drawn a thin line of crimson across Lori's tanned skin, but she seemed remarkably unconcerned about the possibility of dying.

"Right now you're all thinking that you didn't know I was capable of influencing people who hadn't gotten a good look at me. You're wondering what else I can do that you didn't know about, but what you should be worried about is the fact that those people out there are now close enough that they can see inside our vehicle. They can see that you're holding a knife to my throat, and they don't like it. You've now missed your opportunity to kill me. If you hurt me now you'll have a riot on your hands."

I looked around at the people pressed up against the van windows and realized that Lori was right. There were a few men who had their phones out as though calling 911, but most of them looked like they wanted to take matters into their own hands.

"Get your knife away from her throat!" I hissed the order at Polly, but she didn't move until Tiffany nodded at her. Even then she didn't obey very quickly, obviously unhappy that Lori had been able to turn the tables so completely on them.

"You're now going to hand Adri the keys to my handcuffs so that she can free me, and then I'm going to step out of the van and walk away without any of you trying to follow me."

Again another nod from Tiffany, and slow, angry compliance from Polly. I took the keys and unlocked Lori's wrists. It would have been too hard to get to her legs with only one hand, so I just handed her the keys to the leg irons and let her unlock herself. While she did that I pulled out my latest burner phone and handed it to her. She looked at me with derision.

"Do you really think I'm dumb enough to accept something that will let you track me?"

"It's got the number to my RV programmed in it. You've got no money and no way of communicating with the rest of the world. You're going to want a way to confirm that your father is released."

Lori looked at the phone for several seconds before nodding and accepting it. "You've got four hours to free him. After that, I'll start hunting your people down and making them pay for keeping him locked up."

"I'm not the one you need to be threatening, Lori. I'm the one who made sure that the two of you were treated humanely. I'll call and order his release within the hour."

She nodded, not exactly satisfied, but apparently willing to give me enough rope to hang myself if that was what I wanted to do. She started to reach for the door, but then stopped and looked over at Tiffany.

"You three empty out your pockets and give me all of the cash you're carrying."

Mohawk looked like she was going to argue, but I stopped her with a look. "Just do it. I'll make sure you're reimbursed."

Lori didn't like that. "I don't want your money, just theirs. If you reimburse them then it defeats the purpose."

"Does it? The purpose I see is making sure that you have enough money that you won't have to steal from someone out there. I'm willing to fund that purpose as long as you're willing to let bygones be bygones with Tiffany and her people. I don't want you hunting them down at some point in the future to extract revenge."

"Why should I care what you want? They imprisoned me and drugged me senseless. They should have to pay for that."

"Be careful, Lori. Once you start down the path of justice above all else you're putting yourself in a very difficult position. What you did in coming to Sanctuary was just as bad. Tiffany's people took away your freedom, but you came intending on taking away Alec's free will."

"So I should show a little mercy to them in hopes that Alec will show me mercy in return?"

"I couldn't have said it better myself."

Her hand was suddenly at my throat, not gripping hard enough to stop me from breathing, but with enough strength that I knew it would take very little effort for her to kill me.

"You're forgetting that your threat is predicated on my believing that Alec Graves is still alive and able to come after me. He's obviously not or he never would have allowed you to come here without him."

I knew I should be scared, but part of me was just too tired to feel the level of fear the situation called for.

"My threat is predicated on Alec being alive because he *is* alive, Lori, but even if he wasn't, if you kill me or come after Tiffany's pack you'd still end up dead. There are more than enough female wolves and hybrids under our command to see the job done."

Her grip loosened slightly as she tried to reconcile my surety with her reading of the situation. "You're an interesting individual, Adriana Paige. You're either a psychopath, or you really believe what you just said. I'm actually inclined to believe you simply because I don't believe that a man like Alec Graves would let himself be taken in by a psychopath."

"Good. I'm not lying, so it makes things a lot easier for both of us if you believe me when I tell you the truth. Do we have a deal?"

"What, two hundred dollars in return for letting Tiffany's people go unpunished?"

"No, your freedom in return for theirs and a promise that you're not going to do the kinds of things that will make Alec come hunt you down at some point in the future. If it's all about the money, I can make sure that you've got enough to really start over. How much would it take to make you do the right thing, Lori? Five million dollars? Ten?"

"It's not about the money! Don't follow me!"

MARKED

Lori threw down the cash and threw open her door, stepping out into the crowd of people—mostly men—who looked at her with desire in their eyes, but who made no effort to mob her like I half expected them to. It was the moment of truth and I did the only thing I could; I jumped out of the SUV and followed after her.

The further Lori walked the more of her admirers she released—by the time we turned a corner and were no longer within sight of Tiffany and the others, she only had two guys still trailing along behind her.

"I told you not to follow me."

"I prefer to think of it as accompanying you—besides, I figured you were talking to the Del Rio ladies. Given that I'm the reason you aren't still passing your days in a chemically-induced coma, it seemed only reasonable that you wouldn't just lump me in with them."

"I could make you stay here."

"Hurting someone who helped you? That's pretty dark."

"I wouldn't have to hurt you. These two gentlemen would gladly hold you here for the next hour if that was what I wanted them to do. Besides, you don't know anything about me."

The two guys following half a step behind Lori were nodding like their heads were going to fall right off of their necks, and one of them slowed slightly as though considering acting on her implied desire, but I shot him a dark look that sent him hurrying to catch back up with Lori and the other guy.

"I know a lot more than you think, Lori. I've been listening and putting the pieces together. Back there they said that you and your dad didn't have very much money saved up."

"What of it? Are you feeling the need to lord over me just how much money your sweetie has squirreled away?"

"Miss Lori, is this chick bothering you? Do you want us to do something about her?"

This was the other guy, the shorter one, and the way that his voice dripped with the desire to please her turned my stomach.

"Yes, she's bothering me, but don't do anything about her unless she physically attacks me."

Both men nodded as though it was perfectly normal for them to be following around a strange woman they'd only just met. Momentarily reassured that I wasn't going to have to fight off several hundred pounds of angry male, I picked my pace back up in an effort to close the distance between us.

"I'm not trying to lord anything over you, Lori. I was actually trying to give you a compliment. You could have made out like a bandit at any point, but you chose not to. You could have easily crashed some high-profile society party and convinced half the billionaires in any given state to hand over half of their net worth, but you didn't. I think that says something good about you."

"Not as much as you think. I considered doing something like that, but it would never have worked. Guys like that love their money more than just about anything else. As soon as they left my presence they would have started questioning their decision to give me money. I would have been looking at a massive set of lawsuits from each and every billionaire I conned. Not only that, it would have blown my cover wide open."

"Interesting, and did you consider conning people for smaller amounts? I'm sure you could have figured out a way to fleece a few billionaires for a million here or there? That wouldn't have left them as likely to second-guess their decision to give you money..."

"Yeah, I thought about it, but my dad didn't like that idea. He said it was still too risky."

My gun was shifting around more than I wanted it to. It was too late to shove it down my pants now, and I couldn't keep up with Lori's current pace with both of my hands in the sling currently supporting my left arm, so I jammed the gun underneath my left arm and just did my best not to let my left arm sway too much as I walked.

"What about the trip out here?"

"What about it?"

"You could have gotten away from Tiffany and the others at any point—why didn't you?"

Lori turned right, seemingly at random, and headed past a pair of banks and a bakery. "I don't know. Maybe I was waiting to see what you would be like in person before breaking out."

"Maybe, or maybe you knew that getting away from your captors would have involved a lot of innocent guys getting hurt or killed. You didn't act to get away until it looked like Mohawk and Polly were going to kill me, and even then, your first concern seemed to be making them back off. You didn't decide to make a run for it until you realized just how completely you had control of the situation."

Lori stopped and rounded on me, sticking her finger into my sternum with enough force I was going to have a bruise later. "Why are you so determined to paint me as a decent person when every other person in the world is convinced that I'm too far gone to save?"

"Because I need you to be a decent person. I think you've been on the fence for a while. I think you enjoy manipulating guys and making them do what you want, but something—either your father or some inherent goodness—stopped you from becoming completely narcissistic. More importantly though, I think what happened in Nephi scared you to death and you're afraid of what you might become."

"I should have known. This whole time you were just hoping that I would fight your battles for you. You're just like everyone else, just in it to see what you can get from me."

"I'm not going to lie to you, Lori. I do need you, but you need me too. I need you to help me fight off the Coun'hij, but you need me to let you stay close enough to Alec that you'll always have someone around who's capable of stopping you from becoming the monster we both know you're capable of becoming."

I expected her to go storming off, but she didn't. "You're not talking about just lurking around in the background, are you?"

"No, not if you need more than that to avoid going off the deep end, Lori. If you prove that you're competent and trustworthy then Alec will move you into his inner circle."

"You shouldn't make that kind of offer, not to me."

"Why? Aren't you trustworthy?"

Lori looked away from me, unwilling to meet my eyes. "Haven't you stopped to wonder how Del Rio ended up with so many female hybrids? As much as you or I might wish things were different, statistically speaking it's a man's world. There are women hybrids, but we're only half as common as male hybrids. In a pack the size of Del Rio we should have had two or three female hybrids tops."

"Actually, I didn't think about that at all."

"I guess you have a few blind spots too. Daddy has been actively recruiting female hybrids and wolves into the pack for the last six years. Before that we had roughly the same ratios of females to males that you would have seen anywhere else."

"Six years ago? Was that when…"

"Yes, that was when I first manifested my ability. Once my father realized what I was capable of, even *he* took steps to try and make sure that he could stop me if I ever got out of hand."

"Maybe there was another reason…"

"I doubt it. Our lives would have been much easier if all of the main players in the pack were male. The only reason to bring in people I couldn't manipulate was because he needed them to serve as a counterweight to me. You can see how it might be a little hard for me to trust that you have my best interests at heart given that even my own flesh and blood doesn't trust me."

I shrugged. "Trust is one of those things you have to build up piece by piece, Lori. I'm giving you the opportunity to start winning our trust, I can't make you take it though."

She sighed. "What I did in Nephi bothered me, but not as much as you think. The Coun'hij enforcers deserved what they got, even if it felt a little wrong to completely take away their free choice like that. Mostly I just felt bad about the innocent wolves who got hurt or killed taking the enforcers down. Next time I won't make that mistake. I'll use the enforcers to kill each other, but not all of them. I'll keep a few around so that I always have resources to throw at whatever else might pop up."

She looked at me again and cocked her head to one side. "You still want to give me a job now that you know that?"

"Yes, I do." It wasn't a lie, but I was going to be very careful about who I put in her power. Lori was sounding scarier by the second, but I needed her if I was going to save Alec.

"Fine, I'm willing to entertain the idea. No more guards, and no more drugs. I go where I want to go when I want to go there."

I shook my head. "If you're signing on with us then you're signing on under the same terms as everyone else. You take Alec's orders and go where he wants you to go, when he wants you to go there. When Alec isn't available you'll be taking my orders as if they were Alec's. You'll be treated with respect, but you will have an honor guard of females responsible for both protecting you and making sure that you're behaving yourself. I'll give you your own RV and a generous stipend, but you'll be expected to mostly keep to yourself and avoid any interactions with males other than Alec."

"You offer me a very pretty cage, but it will be a cage nonetheless."

"Stop and think about the situation from my end of things, Lori. You're not just every leader's biggest fears made flesh, you're every woman's worst nightmare. If I let you just wander around and interact with anybody you please then Alec and I will have half our people up in arms convinced that you're arranging some kind of coup d'état and the other half of our people will be up in arms worried that you're manipulating their boyfriends or husbands.

"The truth is that there is a very good chance you're going to have somebody come after you the first time their boyfriend breaks up with them because they'll be convinced that he secretly wants to date you. The guards are as much for your protection as anything else."

Lori looked at me for several seconds. "You only have one thing that I want, Adriana Paige. I've spent a good chunk of my life knowing that I could have any guy I wanted. Once I realized that, they all became completely undesirable. Part of that is the same thrill of the hunt that all women enjoy, but part of it is because as long as I can manufacture a man's feelings for me those feelings are less than worthless. There's only one straight man who has ever resisted my advances."

It was a good thing that we were standing still or the sinking sensation in my stomach probably would have made me trip.

"You want Alec."

"Indeed, I do. He's rich, powerful, considerate, and completely immune to my power. You can hardly blame me for wanting him."

"No, I completely understand the appeal, but you haven't answered my question. Do we have a deal?"

"What, no additional restriction that I not interact with Alec either?"

"You wouldn't honor it even if I tried, but I'm not going to ask because I know Alec is his own person. Either he'll continue to choose me or he won't. I can't stop him if he chooses to leave me, all I can do is try to be the very best fiancée I can be and remind him every day why he chose me in the first place."

"You're not nearly as confident of that as you're trying to pretend you are."

She was right. Looking at her, still drop-dead gorgeous despite the fact that she needed a shower and didn't have any makeup on, it was hard to see a future where Alec didn't eventually choose her over me. In the end though, it didn't matter. I would rather see Alec alive and with her than lose him to Dream Stealer. I needed her if I was going to save Alec, the only question was whether I could keep her under control for long enough to aim her at the Coun'hij before she turned on me.

We shook on our agreement and I tried to ignore the little part of me that died in the process.

Chapter 17

Adriana Paige
East Side
Kansas City, Missouri

Now that we were theoretically on the same side, Lori gave me back my burner phone and I called Donovan on his latest prepaid phone. He promised to procure another RV as well as sending a car filled with capable female shape shifters to pick us up at a prearranged location in an hour.

Lori gave me a curious look at the timing, but I wasn't going to get into the habit of explaining my every move to her. I asked her to dismiss her bodyguards with a request that they not talk about their time with us, and then we set off on foot towards downtown Kansas City.

It took us forty minutes to get to the section of town that I wanted, and by then it was much too late for two young ladies to be out on foot by themselves, but I knew Lori would be able to handle almost any conceivable threat we might run into so I just focused on putting one foot in front of another and not falling asleep mid stride.

"You do know that without me here to manipulate people's emotions you would have been raped three times already tonight, right?"

"I suspected as much—thanks for doing your job."

"You don't like me very much, do you?"

"Are we really having this conversation? You just told me that you were going to try to steal my fiancé."

"Yeah, I don't expect you to like me—most girls don't—but I'm still trying to understand why you gave me a job anyway."

I rubbed my eyes and wished that I was safely back in my bunk, a bunk that could very well be hosting one of Tiffany's people as we spoke. That was a depressing thought. Oh well, I could always just go into the bedroom with Alec and sleep there, even if that never seemed as restful as the nights where I slept in my own bed.

"Look, I don't have to like you to give you a job. The fact of the matter is if it were completely up to me, I probably would have kicked you to the curb, but this is bigger than just Alec and me. A lot of people are going to die if we can't overthrow the Coun'hij."

"I would venture a guess that a lot of people are still going to die even if you do manage to overthrow the Coun'hij."

"The proper statement is that a lot of people are going to die even if *we* manage to overthrow the Coun'hij—you're on my side now, remember?"

"Fine, people are still going to die even if *we* succeed in bringing down the Coun'hij."

"Yeah, but in that case it will be their people dying rather than our people."

"So it's just a question of us or them?"

I suppressed the urge to tell her that she was being childish. "Lori, you yourself said that you felt worse about the innocents that got killed during the fight in Nephi than you did about the enforcers. This is just that same thing on a larger scale. The Coun'hij has been taking away people's rights for centuries. We aren't fighting for money or power, we're fighting to give our kids a chance to grow up in a world where they don't have to worry about being killed by someone like Agony because they were in the wrong place at the wrong time."

"You sound like that's not just hypothetical…"

"It's not."

"Who was it and what happened?"

"Her name was Alison. There were others who died at the same time, and Jess lost her memories, but Alison got the rawest end of the deal because unlike the boys, she never did anything to hurt anyone. Agony came through a little while after I moved into Sanctuary, and when he didn't manage to force Alec into a fight, that was his last big play. He murdered our friends and dared us to do something about it."

"I'm sorry."

"Are you really, Lori? Because so far you don't seem like you really get it. I'm not going to go back on my offer of a place to live and access to Alec, but if you really want to be pulled into the inner circle you're going to have to gain some real empathy. Alec will be able to use you either way, but you're not going to impress him talking like you are now."

"I think you're actually serious…"

"You know I am—you'd be able to tell if I was lying."

"Why would you help me in my quest to steal Alec away from you?"

"I'm not, I'm trying to help you become a better person. Now be quiet. I need to make some phone calls and we don't have very long before Donovan's team picks us up."

I dialed Jaclyn's number first because I hadn't heard from her since the day Alec had been shot, and because, right about now, I couldn't think of anyone better suited for keeping Lori in check. Unfortunately Jaclyn didn't pick up, which meant I was back to square one when it came to how to keep Lori safely contained.

"Jaclyn, it's Adriana Paige. We need to talk—preferably sooner rather than later. There have been some developments and I'm not entirely sure that your mission is necessary anymore. We've got another way and your ability would be especially useful back here right about now. This is a burner phone, so don't bother calling me back on this number. You can reach Alec and me on his normal number—we've got a communications system up and working for inbound calls again."

"Jaclyn Annikov?"

I nodded as I dialed Tasha's number. I was surprised when a man answered her phone. "What?"

"I need to talk to Tasha."

"She's not here." The voice was familiar sounding, but I didn't know anyone who could manage to sound that emotionless.

"Grayson, is that you?"

"Yeah, Adri, it's me. What do you want?"

"What's going on? Why do you sound so different?"

I half expected him to get angry with me. A hybrid as dominant as Grayson wasn't usually very willing to sit and play Twenty Questions. In a way, I almost hoped that he would get angry with me. The dead, monotone voice he was currently using was unnerving.

"I'm not going to answer that question. What do you want?"

"I want you and Tasha to gather everyone up and come meet us. We have good intel with regards to where the Coun'hij is based and I want to reassemble our strike teams. How soon can you all be on the road?"

"I can't help you, Adri. You'll have to find someone else to do your dirty work."

"Can't or won't?"

"I suppose you're right, I could help you, but I'm not going to."

"I don't understand what's going on, Grayson. Tell me why you're acting so weird and where Tasha is!"

"You're right, you *don't* understand what's going on. Don't bother calling this phone number again, Adri, nobody will be around to answer it."

I threw my phone into the side of a building with enough force that it looked like it exploded when it hit.

Chapter 18

Adriana Paige
Interstate 64
Western Kentucky

My hand had started shaking whenever I didn't have anything in it. I'd had Donovan give me his professional opinion, but all he could recommend was a vitamin supplement, meditation for my nerves and more sleep. I followed his advice on the vitamin supplements, but the other two items were just not going to happen while everything around us was one ill-timed sneeze from blowing up in our faces.

Lori had caused an even bigger stir than I'd been afraid of—it had been all Mallory could do to find enough women to fill out a guard schedule for the fourth RV. At one point it had looked like we were going to lose our few volunteers simply because there weren't going to be enough of them to take her down if it became necessary to do so.

In the end, Dominic had to take a ten-hour shift each day and Mallory had to sign on for a six-hour shift to make everything work. Even that wasn't going to be sustainable long-term. We needed to convince some of our remaining females to help out with guard duty, that or meet up with more of our people. I figured that Rebekka and her daughter would be tough-minded enough to stand guard over Lori, but unfortunately they hadn't called to check in for quite a while.

Throwing my phone against the wall after talking to Grayson had been foolish. I should have thought to call Rebekka and ask her to meet back up with us, but at the time I'd just been too frustrated by the fact that Jaclyn had refused to pick up and Grayson had refused to even talk to me.

Part of me wanted to stop somewhere and call them now, but that would have been a major mistake. The Coun'hij was getting closer and closer to tracking us down, and Donovan was fairly certain that any outbound calls with encryption would lead them right to us.

We could still take inbound calls, but even that was getting more spotty and dangerous. None of our hackers were quite sure what had happened, but the Coun'hij hackers seemed to have found a way to strip away much of the benefit of our communication suite. The risk monitor running on the tablet in Alec's room rarely ever dropped below sixty percent lately, even when I wasn't actually on a call, and occasionally spiked up above ninety percent for no discernable reason. When that happened the equipment went into a low-power standby mode until our hackers could implement more of their techno-wizardry and throw the Coun'hij a little further off of our trail.

That meant that our communications capabilities had become so intermittent that I was losing any real feel for how the war was going. Some of my people seemed to have given up trying to check in and now I was having to try and keep track of them through rumors.

I was pretty sure that we'd lost a group sometime the day before. There had been some kind of massive explosion in a small town in Colorado that the media had been covering for almost fourteen hours straight. Almost three hundred people had been killed and nobody seemed to have any real idea what had caused it.

Donovan was convinced that it was the Coun'hij covering up a massive fight between our people and theirs. I had a hard time believing that any of our teams could have put up that much of a fight, but I wasn't going to second-guess him. All I could do at this point was try and figure out who we'd lost.

All that would have been enough to bring me to my knees, but when you threw in the fact that

Alec's condition seemed to be decaying much faster than last time around, it was all I could do to pull myself out of bed in the mornings.

Alec's phone—my phone now—started ringing, and I reflexively looked over at the tablet. We were a little above eighty percent risk—it would have to be a quick call.

"This is Adri—what do you need?"

"Adri? Where is Alec?"

"Jess, is that you?"

"Yeah, it's me. Where is Alec? I really need to talk to him."

"He can't come to the phone right now—tell me what you need and I'll pass the message along. Unless it's something I can take care of myself. In that case, I'll just make it happen."

Jess suddenly sounded uncertain. "How have you been, Adri?"

"Honestly? Not great. We've had a series of reverses that none of us saw coming. Things are pretty stressful right now. I'd love to catch up and find out how your trip with Wyatt has been so far, but I'm afraid I just can't—not today."

"I really don't think this is something you can help me with, Adri. How long will it be until Alec can call me back?"

"Jess, right now we don't have the capability to make outbound calls without alerting the Coun'hij as to where we are. You're going to just have to trust me to pass the message on."

"I could call back…"

"You could, but the odds of you catching Alec are so close to nonexistent that you would be wasting your time. Just tell me what you need. Please."

"I've...well, there are a lot of things I've learned since I arrived here. Alec needs to know this stuff, but I've promised not to say anything to anyone other than Alec. He needs to be down here—he really needs to be down here. A lot depends on it."

"You're going to have to give me a lot more to go on than that, Jess. A lot depends on Alec being up here with us."

"I *can't*, Adri."

"What kind of timeline are we working with?"

"Alec needs to be in Florida later today."

"There's no way that is happening, Jess. It's not physically possible to drive that fast and trying to take some kind of flight would just result in a big fight with the Coun'hij."

"You'll be able to fly—we can make it so that the Coun'hij won't be able to track you for the next few hours."

It wasn't much to go on, but I'd spent the last several days getting a crash course in what it took to drop completely out of sight from Dom and Donovan. There only one possible explanation for her certainty.

"You've got access to someone with an ability, a really powerful ability. That's how you're going to smuggle us aboard a plane."

"Yeah, there's someone here who can make that happen."

It was an answer to a prayer I hadn't consciously voiced. We didn't know how the Coun'hij had managed their recent breakthroughs, but I was pretty sure that if we could fall off of their radar—even for a few hours—that it would make all of the difference in the world.

"Jess, I need you to have your person there mask us for a few hours right now. The Coun'hij is breathing down our necks. If your people can get us clear of this current round of craziness, then in a couple of days you can call me back and we can work out something as far as a trip down to Florida."

"I'm sorry, Adri, it doesn't work that way. I don't have that much pull down here. This is a one-time offer and it's only valid if you're using it to come down here."

"Really, Jess? That's how you want to play things? You do realize that Andrew is here with us, right? Even if you've switched sides and don't care about the rest of us, surely you still care about him…"

"That's not fair, Adri. My hands are tied."

"Well, so are mine. Alec can't drop everything and just fly down to Florida on nothing more than your say-so. Don't bother calling back if this is all you're going to do—you've wasted precious call time that I should have been spending with people who are loyal to Alec."

I looked over at the tablet and saw that it was at eighty-six percent. I'd spent too long on the phone with her already. I started to hang up, but Jess stopped me.

"Please, Adri. Everything depends on Alec being here later today. You have no idea what it took for me to get permission to call you. I wouldn't have done any of this if it wasn't important."

"You're right, I have no idea what it took because you're not telling me. You have a very narrow window in which to explain, but you'd better start talking fast or it will close forever."

"I can't tell you any of that, Adri! I want to, but I can't."

"What *can* you tell me, Jess?"

"I can tell you that it's wrong for Alec to try and restore the monarchy."

"That's insane, Jess. You of all people know how terrible the Coun'hij is. Oblivion took *everything* away from you. Alec has to restore the monarchy if there's ever going to be any hope of the shape shifters having normal lives."

"I didn't say it was wrong for Alec to want to stop the Coun'hij, I said it was wrong to try and *restore the monarchy*, Adri."

There was a pause as someone said something that was too low for me to catch, and then Jess sighed. "I'm sorry, Adri. I really wish I could tell you more, but I can't. If there is any way for you to convince Alec to come down to Florida, then please do it."

She hung up before I could get off any kind of parting shot, and I was left with a monitor that showed an eighty-seven percent risk profile and a bad taste in my mouth. I wondered if it would have made any difference if I'd just come clean with Jess and told her that Alec was currently unconscious and under attack from Dream Stealer.

We'd reached the end of our resources. There hadn't been any word out of Jasmin—not surprising considering the fact that she'd been headed into a fight she couldn't possibly win—and nobody had managed to capture a mentalist vampire yet.

Mallory had us headed east in the hopes that we'd be able to capture a mentalist in one of the higher-population areas along the coast, but we all knew that was a long shot. It had seemed so simple back before the Coun'hij had been hot on our tail, but now all I could think about was the fact that stopping to hunt vampires would probably mean that we would have kill teams in the area hunting *us*.

Maybe if I'd come clean with Jess then Wyatt's people would have had a solution, but I didn't think so. It had been hard enough to believe that some fringe group that had spent the last hundred years flying under the radar would have two hybrids with major abilities in their ranks. The idea that they might have a third hybrid with a power—a hybrid who could track down Dream Stealer or kill him from a distance—in addition to Grayson and Jess' mystery 'cloaking' hybrid, just boggled the mind.

I felt reasonably comfortable in my decision not to tell her, to control the rumors that would have started spawning as soon as I began admitting that Alec was fading fast, but there was a tiny part of me that was worried I'd been wrong, that I'd just sentenced Alec to death despite my best intentions.

I looked over at Alec and my stomach knotted up the tiniest bit more at how pale he'd gotten. I stood up and crossed over to his bed, taking his left hand in mine as I wished there was something productive I could do.

I couldn't make any calls out to the rest of the world, and the monitor was now showing an eighty-eight percent risk profile despite the fact that I wasn't even on the phone with anyone. Even if someone called in I would probably have to ignore their call—I was completely useless. Donovan, Mallory and the rest all looked to me for direction, but I had no idea how to stop the disaster I could feel us sliding towards.

Lori was a ticking time bomb that could destroy the Coun'hij for me if I could hunt them down before she went off, but the odds of accomplishing that were getting slimmer by the hour.

I must have closed my eyes and started to nod off sitting up, because the sound of my phone ringing made me jump. For a second there it had felt like something had been pulling me down a long dark tube. I'd been terrified of what was happening, but at the same time it had felt oddly right to be headed wherever I was headed.

I went to hit the 'ignore' button on my phone, and then realized that it was Isaac who was calling. The monitor had dropped back down to eighty-six percent—still too high to risk a call of any length, but I hit accept regardless. I'd promised Alec.

"Isaac, is that you?"

"Adri? Where is Alec? I'm sorry, but I don't have much time and I really need to talk to him."

Isaac sounded worried and stressed, but he also sounded like home. Isaac had been different lately, more angry and unbalanced, but in my heart he was still the same guy who had accepted me into the pack over Jess' objections. He was still the guy who had risked death to come watch out for me while I'd been in New York.

"I'm sorry, Isaac. Alec isn't available, but he made me promise that I'd pick up no matter what the next time you called."

I'd been trying to sound as normal as possible, but apparently I hadn't succeeded, because there was a change in Isaac's voice when he responded.

"How long will it be before Alec can call me himself and talk to me?"

Maybe someone else would have started to resent the fact that everyone wanted to talk to Alec, that I wasn't good enough to solve their problems, but not me. Nobody was more conscious than me of just how poorly I was doing when it came to filling his shoes.

"I don't have an answer for you on that one, Isaac. Why don't you just tell me what you need and we'll see what we can pull together for you?"

Even I heard my voice catch on that response, there was no way that Isaac could miss it.

"What's going on, Adri?"

I suddenly wanted to just start crying. Part of me wanted desperately to just hand all of these problems off to someone else. Isaac had always felt so solid and strong. He wasn't strong enough to take over and do everything that Alec was supposed to be doing, but surely he couldn't do any worse than I was already doing.

"The Chicago pack is in ruins. Nobody has heard from Shawn or Ulrich in days. The Coun'hij has kill teams scouring the country for our people and they are scary good at finding people they shouldn't be able to find. My two best weapons are Jaclyn who refuses to pick up her phone, and Grayson who told me directly the last time I called him that he can't help me with any of my problems."

"That's not what I was talking about and you know it."

I don't know what I expected out of Isaac after listing my problems off like that, but that wasn't it. I'd just been more honest with him than I'd been with anyone else for days, and he was acting like I was trying to jerk him around.

"Sorry, Isaac, that's all you're going to get unless you're ready to come meet up with us so that I can tell you in person. I'm not saying any more over a phone line regardless of how secure you or anyone else tell me it is."

"Where is Alec?"

There was something to his tone that put my back up even further than it had been, but that was okay, it was better for me to be angry. Anger had its own set of dangers, but at least anger made me want to keep fighting rather than just giving up and waiting for the end to come.

"Not another word, Isaac, or I'll hang up on you right now and Alec can just deal with the fact that I broke my promise to him."

"He's not dead." There was an element of concern to Isaac's voice despite his certainty. It was reassuring, like maybe the old Isaac was still there underneath everything. All of the warm, fuzzy feelings in the world couldn't change the fact that the monitor had just crept up to eighty-nine percent though. I needed to get Isaac off of the phone.

"No, he's not dead. What do you need? I've got problems here that need to be dealt with."

"I'm in Louisiana. Those kill teams chased us here and then Onyx backed us into a corner. I'm about to go fight Onyx, but I know that I can't win. I was hoping that Alec could come put him down for me."

The monitor hit ninety percent and started flashing a warning that the call would be dropped in the next few seconds in order to stop the Coun'hij from locking in our position. I closed my eyes for half a second and then cradled my phone against my shoulder so that I could hit the override button on the monitor. It was risky, but this was Isaac and he'd just told me he was up against a fight that he couldn't win. I had to try and do something to help him. I desperately ran through a list of the people still calling in on a regular basis, people who might be located close enough to Ash's old home to get there in time.

"That's not going to happen, not with everything else that's going on right now, but I might be able to get some hybrids down there to help you out. I think that there are two from the Tucson pack I could shake loose along with four or five wolves."

My override had spurred Donovan's beleaguered hackers into a frenzy of activity. The risk profile was still holding steady at ninety percent, but I knew they wouldn't be able to protect us for much longer. I needed Isaac to say yes and then give me an address and a time.

Isaac sounded frustrated. "No, that isn't going to do the trick. You can't just throw bodies at this guy. He's got an ability that drops people from a dozen yards away. Sending a dozen hybrids wouldn't be enough, you'd just end up with more corpses on our side when all was said and done. I need Alec, he's the only one who can definitely neutralize Onyx."

I felt like I'd just been punched in the gut. Alec couldn't help Isaac out, but there was another option if I was willing to use it. Lori would be just as effective against Onyx as she would be against any other male. The question wasn't whether Lori could save Isaac, the question was whether she would keep Onyx alive and use him as her own personal weapon.

I opened my mouth to tell him that help was on the way, but that wasn't what came out. "I'm sorry, Isaac, I really wish there was more that we could do, but there isn't. Are you sure that there isn't some way to get the three of you out of there?"

"Not one that would let me live with myself afterwards. What about if I stall for a day or two?"

The shakes were back, but this wasn't stress or malnutrition. It was just the natural result of abandoning my friend. A tiny part of me had been trying to convince myself that we couldn't have gotten Lori down to New Orleans quickly enough, but that excuse was gone now that he'd offered to stall.

"It wouldn't make any difference. I wish it would, but there's just no way. Can you think of anything else that we could do from here that would give you a chance of getting out of there?"

"Crap. No, there isn't any other way."

"Are you sure, Isaac? I...we could really use your help back here. There aren't very many people I can trust right now."

I tried to put all of my need into the words, tried to convince Isaac to save himself since I was unwilling to risk everything to save him. It seemed like I'd almost reached him—his voice changed slightly, got a little softer—but that hope lasted only until he responded again.

"No, Adri, I just can't do that. I'm sorry, but you'll be okay. You seem like you're keeping the wheels on, just don't let on to anyone else the true extent of our problems. I'm not going to tell anyone, but if word gets out we're all going to find ourselves pretty much screwed."

"Go teach your grandma to suck eggs, Isaac. You caught me in a weak moment or I wouldn't have even told you as much as I did."

"Just make sure that you tell Alec that I'm sorry. Oh, and if Ash doesn't manage to bring Onyx down, promise me that you guys will find a way to take him down soon. He needs to be stopped before he can do more damage down here."

There were tiny dark spots on my jeans. Somehow I'd started crying without realizing it.

At least I could make sure that Isaac knew that Alec didn't hate him. It was a terribly small thing to give someone headed off to die.

"Alec already knows. He wanted me to tell you that he's already forgiven anything that needed forgiving. He hopes that you know how sorry he was that he couldn't have done more to save Jess. He still considers you one of his closest friends."

"I feel the same way. Do I have your promise that you'll see to Onyx?"

"Yeah, even if I have to pull the trigger myself. We're going to bring the Coun'hij and everyone who's been supporting them down or we'll die trying."

I didn't even have to think twice about my response, but that didn't surprise me as much as it should have. I'd been willing to do a lot worse in my quest to save Alec; it didn't seem fair to deny Isaac this one last request. Not when Donovan had the cash and the contacts to arrange it.

"The old Adri wouldn't have approved of assassination."

He was right, but that didn't matter. For a split second my mind was pulled down a different path, one where Alec's principles hadn't stopped us from taking full advantage of all of our resources. Onyx could have been killed years ago, shot from a mile away. Agony could have been assassinated as he was leaving the estate the first time he and Oblivion paid us a visit. We could have killed pack leaders all over the country who supported the Coun'hij and instituted a reign of terror that would have eclipsed anything the Coun'hij had done so far.

It was surprisingly seductive. It wouldn't have saved Alison, Jack and Sam—it wouldn't have even saved Jess' memories, but it might have saved Jasmin and Ben. If Agony's visit had been cut short then maybe Jasmin would have been able to convince Ben not to run off to New York.

I wondered how often Alec had sat alone in the darkness considering the very course I was considering in that moment. It would be so easy to remove the obstacles in the path he'd chosen, but despite the allure, I knew—just as he must have—that becoming the Coun'hij wasn't the answer. It might result in our beating them, but we'd never be able to replace them with something better if we went down that path.

It was odd, but in that instant I felt closer to Alec than I ever had before. There were very few people who could understand the temptation that was calling out for me, but he was one of them. Maybe it was true that there was a silver lining in every storm cloud. As terrible as having Dream Stealer attack Alec had been, without it I never would have really understood what it was to have the power to save someone you loved and yet still not use it because to do so would be wrong. I understood Alec in ways now that I'd never understood before.

I also understood some of what made us different. I would fight Alec's war for as long as I could, but if I ever truly became convinced that our war was hopeless then I would choose an option that would have been anathema to Alec. I would go to ground with as much cash as I could scrape together and then I would fulfill my promise to Isaac.

I'd hire it out if I could, but if that didn't work then *I* would learn how to shoot. I would kill Onyx and then I would work my way through as many of the sympathizer packs as I could before they finally caught up with me and I went to join Alec in the oblivion that waited for us when we died.

"Yeah, well, I swore a promise back in Chicago. Besides, it's been a rough couple of weeks. There are worse things than putting a bullet in the head of the kind of people we are fighting. Take care of yourself, Isaac. I'll pass on your message."

"You too, Adri."

The monitor was flashing at me as I hung up. Ninety-eight percent. I'd fulfilled what I was starting to believe would be Alec's last request. The only question was what that was going to end up costing us.

Chapter 19

Adriana Paige
Interstate 64
Western Kentucky

"You simply spent too much time on the phone, Mistress Paige. The communications suite is of no use to us now. The Coun'hij has localized us. They know where we are to within twenty or thirty miles."

"I'm sorry, Donovan, it was Isaac; I was trying to fulfill Alec's last wish."

It was like I'd slapped him. "I refuse to accept that."

"I'm not going to pretend that I've known Alec for as long as you, Donovan, but this isn't easy for me either. Look at him! Really look at him and tell me that you think he's going to make it another week."

It was cruel. Donovan had raised Alec. He was the last person who should have been forced to stand by and watch, powerless, as Alec slowly slipped away from us.

Alec's breathing had become shallow and fast, but that didn't scare me even half as much as the fact that he'd stopped fighting the restraints that we'd put on him so that he wouldn't damage anything if he started flailing about in his sleep.

"Very well, Mistress Paige. I admit that Master Alec appears to be on his last legs. What do you propose? I've been texted alerts that there are road blocks being set up on all of the major roads within thirty miles. We are quickly being surrounded and even if we succeed in breaking out of the perimeter we'll be on the run and likely be forced to deal with local and possibly even federal law enforcement. Even our resources have their limits…"

"We'll use Lori, but we won't try to break through the blockades. She'll be in the first vehicle and she'll simply tell any police at the blockade that our group isn't the one they are looking for, that it's all been a colossal mistake."

"And if there are Coun'hij enforcers there?"

"Then she will tell them to kill each other. I want her guard doubled, and I want them within arm's reach of her the entire time. If she so much as blinks wrong then we're going to be forced to kill her."

"We can't continue on like this forever, Mistress Paige. Sooner or later you're going to have to decide whether or not you can trust her."

I gave Donovan a sad smile. "She's just too dangerous, Donovan. If Alec was conscious and able to keep her honest then things would be different. Ditto if she had a better history. As it is, there is just too much chance that she's going to turn on us at the worst possible time."

"Very well, I'll begin using one of the burner phones to make the arrangements with Mallory. With any luck she'll already be there in the vehicle with Lori."

"Thanks, Donovan. Make sure that she lets Lori know that we aren't going to stand for her collecting any pawns. The humans are all to be allowed to go back to their normal lives with nothing more lasting than an order not to report that we were ever in the area. Any enforcers are to be killed on the spot."

Donovan nodded. "What about once we are past the blockade? We're going to need to leave the communications suite off for an extended period of time still if we're going to remain under the Coun'hij's radar. I'm not sure that goal is compatible with the amount of time Master Alec has left."

"Once we are outside of the Coun'hij's secure perimeter, I'll be taking Alec with me and breaking off from the rest of the group. I'll need one of the SUV's and some cash. Eighty thousand dollars should be more than enough."

"No."

"Excuse me? You agreed that I would be giving the orders around here, Donovan, you can't go changing the rules on me now."

"Is that so, Mistress Paige? Not even if you change the rules yourself? I will not let you take Alec away from the safety of the group."

"There isn't any other choice, Donovan. I have to do this."

"You're going to try and rejoin him in his dream, aren't you? Even though he didn't want you to risk it."

"Of course I am, but this is bigger than that. Part of what is keeping Lori in line is the idea that there are some lines that she can't cross, lines that will cause Alec to come after her. We can pile women around her until they are twenty deep, but all it would take is her getting her hands on a male hybrid with the right power to foil all of our security efforts.

"Alec is the one person she'll always have to be worried about. As long as you can make sure that she doesn't get her hands on Puppeteer or Dream Stealer she'll know that Alec could always cut through her defenses like they didn't even exist."

"But how will she continue to…ah, I see. You wish to introduce an element of doubt as to Master Alec's ultimate fate."

"Yeah. It's risky, but there will always be a chance that I succeeded in besting Dream Stealer and maybe that will be enough to keep her from giving into the worst inside of her."

"You really think that Alec would stay away from his people if you succeeded? He's not the kind to shirk a responsibility."

"I know, but there is a chance that I can convince him that he'll be able to do more good striking from the shadows. If the Coun'hij believes that he's dead then there is a chance that they'll lower their guard. Don't you see, Donovan, this is the best of both worlds. Regardless of whether I succeed or fail, Alec will still have created a legacy that has a chance of doing you some good. I've told you that I'm going to do my best to convince Alec to disappear if he survives, so you'll always have to wonder. Every time a group of vampires turns up dead you'll wonder if it was Alec."

"You'll have to make arrangements to make sure that your corpses don't turn up if you fail. That would ruin everything."

"I know. Program Sergio's number into my phone. I won't use him, but I'll get him to give me a list of people he thinks are trustworthy. I'll have one of them dispose of us."

Donovan looked different in that moment. Despite the gray hairs and wrinkles, he looked like a lost little boy. "Master Alec would never have contemplated something like this. If you're successful you will have turned him into something uncomfortably close to a religious figure."

"I know, he never would have wanted that for himself, but it's the best thing for our people. If things go as badly for the rebellion as I suspect they will, then they are going to need something bigger than themselves to believe in. If that means you and Mallory have to create the church of Alec Graves, then so be it."

Whatever Donovan was about to say was preempted by the ringing of the burner phone on the table next to Alec.

"I thought you said this was a clean phone, Donovan. We can't afford to get traced right now."

"I just pulled it out of the manufacturer's packaging myself this morning, Mistress Paige. It's as clean as it's possible for one of our phones to be. There is no possible way for the Coun'hij to have that number."

I frowned at the phone. Lately all of the surprises in my life had been bad ones. That didn't stop me from answering the phone though.

"Yeah?"

"I won't use names, that would be incredibly imprudent."

It was a man's voice, one with a slight accent I couldn't place, one that was vaguely familiar.

I cleared my voice, unaccountably uncomfortable. "Fine, no names, but you're going to give me an idea who it is I'm talking to. Where did we first meet?"

"I'm not sure that telling you that would mean anything, but more recently we ran into each other in a Manhattan park. I apologize—it was an unexpectedly stressful night and I wasn't at my best."

It was the old man, the one who had saved Isaac, Jasmin and me from the werewolf. I recognized his voice now, but I still wanted to be sure.

"Who were you expecting to see that night?"

"Your friend from south of the border. To be honest I'm still not sure of long-term implications of that change, but we've come much too far to try and pull out now. There's nothing to do but continue forward the best we can and hope that things turn out okay."

"What do you mean by that?"

"I'm sorry, that's not something I can tell you right now."

"Then why did you call?"

"I called because you're about to make a very big mistake. You're planning on taking your fiancé and leaving your friends. That's the right decision, but you need to go now, within the next fifteen minutes, or everything will unravel."

"How could you possibly know what I have planned? Do you have some kind of bug planted in here?"

"No, my dear. There are no bugs in your vehicle. As to how I know, you're already starting to suspect, but something is holding you back from believing."

"If what I suspect is true, then you should have called ten minutes ago before I told my friend my plan. It would have done a lot to increase your credibility."

"Would it? I think you're just stubborn enough to get everyone you care about killed just to prove that you make your own decisions. I needed to call now, after you'd already made up your mind, not earlier when the decision was still uncertain."

"You're asking me to take a lot on trust for someone I've met only once, twice if you're to be believed."

"Indeed, but I did save your life the last time we met. Surely that buys me some kind of credibility. If I'd wanted you or your friends dead, I could have easily accomplished that very thing merely by failing to intervene on your behalf."

"That's fair, but before I decide one way or another I need to know why you're doing this."

"I'm helping because I'm an incredible fan of you and your fiancé both."

"That's not much of an answer."

"I'm sorry. There is more to my reasoning than that, but the rest of the answer isn't something that you're capable of understanding. Will you heed my advice?"

"Yeah. Call me crazy, but I will. Anything else you want to tell me?"

"Only that you and your fiancé must go by yourselves. Anyone you bring with you will be killed and could very well result in everything being thrown off."

Donovan looked like he was going to pop a cork. He'd been obviously unhappy with the idea of me taking Alec away from him and his displeasure had only gotten worse as my caller had told me that I needed to leave even before I'd been planning on leaving. The idea that I might actually agree to this, might deliver Alec into the hands of someone Donovan didn't know or trust, was obviously too much.

I sighed. "You don't ask for much, do you?"

My sarcasm seemed to throw him for a loop. "I would not ask it if it were not vitally important."

"Yeah, I know. I wasn't planning on taking anyone else with us."

"Good, this isn't the last time we will talk."

"Yeah, unless we're off your script more than you think. All right, unless you're going to tell me something else—something useful—I need to go deal with an impending mutiny."

Donovan waited until I hung up before speaking. "I know that I agreed to follow your orders, but I must protest this decision in the strongest way possible. This is likely one gigantic trap."

"It's a possibility."

"And yet you are going to go through with your plan of leaving the rest of the convoy?"

"Yes, Donovan, I am. I can't explain why, but for the first time in weeks I feel like I'm doing the right thing."

"You're acting on faith, Mistress Paige. I understand the desire to put your fate in the hands of someone else, the desire to give up the crushing responsibility that you've been forced to bear, but this isn't the right choice. Don't give up now."

That hurt more than I'd expected it to. I'd thought Donovan had been proud of me, thought that he'd been happy with my efforts not to collapse under the stress this time around. Apparently I'd been wrong. I'd given up once and therefore I'd failed to measure up. I knew I was no Alec Graves, but apparently I was much less in Donovan's eyes than I'd realized.

"It's nice to know how you really feel, Donovan. Now that we have that out of the way, are you going to tie me up on the bed next to Alec or are you going to get out of my way? Those are your only two options, because I'm done talking about this."

Donovan stared at me with a stiffness that he hadn't displayed since my first few days at the estate. Donovan was always a little stiff with everyone, but this was more than that. This was Donovan's way of retreating into propriety, his way of keeping everyone around him safely confined in little boxes where they belonged.

"I will not break my sworn word, Mistress Paige. Nor will I attack a woman who has offered me no harm, no matter how much I might disagree with her actions."

"Well then, I guess we're not as different as we might have thought. You've got your own brand of blind faith too, yours is just in the rules of courtesy."

I brushed past Donovan without another word. I knew that if I survived I was going to regret what I'd just said, but I was too angry to care right then.

"James, could you please strap Alec to the rigid stretcher that has wheels on the ends of the handles? I'm going to need to move Alec and that's the only way I can think of to do it by myself, especially since I only have one working hand."

He gave me an odd look, but he didn't argue, which was a miniature miracle in and of itself. I pulled my phone back out as I walked up to Ruby who was driving again.

"Ruby, be looking for a spot where we can safely pull off to the side of the road, please. It doesn't need to be for long, but it needs to happen in the next five minutes."

Ruby opened her mouth as though she was going to ask me what was going on, and then closed her mouth again and simply nodded. Addison wasn't as timid.

"Where are you taking Alec?"

"Despite knowing full well that we are in the middle of a secure perimeter established by the Coun'hij, a perimeter that she can't possibly escape on her own, Mistress Paige is going to leave the convoy and strike out on her own with Master Alec."

I shot Donovan a dirty look, but before I could respond Addison jumped back in. "No, that's not acceptable. Samantha would never countenance something like that."

"In case you've forgotten, Samantha Graves is currently in a coma, and up until recently she couldn't have cared less about what happened to Alec or Rachel either one. I don't think her wishes should weigh into this decision."

"She's back now and eventually she's going to wake up again. When that happens I'm not going to be the one to tell her that you ran off with her son and got him killed."

A phone was ringing, but I ignored it.

"Fine, then don't tell her. I'm sure Donovan will happily tell her how foolish I was."

"I don't know why Donovan has let things get this far, but I'm not going to just stand by and let you walk off with Alec."

"Don't try and stop me, Addison. I'm warning you."

"You don't have your precious gun, Adri. I may be old and half crippled, but I'm still a shape shifter. I'm still going to be more than strong and fast enough to stop you."

I shifted slightly, moving my weight over the balls of my feet.

"Stop right now!"

James didn't sound amused at the fact that his mom and I had been seconds away from trying to kill each other with our bare hands. He held up a burner phone, brandishing it as though it was a magic talisman that could force the two of us into compliance with his will.

"Go ahead, Rach. I think we've got their attention finally."

Based on the looks on Addison, Andrew and Donovan's faces, I wasn't the only one he'd taken off guard. It wasn't until I heard Rachel's voice that I realized the phone was on speaker mode.

"What just happened, Adri?"

"Addison just threatened to throw down against me."

"No, that's not what I'm talking about. Something big just changed."

Donovan cleared his throat. "Mistress Paige just took a call from an unknown individual who counseled her to leave the rest of us and strike out on her own. She wants to heed his advice against the better judgment of every other person here."

"Hmm, so that's not what changed. For a minute there I was worried that you'd decided to stay with the rest of the caravan. You're still taking Alec with you, right?"

I was experiencing a weird sense of déjà vu. It took me a couple of tries to respond. "Yeah, that was my plan. Are you saying that I'm right? That I need to leave just like I'd originally planned on doing?"

"Five minutes ago I would have said yes, but I'm not so sure now, Adri. You've changed everything somehow. All I know is that before everything went dark, you leaving was the best path. Now I'm not so sure. You're still planning on taking James, right?"

"I was never planning on taking James. This is supposed to just be Alec and me, especially after the call I just had. He said that anyone else I brought along would be killed."

Rach didn't seem to hear me. "James, you'll go with her, won't you?"

Donovan didn't give James a chance to respond. "Mistress Rachel, your place is with us. When will you be returning home?"

"I'm not sure I'll ever be returning home, Donovan."

"That is unacceptable. Your mother needs you."

For the briefest of moments the hurt child seeped through Rachel's newfound confidence. "My mother has never needed me, Donovan. I doubt she even knows that I'm gone."

"You're wrong, Mistress Rachel. She is much improved, she seems to be back to her old self and she's going to need you even more once Alec is gone."

Rachel was silent for several seconds. "You do know your audience, Donovan. Out of all the things you could have possibly trolled out there to shake my resolution, that is the only one that had a chance of succeeding."

"Have I succeeded? Will you return to us?"

"No, Donovan. We all have sacrifices to make—apparently mine are more numerous than I'd realized."

"I will not allow Mistress Paige to take your brother away."

"Poor Donovan. So scared of facing a future without your wards, a future where you've failed in the task my father laid across your shoulders so many years ago. You can't save Alec now. Nothing you can do will stop the inevitable from playing out. You need to let Adri take him away. Her plan is the best option we have left to us."

"It will work then? She'll convince everyone he's still alive even after he's dead?"

Donovan sounded like someone who'd lost their faith, someone who was desperately looking for *something* to believe in.

"I can't see that, Donovan."

"What can you see, Rach? If I go with Adri am I really going to die like she said?" James sounded oddly detached. There was none of the anger that had characterized him for so long.

"I don't know, James. I know what was supposed to happen a few minutes ago, but that's gone dark to me and with every second that passes we are further and further away from the future I thought I could see."

"You're not coming off as a very good seer, Rach. If you really want to convince people to go throw themselves into hopeless situations you need to practice your delivery."

"I never said I was a seer, James. I'm not here to take away people's choices. I'm just trying to nudge you all to the best possible outcome."

"The best outcome for who?"

"I'm not sure. Will you go with Adri?"

"In the future you could see before everything went dark, did I survive what comes next?"

Rachel's voice was strangely gentle when she answered. "It doesn't matter, James. The future isn't set in stone. The real question is whether or not you trust me when I say that you need to go with them or things will go much worse for everyone you care about."

Addison apparently felt like the conversation had gone far enough. "Nobody is going anywhere. Alec is staying here, as is my son. If you really think you can…"

"Be quiet, Mother. I'm going with them. Ruby, get this bus pulled over. Adri, call up Mallory and get us a car. You heard Rachel, we're getting further and further away from the future she's trying to guide us down."

Chapter 20

Adriana Paige
Interstate 64
Western Kentucky

Donovan and Addison weren't any happier about the fact that I was leaving and taking Alec with me, but now that I had James backing me up there wasn't anything they could do about it. We'd been all getting along and living by the rule of law for so long that I think we'd nearly forgotten that James was the only healthy hybrid left among the core leadership group. Now that his mind was made up, even Addison could see the futility of trying to argue with him.

My call with Mallory was short and to the point. I asked her to detach a single SUV and have it stop behind our RV while the rest of the convoy went on ahead, albeit at a much reduced speed. The vehicle exchange went without any problems, and five minutes after James had decided to throw in with me, the SUV's previous occupants were safely inside of the RV with Donovan and the rest, and James, Alec and I were driving cross-country with the SUV's lights off.

We drove the first half hour in silence, James because he was concentrating on picking a path through the terrain that wouldn't leave us with a flat tire, and me because I was so worried about what the jostling might be doing to Alec. Once James found a small country road things got better and he was able to speed up at the same time that the ride got much smoother.

"I'm sorry you didn't get a chance to say goodbye to Dom."

James shrugged. "It's for the best this way. I'm not a huge fan of big, mushy goodbyes. Hopefully if I survive this, Dom will forgive me. Anyway, you heard Rachel, we didn't exactly have very much time. Where are we headed by the way?"

"I'm not sure. Really, we just need to find a city. It doesn't matter which, just one that is big enough that Alec and I will be able to disappear for a month or so. Once you drop us off you can go to ground yourself for a couple of weeks, after which Donovan should have Alec's phone up and running again. You should be back with Dom before the month is over."

"What about this town?"

It took me a couple of seconds to realize what he was talking about; my eyes just weren't as good as his, so it was a lot harder for me to pick out the darkened silhouettes of the buildings that were just now rising up from the horizon.

"I don't know, James. The entire town doesn't look like it has any buildings over two stories. That feels like the kind of place where people pay attention to their neighbors. Not only that, we're still awfully close to where we left everyone else. The last thing I want is to still be inside of the Coun'hij's perimeter if they decide to do some kind of door-to-door search."

"Doesn't that violate the Constitution?"

"Probably, but I'm not sure that would stop the Coun'hij, not when they might be able to just scent-track me to my door."

"Good point. Do you mind if we go ahead and stop for gas here even though it's not your final destination? We're down to just over a quarter tank, which isn't going to be enough to make it very far if we do end up with a kill team trailing us."

"Do you think there's even a working gas station here? The closer we get the more I realize just how dead this town looks. Shouldn't there be more lights?"

James shrugged again. He was nothing if not laconic, but after a second he went ahead and answered my question.

"The buildings we're headed towards seem to all be industrial construction, and most of them look abandoned. I think things will start looking a little more lively once we get into the center of town."

"Okay, but let's not get too deep into the town. I'm perfectly happy with a quiet gas station on the edge of everything if we can find it."

"Noted."

As it turned out, the first gas station we came across fit the bill well enough that I motioned James to go ahead and turn into it. James climbed out and started pumping gas without having to be asked.

I was feeling pretty good about how things were going—right up until the white and blue police car pulled in behind us. I tried to act casual, tried not to draw any attention to myself, but I instantly started shaking.

There was a good chance that this particular cop wasn't even looking for us, but all it would take was for him to see Alec. One glimpse of an unconscious, restrained man in our backseat would be more than enough to get us hauled in for questioning.

I tried to keep a surreptitious eye on the young-looking police officer out of the passenger side mirror as he started fueling up his vehicle. The SUV's tinted windows were a godsend inasmuch as they stopped anyone from being able to look inside of the vehicle, but right now they also meant that James couldn't see me trying to get his attention.

It boggled the mind that he hadn't already seen the police officer. If nothing else, by now he should have been able to smell the gun oil on the cop's gun.

"James. James, can you hear me? There's a cop behind us!"

Apparently I'd managed to be just loud enough for James to hear me without alerting the cop. James stiffened slightly and then casually looked over his shoulder. He stopped the flow of fuel into the SUV and turned to rack the hose, but he was actually moving *too* slow.

It was understandable. In a crisis situation, with all that adrenaline surging through their system, it was even harder for a shape shifter to avoid moving with the kind of preternatural speed that gave them away as being more than just human. James was trying to move slowly enough not to draw attention to himself, but he'd gone too far the other way, and I watched as the police officer behind us looked up and saw James slowly put the nozzle back into its receptacle.

The officer stepped away from his vehicle, moving in our direction, as James opened the driver's-side door.

"Evening."

"Evening, officer."

"That's a nice rig you've got there. Looks like you're from out of state—what brings you through our little town?"

"We're visiting some family in New York."

"Oh, that's great. What's the occasion?"

James stopped with one foot inside the vehicle. I wanted to reach over and pull him into the SUV so we could make a run for it, but I knew he was right. Leaving would just guarantee that we would have the police after us. The only way forward was to make nice and hope that we didn't make the officer's Spidey sense start tingling.

"My brother just had his first child, and my wife is really good friends with my sister-in-law, so I'm taking a week and a half off under protest so we can go out there and help them with the new arrival."

James was an even better liar than I'd realized. He put exactly the right amount of unhappiness into his voice when talking about being forced to take time off of work, but rather than just walking on in to the convenience store like I'd been hoping he would, the police officer was walking up to my door.

"You headed into a busy time at work? What is it that you do?"

"It's always a busy time at work. I work in finance. Nothing big ticket or anything—I don't have enough experience for the really high-profile stuff, but so far it's paying the bills."

"That's all any of us can ask for, right? Still, with a job like that I'm surprised you didn't save yourself the hassle of driving. It's got to hurt putting so many miles on such a nice car."

An edge had crept into the officer's voice. He was suspicious of us—probably had been suspicious of us the entire time.

"I would have loved to have flown, but Alice has a phobia of flying, and there was no way I was going to get her on a bus, so this was the only option."

"That's a real shame that she's got a fear of flying...what's the technical name for that?"

James shook his head, a perfect picture of innocence, but I could tell by the way his fist tightened around the steering wheel that he knew the game was nearly up.

"I never can remember. I can do net present value calculations in my sleep, but all the Latin in the medical terms just goes in one ear and out the other."

"Why don't you ask your wife to roll down her window so that I can ask her what the proper name of her particular phobia is?"

I wanted to scream, but James' expression didn't change in the slightest. "You heard the nice man, Alice. Roll down your window so that you can tell him the name of your condition."

The window came down with the perfect smoothness only found in top-of-the-line vehicles, and as soon as our eyes met I knew that he'd seen my face before. My time sense ratcheted to high alert as the officer stepped backwards to buy himself room to draw his gun.

It felt like he was moving in slow motion and I seemed to have forever in which to analyze and discard countless plans. James was on the other side of the car from us, which meant there was going to be very little he could do. Hybrids are fast, but he wasn't going to want to shift forms if he could avoid it, and even in his hybrid form he wasn't going to be able to outrun a bullet.

"Show me your hands! Now!"

I put my right hand out of the window. "The other one is broken."

It was as though he couldn't hear me. Maybe it was all of the adrenaline in his system, or maybe he just didn't believe me.

"I said show me your hands!"

"I can't! This hand is paralyzed—it doesn't work anymore."

That finally seemed to get through to him. The police officer blinked and then pointed at my door with his gun. "Open your door from the outside and then come out and face the car."

I looked at James, who had both hands pointed straight up.

"Don't look at him, look at me! Now do what I told you to do."

I nodded and reached around so I could open my door. Once I was standing against the side of the car, the officer motioned James around to my side of the SUV, and then he cautiously approached us and started frisking James. I was desperately trying to come up with a plan that didn't end with us getting shot or imprisoned, when James suddenly spun in place and made a grab for the officer's gun.

Even with my time sense ramped all of the way up, I still almost couldn't follow James' movements. He grabbed the gun with one hand and the officer's wrist with the other, and then threw the poor man into the side of our vehicle with enough force that I was half afraid he'd broken the officer's neck.

As the gun hit the ground, James picked the officer up and carried him back to the police car. "Get back in our car, Adri!"

My shakes hadn't ever gone completely away, but they were back now with a vengeance. It took me two tries to get my door open. By the time I managed to pull myself inside of the SUV, James was back and he had the officer's radio in one hand and a police-issue gun in the other.

I reached out for the tough-minded persona that had gotten me through so much in the last few weeks, but she'd deserted me. Fighting against the Coun'hij was one thing. Being an accomplice to knocking a police officer unconscious was something else altogether. The police officer had just been doing his job. I felt like we'd crossed a line we couldn't ever come back from.

James dropped the gun onto his lap and then set the radio on the center console. "Just focus on your breathing, Adri. He's going to have a massive headache when he wakes up, but other than that he's going to be okay. It's his own fault really. If he'd followed procedure and called us in I wouldn't have even tried something like that, not with a dozen other cops on the way. He must have been fresh out of the academy."

"What do we do now?"

"We get as far away from the scene of the crime as we can without drawing attention to ourselves and we listen to his radio so that we will know if someone saw what just happened and calls it in."

"How can you be so calm, James? You could have been shot. And we're now criminals."

James started the SUV into motion without putting on his seatbelt. "I'm not skilled with hand-to-hand in human form, but weapon control and disarmament is something that Donovan made all of us practice years ago. As for the part about being criminals, he recognized your face, Adri. You're already a wanted woman."

"I think I liked it better when you didn't talk as much. In fact…"

James shushed me as the radio crackled to life.

"All units, we have an officer down at the Gas and Grub on Second Street. The officer involved appeared to be making an arrest at the time he was attacked. The perpetrators are in a black SUV—probably an Escalade—and were last seen headed north."

James muttered something I was pretty sure Dom wouldn't have approved of, and then pulled the SUV into a dark alley. "Time to lose this ride—grab your gun and whatever cash Donovan gave you—leave everything else. I'll grab Alec."

I reached back for the small black backpack purse that had all of the liquid assets, and then opened up my door and climbed out.

"Our fingerprints are going to be all over this vehicle, James. They are going to know we were here and it's going to be pretty hard to get away on foot…"

"I know, but we're going to have to deal with one problem at a time, Adri, and they've made our car."

James produced a blade from his pocket and sheared through the nylon restraints holding Alec to the stretcher. Alec had lost so much weight since Dream Stealer had first attacked him that James was easily able to pull him out of the SUV using just one hand.

"Now stand here next to me and we'll carry him between us. It's still not perfect, but it at least has a chance of looking like we're just three friends out for a stroll—that or two friends carrying a third friend who's so drunk they passed out."

"You think that will really work?"

"I don't know—depends on how close they are. I'm sure I don't have anything better than that though, and we need to get moving while I look for another vehicle to steal."

James grabbed the police radio and hung it from his front pocket, and then we took off with Alec's arms slung over our shoulders and James supporting all of Alec's weight with an arm around his waist.

We headed east and made it two blocks before I saw the first set of flashing lights. The sirens had been headed towards the gas station since before we'd even started out on foot, but they'd somehow managed to almost become background noise even just after such a short time. Seeing the lights made me freeze up, but James just shifted his arm from Alec's waist to mine and pulled me along.

"You can't stop, Adri, we don't want to draw attention to ourselves."

James turned right, putting a building between us and the police car that had turned onto our street a moment before.

"They're responding too fast. A town this small shouldn't have so many cops on call, not on such short notice. Come on, we're going to have to travel through the center of the block if we're going to have any chance of getting outside of their search perimeter—it's only a matter of time now before they find the car."

I followed James between two dark houses and then watched as he stripped down to his ha'bit and shifted into his hybrid form.

"Is this a good idea, James?"

"No, but it's the only way we're going to be able to travel fast enough. Right now they are running two search patterns, one assuming that we are still in our vehicle, and one assuming that we are on foot. Once they find our vehicle they are going to collapse down to just one search pattern and they know exactly how fast two people on foot are capable of moving. We've got to move faster than we have been. Put my clothes in your backpack and clip the radio to your belt. We need to be moving."

James slung Alec over his massive shoulder with one arm, and then used the other to pick me up. James waited just long enough for me to wrap my good arm around his neck and then we were off.

I wouldn't have believed it if I hadn't experienced it for myself, but James tore through the yard we were standing in and then cleared the six-foot privacy fence in a powerful leap that shouldn't have been possible while carrying one person, let alone two. The next yard had a German Shepherd in it, but the poor dog only got one bark out before James let out a deep, menacing growl that shut it up.

It was hard sometimes to remember just how powerful and graceful a hybrid really was. Lately everything had been about the hybrids with abilities. People like Jaclyn and Lori, like Grayson and Puppeteer. I'd had to mold all of my plans around the heavies who had no counter, but in doing so I'd lost sight of just what a single, 'normal' hybrid was capable of.

James was already breathing hard from the added strain of sprinting while carrying several hundred extra pounds, but he didn't seem to be slowing down at all yet. Motion-activated lights flashed on in some of the yards that we passed, but we were moving so fast that I was confident very few of the people living on the block had looked up in time to see anything more than a dark shadow disappearing over their fence.

We jumped a low set of bushes and then James skidded to a stop behind a storage shed.

"What's going on?"

"I can hear a car headed this way, sounds like what the local police department drives."

"You can actually tell different cars apart just by how they sound?"

"Yep. You can too; you've just never stopped to think about it."

Before I could respond to that, a police car drove by slowly with its lights off. Score another point for James. Even if I'd had James' speed and strength, I would have just kept running blindly and been captured eventually.

James stood up and darted across the road as if Alec and I combined still weighed nothing. I'd been wrong, he had been slowing down, but our pause—brief though it was—was sufficient to give him back most of his speed, and this block was full of yards with fences that were only five feet tall. We blurred forward so fast that my eyes started tearing up, but I wasn't about to complain, not when our very survival relied on James' speed.

We worked our way across ten more blocks, sometimes pausing at the edge of the street before running across, but with each block we covered the police presence seemed to get further and further behind us.

After ten blocks I started to lose count. I'd been trying to support as much of my weight as possible so that James could use his arm to help balance himself, but I was starting to get tired. It was harder than I'd expected it to be with only one arm. I couldn't give myself any kind of break so my weight just seemed to grow with each passing second.

As we crossed another street and reached what I thought was block fourteen, the radio crackled back to life.

"We've located the suspects' vehicle. They can't have covered more than a mile and a quarter. I want a cordon from Saint Clair all the way down to Hummingbird and from Vexor Avenue all the way over to Redwood Street. We've got enough cars to put bodies on alternate intersections and K9 units are on their way to the abandoned vehicle as we speak. Hold the line for another half an hour, boys and girls, and we'll have these pieces of scum in cuffs."

"Is that good?"

James nodded. He was back to breathing hard enough that I thought for a moment that I wasn't going to get any more of a response than that, but in between gasps he choked one out.

"I think so. I don't know the local street names, but we're coming up on two miles now. That should put us outside of their perimeter, which means that we can go to ground pretty soon and start looking for a car to steal."

"Do you think they've pulled down the road blocks?"

"No, not yet. They probably won't pull them down until they catch us, but I'll try and steal something that can go cross-country."

I started counting again, partly so I would feel like I had something to do and partly in the hopes that it would distract me from the burning sensation in my arm as my muscles started to shake. We made it four more blocks before James slowed again. At that point a terrible thought hit me.

"What about the dogs, James? Are they going to be able to track us?"

"Yeah, a dog will track a shape shifter. They may have a little trouble with the spot where I shifted, but a good dog will figure it out and follow the new scent trail because there isn't anything else leaving the spot. That's part of why we need to steal a car."

"How much further can you run?"

"Not much further—at least not carrying both of you like this. If it was just me, I could go for a few more miles at this pace, but we're starting to get pretty close to that industrial section of town that we saw on our way in. There aren't going to be many cars out there, so if we don't find something soon we're going to be out of luck."

"You're just full of good news."

"Given what we're up against, I think I'm being positively optimistic."

There was a hint of laughter to James' voice and I found myself revising my opinion of him slightly. I'd always assumed that there was more to him than met the eye—it was the only explanation given that Dom liked him—but this was the first time I was getting a chance to see this side of him. He was surprisingly likeable when he wasn't glowering and angry.

"Are you actually having fun, James?"

"You'd be surprised just how liberating it is to go into a situation that you don't expect to survive, Adri. Once you get over being sad about all the things you aren't going to get to do, it becomes kind of fun to see what you can get away with during the time you have left. Now hush, I need to find a vehicle that is old enough I'll have a chance of stealing it without any tools."

We made it two more blocks with James frowning at every car that presented itself, before the radio clicked back on. *"All units, the*

FBI will be taking over the manhunt. You'll be taking your orders from Special Agent in Charge Cruthers."

The voice on the radio didn't sound particularly happy to have someone else muscling in on the party, but it also didn't sound like they had much choice but to cooperate. A second later a new voice took over.

"Your estimates regarding the suspect's speed are drastically low. In the time involved, it is very likely that the perpetrators have gone nearly three miles. The dogs are headed..."

There was a pause as someone whispered something into the new arrival's ear. I caught something about a radio and an injured police officer, and then suddenly our radio started squealing. James stopped and set me down so he could rip the radio off of my belt and tear it in half. That didn't stop the terrible screech coming out of the radio, but James then threw the radio against the ground with enough force to leave a dent in the asphalt and that did the trick.

"What just happened?"

"They realized that the officer we disabled was missing his radio and cut it out of the circuit."

"I didn't even know that was possible."

James picked me back up and started across the street at a sprint. "We could still listen into their frequency if we had another radio, they haven't done anything to encrypt their signal, they just sent a kill signal to this particular radio. Honestly, I'm surprised that a town this small has that kind of tech, but that's not our main problem."

"What do you mean?"

"We've only been on foot for about ten minutes. Expanding the perimeter out to three miles from our car is crazy. That's barely over three minute miles. That's my best speed over a medium distance on my good days when I'm by myself, running unburdened."

"You mean they know you're a hybrid?"

"Yeah, if that's a real FBI agent then I'll eat my socket wrench. The Coun'hij must have found a way to impersonate the bureau. We've got a kill squad in the area and if they haven't already picked up our scent trail they won't be more than a minute or two away from picking it up. We've probably got no more than seven or eight minutes before they catch us. We have to find a vehicle right now."

James jumped us over another set of hedges and then suddenly we were face to face with a large, eight-foot chain-link fence that was topped with razor wire. For a second I almost thought that James was still going to jump it, but at the last second he slashed out with his right hand and sheared through a large section of links.

The opening he'd created was more than big enough to let me through, but it was still too small for a hybrid. I dropped down to the ground and pushed through the fence as I felt a flare of energy behind me and turned to find that James had shifted back to human form.

I looked around as James followed me through the opening in the fence. I must have lost count of a few blocks somewhere along the way because we weren't just *near* the abandoned industrial section of the city, we were actually there.

I was standing in the middle of a large open space that was full of weeds and piles of metal, scrap or otherwise. More importantly though, I could see a large flat-bed truck thirty yards away from us.

"What about that truck, James? Is that something you can hotwire without any tools?"

James manhandled Alec through the hole in the fence before looking in the direction I was pointing. "Yeah, assuming that it still runs and that it's got enough gas to get us more than ten or fifteen miles, it should work. Come on."

James shifted forms again and threw Alec over his shoulder as his long, hybrid legs ate up the distance between him and the truck.

I followed along as best I could, carefully dividing my attention between the ground in front of me and James' actions as he reached the truck. James put his fist through the driver's-side window, shattering it with a casual display of force as he lowered Alec to the ground.

As I picked my way around a piece of machinery that looked like it belonged on a farm back in the early eighteenth century, James used his claws to tear through the plastic sheath around the steering column. A second later he'd also slashed through a bundle of wires and then he shifted back to human form and pulled the door open.

The sound of howling wolves told me that the Coun'hij was getting closer. I hurried forward and stopped next to Alec as James started twisting wires together.

"I wish Dom was here, she's better at this kind of stuff; I'm much more at home working on an engine."

A second later James struck two of the wires together and the engine roared to life as a long, blue spark shot from one wire to the other. The engine turning over was one of the most welcome sounds I'd ever heard, but it nearly cost James his life because it covered up the sound of the approaching shape shifter.

James had just bent down to pick up Alec when something—probably a stray breeze—tipped him off to the fact that we had company. James straight-armed me, shoving me to the ground at the same time that he threw himself in the opposite direction.

The thing that hit the side of the truck had started out as a slender, gray form that sliced through the darkness with the speed and grace you only saw from a wolf, but by the time it collided with the driver's door it had shifted to a six-and-a-half-foot-tall tower of muscle and claws.

The force of the impact rocked the heavy truck on its suspension, but I hardly noticed because of the sudden lance of pain that pierced my leg. The hybrid had speared me with one of his toe talons, but it was nothing more than an afterthought—he didn't have time for more than that because James had already shifted forms and thrown himself at the enforcer.

Watching two hybrids fight had always been a surreal experience, but for the first time I could remember I was actually able to follow what was happening. James shoved the other hybrid back into the truck as his claws tore into the enforcer's arms and chest. I somehow retained enough presence of mind to roll to one side, putting more distance between myself and the fighting. The ferocity of James' attack was sufficient to keep the enforcer off balance for a fraction of a second, but James was slightly shorter and less bulky than his opponent.

The enforcer blocked one of James' slashes and then ducked under the next attack and suddenly they were circling each other nearly ten yards away from the truck. They were both bleeding now, but James was continually falling back before his enemy's onslaught.

James was the one circling now, trying to work the perimeter, dashing forward and back in an effort to create an opening in the enforcer's defenses, but with every second that passed he was picking up new wounds. The enforcer suddenly blurred into motion, slapping aside James' claws and then sinking his fist into James' side.

Before James could react and try to get his other hand into play, the enforcer grabbed his wrist and threw James into a pile of large metal pipes. It took a lot to break even the smaller bones in a hybrid body, but I heard something snap inside of James as he collided, and I knew he was going to be even more outclassed now than he'd been up to this point.

I could still feel blood trickling out of the hole in my leg, and I knew I'd already lost too much blood, but that all paled against the fact that James was only seconds from death and with him gone, Alec and I would be following him within heartbeats.

Somehow my pistol had made it into my hands without a conscious decision on my part to pull it out of my waistband. I knew next to nothing about aiming a gun, so I didn't aim it; I just pointed it in the bigger hybrid's direction and pulled the trigger.

The kick as the first bullet left the gun was startling. It wasn't painful, but between that and the shockwave of sound that washed over me it felt as though I'd been struck. A tiny part of me tried to drop the gun, but the cold, in-control persona that had gotten me through everything that had been thrown at me since Alec had been shot was in the driver's seat and she calmly pulled the trigger again and again.

My time sense was as hyped up as it had ever been—I was actually able to see the path the bullets took through the night sky, a dull-gray bar of distortion no bigger around than a pencil. It made it incredibly easy to adjust my aim. The first bullet had missed, but it had still served a purpose in that it had stopped the enforcer from going after James. The second bullet took the massive hybrid in the chest, but after that he started moving towards me and things got harder.

He was moving erratically so as to make it harder for me to hit him or else he would have been on top of me after the third and fourth shots missed, but then I managed to anticipate where he was going and I shot him twice more in the chest.

The enforcer was less than two steps away from me when James crashed into him from the side, slamming him into the side of the truck with so much force that the driver's door crumpled like cheap tin. This time I heard bones break inside of the *enforcer's* body, but that was all just an afterthought. James' claws punched into the enforcer's chest and a second later the bigger hybrid dropped bonelessly to the ground in a way that I knew meant he wouldn't be getting up.

James ripped the ruined driver's door free of the truck, picked Alec up—heedless of the damage his claws were doing to Alec's fragile human flesh—and slid him into the cab of the truck.

"Get up, Adri, those shots are going to have every cop in the city here within seconds."

I slipped my gun into my sling and tried to get to my feet, but my right leg just wouldn't work. A second later James was there, now in human form, and I was being tossed into the truck next to Alec.

"Adri, you're going to have to apply pressure to your leg, if I stop to bandage you we'll be caught for sure."

I couldn't get the words I wanted to come out, so I settled for just nodding. I felt remarkably numb considering what I'd just been through, but something told me that James' orders were important. I pushed against the hole in the top of my leg with my one good hand, but that wasn't going to do anything about the hole in the bottom of my leg.

I unexpectedly found my voice and turned back to James. "It's not stopping—I'm still losing blood out of the bottom of my leg."

"Crap! You should have said something. Here, stick your hand underneath your leg and I'll apply pressure from the top."

I got my hand underneath my leg and then nearly passed out from the pain as James reached over and pushed down with a good chunk of his two hundred pounds.

"I'm sorry, Adri. I know that probably hurts, but you've already lost a lot of blood and I need to keep enough inside of you that I'll have enough to work with once we finally get a chance to stop and work on you."

James had looked away from the road to check on me, so I was the first to see the huge, furred figure step out of the shadows and onto the dirt road in front of us. My gasp brought James around though and he stepped on the accelerator, obviously intending on running over this latest member of the Coun'hij kill team.

The ancient truck leaped forward as the engine roared in protest, and then we were practically on top of the enforcer. James threw himself towards me at the last second, trying to make sure that he was out of the reach of the hybrid, and I realized that he'd never actually expected to be able to hit the enforcer.

He was right. The red-furred hybrid spun to one side just before the truck would have smashed into him, and then slashed at James. I saw it all happen in painful slow motion. His claws took James in the leg, tearing through skin and muscle, but even I could tell that it wouldn't be a lethal injury. I thought for a split second that James' plan had worked, that we were going to be able to get safely past the hybrid, and then a jolt of energy surged out of the enforcer's claws.

I only caught the fringes of the shock, but it was still enough to make my heart stutter and to force every single one of my muscles to simultaneously contract as though my body was trying to rip itself apart. It was much, much worse for James.

The hand that had been pressing against the top of my thigh shot up and hit me in the face hard enough that I saw stars, at the same time that James jerked the wheel to the right. There was a single crystal-clear second in which things were quiet enough that I heard James stop breathing, and then we slammed into the side of the building at more than thirty miles per hour.

The crunch of broken metal and shattering bones was nothing less than horrifying. James was ejected from the car just as my torso hit the dash with enough force that I felt most of my ribs break. Alec hit a split second later, and the sound made me want to be physically sick, but I couldn't seem to conjure up the determination required to get my body working well enough to check on him.

The seconds leading up to the crash seemed to be seared onto my mind. We'd hit the building at a shallow angle—in fact, if James had been able to cut the wheel a little more to the right we would have gone in through the door we'd just shattered rather than slamming to a stop against the structural steel that had supported the door's hinges.

MARKED

The image of the door being flung out of our path a split second before the truck wrapped itself around the large steel support played itself over and over in my mind. I'd already been in shock from the fight. I didn't think it was possible to go into double shock, but my mind felt like it had stripped a gear. It spun over and over again without ever catching on anything.

The sound of the truck's passenger door being ripped off of its hinges brought me back to myself enough that I was able to turn my head and meet the red hybrid's eyes. They were an inhuman yellow that seemed to show no remorse for what he was planning on doing. The hybrid reached towards Alec with claws that gleamed in the faint moonlight.

"Not so fast."

The words came a split second before a dark-skinned hand grabbed hold of the hybrid's wrist and threw him deeper into the darkness of the building. It all happened so fast that even with my augmented time sense I was still left confused and struggling to put the pieces together. I had vague impressions of a clean-shaven head, but that didn't make any sense. No human could possibly be strong enough to pick a hybrid up and throw them like that.

Even a shape shifter in human form or a vampire would have a hard time casually slinging around that much weight, but the flashes of action that had stayed with me confirmed that my savior was male and undeniably human-looking.

Whoever he was, he turned and shot after the enforcer with a speed that was every bit as fast as any hybrid I'd ever encountered, and it only took a moment before he was deep enough into the building that I had no hope of following the fight other than by the enforcer's growls and the sound of flesh impacting against metal.

Just as I started looking down to check on Alec, I saw the first of the odd, blue flashes of light. At first I thought what I was seeing was the result of the red hybrid cutting loose with another massive charge of electricity, but the flashes went on and on. It was still possible that what I was seeing was the Taser-like power the hybrid had displayed when he'd incapacitated James, but I was having a hard time imagining a situation where any living being would be able to absorb those kinds of repeated shocks and still be able to go on fighting.

Still, there was something almost electrical in the hue and cadence of the light pulses I was watching. It reminded me of the time in Minnesota when I'd been sent into the shop class with a question for one of the students from my English teacher. The flickering shadows dancing across the ground reminded me of watching someone use an arc welder.

It was the feeling of blood pooling in my shoe that finally made me realize that I was fixating on stuff that wasn't important. James was still out of commission, Alec was quite possibly critically injured, there were police doubtlessly headed in our direction, and if I didn't force myself to focus, I was going to bleed to death before anything else could happen.

I pushed myself back off of the dashboard and a scream tore itself free of my throat despite my best efforts. Somehow my shock had cushioned me from the pain of multiple broken ribs, but it wasn't up to the surge of agony that moving brought on.

Screaming was an even bigger mistake than I'd expected it to be, it left me feeling even more light-headed than I'd been a second before and I suddenly realized that my breathing was shallow and fast. No matter how hard I tried I couldn't seem to get enough oxygen into my bloodstream.

It was now a race to see whether blood loss or asphyxiation did me in first. It was funny in a bitter, macabre kind of way, but I didn't have the breath to laugh, so I tried to school myself to seriousness—it wasn't working until I saw another hybrid step out of the darkness and approach the truck. I didn't recognize him, but I knew he was another enforcer. None of our people would have been able to get there so quickly—even assuming they realized what was going on.

The enforcer stepped over James, and headed directly towards Alec and me. He was less than three feet from the truck when something caused him to spin around and raise his claws. Despite the pain and the fact that my vision was starting to go fuzzy, I managed to turn my head far enough to the side to see what had made the hybrid so skittish.

It was another human, but one who looked vaguely familiar. Some tiny part of me must have been hoping against hope for the appearance of another ally because when I looked back and saw that the enforcer was now relaxed I felt a surge of disappointment that couldn't be denied.

"What are you doing here? Nobody told me to expect backup—especially not you. Don't tell me that you're here to steal the kill. I've worked hard for this and taking down Graves is the kind of thing that will make people sit up and take notice."

The approaching figure, small and frail in comparison to the muscled bulk of the hybrid just outside of the truck's cab, shook his head.

"Good. You can slit the girlfriend's throat if you want—that or their bodyguard is right over there. Plenty of killing still to be had if that's what you're here for."

I couldn't feel my right hand anymore, couldn't feel much of anything from the neck down, but my approaching death had finally thrown everything into stark clarity. I was amazed at how sensitive my hearing had gotten. I could hear the fear in the enforcer's voice as easily as I could see the waning flashes of light still coming from inside the building.

It seemed odd to me that the two latest arrivals would be more concerned with killing me than with helping their comrade in arms, but then again the Coun'hij's forces had always been more like a group of professional bullies than a real army.

I could feel the moment of hesitation as the hybrid tried to come up with a way of getting to Alec without exposing his back to the man who had nearly arrived at the truck. Hunger for the kill finally won out over fear and self-preservation.

The hybrid sank the tips of his claws in my leg and turned me towards him. It should have been excruciating, but I still seemed to be dead from the neck down. I expected him to toss me out of the truck, but just as his muscles tensed up, the new arrival put his hand on the hybrid's arm. There wasn't any crackle of electricity or rush of metaphysical power. There was no reason to think that the simple gesture was an attack, but the hybrid instantly dropped to the ground.

The new arrival stepped up to the cab of the truck and I finally realized why he'd looked so familiar. It was Oblivion.

I started to scream as he reached for me, but it didn't do any good and I was left to wonder whether it would hurt to have my memories torn out of my mind.

"He remembers nothing. He's like your friend Jessica."

The chorus of voices that I heard inside of my mind was exactly as I'd remembered it from the one and only other time when Oblivion had touched me. Each word was spoken by a different voice and they ran together with odd, choppy intervals between them.

"I don't understand…"

"He doesn't belong to the Coun'hij anymore. He's a child once again; you have an opportunity to win him to your side now if you show him kindness and are fair. Don't punish him for his past sins, that person is already dead."

"You're giving him to me like he's some kind of puppy? What am I supposed to do with him?"

"You can make him yours or you can cut him loose and let him return to what he was. His name is Drake."

I'd been light-headed before I'd started talking—now I felt like I was floating on a cloud. I wasn't sure if I asked my next question verbally or if Oblivion just plucked it directly out of my mind.

"Why are you doing this?"

"I was sent here."

I weakly shook my head. "That's not what I meant and you know it."

Oblivion reached forward and ripped a swath of material off of the bottom of my shirt. He was surprisingly gentle, but he still jostled me enough that it sent lances of pain through my chest. I gasped, partly from the agony, and partly from the realization that I wasn't paralyzed. Apparently my mind had just been trying to cushion me from the tide of agony I'd been experiencing.

The gasp sent another tsunami of pain through me and I lost several seconds. By the time I was able to focus on anything more than just the burning, Oblivion had tied the scrap of fabric around my leg, using it as a makeshift bandage. I wanted to laugh again. That wasn't going to save me now, not after all of the blood I'd already lost, not with a collapsed lung. I was still going to die, all Oblivion had done was stretch out my suffering a little.

"Why are you here? Why are you helping me?"

"I'm doing this because out of all that is bad in the world, there is nothing quite as wasteful as killing."

"You've killed before—I saw it in the memory you shared with me."

"Indeed I have. I've done many terrible things so far in my life and I know as surely as I know the sun will rise tomorrow that I will do yet more terrible things before I die. Some of them worse than anything I've done so far."

"If you know they are terrible and you do them anyway then you're no better than Dream Stealer or any of the rest of them. I only wish that I had the power to stop you."

"You do, Adriana Paige. You have had it for weeks now, but after tonight you have it more than ever. If you want me to be stopped simply let it be known far and wide inside of the resistance that I helped you not once, but twice. Puppeteer and the others will see me dead within hours of a rumor like that reaching their ears. You are uniquely placed to stop me now. There are no other witnesses of tonight's events. Now you must ask yourself how much of my guilt you'll share if you don't stop me."

Oblivion pulled his hands away from me, making further communication impossible, and then turned and walked away without looking back.

I wanted to yell after him, to beg him to call an ambulance, to plead for his help, or failing that to curse him for leaving me here to die, but I didn't have the breath to spare for any of that. I watched him walk away and felt myself getting weaker with every shaky, weak beat of my heart.

The fighting from inside the building had nearly died down now, but I could hear other sounds from further away in the darkness. The howls of approaching wolves and hybrids were something that I'd been expecting, but there were other sounds that I didn't recognize, foremost among them a kind of hissing cough that made my blood run cold.

I could hear sirens again too, but I knew the police were never going to make it to me, not with one or more Coun'hij kill squads in the area. I'd be dead—from natural causes or otherwise—long before the police ever made it to me. There was just one thing left for me to try and do before I died.

This wasn't how I'd planned to try and rescue Alec. None of the necessary pieces were in place to turn him into a religious figure, and I probably wouldn't last long enough to even find him inside of the jungle—let alone fight and kill Dream Stealer—but I had to at least try.

I pulled myself over so that I fell lengthwise across Alec. As the darkness came for me I remembered that I didn't even know how to connect with Alec's dream. Everything I'd done inside of the dream up until now had been nothing more than an accident.

Chapter 21

Adriana Paige
Unknown Dreamscape

I sucked in an experimental lungful of air and not only did it not hurt, I wasn't short of breath. I couldn't think of any better proof that I was either dreaming or dead. All that was left was to open my eyes and see which it was.

The dark jungle surrounding me was similar to what I'd seen the last time I'd shared Alec's dreams. The plants had the same long thorns and razor-edged leaves that I remembered from before and they gave off the same light-eating darkness, but everything felt colder than it had the last time. My breath clouded the air before me, and the aura of decay that had turned my stomach was even worse now.

I dropped down to my knees and sank my fingers in the cold dirt, hoping against hope that touching more of the substance of the dream would make my special vision reappear and confirm that this really was Alec's dream, albeit a darker, more chilling version.

No such luck. The dark loam sucked the warmth out of my hand without sparking the threads of light into existence. It wasn't until then that I realized my left arm still wasn't working. I shouldn't have been surprised, but somehow I'd been hoping that it would be back to normal, that it would be healed just like my ribs and legs were healed.

Apparently that particular injury had been a part of me for long enough that I subconsciously expected my arm not to work. That was too bad—it had been all I could do to survive my last fight with Dream Stealer when I'd had the use of both of my arms. I stood even less chance this time around, but then again it didn't actually matter whether I survived—all that mattered was that I kill Dream Stealer before my wounds back in the real world killed me.

I could feel something moving around in the darkness, no doubt drawn by the unearthly white light I was giving off, but it was surprisingly easy to conjure my dream replica of Alec's sword. This time I envisioned it with the monofilament edge to start out with, and as it flared into existence with the same clean glow as last time, I took an experimental swipe at a nearby tree. My sword sliced through the eight-inch trunk with only the slightest hint of resistance and I smiled.

If Dream Stealer's shadow creatures with their compound eyes wanted to attack me then so be it. I was as ready as I could be.

I closed my eyes and tried to reach out with all of my other senses. I could feel a slight tugging coming from off to my left, so I started off in that direction, first at a brisk jog, and then faster and faster as the weight of the passing seconds and minutes continued to bear down on me. It would be a cruel twist of fate for me to find Alec but die before I was even able to begin fighting Dream Stealer.

I started breathing hard after only a few minutes—I'd never been any kind of distance runner and was actually surprised that I'd made it so far before the exertion started to catch up with me. Except as I stopped and gingerly leaned against a tree to catch my breath, I realized that I was still thinking about things as though I was in the real world.

Back in reality I might be unathletic and easily winded, but there was nothing to say that I had to be that way here. In fact, I was starting to suspect that the only reason I'd manifested as a blonde-haired, blue-eyed seventeen-year-old girl was because that was how I thought of myself.

I gathered my scattered thoughts and forced myself to envision an Adri who was stronger and faster than the one I'd actually spent the last seventeen years crafting for myself. I imagined hard, wiry muscles running up and down my legs and a left arm that worked. I imagined a me who could run for miles without getting tired, and then I *pushed* with everything I had, trying to force my vision into being here in this pseudo reality.

For several seconds nothing seemed to happen and then all of a sudden I felt my mind catch on something and a jolt of pain exploded inside of my mind. I bit back a scream and then suddenly realized that I wasn't gasping any more. My body was different too, leaner and harder, but my left arm still refused to respond to my will. There had been a moment where I'd almost been convinced that I could feel a phantom pain out at the edges of my fingertips, but that was gone now and I didn't have any more time to waste trying to bring back a dead limb.

Now secure in my ability to summon my sword back into existence whenever I needed it, I banished it so that I could run without worrying that I would trip and decapitate myself. It still wasn't enough though. The leaves and thorns were taking pieces out of my flesh and the faster I ran the worse that got due to the fact that I couldn't see far enough to dodge the vicious plant life.

I considered a dozen different solutions, everything from replacing my skin with some kind of hard exoskeleton to trying to teleport myself directly to wherever Alec was being held, but in the end I just forced a clear, vegetation-free path into existence with my mind and continued to run.

Each change I imposed on myself or my surroundings seemed to extract a price—an initial, heavy price followed up by an ongoing low-level drain on my battered mind—but it couldn't be helped, not if I wanted to get to Alec in the short time I had left.

I let the jungle close back into place behind me as I ran, which seemed to help take away some of the load, but I could still feel my strength trickling away with each passing second. It felt like I'd been running for hours by the time I started breathing heavy again, but I knew that couldn't be the case, not at the speed I was moving, not unless the jungle had gotten much bigger than it had been the last time I'd been here.

My legs were starting to burn too, so I slowed down to a walk, which was when they struck.

Both shadows came out of the underbrush with a speed that was all the more incredible considering my altered time sense, but I heard them at the last second and when I held my hand out my sword flared into existence without any problem.

I threw myself to the left in an attempt to get out of the way, but I let my sword hang in the air behind me like a glowing tail that traced the arc of my travel. The closest shadow managed to get a claw into the outside of my left leg, but it had too much momentum to bring itself to a complete stop before it stumbled into the impossibly thin edge of my sword.

The pain of the shadow's claw tearing through my flesh was strong enough that I couldn't stop from crying out, but a split second later the shadow fell to the ground, cleanly sheared into two separate pieces.

I hit the ground hard, but I had enough presence of mind to let my sword go and it flickered out of existence an instant before the actual impact, which is the only thing that saved me from the same fate as the first shadow. I'd known I was in for a rough landing—it couldn't be otherwise considering the fact that my left hand was unable to catch me—but the shadow getting its claws into me had thrown me even further off than I'd expected.

My head collided with a rock hard enough that I saw stars and everything started to go dark, but I knew I couldn't afford to pass out. I clung to consciousness with every ounce of fight I had left, and rolled onto my back just in time to see the second shadow throw itself at me.

I acted without thinking, and for once my instincts worked to my advantage. Rather freezing up like I would have in the real world, I willed my sword back into existence and angled the softly-glowing tip so it took the shadow in the center of its chest, just below the base of its neck.

I'd spent enough time around shape shifters to know that particular strike was a paralyzing blow. It did everything I could have hoped for—the shadow that hit me was paralyzed from the shoulders down—but that didn't do anything to reduce the force of the impact as it landed on me.

For several seconds I couldn't breathe, partially because of the sheer weight pressing down on my chest and partially because I'd had the wind knocked out of me, but I finally managed to roll the creature off of me and draw in a huge gasp of cool, welcome air. I was bruised and there was blood trickling down the side of my face where the shadow's claws had come within less than half an inch of destroying my right eye, but other than that I was okay and I staggered off in the direction I could still feel the pull coming from.

A few minutes and several miles later I got close enough to see the foreboding stone pyramid rising out of the jungle. I slowed my pace and forced my sword to reappear in my hand, but I couldn't bring myself to slow very much—not when I knew that Alec was probably suffering as he waited for me to arrive and free him.

The pyramid was hollowed out in a way I wasn't sure was actually possible in the real world, with burning torches scattered around the perimeter and a pair of large metal braziers on either side of the stone altar providing a flickering, multi-pointed set of light sources.

I took in all of those smaller, unimportant details in bits and pieces. I noticed that the creeping vines were blood-red in the firelight, and that the altar was nearly as tall as I was before my mind finally relented and let me register the most important part of the scene.

Alec was on the altar, nailed to it with metal spikes through his arms and legs along with a single larger spike that went through the right side of his chest. The spikes had been shoved straight into the stone of the altar and they widened at the top such that the only way Alec would be able to free himself would be to lift himself up off of the stone slab, ripping the thicker ends through his flesh in the process.

There was so much blood pooled on the stones around the altar that for a second I thought Alec might really be dead despite his assertion that he couldn't be killed inside of his own dream. I rushed forward and used my sword to slice through the spike that was pinning his right arm to the stone, cutting through it down next to the altar.

Alec screamed as the spike shifted. It was a terrible sound, but it was the first evidence that he was still alive—I hadn't even been able to see his chest moving before then.

I grabbed hold of the spike and pulled it out of his arm. "Hold on, Alec. I just need a few seconds and I can cut them all."

He weakly shook his head. "Just my arms and legs. I'll pull the one in my chest out."

I worked carefully, not wanting to accidentally cut Alec with my sword, but even so it only took another twenty seconds for me to slice through the remaining three spikes in his appendages. Once that was done Alec didn't move for several seconds as though marshalling his strength.

"Alec?"

His only answer was to reach up to the last spike and rip it out of the stone with a single herculean effort. He rolled off of the altar and collapsed to the ground next to it, breathing heavily as though he'd just finished a marathon. I made as if to go to him, but he stopped me with a gesture and I was left to watch from several feet away as he began pulling himself back together, bit by bit.

I'd known that the physical torture was carried out solely as a way of breaking Alec mentally and spiritually, but somehow I'd forgotten that when faced with the sheer scope of his injuries. It wasn't until I tried to take another step closer to him and he opened his eyes to glare at me that what he'd been through really started to sink in.

It wasn't Alec looking out at me through those eyes, it was someone else—something else, something that had more in common with his beast than the man that I'd grown to love. The thing that looked up at me didn't view me as a friend, it viewed me as yet one more thing that was going to try and hurt it.

I watched as whatever was left of Alec tried to master the thing that he'd turned to for strength when the torture had grown to be too much, and I realized that there was no guarantee that Alec was going to come out on top in this particular fight.

"I'm so sorry that I didn't come sooner, Alec. Was it like that every time? Did you have to tear yourself off the spikes each and every time Dream Stealer left?"

He nodded shakily as though just now remembering how to execute that particular motion. I longed to run to him, to take him in my arms, but I knew that now wasn't the right time, that I would be risking pushing him further away if I did that.

I watched as he closed his eyes and began shaking with the fine tremors of a shape shifter trying not to transform. I needed something that would remind him who he was...and then suddenly I had it.

"I talked to Isaac. I think it was last night. It was probably a mistake—that's how the Coun'hij was able to track us down to a small enough area that they decided it would be worth it to throw up road blocks on the interstate. I took his call though because I know how much he means to you."

Alec's eyes had popped back open and he was looking at me, but his eyes were too pale. They were the eyes of his beast and he was looking at me like I was going to be his next meal.

"I told him that you'd gotten his message, that you accepted his apology, that anything that needed to be forgiven was long since buried, and that you were sorry you couldn't take his call yourself. He's in trouble, Alec. He's in New Orleans and he called to see if you would come down and depose the head of Ash's old pack. I told him I could probably get some more hybrids and wolves down there to help out, but he said this other guy—Onyx is his name—is just too powerful for that."

I could feel the tears starting to trickle down my cheeks, but I didn't try and wipe them away. They were long past overdue.

"I told him that we couldn't help him even though we could have. I lied to him because I was scared of what would happen if Lori got her hands on someone like Onyx without you being around to slap her down. It was the hardest thing I've ever had to do, Alec, and I'm still not sure I did the right thing. The whole time I just kept wishing that you were around to tell me what to do, that you were there for me to lean on.

"I didn't even ask about Kristin and Ash. For all I know they're both dead—Jasmin too. Jaclyn hasn't been picking up her phone and Grayson is refusing to help me—I've basically single-handedly destroyed everything you've built in just the last week or two."

The tears were streaming down my face now, leaving warm, salty tracks, that were for Alec and Isaac as much as they were for Jasmin and me.

"I'm so sorry, Alec. I did the best I could. I promised Isaac that I would avenge him, that I would put a bullet in Onyx, but it looks like I'm not even going to manage that. I told Donovan though. He'll probably make sure it happens just so he can keep Onyx out of Lori's hands. There's that at least."

"How long has it been?"

Alec's voice still sounded rusty, like it hadn't been used for anything other than screaming for many days, but he wasn't shaking anymore and his eyes were back to the same clear blue that I'd fallen in love with months ago.

"I'm not sure. I didn't retreat inside of myself this time, but there was just so much going on. A week maybe—not more than a week and a half."

"It's funny, but it feels like a lot longer than that to me. You said you wouldn't come in here unless you didn't have any other choice, Adri."

"I don't have any other choice, Alec. Your body is starting to shut down. I figured that you only had another few days at most, so James and I took you away from the convoy. I was hoping I could take you some place quiet and then arrange things so that even if I failed there would be some doubt as to what had really happened to you. I thought maybe it would be enough to convince everyone that you were still out there fighting for them."

Alec's smile was only a shadow of his normal grin, but he was still smiling and that, more than anything else, told me that he hadn't broken under Dream Stealer's torture. It had obviously been a near thing and he might bear the scars of what he'd been through for the rest of his life, but he'd refused to give in. In the end, even Dream Stealer hadn't been able to break Alec's indomitable will.

"I'll bet Donovan wasn't happy about that."

"He wasn't, but Rachel and I convinced James to back me, so there wasn't anything Donovan or Addison could do about it. It was a good plan, but a police officer recognized me when we stopped for gas and we had to make a run for it."

"What happened, Adri?"

The concern in his voice told me that he already had a pretty good idea, but I forced an answer out anyway. "I'm dying, Alec. You and I are lying in the bed of an old pickup truck. I have broken ribs, a punctured lung, and I've lost a dangerous amount of blood. Even if the Coun'hij doesn't find us I'm still not going to make it. You see, I had to try again—I'm not going to get another chance."

Alec pulled me down into his arms and for the first time since he'd been shot I felt well and truly safe. Being with Alec didn't change any of the hard realities of life—I was still going to die, he was still trapped inside Dream Stealer's nightmare—but being inside the circle of his arms helped me see that there was more to life than just living and dying.

'Until death do us part' was never going to be enough for me—not when it came to Alec. I didn't know what I believed when it came to the afterlife, but Alec made me want to be more than I was, made me want to be better than I would have been on my own. I wanted to be as good as I could possibly be just so I would have a chance of being with Alec if there really was some kind of afterlife.

If for no other reason, Alec deserved to be king simply because he was so good at getting the best out of people. I wanted to stay there in his arms, but I didn't know how much time I had left.

I pushed back from Alec and picked up my sword. "Come on, we need to find Dream Stealer—I'm going to kill him before I run out of time. Can you feel him? Is he here?"

Alec shrugged uncertainly. "Things have changed since you were here last. He's gotten stronger since then, better at masking his presence, and this place is always more his now than it is mine. He might be here right now, or we might have hours still before he comes back."

The tentative response made me angry, not at Alec, but at Dream Stealer for having robbed

Alec—even temporarily—of his normal, effortless control in almost any circumstance. Alec stared at me blankly for several seconds before shaking himself as though surfacing from a long dive.

"There is so much that I need to tell you, Adri. I'm so sorry to have pulled you into my world. If not for me you could have lived a long, full life somewhere safe."

I shook my head. "I'm not sorry that I fell in love with you, Alec. I don't even wish that I was sorry. I'm not excited about the fact that I'm going to die, but everything that has happened has been because I love you. It's okay—you don't need to say anything. If we end up having time after Dream Stealer is dead then we can talk, but I want my last moments to be dedicated to giving you that gift."

Alec closed his eyes for several seconds, visibly forcing his emotions back into a tiny corner of his mind, and then he opened his eyes and gave me a crooked smile. "What's your plan?"

"The only thing I can think of is for us to go back to the bars that lead outside. Since we don't know how to find Dream Stealer we might as well hack them to pieces so that you'll still be able to get out even if I fail. More importantly though, last time when I touched them something happened to me. I could see everything, including the golden threads that Dream Stealer is using to steal power from you so that he can create this place. If my vision changes again when I touch the bars then I'll be able to find Dream Stealer, if he's here."

"If that's what you want to do then we should get started—I'm pretty sure Dream Stealer isn't here though, he's not the type..."

Whatever Alec had been about to say was interrupted by an earthshaking impact as a figure made out of black fire dropped down from the top of the pyramid.

"Please don't go—I'd really like to know more about these visions that you're having."

My blood turned to ice water inside of my veins. I would have said that nothing could have been more terrifying than Dream Stealer had been when I'd last faced off against him, but apparently I would have been wrong.

He was bigger now than he'd been before, and he gave off a sense of wrongness that spoke to the primitive part of my brain that wanted to run screaming out of the room anytime I saw a spider. I could have sworn that he was getting bigger as he slowly moved towards us too—even the massive stones that made up the foundation of the pyramid seemed to groan and crack as he moved across them, but I couldn't tell whether that was a function of his size or if it was because he was too much of an abomination for even this place to bear.

Dream Stealer looked like some kind of evil pagan god and a tiny part of me was screaming that I should be bowing down before him and begging for mercy. His presence was so overwhelming that I might have even done it if not for the fact that I could feel Alec at my side and see the pure white light radiating out of him. If Dream Stealer was a dark, unholy demigod then Alec was an angel made out of an unquenchable fire.

Alec shifted to his hybrid form and was suddenly a hundred times more impressive, but he was still such a small, frail figure to match itself against the four-armed monstrosity that was nearly close enough now to attack us.

"Spread out, Adri. We're going to have to come at him from opposite sides if we're going to have any kind of chance of beating him now."

I nodded without taking my eyes off of Dream Stealer, and then held my sword out to Alec. "Take this. Don't let it get in your way or anything, but it's sharper than your claws."

"It may be sharper than my claws in the real world, but it's not sharper than my claws in this place, Adri."

There was a hint of laughter in Alec's tone that was almost enough to convince me that we might have a chance. Then again, even if we didn't have a chance there still something about fighting with Alec at my side. This was something that could never happen in the real world—I was simply too outclassed there—but I found that I was looking forward to it now that it was about to happen.

I expected some kind of threat out of Dream Stealer before he attacked, but he simply waited for us to circle around so that we were on opposite sides of him and then threw himself at Alec with such blinding speed that I almost wasn't able to follow their exchanges.

Alec threw himself to the side, ducking the longer upper arm on Dream Stealer's right side, and then knocking the smaller arm to one side as he sliced long gouges into Dream Stealer's side. My heart felt like it was going to burst with pride at the fact that Alec had managed to draw first blood against such a terrifying foe, but I didn't let that slow me down as I darted in and took a slash at Dream Stealer's upper left arm.

I expected Dream Stealer to yank his arm out of the way, but he simply turned my attack to one side with his claws. Not only did my blade not cut through his claws, the force of his block nearly ripped my sword free.

I'd been expecting to primarily be serving as a distraction, something to give Alec a fighting chance, but Dream Stealer reversed direction and slashed at me almost faster than I could compensate for. I threw myself backwards with all my might, but he still managed to nick my left shoulder. I didn't feel any pain from the wound, but he started a steady trickle of red working its way down my arm.

Dream Stealer would have killed me then—before I had a chance to roll back to my feet, but Alec dove forward and slashed the side of Dream Stealer's leg. It was a clean, deep cut, one that would have completely severed Dream Stealer's leg if not for how massive the limb was. I'd been hoping to see the spray of crimson that would have indicated that Alec had opened up a major artery, but instead all he was rewarded with was a steady drip of what looked like liquid black fire.

The fluid didn't seem to be harming Dream Stealer's flesh, but I could see where it was eating into the stone, leaving small, star-shaped cracks in the rock wherever it splattered. Several drops landed on Alec and he hissed in pain as he tried to get back out of range of Dream Stealer's counterattack.

Alec would have failed if he'd done even the slightest bit less damage to Dream Stealer's leg. Instead Dream Stealer was forced to pull up short as his leg threatened to buckle underneath him, but even so the tips of his claws drew thin lines of crimson across Alec's back. It wasn't a killing blow—he hadn't even managed to bleed Alec very badly—but it was proof of just how closely the three of us were matched.

All of that flashed through my mind as I stepped forward and to the side, trying to get in behind Dream Stealer where his arms would have a harder time reaching me. I felt like I was moving with glacial slowness in comparison to the sharp, violent motions of the other two, but

I'd picked my time with a perfection I never could have matched in the real world.

Dream Stealer spun back towards me, rotating on his undamaged leg, but my sword was already up in the perfect position. The slender length of white light sheared through Dream Stealer's upper arm just above the elbow with only the faintest tug of resistance.

I had a split second to glory in the strike, in my accomplishment, and then the rush of flaming black blood splashed onto me.

The pain was beyond anything I'd ever felt before. I tried to scream, but my skin seemed to have pulled tight against my jaw, restricting my ability to open my mouth. The entire front half of my body from my waist up seemed to be one large mass of burning agony. It should have shorted out my nervous system and left me unable to feel anything, but I was still able to feel the impact as Dream Stealer's lower arm slammed into me with enough force to launch me more than thirty feet.

I couldn't hear anything out of my right ear and I was almost positive that my eyes had been destroyed, but in the instant of impact I felt something change inside of me. The darkness was suddenly replaced with an infinite number of glowing gold threads.

I was still sailing through the air when Alec threw himself forward and drove the claws on his right hand into Dream Stealer's back. Alec pulled down as though planning on pulling himself up higher on Dream Stealer's back, but the unnatural sharpness of his claws worked against him now—his claws sheared through bone and muscle without encountering any resistance and Alec stumbled as Dream Stealer spun and slammed an elbow into the side of Alec's head.

I collided with a tree at the precise instant that Alec's feet left the ground, and not even the pain as dozens of thorns pierced my flesh was enough to distract me from my fear that Alec's neck had just been snapped. Alec sailed backwards, and for the first time I noticed that this time the threads of light running from Alec off to the bars in the distance were matched by an almost equal number of thick threads that ran back from the bars to Dream Stealer.

It all suddenly made perfect sense. Dream Stealer had become stronger since the last time I'd seen him because he was draining Alec like some kind of metaphysical parasite. Dream Stealer was even moving better than he had a few seconds before as stolen energies supercharged his healing process.

Alec's flight was interrupted as he collided with the stone blocks of the temple. He dropped to the ground, landing in a three-point stance, and then charged back toward Dream Stealer. I wanted to yell to Alec, to tell him what was going on, but my mouth still wasn't working.

My back had stopped hurting, and even the burning across my chest seemed to have subsided into something that could almost be ignored. There was no way of knowing for sure whether that was because I was dying or if the thorns were just coated with some kind of numbing agent. Either way, I didn't have much time left before I'd no longer be able to act.

I looked down and realized that my sword was still dangling from my right hand. I took a deep breath and then slashed through the two-foot trunk of the tree just below my feet. Even as I did it, I knew that my actions were insane.

The jolt as the free end of the trunk dropped down and slammed into the ground took my breath away. For a second I thought the tree was going to fall over in my direction and crush me, but after a second that seemed to stretch out to eternity, the tree slowly started toppling to the side.

Just before the top of the tree crashed into the ground, Alec reached Dream Stealer and the two of them exchanged raking slashes. Alec was moving more slowly now, while Dream Stealer even seemed to be regenerating the arm that I'd cut off. There wasn't any time to waste.

I laboriously pulled myself off of the thorns, but my right leg refused to work when I tried to climb back to my feet. I nearly despaired until I saw the tiny thread that ran between Alec and I. The pulses of light moving between us offered a possible solution. I reached out with the same part of my mind that was responsible for manifesting my sword, and used it to reach for the energy pulsing on the other end of the thread.

The thread suddenly brightened nearly to the point where it was painful to look at, and something in my pelvis shifted as nerves that had been severed reconnected. The feeling was pure bliss and a part of me wanted to pull more power down through our link, wanted to drink it all in until I glowed brighter than the sun, but in that instant Alec stumbled, his light dimming, flickering as more light was pulled from the rest of the threads running from his body out to the real world.

That stumble nearly cost Alec the fight. He'd been charging forward in an effort to get inside the reach of Dream Stealer's upper arms, but his misstep robbed him of valuable speed and even I could see he wasn't going to make it in time. Alec twisted away at the last second, jumping over one of the lower appendages, but he still wasn't able to escape completely unscathed.

Dream Stealer connected with another blow—this one more glancing, but still more than enough to knock Alec back into the temple, and Alec was slower to get back to his feet. I heard screaming and realized it was coming from me as I sprinted forward on my newly-healed leg.

Alec was in motion too, moving with a hitch that told me that last impact had broken one or more of his ribs, but still moving with a speed that I'd never seen anyone in the real world match. Somehow, in the middle of the fight, Alec had figured out how to modify his own body and grant himself more speed and strength.

Dream Stealer launched a blindingly fast swipe at Alec that seemed impossible to block or dodge either one, but Alec threw himself into the air and landed on Dream Stealer's right arm, digging in with the talons on both feet and the claws on his left hand.

I expected Alec's claws to rip free of Dream Stealer's arm just like they'd done a few seconds before when Alec had shredded Dream Stealer's back, but Alec must have returned them to their normal level of sharpness because rather than tearing free, they provided him with the leverage he needed to scramble further up Dream Stealer's arm.

Dream Stealer brought his left arm over, intending on using his newly-regenerated claws to impale Alec. I screamed a warning, but Alec simply brought his right hand up before him and in the split second before impact I saw Alec's claws lengthen out to more than double their normal length. They sliced through Dream Stealer's flesh with the ease of a monofilament edge, and then Alec screamed as liquid fire washed over him.

I knew the agony he was enduring—I fully expected for Alec to lose hold of his grip on Dream Stealer's arm, but instead he launched himself forward, the massive muscles in his left arm and both legs propelling him like an arrow towards Dream Stealer's throat.

For one perfect second I thought Alec was going to succeed. Not even Dream Stealer could survive a beheading and there was no way that Dream Stealer was going to get either hand in position to knock Alec away. An instant before Alec's claws would have sliced through Dream Stealer's neck, large spikes of what looked like obsidian shot out of Dream Stealer's shoulders, neck and upper chest.

Aimed as if by magic, the glassy thorns impaled Alec and then continued growing so that they lifted him up and away from Dream Stealer's vulnerable flesh. The scream that was torn out of Alec was partially pain and partially rage at having been bested. Still sprinting, I watched as Alec flailed helplessly away against the spikes immobilizing him. His claws, even the monofilament edge of his right-hand set, didn't even mark the dark glass, and the slick black material didn't provide enough friction for him to lever himself off of the cruel points.

"And what about you, little one?" Dream Stealer turned towards me as I reached my goal. "What will you do now that young Graves is finally helpless?"

"He's not helpless as long as he still has friends!"

Dropping my sword, I reached up and closed my fist around the cable-like mass of glowing threads that connected Alec to the bars, and then clamped down with every ounce of strength I could muster.

The effect wasn't quite instantaneous—not to my amped-up time sense—but there was a noticeable dropoff in the light from the billions of threads that made up the substance of the jungle around us. More importantly, with me stopping the flow of light away from Alec, he brightened noticeably and the flow of some of the threads connecting him to the real world reversed direction and energy started flowing away from Alec rather than solely towards him.

Most importantly of all, the black light and flame coming from Dream Stealer immediately started dimming.

"No! How are you doing that? It's taken me weeks to figure out how to tap into his power, how are you stopping the flow so easily?"

I gave him my best cold smile. "Wouldn't you like to know?"

Dream Stealer charged towards me with a howl of rage, but I reflexively pulled more light along the thread connecting me to Alec and it was suddenly child's play to skip to one side, effortlessly avoiding the four-foot claws that otherwise would have ended my life. Dream Stealer spun in place, somehow less than he'd been even just a few seconds previously, but still very much capable of ending me if he got his claws on me.

Alec seemed to have reached a kind of equilibrium. He was brighter than I'd even seen him before, but most of the light coming in from the outside world was being redirected back out along other threads that were likewise running to the outside world.

Dream Stealer took another swipe at me and this time I jumped over the attack and ran partway up his arm before I felt something moving underneath his skin. A new set of obsidian spikes burst free from Dream Stealer's skin, moving faster than even the ones that had succeeded in spearing Alec, but I was already sailing away from Dream Stealer, completing a perfect backflip and then landing with the threads between Alec and the exit still tangled around my fingers.

"What happened to your sword, little one?"

Some of the concern had disappeared from Dream Stealer's voice. We were locked in a stalemate, but it was a stalemate that favored him on every level. As long as I maintained my grip on the threads that had been powering him, he would continue to shrink back down to something closer to his real size and strength, but as long as my only hand was occupied with the threads I couldn't attack him. I was fighting a purely defensive war, one where I had to dodge every blow in order to go on surviving. He only had to get lucky once.

The next attack came even closer still and I reeled away with fresh trickles of blood running down my left arm.

"How long can you keep this up? You're slowing already. It's only a matter of time now, little one."

He was right, but not in the way he thought. I was slowing, but the real problem was that my real body was still gasping for breath, still on death's doorstep. I needed to finish this now.

I reached through the thread connecting me to Alec once again and gulped down all of the power I could hold. It was a heady feeling. The world around me slowed even further as Alec, still writhing in pain on Dream Stealer's spikes, dimmed back down to a dangerous level.

Dream Stealer charged me again, but this time I ran forward to meet him. I waited until the last second and then threw myself down as though I was sliding into home plate. His claws passed over me, mere inches from my face, and then I was passing under him—too fast for even me to take advantage of the moment.

Still drinking down Alec's light, I let go of the threads I'd been holding onto and conjured my sword with one clean motion. On one level it was ludicrous to think that something as tangible as my sword could shear through the intangible cable that Dream Stealer was using to drain Alec, but my sword wasn't just a sword, it glowed with the same pure, white light that I did.

Out of the corner of my eye I saw Alec's light dim even further as a blinding flash of energy shot down the thread I'd just released, but most of my focus was on the silvery thread that connected me to my sword. I pushed light down that thread at the same time that I envisioned a weapon that was sharp enough to cut through spirit as well as the coarse matter that I'd originally created it to rend.

The light from my sword was blinding as I whipped it through the air, but even through the afterimages it left on my retinas I was still able to see it slice through the threads that bound Alec to this nightmare.

I started turning back around to face Dream Stealer, my sword held high and a smile on my face, when I felt a slight tugging at my chest followed by an inability to breathe. My impossible speed hadn't been enough to save me, not when I'd held still to cut the threads, not once Dream Stealer had—even momentarily—access to the enormous well of power inside of Alec.

I'd turned thinking I still had plenty of time to get set before Dream Stealer would be able to turn around and attack me, but I'd been wrong and the sight of his claws ripping through the right side of my chest, my blood shimmering in the air, was enough of a shock to make me lose my grip on the energy I'd been siphoning away from Alec.

The light and power that could have saved me shot back down the thread, racing to Alec and leaving me a weak, dying husk of what I'd been. That jolt of energy, combined with the backlash from the thread I'd just cut, momentarily turned Alec into a being of such incandescence that I expected to feel heat coming off of him. I turned away, even my unique vision overloaded as I heard the sound of fine crystal shattering.

When I was next able to look at Alec he was standing in front of Dream Stealer, shards of obsidian still protruding from his body where he'd cut himself free, and his fist inside of Dream Stealer's chest. The two stood there frozen for several seconds, Alec taller and more powerful than I'd ever seen before, and Dream Stealer a dark, tiny shadow of the thing that we'd been fighting just seconds before.

"What I do now is merely justice. The crimes you have committed demand death to restore the balance."

Dream Stealer laughed weakly. "I begin to see why he's so scared of you. Again and again we underestimate you. We all thought Brandon was merely a fluke, but then you killed Cyrus. I should have known better, but I was so blinded by rage that I thought I could beat you by myself."

"Who's scared of me? Who are you talking about?"

I wanted to smile, wanted to cheer for joy, but I just didn't have the strength. I could feel my life leaking away from me, both inside the dream and in the real world, but I forced myself to stay there, forced myself not to go into the yawning void I could feel opening up underneath my feet. More than anything else I wanted to see Dream Stealer die, wanted to know for certain that I'd been successful, that Alec was finally safe.

As I watched I could see the darkness bleeding out of Dream Stealer. It wasn't a burning fire any more—it was really little more than a mist that evaporated away as it left his body. Only the longer I watched the more I realized that wasn't right. It wasn't evaporating, it was soaking into Alec. I felt a moment of terror at the idea that Dream Stealer might be trying to possess Alec, but then I realized that the mist was turning from darkness into light in the moment that it touched his skin.

With each droplet that Alec absorbed he became brighter and taller, and Dream Stealer became smaller and more feeble. Dream Stealer started coughing violently and then when he looked back up, Alec's hand still buried in his chest, he was no longer a creature of shimmering darkness, he was merely a man.

I couldn't have said how I knew that the tired, old face was Dream Stealer's, but I knew it. Even stranger, I felt as though I'd seen those careworn, Native American features before now, felt as though they were as familiar to me as my father's face had been before he'd been taken away from me.

Alec grabbed Dream Stealer's right shoulder, sinking his claws into Dream Stealer's flesh as he shook him. "I want a name. Who's scared of me? Whose orders are you taking?"

Dream Stealer started to laugh, but that triggered another weak coughing fit. "I don't actually know his name, none of us do. I call him the Scientist, but I do have a name for you—mine. It's Taggart. I want at least one other living person to know it now that Cyrus is gone."

Dream Stealer—Taggart—looked over at me and smiled. "At least I deprived you of her. He's convinced that you can't win without her."

Alec shook his head. "You came very close to breaking me, but in the end you gave me access to power I never realized was possible. Look at her and see your hopes dashed as you dashed the hopes of so many over the centuries."

It started out small, no more than a feeling of warmth in my stomach, but it rapidly grew into a fire of such heat that I thought I was going to be consumed. I looked down and saw light pouring into me from the thread that connected Alec and me—healing, life-giving light.

For the first time in minutes, I opened my eyes and saw more than just threads and darkness. I saw Alec looking at me with gratitude and determination. I started to pull myself to my feet and then nearly fell when my left arm refused to respond.

Alec's brow furrowed even more and the amount of light flowing down the thread doubled and then redoubled again. It was far more power than I'd been able to pull in myself and my form started to waver as though I was nothing more than a mirage, but my arm still refused to respond to my will.

I looked up at Alec and shook my head, but that merely caused him to send even more light to me. I was shaking now and it felt like my skin was losing the battle to keep the raging energies inside of me, but even through the euphoria I was still able to see Alec's light faltering, was able to see some of the threads powering him begin to flicker.

"Stop! It's not worth it, Alec. I'll be fine like this."

Forcing the words out was one of the hardest things I'd ever done, and not just because being full of light was the most addicting feeling I'd ever experienced. There at the end I'd felt sensations start to shoot up and down my left arm. Now that I'd gone for days without the use of my arm I wanted it back more than ever, but I was fairly certain I knew what was on the other end of all those threads and I wasn't going to sacrifice one of my friends simply to regain the use of a limb.

I looked up at Alec with tears in my eyes, but I forced a smile on my face so that he would think they were tears of joy. I got a hesitant smile back in return and then realized that I could feel Taggart slipping away.

"His heart! Now, Alec!"

Alec ripped his claws free of Taggart's chest, but I could still feel Taggart turning to metaphysical mist. I acted out of instinct, willing him into place, refusing to acknowledge a reality in which he was able to escape. What I was attempting was beyond me, but I wasn't just relying on my natural abilities, I was still full of light and energy. Not as much as I'd been holding just seconds before, but still far more than any human should ever be offered.

I clamped down on Taggart's essence and rooted it to this reality, to the jungle where he'd tortured Alec and paralyzed me. He could feel what I was doing—I could feel him fighting, but he was weak and dying.

He turned towards me and gave me a sad smile. "And so I am truly bested and the world will be shattered as a result. Beware the werewolves. When they start acting in inexplicable ways you'll know that the end is near."

I watched the light in Taggart's eyes go out and couldn't explain why I was crying. Alec finally lowered the limp body to the ground and I threw up an instant later.

Dream Stealer had been a terrible person, but somehow my world felt a little smaller and colder than it had been before his death.

Epilogue

Adriana Paige
Galt Oil Field
Western North Dakota

By all accounts I should have died—or at the very least woken up in a hospital under a police watch—and Alec should have died with me. Alec and I had come back to ourselves at the same time, surrounded by silence so profound that I'd been worried James hadn't survived.

I'd been wrong—James was okay, albeit a little worse for the wear after having been electrocuted and then ejected from a moving vehicle. Both Alec and I were healed from all of our injuries, everything but the paralysis in my left arm—that was still unchanged.

Drake, the guy Oblivion had wiped clean and then abandoned, came back to consciousness about the same time that James did. Interacting with him was odd in ways that I was still getting used to. Oblivion seemed to have taken more from Drake than he had from Jess. Drake knew how to walk and talk, but other than that it was like dealing with a small child. He had zero background knowledge, which meant that he was very disoriented, but he was also incredibly trusting. I told him our names and then gave him the option of coming with us or us leaving him somewhere safe and he asked to come with us.

The four of us took more than half an hour to walk back to the SUV that James and I had ditched at the beginning of our run from the police. Looking back at the trip, it wasn't the smartest thing to have done, but having Alec back had made me feel so secure that I hadn't even thought twice about the possible risks.

After everything else we'd just been through it hadn't seemed possible that the local police department or even a Coun'hij-suborned arm of the FBI would be able to stop us, not when Alec was capable of dropping them all in their tracks.

The SUV was exactly where we'd left it. We drove through the night and then once it was light outside James checked it for tracking devices and pronounced it clean. I fell asleep in Alec's arms for the first time in far too long and was content in ways that I'd never been content before.

Alec was back and I'd been key in bringing that about. Having him back was the most important thing, but I was surprised to find that on some level I'd been hungering for a chance to prove myself. Alec had never uttered any words of reproach about the fact that I'd always been the weaker partner, but it was still something that had unconsciously been weighing on me.

That weight was gone now. I couldn't stand next to Alec on the battle line in the real world, but I had my own kind of strength, an important strength. I'd held things together in his absence and I'd helped kill Dream Stealer.

I was still inexplicably conflicted about that last part. It made no sense for me to feel the same kind of gaping hole inside of me now that I'd felt when my dad and Cindi had died, but there was no point denying that it felt almost exactly the same as when I'd first learned of the accident—worse maybe.

There were new shadows behind Alec's eyes that hadn't been there before he'd been shot. It was all too likely that he was suffering from some kind of post-traumatic stress disorder. The timing was bad—we still had a war to fight. Puppeteer was still out there and while the ranks of the Coun'hij's enforcers had been depleted, we'd lost a lot of people too.

Part of me wanted to tell Alec to take some time and put himself back together, but I knew he would refuse, just like he would have refused the behind-the-scenes role that I'd wanted everyone to believe he'd assumed if we never came back.

MARKED

Alec started making calls that next morning when we stopped at a hotel to shower and change clothes. Knowing that the Coun'hij could be tracking us made me a little nervous, but Alec seemed to think that the loss of Dream Stealer had probably thrown them into disarray.

Alec still referred to him as Dream Stealer, but I couldn't think or talk about him without using the name Taggart. Alec had noticed that, but he seemed content to let me work through my demons on my own if that was what I wanted. For now that *was* what I wanted.

We started heading north once we got back in the car, but Alec was unusually reticent about our destination. All he would say was that Mallory, Donovan, Dom, and Addison were all still alive and that we would be meeting up with 'them' soon.

The where turned out to be a small group of oil rigs in North Dakota. Contrary to what I'd been expecting, the first set of arrivals didn't include a quartet of massive RV's. Instead the convoy that pulled into the shadows cast by the pumps was a motley collection of vehicles, most of which looked like they were on their last legs.

When Isaac got out of the lead vehicle I ran to him and wrapped my arm around him as a new set of tears started rolling down my face. After a second Isaac returned my embrace, but there was a new hesitancy to his movements, something more than just the normal concern that he'd accidentally break me if he squeezed too hard.

When Jasmin, Ash and Kristin got out of the next two vehicles I thought I might start hyperventilating. Having so many friends I'd given up for dead turn up alive and well was the best kind of surprise that Alec could have possibly given me.

Outwardly everyone was exactly the same as I remembered, but beneath the surface I could see that things had changed. Kristin had the same kind of darkness lurking behind her eyes that I now saw so often when I looked at Alec, but that was hardly surprising given what she'd been through before Alec and I had finally managed to kill Taggart.

Ben was still unconscious and Jasmin had an air of hopelessness to her that was completely at odds with her usual quiet confidence. Nearly as shocking was the fact that she'd arrived accompanied by a vampire named Geoffrey.

Alec had apparently been aware of Jasmin's unorthodox choice in traveling companions, but nobody had thought to warn James. I thought for a second that he and Jasmin were going to come to blows, but in the end James backed down despite obviously being unhappy about it. There was a new order inside of the pack now and Jasmin was unarguably dominant to James.

Only we weren't really a pack anymore because Jasmin had her own pack—a ragtag batch of submissives, but they were undeniably ready to back her play when it came to protecting Geoffrey, even if it brought them into conflict with James.

Isaac was a pack leader now too, which was shocking on a number of levels. He'd never wanted to be the one in charge and was obviously still getting used to the idea. The fact that he seemed to be paired up with Ash's sister was likewise unexpected, but the biggest change was the way that Isaac held himself and the way that everyone treated him.

Gentle, controlled Isaac was now an object of fear. Whatever had happened in New Orleans had left its mark on Isaac, because nobody seemed more worried about him losing control than he was. I tried to ask Alec what had happened, but all he told me was that Isaac had manifested a power.

It was yet another impossible event. Mallory had looked Isaac over when he'd been born and declared that he had no possibility of developing an ability, but it was no more impossible than Jasmin manifesting a hybrid form after all these years. I was starting to realize that we'd never really understood the rules the world ran under.

I caught Alec and Isaac off by themselves a little while after the pizza we'd ordered arrived. They seemed comfortable with each other in a way that hadn't been the case since before Alec had first manifested his power.

Alec accepted the slice of pizza I brought him and then stared off into the distance for several seconds before turning to Isaac. "Andrew is okay. He's had a rough time of things, but he made it through the last round of fighting unscathed."

"Thank you, I've been meaning to ask how that went."

"It was bad—really, really bad. Donovan will be here and able to fill us in in a few minutes, but we're going to need you now more than ever. Your ability may be our only chance of taking Puppeteer down."

"Isn't there another way?"

"Not that I see. If there is then I'll take it. What I can promise you is that I won't let you lose control."

Isaac nodded slowly. "I appreciate that. To be honest I've thought about little else since the fight in New Orleans. I came here ready to swear fealty to you if that was what it was going to take for you to agree to control me."

"You don't need me to control you, Isaac. Out of all the people who could have manifested your power, you're the only one I trust to keep it under control on your own. You don't need me, but I will serve as a safeguard for you if that's what you want. Fealty or no—I'll still do it. I owe you at least that. I'm sorry I couldn't be there when you needed me."

Isaac shrugged. "You had valid reasons. It's hard to believe that we're coming to the end of

the war. It's only a matter of time now until we find Puppeteer and then it's just a matter of mopping up a few enforcers."

The shadows were back in Alec's eyes. "I wish that were the case, but now more than ever I'm convinced that we're only at the start of the fighting."

Acknowledgments:

Publishing a novel is a much smaller undertaking than filming a movie, but there is still a tremendous amount of work that goes into the undertaking and it's only right that those individuals who helped make Marked a reality be recognized.

My wife Katie usually gets named last, but the truth is that she's the first one to help out and her help continues on until long after the publish button is pressed on the last retailer. The only reason I'm able to put in such long hours writing is because Katie puts in even longer hours taking care of everything else in our lives. That by itself would be more than I could rightfully expect, but she goes even further by serving as my very first reader, my sounding board and my cover designer.

Most spouses would have pulled the plug on this endeavor a long time ago, but Katie keeps looking for ways to make it work, for avenues that will let us keep going just a little bit longer so we can get a few more books out. Thank you, Katie.

Once Katie got done with the manuscript for *Marked* it then went to my editors RJ and Amy, who—as they always do—performed small miracles getting this book into a state where it was fit for human consumption. Thank you both for you amazing work and for both being willing to tackle each new book as I write it.

From there, *Marked* went to a very special group of four ladies who are some of my absolutely most dedicated fans. Heather, Janelle, Jenine and Mei serve as my very first group of advance readers these days, taking the book once it's through the editing process and providing additional feedback and editing catches. This group often turns a manuscript around in just a few days and each one they touch turns out better as a result of their efforts. I'm profoundly grateful to all four of them for their help in making *Marked* a reality.

Next comes my broader group of advance readers and bloggers, many of whom have been with me since the beginning, all of whom are appreciated for their feedback and help, reviews and support. Mom, Dad, Matthew, Shalese, Lachele, Mark, Mimi, Kim, and Merissa, thank you all for your support and help!

Lastly, I want to give a big shout out to my readers. When you tell a friend about the series or leave a review of one of my books it helps make it so that I can continue writing full-time so that we can all find out what is going to happen next.

About the Author:

Dean Murray is a prolific author with dozens of novels across multiple pen names and more than half a million copies of his work currently in circulation.

Dean started reading seriously in the second grade due to a competition and has spent most of the subsequent three decades lost in other worlds.

Things worsened, or improved depending on your point of view, when he first started experimenting with writing while finishing up his accounting degree.

These days Dean has a wonderful wife and two lovely daughters to keep him rather more grounded, but the idea of bringing others along with him as he meets interesting hew people in universes nobody else has ever seen tends to drag him back to his computer on a fairly regular basis.

Keep up to speed on Dean's latest projects at deanwrites.com.

The Greater Darkness:
(Writing as Eldon Murphy)

Something powerful is stirring in the darkness. Something so ancient that even creatures who've been alive for hundreds of years have long since discounted this new threat as nothing more than myth.

Normal humans will be caught in the crossfire, but then that's always the way of things. Geoffrey has no memory of his past life or any idea how to survive in the violent, dangerous world in which he's trapped. Despite his best efforts, he's about to find himself in the middle of a conflict that threatens to sweep away everything, and everyone he's been fighting so hard to protect.

Bound

The only thing worse than having no family at all, is having a family that is out to hurt you. That would all be bad enough for a normal 17-year-old, but it's even worse for Alec Graves. A shape shifter's pack, his family, is the only thing stopping the other preternatural creatures out there from killing them.

Alec's pack isn't just neglectful, he's pretty sure that his father wants him dead. Alec is about to be sent to the front lines of a war between his people and everything else that goes bump in the night. His only chance of survival is to convince everyone around him that he's the perfect soldier, but there are lines that Alec won't cross, not for any price.

Publisher's Note: *Bound is the first in Dean's new Dark Reflections novels, an alternate timeline set in the same world and featuring many of the same characters, but with a profoundly different backstory.*

Frozen Prospects

The invitation to join the secretive Guadel should have been the fulfillment of dreams Va'del didn't even realize he had. When his sponsors are killed in an ambush a short time later, he instead finds his probationary status revoked, and becomes a pawn between various factions inside the Guadel ruling body.

Jain's never known any life but that of a Guadel in training. She'd thought herself reconciled to the idea of a loveless marriage for the good of her people, but meeting Va'del changes everything. Their growing attraction flies against hundreds of years of precedent, but as wide-spread attacks threaten their world, the Guadel have no choice but to use even Jain and Va'del in their fight for survival.

CHET:
Whispers From The Past
By Larry Murray

30 years ago Charles Tucker lost everything that made life worth living. A brutal car accident killed his son. A short time later painful cancer took his wife.

The arrival of the Saunders family casts Charles' life into turmoil, tearing open unhealed wounds. Without his help the Saunders' financial troubles threaten to destroy them, but helping them risks destroying everything Charles spent a lifetime building.

Over all the turmoil looms Chet, the battered old '64 Chevy pickup that carried Charles' son to his death. For 29 years Charles blamed the old pickup for his devastating losses, locking Chet away in an old barn.

The most intriguing mysteries refuse to stay locked up. Solving this one promises an enchanting adventure for the whole family.